OLIVE

We hope you enjoy this book. Please return or renew it by the due date.

You can renew it at www.norfolk.gov.uk/libraries or by using our free library app.

Otherwise you can phone 0344 800 8020 - please have your library card and PIN ready.

You can sign up for email reminders too.

Withdrawn for sale

NORFOLK ITEM

30129 085 997 295

NORFOLK COUNTY COUNCIL
LIBRARY AND INFORMATION SERVICE

D1342374

Praise for OLIVE

'It's a corker . . . Warm, nostalgic, moreish'
The Telegraph, DEBUT NOVEL OF THE SUMMER

'This tale of four young women trying to sort out the dilemmas
of motherhood will bring relief and recognition to many. It's
a lovely book – thoughtful, searching, funny, and honest'
Elizabeth Gilbert

'It'll give a voice to countless women, it'll give them courage,
they'll feel empowered to defend their decisions . . . A
profound issue wrapped inside an accessible, highly engaging
novel'
Marian Keyes

'A tale of navigating being an adult while facing major milestone decisions, it is a must-read'
Hello

'Funny in parts, painful in others, thoughtful throughout, it
explores many dilemmas, with characters who feel utterly real'
Sophie Kinsella

'A witty, tender portrayal of female friendship under pressure'
Mail on Sunday

'Olive is the best friend every young woman needs, and one
I wish I'd had. Gannon gives us an important book, reminding
her readers of the beauty in our individual paths'
Christina Dalcher

'I suspect a lot of women will feel relieved and seen when
they read it'
Holly Bourne

OLIVE

EMMA GANNON

HarperCollins*Publishers*

HarperCollins*Publishers* Ltd
1 London Bridge Street,
London SE1 9GF

www.harpercollins.co.uk

HarperCollins*Publishers*
1st Floor, Watermarque Building, Ringsend Road
Dublin 4, Ireland

This paperback edition 2021

1

First published by HarperCollins*Publishers* 2020

ISBN: 978-0-00-838273-5

Set in Berling LT Std by Palimpsest Book Production Limited, Falkirk, Stirlingshire

Printed and bound in the UK by CPI Group (UK) Ltd, Croydon CR0 4YY

MIX
**Paper from
responsible sources**
FSC™ C007454

FSC
www.fsc.org

Prologue

Editor's Letter
Published 18 January 2020,
from issue #24 of .dot magazine

'The Mother of all Choices'
by Olive Stone

I am the same age as my mother when she had me. Thirty-three. If I turn my face a certain way in the mirror, I can see her looking back at me – we have the same chin, thick dark hair, and a mole more or less in the same place above our lip. But I am miles away from who she was then. We might look the same, but in all other ways we are not. I was told when I was little by my grandmother, Pearl, that when you turn thirty, you are suddenly gifted a new kind of respect for yourself. 'You will care less, as if by magic, my dear,' she would say. 'Being young is terribly confusing. Quite awful really.'

It's true that as you grow older, you know yourself better.

You leave bad parties slightly earlier. But then, the down-sides: your bones are slowly beginning to disintegrate, a natural decline in bone mass, though consuming vegetables, protein and collagen might help. You start to realize exercise is no longer about vanity, but necessity. Your metabolism changes too, sadly starting to slow down. You start to realize you 'should' go easier on the cheese boards, but you won't because brie is everything. Then there are the hangovers! Drinking two bottles of Prosecco doesn't feel like having a beaker of lemonade any more – it fizzes and pops and aches in your head the next day; but fortunately you have more willpower now to 'get on with it'. Rumour has it your libido changes too; it ebbs and flows and tends to dry up a bit, and of course you'll start noticing a few more lines on your forehead and around your mouth that seem to be slightly more prominent than before, but you also think it looks cool. A sign that you know more stuff. You might feel the need to chuck out your entire wardrobe and start again, to reflect a new chapter in your life, a new confidence, a new relationship with your body. You slip into your new skin like a snake who's finally come home. On the whole things start to seem easier and plus, you have a bit more cash now. This is everything grandmother Pearl foreshadowed.

And then bam – even though I should have seen it coming – babies are suddenly on the brain. There is an abrupt tap on the shoulder from friends, family, society and suddenly it's the number one topic of conversation. Babies. Babies. Babies. When. When. When.

When I was twelve, in 1999, I remember being obsessed

with snipping cut-outs from my mum's old Argos catalogues and sticking them into the blank pages of my notepads. Notepads were the only present people bought me or put in my stocking, because I was always doodling as a tiny kid. I would have stacks of them: beaded ones, velvet ones, bright pink ones, furry ones, holographic ones, and secret diary ones with a lock and key. But I had stopped writing and started making collages instead. I would neatly cut around pictures of products I found interesting from the flimsy thin pages of Argos, and Pritt-stick them inside the blank pages. Navy-blue patterned plates. A big wooden rolling pin. Hand-painted tea cups. A garden slide. A stylish armchair. A woollen throw for the sofa. A picture frame designed for four landscape-shaped photos. I would trim carefully around each one with big kitchen scissors, in circular motions, around the plates, bowls, crockery. I would stick them into the blank pages, designing my life in detail from an early age. I believed I would have these perfect little things in my home when I was older. I would have a garden. I would live in a big house, bigger than my mum's. I would have a husband. I would have a baby too, probably. Or two. Or three! Because that's what you do. My friends would come round with their babies. They would all play together. We would go to the beach and tell them not to eat the sand, while we drank tea in flasks and reminisced about the good old days. That's what grown-ups did. When I am an adult, I would think, everything will be good. I will finally be free. Adulthood = Freedom.

I painted a picture of my Big Bright Future through the

lens of an old Argos catalogue, and today I am inside that distant future; in the painting, living and breathing it. But I don't have the hand-painted tea cups, or the navy-blue patterned plates. I don't have a garden slide. And I don't have the baby either.

Looking back, perhaps the baby thing was always more of a blurry idea; one that I could never totally zoom in on. I could only really imagine it hypothetically. The idea of becoming a mother was something passed down to me – from my mother, and her mother's mother, over centuries and centuries of social conditioning. It seemed like a no-brainer. Like all the other milestones in the how-to-be-a-person manual.

Turns out that you can't Pritt-stick a life together as a child and then hop inside it when the time is right like Bert from Mary Poppins.

And so now, sitting here in 2020, typing this, I realize that I imagined a different thirty-three-year-old to the one I have actually become. This woman who has no sign of 'twitching ovaries', or fertility flutters, or random broodi-ness. I hold babies and, sure, they're cute, but I give them back and don't feel any biological shifts or urges. I see pregnancy announcements online and press the heart button but feel zero jealousy. I picture myself twenty, thirty years into the future, with silver in my hair, walking on a beach with a partner, writing in the evenings with a glass of wine, and multiple nephews and nieces visiting me in my cosy home. There might be no children of my own in my future, but why should this cause me any worry?

So why am I telling you all of this? Last month's issue was all about exploring different variations on adulthood and motherhood. This whole issue of .dot is dedicated to exploring what it means to be child-free, by choice, and all the other myriad ways we might decide to live our lives. We hope you love this issue as much as we do, but we realize this is the tip of the iceberg: we aren't done talking about these issues! The decision to have kids might be one of the biggest choices we ever face, and we should be talking about this in all its complicated, nuanced depth.

Thanks as always for choosing to read .dot, and we look forward to reading your letters and tweets.

See you next month,
Editor-In-Chief, .dot
Olive x

Part One

'You know what gets to me? The knowing, smug
smirk that so often accompanies the words:
"You'll change your mind."'

Kym, 35

1

2008

'WAKE UP OLIVE.' Bea jostled me awake gently, and I drifted from my dream into the vibrations of her deep, velvety voice. She had plonked herself down on the bed next to me, her curvaceous body cushioned softly on the mattress. Through half-opened eyes, I could make out the outline of her head of huge, tightly curled hair. I had an unused face wipe stuck to my forehead and a pounding headache. I peeled it off and the sunlight streamed into my eyes. Bea had waltzed on in and opened my blinds again. There was no such thing as privacy in this house, and to be honest, that's the way we liked it. The real world was a maze offering too many choices, too many narrow alleyways, too many wrong turns. Everything in this old and painted-over Victorian semi-detached house felt safe. We paid bills together, we ate together, we ran errands together, we were partial to a group nap. This was our much-loved university student house, and we would be leaving here forever in a few short hours.

'Ugh?' I said, moaning. I picked up my phone with one crusty eye open and saw my ghastly reflection looking back at me on the screen. My skin was still clear and smooth but my face looked puffier than usual and my green eyes were blackened, like a panda's, with eyeliner smudged all down my face. My long black hair was knotted on one side, and there were sticky drink stains along my pale arms. I sniffed. Yes, it smelt like Sambuca. I had obviously attempted to clean my face with the wipe and failed miserably. I looked at the packet on the floor and realized it wasn't even a face wipe, it was one of those kitchen wipes that you clean surfaces with.

'Have you definitely packed everything?' Bea asked, as she picked my underwear up off the floor and flung it into a carrier bag. She lay down next to me, so both of our heads were on my pillow.

'Yes. Everything is done. Just a few tiny bits left in a few drawers. Oh my god,' I croaked, 'I sound like Deirdre Barlow. I must have smoked.'

'I did try and stop you. Those horrible Marlboro Reds,' Bea told me, closing her eyes and shaking her head.

'I had such a good time last night . . .' My voice shook, I was about to cry. 'I don't want us to leave, Bea. I don't want this chapter to be over.'

'Oh Ol. You just need a perspective change. This isn't the end. This is the beginning,' she said, and stroked my unwashed hair.

'I want to stay here for ever.' I nuzzled into her big comfy bosom. 'It's the end of an era. Us four, in this house together. They've been the best years of my life.' I put my hand on

10

hers. She smelt of Ghost perfume. Her cashmere jumper felt so soft. I just lay there, and inhaled her, my best friend. Past boyfriends had sometimes commented on how touchy-feely my friends and I were. We'd often pass out almost naked in each other's beds. They never seemed to properly understand the intimacy of women.

The four of us had gone through the same phases over the years: like wearing all black because it seemed more chic; sporting the same gold friendship jewellery; we even got the same tattoo of a slice of pizza under our left boobs on a holiday in Australia (I know, what?). We all passed our driving test the same year, lost our virginity within a few months of each other, grew up with and quoted the same TV box-sets. It definitely felt like the stars had aligned when we all ended up going to University College London to study together. We had made a pact, as a four, that UCL would be our first choice. We all wanted to go to the big city together. But we had to get the right grades at A level first, and that was going to be tough because we had spent so much of school pissing about, going to house parties with boys and smoking too much weed. But results day turned out to be one of my favourite days ever. We ripped open the envelopes together, and screeched when we knew we'd be staying as a close unit for another three years. Maybe fear really is the only motivator in life.

We've shared all the same big milestones, the highs and the lows of new boyfriends, break-ups and family dramas. Our lives have pretty much mirrored one another's exactly; with peaks and troughs, like lines on a graph.

'It's been an amazing chapter, babe. But . . . it's time.' I could tell Bea was sad, but she was also being optimistic. That's Bea all over – the glass is always half full. The constant exhale of everything will be fine. She patted me, and then unclasped my hand, peeling herself away from me. Her presence always felt so motherly, so safe.

'I know, but let me wallow for a bit, Bea. Zeta isn't coming to collect me for ages yet.' My older sister Zeta was driving down from teaching a workshop in Bristol in her battered old Mini, so she would be late. She always was – she was notorious for it. It wasn't that she was scatty, just that she was an intensely dedicated charity volunteer, and if someone needed her for something, she would be there for them. She never felt as if she could say no, even if it meant saying no to her own family sometimes. I was glad my big sis was going to come and get me and help with my bags, but it wasn't exactly her priority.

'C'mon. Have a shower. I'll take that big suitcase downstairs for you,' Bea said, as she rolled up her sleeves.

'Don't take it down yet,' I said, tears glistening in my eyes.

'Ol. Look. It's OK. I'm sad too. We all are. But c'mon, you need to get showered.'

I suddenly had a flashback to the previous night. The barman had given us all endless free shots because he fancied Cecily, Bea had ended up doing the worm on the dance floor, and Isla had stolen someone's sombrero.

'How are you not hungover?' I heard a moan from outside the door, directed at Bea. 'Are you an alien?' Cec had appeared in a T-shirt and a lace thong, sucking on a straw in a water bottle. Her blonde bob was still magically intact. Her long legs had streaks of fake tan left on them.

'I *am* hungover. But you know me, I can't lie in,' replied Bea, shrugging.

Cec took a running jump and landed on my bed. On top of me. Her naked bum cheek touching my leg.

'Bea, you're so *odd*,' Cec said, and threw Henry, my cuddly toy, at her. It ricocheted off her chest and squeaked. 'God, I feel rough.' She snuggled in under my armpit, laughing and then said: 'Olive you reek!'

'Make room for me,' Isla croaked at the door, her dark blunt fringe flopping over her eyes, and her glasses wonky on her freckled face. 'Guys, I have the fear. Seriously, did I say or do anything weird last night?' She walked across the room, kicked off her slippers and curled up underneath the duvet with us, spooning Cecily. Isla always gets 'the fear', ever since our sixth-form days when she got hammered at our leavers' do on Bacardi Breezers and asked our only male teacher (poor Mr Simmons) 'to dance', as if she was a character in a Jane Austen novel.

'While you're there, Bea, can you take my suitcase down too?' Cec said, pushing her luck.

'Piss off. I'm not your mum,' Bea laughed, rolling her eyes.

'I don't remember much from last night, you know. We really went for it, didn't we?' said Isla. 'I do have a faint memory of us breaking into that park on the way home.' Oh my god, she was right, we had scaled the walls, and it was all Cec's fault. Her and her wild ideas.

'I swear it was the one where Hugh Grant and Julia Roberts hung out in *Notting Hill*,' Cec said, trying to hold down a burp. Living in London as students regularly allowed for these strange night-time adventures.

'You can pretend it was, love,' Bea said, lifting a heavy bag out of the room.

We had sneaked into a park (could have been someone's private garden, to be honest) and sat on a bench together, underneath some twinkling fairy lights, and reminisced about the last three years living in our special little home. We had played 'Dancing in the Moonlight' by Toploader on my iPod and danced with each other. We sang like out-of-tune cats.

'Guys,' I gulped, then paused. 'Can we always, always make time for each other – no matter what happens?'

Cec swung her arms around me. 'You're not getting rid of me, mate.'

'Of course, Ol, you are such a worrier!' Bea said.

Isla nodded along like a Churchill dog.

As I lay there, hungover in bed, the reality was dawning. We were moving out. Moving on from the disgusting kitchen, the mice, the creaky radiators and the creepy landlord. There was no happier feeling than four of us in the bed. Four young sweaty bodies, entangled, feeling fragile, but excited for the future. They were my home. Home with a capital H.

There was a knock at the door, it was Bea's boyfriend, Jeremy – we could see it was him through the frosted-glass panelling on the front door. Tall, lanky, ego-free Jeremy. Bea had never let anyone in until now; she'd had her fair share of bad boys who she'd kick to the kerb when it all got a bit too real. Jeremy was arty like Bea, an ambitious film student who had already got an internship lined up at Working Title. They were a sweet couple, but we hardly saw him. Apparently Jeremy never complained if she prioritized us over him and she would only see him and stay at his house on Sunday nights, even though he had a giant TV, way better than ours. He never stayed over here either, so the majority of the time she was still ours. Maybe that was why I liked him. But now, she was leaving, and I knew there would be whispers of them moving in together. And the rest.

'Hi girls, so great to see you all,' Jeremy said politely, and swooped down to kiss each of us on the cheek. He then wrapped his long arms around Bea and squeezed her tight, lifting her slightly off the ground. 'Sad day?'

'It really is,' I sighed before Bea could reply, and flinched as he picked up one of Bea's huge duffel bags with ease, swinging it over his shoulder.

'Sorry to be a pooper, but we'd better get going, Bea, you know, to beat the traffic,' he said.

'Good point,' Bea said, looking at us, glumly.

The three of us, the remaining ones, did a last lap of the house, saying goodbye to all the rooms. The kitchen, where we'd made countless disgusting drinks; we had followed that hideous trend of putting Skittles in vodka for a time. Then Bea's downstairs bedroom, with a door leading onto the garden patio (covered in bird poo and old bin-bags ripped apart by foxes), which she'd proudly decorated with one of those giant dreamcatchers hanging above the bed and where we'd often watched back-to-back episodes of *Friends*. The living room, where once we'd staged a private karaoke party; we'd invited everyone we'd met in the night-club queue that evening and the neighbours had complained and almost called the police. Isla's bedroom, on the floor of which we'd eaten many a Domino's pizza, and Cec's room, where she had once dressed up as a giant banana and, having got wedged in the door for hours, ended up wetting herself.

And finally, my room, the biggest, with an old fireplace and wooden flooring. My bed seemed to be the place we all gathered when we were sad. It was the room we'd get ready in before a night out because it had the most floor space. The room where we would sit on the floor and chat for hours. There were nail-varnish stains on the walls and burn stains on the rug from hair straighteners. I loved this room – our communal room.

The doorbell went again. Isla was collected by her second cousin Sarah, who also lived in London. Isla had lost her parents in a freak road accident at a young age, and depended on the kindness of her friends and extended family who had wrapped a web of love around her over the years. Cec was the last to leave, picked up by her mum and dad, Tiff and Todd, in their brand-new Land Rover. They would be going back to their large house in the countryside to warm themselves by the fire. I always felt a pang of jealousy thinking of Cec's family and their luxurious lifestyle, but instantly shook it away. Cec hugged me closely, as she always knew to do when I was feeling vulnerable.

'Are you going to be OK here until Zeta arrives?' she asked me.

'Yes of course,' I said, knowing her question was rhetorical, as Tiff had her hand on Cec's shoulder, and Todd was waiting in the car. They were ready to leave.

'Sure?' She lowered head and scanned my face with her eyes.

'Yes, go on, I don't want to hold you up,' I said, and ushered her outside. I squeezed Cec, and shivered. She got inside the car in the back seat and waved with a sad, tight-lipped smile. Tiff and Todd were in the front, beaming, clearly happy to be reunited with their daughter. I went back inside and shut the green front door behind me, the one we had all opened and closed thousands of times, and it suddenly felt cold, with no people warming up the house.

I sat on the stairs, waiting for Zeta like a lost puppy. The minutes turned into hours, and I didn't enjoy having that much thinking time, alone in a house full of memories, reflecting already on a period of time with friends that I would never experience again.

2

2019

It's been six weeks now since Jacob and I broke up. It feels like a quick snap of the finger, and yet absolutely ages, all at the same time. It's been horrible and everything feels uncomfortable and sticky. My brain keeps going around and round like a broken record: nine years down the drain. Nine whole years.

I close my windows and put my bedroom fan on to the strongest setting. A cheap one from Amazon that makes an irritating buzzing sound. It's a muggy day, and my flat suddenly feels boiling.

I have heaps of washing-up that needs doing. Heading into the kitchen, I turn on the red digital radio that stands on the shelf above my sink, and it blasts out BBC Radio 4. I listen while I put on my Marigolds. The tap splashes some water on my face, and I realize I'm crying a bit too – at least I've held off longer than I did yesterday.

'According to papers today, Millennial women are suffering

from the paradox of choice. They have a multitude of options that can problematize decision-making! Too much choice! Tweet us – do you feel like having too many options is holding you back?'

I turn the radio off. What an annoyingly chirpy voice.

I have the Sunday blues, but I also feel glad that I have an office to go to tomorrow after a depressingly quiet weekend. I posted some old photos of me sitting in the park on Instagram so that people might think I was busy. In reality, I'm not quite ready for human contact. I'm also ninety-five per cent full of booze and chocolate orange and didn't move all weekend except for occasionally putting a cold glass of gin to my lips. I am bigger since the break-up – I feel like a woman made of Play-Doh but it feels strangely comforting. I can grab hold of parts of myself I never could before. My body has changed and morphed, and now I'm my very own teddy bear. My skin is blotchier than usual too. I'm needing half a bottle of something to sleep each night. But I think I've gone through the worst of it. At first I spent many days festering in bed in my own juices, distracting myself by watching Netflix documentaries about climate change, serial killers, and how the world is totally fucked beyond repair, and surprise, surprise, it didn't really help. Then I tried reaching for some positivity: old movies, reading my favourite erotica books, and watching old episodes of *MTV Cribs* on YouTube. I even forced myself to get a haircut, to try and make myself feel better, and the new hairdresser guy gave me a head massage at the sinks that felt so good I burst into tears. Because the only intimacy I can get at the moment is a hairdresser touching my scalp. I messaged the girls about inane things on WhatsApp – I haven't told them about the break-up yet. Telling them would make it real, and I want to talk it through with them in person. But everyone seems a bit preoccupied; no one really replies on the WhatsApp group beyond a few quick emojis these days anyway.

Bea always says to 'give yourself a wallowing deadline' whenever you feel down, meaning that you should wallow intensely, feel it all properly and then decide when to stop. My deadline is up. It's been long enough now. I have to face life again, whatever that means. I start with having a clear-out. My flat is not dirty, but it is certainly messy – there is stuff everywhere. I have ornaments and vases covering every surface, faux plants hanging off every shelf; there is a fruitless fruit bowl full of receipts, bills and paper clips. I have a pile of books gathering dust next to the TV and torn-out recipe clippings from old magazines stacked up on the end of my kitchen counter that I am not planning to read again. I grab two blue Ikea bags and start loading them up with books, old jumpers, pieces of painted crockery and vases that I no longer need. Giving away things to a charity shop every now and again always makes me feel better, like I'm in control of what I let in and out of my life. I call up the shop at the end of my road, owned by a lady called Mrs Farnham who does next-day charity collections. It rings a couple of times.

'Hello?' A croaky man's voice answers the phone.

'Er . . . hi . . . ? I'm looking for Mrs Farnham,' I say.

'Oh – nah she's not in, sorry love. The shop's not doing collections for a few months while Mrs Farnham is on maternity leave.'

'Oh, I see! Is there no one else there that might be able to help?' I ask, politely.

'No, love, I just told ya. Shop's shut while she's off. Shouldn't say "off", should I? Sounds like a holiday.' He laughs.

'Right,' I say.

'Ring back in a few months, I reckon.'

I groan, and hang up.

The following day, I pick up a takeaway coffee in my favourite little café, Kava in Soho, next to the .dot offices. It's my usual morning routine before work. I quickly check my emails at the end of the bar. The press releases I receive get more and more bizarre by the day:

- Amal Clooney Gets Bunions, So Now Everyone Wants Them
- Four Steps to Having Skin Like Paul Rudd
- The Best Bacon-Scented Sex Products (Including Lube!)
- Home Remedies to Grow Back Those 'Barely There' Nineties Eyebrows

Delete, delete delete.

I have a quick scroll through Facebook while my latte gets frothed. Who are all these people? I don't recognize any names. A girl who I remember being really fun at school is now married to a boring basic banker. Another friend from university who I vaguely remember as sleeping with the entire football team has now become a nun and has written a painfully long caption to explain her 'difficult' exit from the online world. Everything is changing. I scroll past photos of five different toddlers, their faces covered in yoghurt, chocolate mousse and baked beans.

I have a quick cigarette outside on the pavement with my coffee in my hand and lean back to relax for a moment, my old faux-fur turquoise coat touching the brick wall behind me. I take big puffs of my cigarette and inhale loudly through my teeth – going against orders from my dentist who has recently told me off for smoking. An anti-fur fashion campaigner suddenly strides up to me with stickers and a placard. He waggles his finger at me and says I shouldn't be wearing fur.

'It's faux fur actually – from a charity shop in Copenhagen.' I exhale some smoke and tuck my long black hair behind my ear.

He wafts the smoke away and opens his mouth to begin his unnecessarily worthy spiel. 'Well, actually—'

'You'll find I am quite ethical, as a person,' I interrupt, tapping my ash on the floor. I know I'm being spiky and defensive, but this is not what I need this morning. I'm going through a break-up for god's sake. People have no manners.

'I'm afraid it's not good enough. Faux fur is made up of synthetic microfibres that never really break down or decompose. Worse than real fur, in some ways. And don't get me started on sequins.'

'Well, are you perfect? I bet you wear leather.'

'I don't wear leather, I'm a vegan.'

'I bet you secretly eat bacon sandwiches when you're hungover.'

'I don't, actually.'

Jesus, what is happening? I'm just trying to drink my coffee and have a cig before I go to work. Life's hard enough without a vegan campaigner banging on and on.

He continues: 'Please take this leaflet and read more about it and please consider your life choices.' He wanders off, to go and find someone else who's doing life totally wrong.

'Maybe I will, maybe I won't!' I call after him, ripping up the leaflet.

This is living in London. No rest for the wicked. No physical boundaries. Constant interruptions. Everyone is so on, on, on. Everything is up for debate and you are always in someone's way. Having said that, I might moan about London, but I also couldn't live anywhere else, ever. Growing up in the countryside in Somerset was idyllic in many ways, especially as I met Bea, Cec and Isla at school, but I also found it incredibly boring. Zeta, Mum and I would cook every night together, eating dinner in our small conservatory overlooking the garden, and knew all of our next-door neighbours and their business maybe *too* well. The air was fresh, and the days were quiet. But, for me, the countryside seems like somewhere you go to disappear and die. Fast-paced city life is in my blood.

A young girl with a long green tartan coat and reddish curly hair walks slowly past me, then turns on her heel, pauses and then comes up close.

'So sorry to bother you, but are you Olive Stone?' she asks, half whispering.

'Yep, that's me.' I take a slurp of my warm coffee, trying not to act totally surprised that I've been recognized. This never happens.

'Sorry, I just wanted to say, your recent piece in the .dot, was . . . amazing. Really fascinating.'

'Oh, thank you!' It feels sad to admit, maybe, but this has really puffed me up. I had written a cover story for .dot magazine called 'Are Men OK?', which had just yesterday been further dissected by a journalist at the *New York Times*. It was a proud moment for me to have my work discussed by other journalists. I had written about the trend of men faking going to work, based on true stories of people's husbands who had pretended to go to work for a whole year (putting on a suit and everything). They would go and sit in the park or sit in a café all day, while running up huge debts on credit cards to cover up their desperation and deception. Some of their partners hadn't known until it was too late and it had totally ruined their lives. It was genuinely worrying. I found thirty-five different case studies – even one that was linked to a friend of a friend.

'Would I be able to email you and send you my CV? If there is ever any work experience?' Curly Hair Girl asks.

'Yeah OK,' I say, with my cigarette hanging out of my mouth, writing down my email address on a scrap of paper, balancing it on my knee.

'Thank you so much. Meeting you has made my day.'

She pauses and tilts her head to look at me. 'You know, some people, like my friends who read your writing, often say you are quite unlikeable. But I like you.'

'Oh?'

'Yeah, I think it's really inspiring. That you put yourself out there. And that you don't care about the reaction.'

'Right. Thanks . . . I think!' I say. I didn't know I was unlikeable. Back-handed compliments really mess with my head.

.dot magazine launched just under two years ago; a new feminist-focused online magazine for younger women that was the brainchild of the founder of a big tech giant in America to try and fill the gaping void left by so many mainstream glossy magazines suddenly going bust. Every viral story that puts .dot more firmly on the map gets more mentions and click-throughs. And for every big story I write I seem to get another promotion, which sort of feels addictive.

I can get away with murder these days – but only because I've worked really hard to climb the ladder at .dot over the years. I've lost count of the number of days I've walked in with unwashed hair, latte in hand, forty-five minutes late. Gill, the editor-in-chief, is normally out of the office and as I am the second most senior to Gill, no one would ever say anything to me about my lateness. I almost wish someone would, to be honest. I'm doing well at work, getting to the point where I'll soon be more than happy with my pay cheque, and it often seems like the only part of my life that I'm sailing through with some element of ease. I think I am in that rare and temporary point in life where I am an 'old young person' and a 'young old person'. I'm bang in the middle: young enough to be cool, old enough to have some experience of how shit life can be. I know I won't be this age for ever, but right now it's working out for me – career-wise, anyway. Now all I have to do is figure out how to freeze time.

I walk into the office, the freshly hoovered soft carpet beneath my Converse trainers. Someone has tidied all the papers on my desk into a neat pile. Everyone in the open-plan office notices me walk in and immediately looks more preoccupied with their work. This still weirds me out. I feel so out of control in my personal life, and yet, in this office people are somehow intimidated by me. Having any sort of influence or power at work is still a huge novelty. I pause. What is that music blasting through the speakers? I have it, it's R. Kelly's 'Ignition'.

I walk over to Judy, a junior subeditor who is wiggling in her seat and bopping her head to the music.

'Judy – R. Kelly is a sexual abuser. Can you turn it off, immediately please?'

Judy stares at me blankly, and turns the volume right down, but not totally off.

I go and sit at my desk, kicking off my shoes. Bloody office politics.

'Here are some packages, Ol,' our receptionist Colin says, chipper as usual, dropping a heavy pile of parcels onto my desk. 'Feels like clothes inside.' He presses down on it with his thumb.

'Yeah. Thanks Colin,' I say, not looking up from my desk.

'Not excited about your new garms?' he says, sitting down on a swivel chair and crossing his legs.

'No. I ordered them from this American website, they took months to arrive, and . . . well, now I don't even need them any more.'

I'd ordered them for Jacob's brother's wedding, months ago when we were still together. These clothes arriving is just another sad reminder of everything that's changed.

'Fair enough. Hey, wanna know something depressing?'

'Not really.' Read the room, Colin.

'It's not proper depressing – more like, funny-depressing.'

'All right, go on.'

'I've just downloaded this app that tells you how many books you could have written if you calculate all the tweets you've written over the years. I've tweeted 5,000 times,' he tells me. 'So that's 700,000 characters. So that's definitely like two books.'

'Why would you do that?'

Colin gets out his phone and goes onto my Twitter page. 'Wow—'

'No. Stop.'

'You've tweeted 52,000 times. So, you could have written, like, fifteen books by now,' he says, deadpan.

I want to whack my head on the desk. I imagine blood going everywhere, splashing onto Colin.

'Can I make you a tea? Also, this new eye cream got delivered today for you all to test out.' He hands me a gold cardboard box. 'You do look a bit tired my love.'

'Cheers,' I say, blankly. 'And yes, two sugars please.'

I'm seeing Bea, Isla and Cec tonight. Maybe I'll take a few boxes of freebies from the office for them; they always seem to love free beauty bits and bobs. I can't wait to see them. I feel like a shell of my usual self. I guess I haven't fully processed the break-up yet. I need some perspective from my mates.

Suddenly my eyes fill with tears. I'd given myself a good talking-to in the mirror this morning. I've done my crying, enough's enough. But clearly the well's not empty just yet. I take myself off to the best place to have a shameless cry: the .dot toilets. They are the newest and fanciest part of the whole office. I take a box of tissues with me and try to cry quietly on the seat of the loo. Twenty minutes later, there's a tap on the glazed glass door.

'Ol? Ol . . . it's Colin.'

'Oh, for god's sake, Colin – not now.'

'Sorry love, it's just . . . your tea is cold and Gill has said she needs you for a meeting.'

'Oh crap.' I look at my phone. Yes, it's 10 a.m. already, time for our weekly features meeting.

'Can I come in?'

'How do you know I'm not doing a poo?' Colin and I have this type of oversharing relationship. We've become quite close friends over the years; he often plays a role in cheering me up or lightening the mood and I have been there to listen to his terrible dates with awful men.

He laughs gently. 'Oh babe, I could hear you crying from outside.'

'OK.' I sniff. I let Colin in and he wraps me up in a big hug.

'Are you OK? Is it Gill? Is she being horrible?'

'No . . . no. It's . . . me and Jacob. We have . . . well, I have . . . ended things.' I sniff.

'Oh no. I'm so sorry.'

'It's OK.'

'Is it . . . OK?'

'No, not really.' I wipe my nose. 'I mean, I just can't stop crying. I've been coming in these loos for a sob every day since it happened; can't believe no one's noticed yet.'

'Do you wanna talk about it?'

'Maybe soon. Not feeling up to it right now.'

'I get it. Don't worry. Shall I tell Gill you've got something else on? I'm sure she'll understand.'

'Actually, that would be great, yes please. Thank you. I just need a bit more time in here, getting myself together.'

'Of course.' Colin squeezes my hand and gives a sympathetic smile.

Grief can knock you sideways. I miss Jacob so much. I feel almost sick at how much I could do with a hug from him right now. I'm constantly trying to fight back tears. I can't imagine anyone ever loving me in the same way. Or seeing me naked, for that matter.

After another thirty minutes, sobbing and squeezing out tears, I look in the bathroom mirror and blot away at my face with toilet roll, removing any signs of dampness. Then I apply more kohl liner around my eyes. Since the break-up I've felt so worried that we've made the wrong choice by ending it. I guess this is being human: we can never be 100 per cent sure about any decision we make.

Jacob moved out 'officially' only recently, after living in his brother Sam's spare room for a month. The idea was that we'd try living apart at first as some sort of 'break'. But it sounded a lot like a break-up from the start. It's been the shittiest time of my entire life. I am stewing in it, sitting in the negativity and depression like a big squishy chair that I can't get out of. Every meal I cook reminds me of him. Everything on TV. Even replacing the loo roll or making the bed in the morning. Everything. I wish I could just delete everything and start again, like picking a brand-new player in a video game.

I leg it out of the office at 5.30 on the dot, itching to get to tonight's dinner. I desperately need to feel the safety net of my best pals, who will allow me to rant and shout and cry and snot bubble. That'll make me feel better. They have always stood up for me. Once, back in the day when you could still smoke inside, they all tapped ash on my ex-boyfriend Billy's head on the dance floor. He was a horrible, verbally abusive arsehole. All the ash just piled up in his hair while he danced. I bet it stank for days.

I'm sweating slightly on the Tube on the way to our usual dinner place, Jono's, a family-run Italian restaurant in Clerkenwell. We stumbled across it one drunken night years ago at uni, and it quickly became our go-to. We always have the same table, a big corner booth looking onto the street. The atmosphere is warm, busy and friendly. We love Jono, the owner, who is always there with a massive smile on his face. He knows us so well now after a decade of the same orders: spaghetti alle vongole (Bea), risotto ai gamberi (Cecily), gnocchi (Isla) and capricciosa pizza (me). We have had countless heart-to-hearts inside, plus countless arguments, countless tears and laughing fits. There are so many trendy new hipster restaurants opening all the time in London, but Jono's will always have our heart. If I'm ever late I know the girls will have ordered my drink (a glass of Fatalone, large), and it will be waiting for me when I get there. The others are never late. Compared to my friends, I guess I do feel a bit . . . behind. I think it's a metaphor for my life.

I rush through the streets of Holborn, panting a bit and stomping past slow tourists who mindlessly dawdle along with no sense of direction. I try not to get run over by an angry cab driver with a cigar hanging out of his mouth who very nearly turns my entire left leg into a squashed pancake. Then a bus goes past me very slowly, wafting toxic fumes up my nose and splashing through a giant puddle which sprays dirty water onto my Converse. 'Arseholes!' I shout. Then, an old woman goes over my foot with her wheelie suitcase, leaving a line of dirt on my shoe.

As I approach the familiar doorway to Jono's, I realize my heart is pounding slightly and my skin prickling – that old underlying anxiety flaring up. It hits me that I haven't seen the girls in a while, and it feels weird. I breathe in through my nose, and out through my mouth a few times. Everyone has just seemed slightly less available, a creeping sense of busyness and life admin and to-do lists, of time being squeezed.

When I arrive, the three of them are sat there, and something immediately feels off. Jono is pouring some tap water into their glasses. They all look like someone's died. Has someone died?

'*Hi guys,*' I say, panting and whipping off my coat. 'Only fifteen minutes late this time, I'm getting better! Sorry. Everything OK?'

'Hey Ol . . .' They all give me big smiles as I go around the table kissing them, saying how lovely it is to see me. I can't help but notice how tired they all look.

'Everything's fine. It's just . . . we're not quite on top form tonight, Ol,' Isla says.

'What's up?' I say, putting my coat over the back of my chair, and sitting down.

'Well . . .' Bea takes in a deep breath. 'Cec is obviously about to give birth any day now, I'm absolutely knackered from being up all night with a vomiting child and Isla has really bad cramps . . . we're not a fun bunch, I'm afraid!'

Cec is in the loo right now. She is weeing every five minutes, apparently.

Isla has suffered with severe cramps and endometriosis issues all her life. Bea has three wild kids who are always plagued with something. This latest ailment sounded like the actual bubonic plague. And Cec, to be fair, is about to pop.

'OK,' I say, trying to hide my disappointment. 'That's fine! Sorry to hear the kids are still poorly, Bea. Shall we have a quick bite then, and maybe just one quick drink?'

'Well,' Bea looks awkwardly at the others. 'We'd actually just decided that maybe we should give this one a miss and head home. Sorry, Ol.' Jono sheepishly puts the bill on the table: £3.00 for some olives, £0.00 for the tap water.

I try and hide it, but I feel winded. 'Oh, that's a shame.'

'I know but,' Bea's phone lights up, 'there's some drama going on at home and I really have to leave. We're all pooped.' I look around the table at their forced smiles.

'My doctor has told me to rest,' Isla says.

'Poor you, of course,' I say, squeezing her hand.

Cec walks slowly over to us from the direction of the toilets, and Jono shouts, 'Bella mamma!' at her as he waves his hands towards her ginormous bump.

'Hey Ol,' Cec kisses me on the cheek, bending awkwardly.

'We've told Ol that we're gonna give tonight a miss,' Bea says.

I know I should be understanding, but we haven't seen each other properly for ages and I really needed some advice and support from my best friends.

'I'm *so* sorry, babe, I will make it up to you,' Cec says. 'Chris is driving over to pick me up right now, bless him. I'm not feeling great. Does anyone need a lift my way?' She plants a kiss on my cheek and puts her cardigan on.

I hope Cec's husband Chris doesn't come into the restaurant. He makes my skin crawl.

'No worries, guys. I appreciate you all dragging yourself out after work. We tried, eh?' I keep my cool and, once they leave, Jono orders me a big glass of wine on the house. Funny how Jono can pick up on my emotions, but not my own friends. But to be fair, they do have a lot on their minds.

Despite life's strange twists and turns, the four of us used to be glued together. We had always been there to lift each other up and out of everything: depression, break-ups, redundancies, you name it. We'd never missed a date at Jono's until recently. Jono's was our time – except for when Isla randomly brought her online date along, who wouldn't shut up about himself and his recent adult gap year before trying to pay for the entire meal in Bitcoin. But still, on the last Thursday of every month, for over a decade, we've gone to the same restaurant and sat at the same table. So why were things starting to slip now? It had felt so simple when we'd first laid down the rules in our twenties, on the day we left our shared house: that no matter what happened, we would make time for each other. Many people make the mistake of kicking friendships aside for the other seemingly more important strands of life, but we all know it's friendship that really keeps you afloat. We weren't going to be those people who let friendships slide. Or were we?

As I go to leave, I look over at another table and see four girls – younger versions of us – sitting, cackling, in shiny dresses, with no wrinkles, their heads rolling back, eyes sparkling and not yet tired by life. That used to be us.

I take my jacket from the wooden coat stand by the door, right next to our window-side table.

'You OK?' Jono says, putting his large hand on my shoulder.

'Yeah,' I sniff. 'Sorry Jono, for taking up your best table

and not even ordering anything.' I gesture towards our empty seats.

'It's OK, Olive. You will always be special customers to me.'

'We wasted a booking – sorry.'

'Don't be silly. You've come here for a long time. You girls have a long special friendship. I've seen it. Hold on to each other.'

'Thank you. I just feel like things are weird at the moment.'

'You must move with the tides: life is full of pushes and pulls.'

'True, Jono. True. I just need them right now.'

'Of course you do.' He pauses dramatically. 'And remember, they need you.'

'I hope so,' I sigh.

'Come back very soon, yes?' he says, wiping down the table and taking away the glasses.

Instead of going home, I reroute to the bar down the road called Mizzi's, and proceed to tell the barman – who co-incidentally looks a bit like Gunther from *Friends* – my life story like a weirdo in a film, while slowly getting red-wine teeth. I don't realize how much I resemble a vampire until I see my reflection in the mirror of the sticky-floored bath-room, and stare with horrified fascination at my bright purple mouth, my lips stained in the corners.

I know how much they all have going on, but I still can't shake the feeling that the girls have let me down. I'm bursting with the need to talk to someone about the break-up with Jacob. Stumbling out of Mizzi's, I sit on a doorway step. I reach for my phone and try to drunkenly call Colin, but his phone is switched off. I type in Zeta's name, but she is on a charity work trip and I know she only has occasional access to Internet cafés. I can't bear to ring Mum and tell her yet, as she just won't get it. I put my phone back in my bag.

When I finally stumble home around 1 a.m., I have a terrible, drunken urge to text Jacob. I type out a message and instantly make a typo. A reminder of how much wine I have consumed.

No. No. I can't.

Maybe I should?

Maybe he'd want to hear from me?

No. Olive. Stop it.

Standing by my front door, trying to fish my keys out of my bag, I notice that Dorothy Gray's light is still on. Dorothy is my eighty-eight-year-old neighbour. Everything else is dark but I can see her fuzzy TV screen; it looks as if a black-and-white film is playing. I've met her a couple of times at the local residents' meet-up or while taking out the bins. She lives in a big house directly opposite my block of flats, and we have a nice old chinwag if we're ever going inside or leaving home at the same time. Her house is ginormous, with its own driveway. She never seems to sleep or, at least, turn out her lights. I hope she's all right. Maybe she just watches TV all night (like me). Each to their own. My curtains are not quite closed, and there is a thin stream of bright light coming from her house into my bedroom. Perhaps it should be annoying, but I feel some warmth from it. Perhaps I'm not alone.

'I always compare the cost of a year's worth of nappies to how much travelling I could do instead.'

Katie, 29

3

2009

I was squatting down, in a sort of 'twerk' position, my knees creaking and trembling. I hadn't done a squat since gym class at school in the late 1990s and it showed. 'Dip' the stick delicately in your 'urine stream', I whispered back to myself, as I held the (now soggy) fold-out instruction manual. Pee in a perfectly straight line? That was like a policeman asking someone to walk along a painted straight line after one too many tequilas. It was impossible to 'dip' anything neatly at this moment, mainly because I was a bag of nerves. I was terrified by the situation. The pregnancy test was tacky and flimsy, and I didn't really trust it. It was purple and white and looked like it could easily snap in half. I was already worrying that it wouldn't be accurate and that I'd have to go back to the store and do this whole shebang again and again. We bought two, Bea and I, in a 'Buy One Get One Free' deal. So here we were, doing it together, sitting side by side in the toilet cubicles in the loos at Foyle's bookshop (of all places). We always joked that our wombs were 'n sync', Justin Timberlake style, but this time we really were. I felt so anxious, hovering awkwardly over an off-white stained loo seat that wasn't my own. I had just peed all over my hand by accident. It was warm and looked syrupy. Quite disgusting really.

'You all right in there?' I shouted sideways to Bea. I didn't hear anything, so I knocked on the partition.

'Mmmm,' she replied, unsurely. I could hear her heeled boots scuffling around on the tiles next to me.

I couldn't even bring myself to wash the pee off my hand because I had to wait for the stupid plastic gadget to show me a result. Germs were lingering everywhere, I thought, bacteria probably climbing the walls. If I was a proper grown-up, I would have anti-bac in my bag – but I forgot. Hurry up, hurry up. On the cubicle wall someone had scribbled, 'Life is beautiful'. And someone has replied 'fuck off with these memes m8' underneath. I shook the plastic stick (like a Polaroid picture?) but I wasn't sure it was doing anything to hurry up the process. It was just flicking small specks of urine onto the floor tiles. Gross.

'Bea?'

'Yeah?' she said, impatiently.

'Remember one line means *not* pregnant, and two lines means you *are* pregnant,' I yelled, hoping nobody else was in the toilets with us.

'Keep your voice down, Ol. I know what the lines mean,' she said.

I laughed. We'd done many lines together, in old skanky party toilets. Now look at us.

Rewind a couple of hours, and Bea and I were having lunch at Fall & Well, a little coffee shop on Denmark Street run by three hot brothers, catching up on life as we normally did on any other Hump Day Wednesday. It was our thing. We used this midweek session to sit and bitch about our jobs (and our bosses) for an hour. I was interning at a celebrity gossip magazine and Bea was a gallery assistant. Both our bosses were similar in their contempt and behaviour towards us: for some reason they wanted to make our lives hell. My boss was called Amie (a pretentious way of spelling Amy, if you ask me). Her nickname behind her back was Amie Hammer because she was as hard as nails. She wore these tasselled, heeled shoes to work, and every time she marched towards you to tell you off, you heard the tassels swishing first. It was a warning sign to get ready for a bollocking. My job was to get 'scoops', to find out if so-and-so was pregnant so we could 'break' the news first. I basically sat on Perez Hilton's website and made sure we copied (paraphrased) the hottest (or grimmest) American news stories onto our site – and I hated it. I wanted to be a writer, and this seemed like the logical first step in 'getting my foot in the door', according to all the career advisers at university. Just go for any old job, they said, as long as you can publish something! Writing horrible stories about reality TV stars really wasn't what I had imagined for myself, even if I did seem to have a knack for it.

'It feels like the better I perform at work, the more Amie Hammer hates me,' I sighed, drinking from my coffee cup.

'Oh Ol, don't worry. It's not you. I guess we just have to suck it up during these early years. The older women up the chain seem to have been told that the only way to "get ahead" is to scream at everyone.'

'You're right. Being the intern is just so hard sometimes.'

'You can't take it personally. They grew up in the "one seat at the table for women" era. Amie Hammer is threatened by you.'

'Ha! I highly doubt that, Bea.'

'She is. You're young. You'll take her job one day,' Bea said confidently, piling more sugar into her coffee.

Mine and Bea's lives have always paralleled, almost exactly. The four of us in the friendship group have gone through most things together, but Bea and I are something else. Our birthdays are just a few days apart, we started our periods at the same summer camp together, we both tried to insert our first tampon in the same bathroom together, we started our very first jobs years later in the same local pub pulling pints; and now we both had jobs that made us cry in our respective company toilets. For so long, we'd moved up the same ladder and our friendship had become more and more solidified on this basis. But today we'd found something brand new in common! Sitting in Fall & Well, we were both complaining about the same bodily annoyances: change in appetite, sore boobs, being grouchier than normal, having annoying headaches and a little bit of nausea thrown in for fun. Oh, and (er, most importantly) a very late period. Upon announcing this, we looked at each other through gritted teeth and realized we should probably check it out, together. We didn't really have time to discuss how we felt about it emotionally – never mind what our boyfriends would think – as we had less than half an hour before we needed to traipse back to the office, aka our prison cells. So, we walked in silence to quickly find some answers. And the answers to modern life's big questions were normally found in Boots.

We walked in and headed to the 'family planning' area at the back of the store – walking past life-size posters of catalogue model babies in shiny nappies smiling creepily at us – and popped the tests in our baskets. I took them to the till. I find it strange that at times of such great personal uncertainty, the cashier knows more about the intimate details of someone's life than their partner or anyone else close to them. Fanny rash? Pregnancy? Fungal infection? They scanned your life's secrets. Beep. Bea went off to look for some mouthwash. The older woman serving me, with two long earrings in the shape of cacti, gave me a wink as she put them in the bag as if to say 'good luck', which was weird, because how could she possibly know what I wanted? Fine, I clearly looked of an age at which buying a pregnancy test was something totally normal and something I might be excited about, but still.

'I'm not happy about this, you know,' I said to the presumptuous cacti-earringed cashier, pointing to the pregnancy tests.

'Er—'

'Yeah, this purchase,' I said, pointing at the offending item with my eyebrows, 'is the opposite of exciting.'

'Oh I see – OK! Well, then. Have a good day.'

Bea and I left the store, and I put one test in each pocket of my big coat. Where should we do them? This felt the same as buying cigarettes back in the day, needing to find a good hiding place to stash our new goodies and consume them privately.

That's when we duck into the flagship Foyle's bookshop on Charing Cross Road, because we knew they had some spacious toilets in there, next to the café on the fifth floor. Whilst everyone else was queuing up to buy their jacket potatoes with salad and coleslaw and skinny lattes, with shiny new hardback books stashed in their bags, we scurried off to the loos to see if our lives were going to change for ever.

When we entered the women's loos on the fifth floor, a little boy – who couldn't be older than two – popped out from behind the door. I let out a scream. Terrifying! Like something out of *The Shining*. He started crying and his mother appeared, with her wet soapy hands still dripping, rubbing them on her jeans. She huffed and puffed and tutted at me, checking her watch dramatically and swiping at his face with a wet wipe. He was inhaling quickly, still crying.

'Sorry,' I mumbled. I literally screamed in the child's face.

'It's OK,' the mum replied abruptly. I stood there like an awkward lemon. This kid's chubby little legs were stuffed into his tiny Converse shoes. I guess he was quite cute. My hand clamped around the pregnancy test box in my pocket.

Time ticked on frustratingly slowly. I waited for the purple line to become a little clearer. I brought the test up close to my face. My eyes crossed over and blurred. Why do seconds seem so stretched out when you are waiting for something important? Bea always told me to 'zoom out' when I became too overwhelmed with daily life. 'Like you would do with your fingers on a photo online, Ol, just breathe and use your two fingers to adjust, in and out,' she'd say. I often get so anxious that I can't find a logical way out of my own muddled-up thoughts, like a spider spasming in its own cobweb. That's why looking at the sky and out to the sea scientifically relaxes humans – because when we look into that deep, deep blue we realize we are insignificant specks. I sometimes found my brain racing around and around like a merry-go-round, and I felt like I was going to be sick but couldn't find a way to jump off safely. Breathe. Zoom out. Switch to bird's-eye view, Olive. Breathe. It's OK, I told myself. This was a *Sliding Doors* moment, but whatever happened, it would be OK.

I heard Bea shuffle out from her cubicle, the door gently closing. When I eventually emerged myself, the door accidentally slammed loudly behind me. I looked over at Bea, who had red cheeks with mascara-stained tears streaking down them.

'You OK?' I asked.

'It's . . . negative,' she said, sniffing.

Oh . . . shit. She actually wanted it to say she was pregnant? Were those tears of disappointment?

I looked down at my hands cupped around the pissy plastic container. 'Me too. Negative,' I said. I couldn't help but sound relieved. I thought of Jacob then, and I tried to imagine what he'd say. If I told him.

Two women, one result, two totally different responses whirring around in our heads, I could feel them clashing in the air. I thought we were in this together, Bea and I; I thought we wanted the same thing. We always did. I felt my utter joy and relief deflate slightly. I was well and truly off the hook – *not* pregnant! Yes! We could carry on living our sweet, sweet lives. Wahoooo! But I couldn't bounce up and down, I had to pretend to look sad. Also: Bea's reaction had really knocked me for six. How did I not know she was trying for a baby? We knew absolutely everything about each other.

Pfft. This was ridiculous. We didn't want kids. We were only in our early twenties. And I thought Jeremy was away all the time for work. She'd be really screwing herself over if she got pregnant now. We hadn't even been out of university that long, and there was so much time stretched out ahead of us to do big crazy things before we settled down. We had parties to attend, careers to smash, hangovers to indulge in, impromptu cinema trips and dinner parties to throw. I had a work acquaintance who had just had a baby and she said that even a trip to the cinema cost her over £50 because they had to book a babysitter on top of the tickets, snacks and car parking. Was that really what we wanted, so soon? Our lives to be put on hold?

After a slow afternoon back at work we went to a small bar just off Soho Square – we both needed a drink after all of that lunch-time palaver. We ordered a bottle of rosé. Then another one. After that we ended up in a dingy basement club nearby, where the barman gave us a free bottle of champagne – I lied and said it was Bea's birthday.

'This is the silver lining eh, Bea – if you'd had a different result you wouldn't be able to drink this delicious ch-champagne!' I slurred, sloshing my glass around.

'Oh sshhhh,' she said, smashing her champagne flute into mine. Luckily they were plastic.

Part of me wanted to ask her about the test, her disappointment: why a baby now, Bea? And why couldn't you tell me? But the bigger, more selfish part of me kept quiet.

So, there we were, marking a real milestone together. Me celebrating – Bea commiserating.

I drunkenly called Cecily on the way home, around 11 p.m., from the night bus. I got off a few stops early so I could get some fresh air. Cec always worked super-late, as a paralegal, so I knew she'd be up reading through a pile of documents that her boss couldn't be bothered to read. Sirens seem to blast past me every ten minutes. Motorbike engines pierced my eardrums. I sat inside a bus shelter to get away from the noise and replayed the whole ordeal to her, my leather jacket perched on my shoulders, with a cigarette in my hand. I was a bit drunk and I realized too late into the conversation that I was being a bit bitchy.

'I mean thank god my test was negative, Cec. And Bea being pregnant would be so weird, it's too early! But she did look very gutted though,' I said, exhaling smoke. I suddenly felt guilty, remembering the intense disappointment on Bea's face.

'Well, I think Bea and Jeremy have mentioned wanting kids one day, but yeah, I agree that it's very early . . .' Cec replied. It sounded echoey where she was; clearly her office was pretty empty as it was so late.

'Yeah. I guess I just assumed we'd both be freaking out. We were both so nervous buying the pregnancy tests because, you know, it was an accident. Well, at least for me? So I was totally taken aback when she looked upset at it coming out negative.'

'Wow,' Cec gasped, joining in. 'I suppose I'd be shocked too. It's a huge change and responsibility.'

'We're only twenty-two,' I said, tapping ash on the floor.

'There's no rush. I'm personally not ready *at all*. I've only just got properly going at work. It's bloody competitive in my office as well.'

'Same! I mean, do you think you will have one, one day though?' I asked.

'Dunno. Not until I'm much older, I think. I reckon I'll have one when I'm like thirty-eight or something? When I'm bossin' it as a lawyer with millions of pounds,' Cec said, laughing.

'That sounds good Cec – and there's no doubt you'll be bossing it. I guess we can just wait and see, can't we?'

'Exactly. And anyway Ol, don't worry about today, and

keep me posted. Right, I'd better sign off, I've got to get through a mountain of stuff and wanna be home by 1 a.m. God help me. Love you.'

'Love you – bye Cec.'

I loved Cec's ambition, her general go-getting attitude. She was a party animal at the weekends and worked super-hard in the week. I loved that we both weren't in any rush to settle down. I was suddenly worried about losing Bea. Terrified that this was the start of the downhill slope. The downhill slope to adulthood and suburbia and staying on the sofa 24/7. Was she going to be getting excited about Tupperware parties next?

It felt like something had shifted. I felt another stab of guilt for judging Bea's life decisions so harshly. But we all know the fear that once your friends start to grow their family, you might become less needed and, then, fully redundant.

4

2019

The office is full to the brim today with extra bodies as our largest meeting room has been turned into a makeshift studio for a shoot. We have partnered with a huge fashion brand for the issue and we've roped all the interns into being the models. Gill's idea, as she says it'll save us money and shows 'diversity'. I pop to the sandwich shop directly below the office to get lunch, and to get away from all the hustle and bustle in the office. Bit lazy of me, but it's nice enough – I just need some peace and quiet. I sit by the window, looking out at all the frantic Londoners, people smoking while speaking on the phone; with stressed-out faces, shouting at cyclists. As I go to take a bite of my crayfish sandwich, a baby starts howling behind me. *Howling.* Wailing loudly and then choking on its own cries. I turn around and see the red-faced baby is in a pushchair, seemingly discarded right in the middle of the café.

'Whose baby is this, please? *Whose baby?*' cries a

waistcoated woman with an Australian accent and short hair. I glance at her chest – ah yes, she has a big badge that says 'manager'.

People look around, confused.

Short-haired Australian woman shouts through to the kitchen. 'Hi Rodge, we have a pushchair here in the middle of the caff and I'm not entirely sure where the mother is. Seems to have been abandoned.'

'The parent, you mean, Rach,' a stern disembodied voice from the kitchen replies.

'Eh?'

'You assumed the gender of the primary care-giver.'

'*Rodge* – not now. I haven't got the time for this.'

'OK, I'll be out in a sec,' says Rodge.

Suddenly there is the sound of running feet coming up the spiral staircase that goes down to the extra seating area below, and a tiny woman with a long swinging blonde ponytail appears, panting.

She suddenly takes the reins of the buggy, keeping her head down, not making eye contact.

'Excuse me – is this your baby?' Rach asks.

'Yes! Sorry, I was *desperate* for the loo,' she says in between breaths. 'I couldn't get the buggy down those stairs . . . and—'

'Madam, you can't just leave your baby alone like that.'

'It was only for a few minutes!' she gasps.

'Long enough to terrify all of us,' Rach says sternly. 'Please make sure you don't do that again.'

I shudder. Imagine that, not even being able to go to the loo without causing some sort of chaos?

I check my watch and realize I need to get back to the office.

Back at my desk, I lean back on my fancy chair, kick off my shoes and tuck into a huge wedge of carrot cake to calm my nerves after the baby fiasco. I'm going to Bea's this weekend with the girls – after much back and forth with calendar checking and WhatsApp chasing. I have my overnight bag underneath my desk and I keep accidentally kicking it and stubbing my toe. I've packed face masks, thick socks, chocolate and a bottle of Pinot Noir. I can't deny my disappointment after the failure of our last meet-up so I'm excited to be having a girly sleepover: a cosy night in, where we can all be together, with no distractions or stresses.

I hear footsteps coming towards me. Gill, the editor-in-chief, saunters past my desk in thigh-high pleather boots over jeans. She throws a newspaper clipping onto my desk, hands on hips.

'I think there's something in this. Maybe we should cover it. You up for it?'

I look down and see a picture of a girl in a red jumper holding a weird-looking dog – with a bold headline: 'MILLENNIALS CHOOSE PETS OVER CHILDREN'.

I laugh. 'Wow – that's quite an assumption.'

'I think it's true, though. Millennials are cash poor and fucked over. Poor sods. Probably can't afford to do the whole kid thing until they're in their forties, or even older, and most of them aren't home-owners, at least in London. But . . . they could have a pet in the meantime and feel like they are moving towards something. Maybe you could interview some people about it? I reckon it'll get a lot of clicks online and retweets.'

'Do you think people might get offended that we're sort of suggesting that Millennials are too immature to have kids?'

'Sure! Ruffle some feathers with it.'

'OK,' I say, picking up the newspaper to look more closely.

'Great! Have a good weekend, Ol.' She lingers, probably waiting for me to ask her what her plans are. She tells me anyway: 'I'm off to a sex club this weekend.'

Too much information, Gill.

'Lovely! Have fun!' I say, forcing a smile before logging back into my computer. I don't quite feel like finishing my carrot cake any more.

I have a couple of gins-in-a-tin from M&S on the train to Bea's, trying not to slurp too loudly. I feel a bit wobbly when I step off the train – I've always been a bit of a light-weight. Bea lives in Surrey and her house overlooks some beautiful countryside. I love walking from the train station to Bea's because you have to go through a big park to get there, and it's gorgeous: ducks on the pond, kids flying kites, and today it has an extra-special glow because the daffodils are out. I look up at the clouds. Even though it's a short train ride, I suddenly feel far away from London's rush.

I always feel so relaxed in Bea's fun, chaotic home – it is the most higgledy-piggledy, disorganized, yet joyful space. There is truly nowhere like it. It is difficult not to trip over all of the unhung framed artwork that leans against the hallway walls, and the mini-sculptures that lie in the middle of rooms. I always stub my toe on a random trophy that holds the kitchen door open. I associate Bea's life with growing up, finding myself through art and books, feeling that youthful sense of excitement, escapism and exploration. Her parents were as wild and carefree as she is now, and they used to let us run riot around their family home when we were kids. Bea's parents, Sonya and Mikeal, were a big deal in the theatre business, and they always had famous dancers and actors seated round their dinner table. They had huge oil paintings of iconic ballerinas and original poster artwork from shows like *Les Mis*. Bookshelves heaving with novels and scripts. Bea ended up working as a gallery curator near Mayfair, a job she got through a family friend, and she's now freelance and works a lot from home or consults over Skype. I still find it bizarre that this is now Bea's life. I live in a 'for now' flat. She lives in a 'for life' home. For so long I had no idea she even wanted kids – or perhaps I'd just never thought to interrogate it – let alone that she'd become a mum of three so young. It's not that she hid her feelings or dreams from me over the years, just that we never really thought to discuss it too much when we were young. I remember the day everything changed; the hopeful pregnancy tests and then the announcement of her first child, Andrew. I was in a state of shock, and now: she has three! *Three* kids. To me it seems insane.

Everything about Bea's lifestyle is madly colourful and vibrant. All her crockery is handmade and she paints smiley faces on all her vases. She has so many pets. It's the sort of home where you wouldn't be surprised if a Shetland pony trotted through the kitchen. The beds are never made, the kids' clothes are always a tinge of pink from mixed-up washing loads, but her home is one where you can't help but feel safe and comforted when welcomed inside. She'd recreated the freedom and vibrancy of her own childhood home. It was at her parents' house that I kissed my first crush at a party in the basement; it's where I tried weed for the first time; it's where I first danced until 5 a.m. to Fleetwood Mac and smoked my first cigarette out of the window. I dropped my cigarette butt, still lit, and burned a hole through her sofa, but Bea just shrugged and said it would be fine. That was the family's attitude towards pretty much everything – there was a sign hanging in big bold letters above the front door that read, 'Home is where the art is'. Bea's mum Sonya gave me my first expensive red lipstick to wear. Her parents would play the piano and offer us posh canapés whilst letting us run around the spare rooms with water guns, shrieking. I sometimes felt bad about having so much fun while my mum was sitting at home sending me strict texts, constantly on medication for her headaches (which made her both snappy and drowsy), sitting in that bare house after my dad left us. My home life was bleak, and Bea's house was my place to escape and feel totally and completely free. I often wonder who I'd be now if I hadn't met Bea.

When I arrive, her back door is already open. They never lock it. Apparently people are nicer to each other in the countryside. They even say 'hello' to random passers-by – strange.

'Hi!' I yell, as I enter through a plant-filled conservatory and kick my trainers off next to a pile of muddy wellies.

'Oh hello, love!' Bea smiles at me from across the kitchen.

I sit down at her big oak table, covered in Emma Bridgewater mugs and plates and scattered newspapers. Bea's kids are all watching TV from a frayed sofa at the other end of the large kitchen.

'Tea?' Bea asks, flicking the switch of her kettle. I go over and give her a hug.

'Yes please! So good to see you,' I say.

'Same! I'm so happy you're here. How are you? Two sugars as usual?'

'Yes please. I'm OK. What's new?' I start eating a biscuit on a plate in front of me.

'See that woman outside the window?' Bea says, subtly pointing towards the window behind the kitchen sink, as she pours the tea. 'She's just moved in next door, did I tell you about her? She's brought up her kid as a vegan apparently, and now the kid has rickets. It's really sad.'

'Jesus – how does that happen?'

'Not enough nutrients, I guess.'

'That poor kid.'

'I know. I feel so sad when I see them, it looks pretty irreversible . . . I mean look, I don't believe in reading parenting blogs or anything, but I think parenting is pretty simple, or at least instinctive.'

'I'm not sure, but that's a bit of a cock-up, isn't it? Giving your kid rickets.'

'Yeah.'

I pause for a moment. 'How do you cope with it all, Bea?'

'What love?'

'The endless pressures of parenting. All the potential mess-ups.'

'Well at the end of the day I suppose all children need is love, education, a goodish balanced diet and some fresh air – that's literally it. It is hard, don't get me wrong. But you get the hang of it,' she says.

This is the biggest difference between us. Bea is just naturally good at life. Good at running a household, good at organizing and planning and preparing. She enjoys it. She has never really understood why I find these things so hard in comparison. Perhaps I keep kidding myself that my friends and I are more similar than we actually are – than we *were*.

Bea just isn't as highly strung as I am, she doesn't get as fixated on things. She believes the answer to a problem is always solved in nature: a walk, a kick around a field, the petting of a soft animal. In Bea's book, you embrace the madness of life and stop trying to control everything by keeping your life clean and orderly. You let the dog sit on the new sofa. You drink the expensive wine. You use your best moisturizer instead of just leaving it to gather dust in a drawer. This was one of my favourite things about Bea: her ability to just go with it, and get on with it. She was always the person who looked after me and swooped in with solutions when life was feeling too hard. Like the time I was feeling low for months at university because I was worrying about my mum (the first time she had told us she was on anti-depressants) and she bought us a house rabbit!

We called him Mr Peterson. He chewed my wires occasionally, but he also would snuggle with us on the sofa when we felt sad.

We slurp our tea and hear the roar of a car engine outside: it's Cecily. She slams her car door and walks past the kitchen window, bump first. We get up from the kitchen bench and race over to her, cooing.

'You are glowing,' Bea says.

'You really are. Wait . . . Are you wearing Ugg boots?' I say.

'Yes – hahaha, they are so comfy.' Cec bursts out laughing.

'You look a lot better than I did at this stage. I remember practically melting into the sofa – no one could move me. I'm so glad you could make it.' Bea kisses Cec.

'I didn't want to miss our last sleepover before I'm chained to my new baby,' Cec says. She gives me a sideways hug.

'Thanks for travelling all the way here. You still got insomnia?' I ask.

'A little bit, god, it's been awful. I'm feeling much better now though – Bea, thanks for your recommendation on that sleeping app. What an idea! Celebs reading bedtime stories. I'll tell you what, it's really helped falling asleep to Matthew McConaughey's voice.'

'Oh yes, it was a godsend when I was having Amelia. I was like a zombie I was so tired – and that was *before* she even arrived!'

'I honestly don't know what I'd have done without your advice,' Cec says, sliding herself onto a stool.

They carry on discussing and comparing pregnancy notes.

Their different symptoms, private jokes, funny moments, advice and anecdotes.

I open my mouth to say something but realize I have nothing to add.

I've noticed that Cecily and Bea have got closer recently; they've been bonding via late-night discussions on babies. Cecily is currently in full-blown preparation mode. She is hoovering up all the parenting blogs, magazines, and any 'advice', which people seem to love dishing out to her. She wants to make sure everything is done correctly. She has paid an obscene amount for an interior designer to Laurence-Llewelyn-Bowen-up her baby's new nursery. It feels a far cry from my carefree Cec, who used to dance around our student house in a thong.

We go to sit down in Bea's spacious but messy living room, Moroccan rugs hanging on the walls, half-used scented candles everywhere, and cushions all over the floor from the kids making a den. Cec shows me a picture on her phone of the monogrammed blanket for Oscar Arnie Pinkington – aka, OAP – and I can't help but laugh. Everything related to the baby has been personalized with initials.

'Cec . . . sorry, but you're naming your kid after a pensioner.'

'Oh Ol, you overthink these things,' Cec says, snatching her phone away grumpily.

'OAP though,' I snort.

'Piss off.'

Bea giggles behind her cup of tea.

I burst out laughing some more and Cec rolls her eyes before her face softens into a smile. She'd picked his name before she'd even conceived. It was always going to be Oscar.

'I can see you've left the price tag on – £75 for that? Ouch,' I say.

I can't help thinking that you could get a cheap flight to somewhere sunny in Europe for £75. That is a lot of money for a miniature blanket that will soon be covered in sick and shit.

'I want everything to be nice for him! It's his first muslin.'

How did our lives diverge so quickly? Every tiny moment of OAP's babyhood is going to be scrapbooked and diarized and Instagrammed to within an inch of his life. The first time Oscar touches his thumb and forefinger together! He's so *clever!* The first time Oscar does a smelly poo! The first time Oscar screams the house down! The first time he eats a bogey!

'It's so weird, being pregnant now and immediately getting all this attention, you know,' Cec says. 'I feel like Mother bloody Teresa or something. People talk to me on the Tube! They stop in the street to let me walk past; people actually smile at me. In London! Can you believe that?'

'Must be quite nice,' I say, running my fingers through the front strands of my hair.

'It is, but it's also a bit sinister. Without a bump I'm just someone else to elbow out of the way and stamp on, and now suddenly for a few months I'm a radiant goddess who can do no wrong.'

'Yeah, I noticed that too. I still keep my "Baby on Board" badge in a drawer in the kitchen to remind me of those times when I felt like a superstar,' Bea agrees.

'Me too,' I say, jokily. They both ignore me.

'At least it's one good thing about being up the duff. I am hating that I can't wear my own clothes at the moment, though. I've been wearing this same grey dress for weeks. It stinks. I do miss my old wardrobe,' Cec says, pulling at the fabric of her dress.

Our phones beep in unison. It's Isla messaging the group chat to say she can't make it. We had kind of anticipated that, as she'd not been replying much when we were organizing timings. She says she's feeling poorly, which might be true, but we all know she's been really down for some time now. The crux is that her and her boyfriend Mike have been trying to get pregnant for a couple of years, and she's now trying IVF. She's been keeping herself to herself, and doing her classic self-defence manoeuvre of withdrawing from everything and everyone. At university, she would withdraw quite often, bolting her bedroom door and putting loud music on. We used to slip handwritten notes under the door, asking gently for her to come down for a cup of tea and a cuddle.

All cosied up on the sofa with more cups of tea spread out on a tray on the ottoman and blankets over us, we arrange to videocall Isla instead on Skype. As the call connects she appears propped up in bed wearing a black beanie and dark kohl eyeliner. Her dark thick fringe looking greasier than normal.

'You OK, love?' Bea says, tilting the screen of her MacBook so we can all see, and turning up the volume.

'Hi guys, I've felt better. Sorry to miss out on tonight, god I miss drinking wine. Thank you for understanding. What are you all up to?'

'Oh, not much! We miss you,' Cec says quickly, leaning back on the sofa in her pyjamas, holding her protruding bump.

'I miss you guys too. I have major cabin fever. But it definitely feels good to be resting and just having some time to reflect. Cec, how are you feeling?'

'Good thanks. The nausea seems to have subsided. Bit uncomfortable now, though.'

'I bet. So soon though! Exciting,' Isla says, forcing a smile. I can tell it's taking a lot for Isla to ask Cec about her bump so chirpily.

I turn the laptop slightly and poke my head into frame. 'What's going on, Isla? We could have cheered you up if you were here.' Bea looks at me, frowning. I return her stare as if to say: 'What? I'm just asking.'

'Oh, hi Ol. It's our IVF – the first round, it hasn't worked . . . my body hasn't responded very well to it.' Isla looks down at her lap. 'We're going to give it another go, but, well . . .' She trails off.

'I'm so sorry,' I say.

'Oh Isla, love,' Bea says.

Isla puts her head in her hands and starts crying.

I sit there wishing I hadn't asked – I hate seeing my friend in pain – but, then again, she needs to talk to someone about this and we're her best friends. She's been keeping everything so quiet.

We all feel like we are trying to do an impossible thing: comfort someone through a screen.

'It's OK, guys. I just need some . . . time, to wallow. Alone.'

'Of course you do,' Cec says.

'Darling, you can't beat yourself up about this,' Bea says. 'It's not you.'

'It feels so . . . personal,' Isla says. 'Like my body is betraying me.'

'But it's not your fault. I have plenty of friends who have had such positive results from their second or third time. I know it's expensive but please don't lose hope.'

'Thanks Bea,' Isla sniffs.

Bea and Cec seem to know exactly what to say to Isla in these scenarios. I feel helpless and muted. How can I not know what to say to one of my best friends?

'What have you got planned for tonight – something relaxing?' Bea asks softly.

'Nothing. Mike is just cooking a lasagne.'

'Nice. We're just gonna curl up and watch a shit film, can't move much . . .' Cec says, holding her back.

'Cool. I'd better go now. Food's ready actually. Have a good time though, guys, I miss you,' Isla says, sounding forced. She hangs up.

'Poor Isla,' I say.

'I feel terrible for complaining about how uncomfortable I feel in front of her,' Cec says, rubbing her bump.

'Don't be silly,' Bea says, snapping her laptop shut.

We snuggle back into the sofa. 'So, guys . . . I . . .' I take a deep breath, gearing myself up to get a few things off my chest. The break-up with Jacob has been swirling around in my brain and now seems like a good time to get their advice, or at least a little pep talk. Round two.

'Aw, I just felt a kick!' Cec yelps, stroking her bump with both hands, her mouth curved upwards with glee.

'No way!' Bea rushes over. 'Let me feel!'

'Come and feel this, Ol,' Cec says, laughing.

She lifts up her jumper, revealing her soft, silky skin. I place my palm on her tum alongside Bea and feel a little upwards push.

'I think it's a foot,' Bea says, smiling.

I smile and stroke her belly, feeling unexpectedly bottled up.

Later in the evening, we settle down to watch a Drew Barrymore film on Netflix and Bea gets out a bottle of red from her fancy wine cabinet. I end up drinking mine and Cec's share. It goes down so easily these days. Bea has ordered us so much takeaway pizza and the boxes are spread out all over the floor. Jeremy, Bea's husband, is looking after their kids in the next room, but Arnold keeps wandering in to show us his new Lego set and six-year-old Amelia wants to play her violin to us. No offence, Amelia, but you're not very good. Arnold, the three-year-old, wanders in and hands me a *Lord of the Rings* action figure that has some sort of dried crust on it. I love you, I think, but please don't touch me with your snotty face and hands.

I'm glad I don't have a hangover, otherwise I wouldn't have survived. Bea shoos the kids out of the room and we are alone again.

'When do they go to bed?' I ask.

'Ha, by eight p.m. normally, but it changes.' There is a noticeable strain in Bea's voice. 'It's so nice when Jeremy is home because I get to hang out with you guys all night.' I get the sense that when Jeremy is around he 'owes' Bea – he can be quite absent. I pour Bea and myself more red wine.

'So guys,' Cec says, clearing her throat. 'Can I read you my list of "the worst things people have said to me whilst pregnant"?'

'Of course,' Bea says, intrigued, turning down the sound levels on the TV.

'I've got a list typed out on my iPhone and I add to it every time something annoys me,' Cec says.

'Go on,' I say, glugging down some more wine.

She clears her throat, smooths down her bob and puts her glasses on.

'Right. Are you all listening? Here's the first one. People coming up to you and just saying, wow you're *big*. Are you sure you've just got the one in there?

'Number two: when people text me just saying ANY UPDATES?? Like, obviously I will tell people when I've given birth.

'Three: Is that all? You look so much further along!

'Four: How much more do you weigh now?

'Five: Are you eating for two?

'Six: Good luck! My labour was absolutely awful!

'Seven: Better get all the sleep you can now!'

I squirm. Before having pregnant friends, I'd definitely been guilty of saying such things. I've been that person who touches a stranger's bump, rubbing my hands all over it and going 'Ooh, it's sooo weird, isn't it?' Cec has made me realize that it was technically akin to reaching out and squeezing someone's boob without asking. Definitely encroaching on personal space.

'So, that's my list,' Cec says, leaning back and rubbing her belly. 'But I'm sure I'll add to it. In general it seems that being pregnant means being stared at and touched more than usual. But then also sort of ignored by men because you're off the table, too. Like one big oxymoron?'

'I felt that too! Like obviously it's not great to be sexually objectified, but also I kind of missed it,' Bea says.

Cec starts yawning loudly. 'Right guys, I think I'm gonna hit the hay. Me and Oscar need our beauty sleep.'

'OK, night Cec, come on, let's fill these up,' I say to Bea, waving my wine glass at her. 'Seeing as Jeremy's got the kids, eh!'

'Ah, I really shouldn't, Ol. I've got to take them to football and swimming tomorrow morning,' Bea says, now also yawning. 'Sorry . . .'

She hugs me goodnight and asks me to turn out the lights in the hallway when I come up. I hear their footsteps upstairs as they brush their teeth. I grab another bottle from Bea's wine cabinet and tuck it under my arm, then nip outside for a cigarette. I stand outside Bea's porch in pyjamas, wellies and Jeremy's big coat, watching the patterns of the smoke coming from my mouth. As I inhale, I feel a gnawing unease. A sense of loneliness settling over me. I want to hear about how Cec and Isla are feeling, I really do. Isla's been struggling for months now and I'm worried about her. But I also want to tell them about Jacob – the exact reason why he and I broke up. I want to tell them how I'm really feeling. I wanted them to stay up past 11 p.m., for god's sake. Everyone else seems to have exciting or important news, while my only update is that my relationship has come to an end.

I sigh and pace up and down on the grass, trying to stamp down on my anxiety and the niggling feeling in my chest that I can't quite make sense of. Perhaps I acted selfishly this evening, perhaps not. We are all at a crossroads, that much is clear, but things are about to change even more. With Cec's impending baby, she and Bea will have even more in common as they talk nonstop about kids, and then if Isla's IVF works out, I will officially be the odd one out. What if I have nothing to talk about with them any more, drifting further and further away? My friends have always formed a part of my identity; they make me *me*. But without them, who will I be then?

I wake up abruptly the next morning, feeling as though my eyes have been closed for all of ten seconds. Shit, why hasn't the alarm on my phone gone off yet? Bea sneaks in and puts a cup of tea beside the blow-up bed.

'It's 11 a.m., babe,' she whispers.

'Oh fuck, really?'

In that moment I feel like I might be Bea's teenage daughter.

'Cec's already gone, she didn't want to wake you. Do you want some pancakes?'

There's the Bea I know and love: a feeder, a mother hen. And right now, to be honest, I'm more than happy to be taken care of.

5

I sit down at my desk at work holding a mint tea in a chipped mug that says 'World's Best Wife' on it. The communal mug cabinet really does have some atrocities in there. Colin wanders over, holding a mug bearing Paris Hilton's face.

'Morning babe. Good weekend?' he asks, taking a sip.

'Yeah, was all right I s'pose.' After I got back from Bea's I just lay horizontal on my sofa for hours watching *Queer Eye*, while Bea was running around a football pitch with her kids and Cec was baby-proofing her house. 'Is it just me that finds weekends actually quite annoying and draining?'

'What do you mean?'

'I dunno, just the pressure of it. Having to face up to real life without the distraction of work,' I say, sighing.

'I know what you mean actually. The stuff you cram to the back of your mind during the week really comes out to play. I pulled a really fit guy this weekend, though, so I'm happy,' Colin says proudly.

'Good for you! You deserve some good news in that department.'

'My trouser department? You bet I do!' he says, knowing full well not to broach the topic of my love life right now.

'I'm just happy it's Monday, to be honest. Sometimes I think .dot is the only place where I actually feel like myself. Like I'm moving forwards.'

'Well quite – .dot would be nothing without you.'

'Thanks, Col. Right, well I'd better live up to my reputation and get on with a few things.'

He air-kisses me and floats off back to his reception desk.

I open the Google home page and crack my knuckles. I need to properly start this assignment from Gill about Millennials choosing pets over motherhood. Let's start with a broad search. I take a deep breath and type 'Do Millennials Want Kids?' into the toolbar.

I love that I'm technically paid a monthly wage to fall down crazy Internet rabbit holes and ask people nosy questions. I love that my Google algorithm has no real idea who 'Olive' is, or anything about my personality, as my searches are always related to the varying topics of my articles. My online search quickly leads me to a blog post called 'Sterilize Me: My Mission to Never Have Kids' written by a young Millennial woman, who goes by the name of Ariana. No surname, no picture. Her profile is anonymous. But it's honest and open, as most anonymous-ish blogs go.

Welcome to my blog. I'm Ariana, and I don't want kids!

[EDIT: You might have seen this blog post get picked by some national news outlets; for any snooping journalists, I am not interested in doing mainstream interviews, or sitting on the sofa next to a certain horrible argumentative man on national TV. I wrote this blog to speak out to other women, I did not do it for online fame.]

I'm 24 years old, and I have been researching ways that I can get sterilized since I was 18. I can't explain it more simply than this: I know, deep deep in my bones that I never ever want to create another human being. It does not appeal to me, my life, my plans. No one will listen to me! They think I will change my mind! Why? The NHS have said over and over that they won't perform the operation. The doctors have said no, because I am so young and 'might change my mind'. But I know I won't. Also: there's a strange double standard going on. If you do decide to have kids, you can't change your mind then, can you! Seems a little one-sided that argument. I feel really unheard right now. And that not wanting kids still feels like a huge awful taboo. The doctors were shocked by my request, and the word got out in the small village where I live, and I have had really horrible notes slid under my door. People are saying that hospital money should be spent on other issues, not my selfish act. Becoming a mother is a very, very serious decision, and so is *not* having them. I wish that I could choose what to do with my own body, and that is to make sure I never have them. Some people are desperate to have kids. I am desperate not to. Please, please, tell me I'm not alone.

@boyo21 Well done for openly admitting that you're selfish.

@sunshine_girl: I used to feel like this too, Ariana. But, I am

43 now and little Gracey came into my life and I've never been happier. I never thought I'd change my mind. Please, don't rule it out.

@planethappy1: Yes it is a very big responsibility but by far the best thing that happened to me. You might hate other people's kids, but seriously you will never feel love for anyone as much as you will for your own child.

@sammy15: lesbian

@lookmum156: fair enough ariana but i think you'll change your mind one day. Doctors are right not to do it.

@saladlover100: bitch whore

@julie_smith: I've known from the age of about 12 that I never wanted kids. I've always found children irritating, even when I was a child myself. I hear you.

@james_smith_90 MUPPET!!

I take in a deep, slow breath. I feel sick at the judgement that people have towards women like Ariana. It still feels like such a dirty topic, a dirty confession. I realize I'm not shocked by her words, even if I've never read anything like this before. And there's no hiding it: I feel intrigued. It's a rush. My face gets closer and closer to the screen until the comments begin to blur. I start typing out a comment:

'Ariana, I just love your honesty. Would you be open to meeting up for a coffee?' Then I notice my username is set to my real name – @olive_stone_ – and I immediately delete it. I also do a quick check that no one is looking over my shoulder.

6

After work, I WhatsApp Cecily and ask if I can come over. I feel as if we didn't really speak properly at Bea's and I'm worried that I was being too jokey and mean.

> Me: Hello babe are you free this eve for a visitor?

> Cec: ooh that's a LOVELY idea. Yes please. Chris is out with the lads, I'm on the sofa, feeling like a whale in thick socks.

> Me: Not a whale. Yay see you v soon.

I have to see her properly before the baby arrives. Nothing beats one-on-one time. I nip home first, and grab a giant frozen tub of home-made macaroni cheese that Zeta made me when the break-up first happened and I couldn't quite stomach anything. They say the best gift to give any pregnant woman, or new parent, is food. Not flowers, because that's just one extra thing to keep alive. I realize on my way over that this is probably the last time I will see her before she is a mum – Cec, being just Cec, on her own. The thought makes me feel a bit teary but then she answers the door and I push out a smile.

Cecily and her husband Chris live in a big Georgian terraced, high-ceilinged, West London house – the kind with sleek white columns in front of the door. The elephant in the room is always that Cecily's house is much nicer than the rest of ours. Bea's is gorgeous but also a kid-infested circus. Cec's looks like an *Architectural Digest* photoshoot. She has a roll-top bath with a marble floor, for God's sake. Her hallway is big enough that it has room for a blue velvet sofa on one side as you walk in. I try not to be too jealous that Cecily's casual sit-down-and-take-your-shoes-off hallway sofa is nicer than my main living-room sofa that took me five years to pay off. It can be awkward when your mate has way more money than you. But she is an award-winning lawyer. I am a not-yet-award-winning writer. We made different choices so it doesn't really make sense to be jealous. But still, it's the easiest thing in the world to compare yourself to others – especially your best friends and their velvet hallway sofas.

She answers the door in a red stretchy maternity jumpsuit and gives me a huge hug, excitedly taking the tub of macaroni cheese from my hands. I hang up my faux fur jacket on her wooden coat stand and kick off my trainers. Cec walks down the hallway; from the back, she doesn't really look pregnant, then she turns to the side and it's like she's suddenly swallowed a giant beach ball. It amazes me how flexible she still is as she squats down to pick up a plate from the lower cupboard in the kitchen.

'Want me to get those?' I ask.

'No, it's all good. I've been going to this yoga class thing,' she says, straining. 'It's good, except for the fact that it's full of mummy bloggers.'

'How do you know?' I laugh.

'I don't. I'm just being a judgemental bitch.'

'You're allowed to be, you're pregnant.'

'What will be my excuse for being a bitch to people after I give birth?' She winks.

'You've had a whole nine months of getting away with anything and everything,' I say, putting my arm around her.

'Yep! And that is the only thing I'll miss about pregnancy.'

She is so rotund now, as if the weight of the huge bump could topple her over, but she's flexing and stretching and bouncing her legs on the floor in a sort of frog-like position.

'Wanna see the Baby Room?' Cec asks, excitedly.

'Yes of course. And, look Cec, I'm sorry if I was a bit off at Bea's at the weekend. I don't mean to make it about me. I just don't want to drift away from any of you.'

'I understand, Ol. There's a lot going on with all of us at the moment. I promise I'm not going anywhere, though. If anything I'll be imprisoned in this house for months and will be desperate for grown-up chat.' She laughs.

We walk down the corridor with her fluffy cream carpet beneath my bare feet and I can already see a big sign on the back wall of his bedroom, lit up, and spelling out OSCAR in pink neon writing. Piles of stuff are folded and stacked up by the cot: nappy bag contraptions and milk thermometers and some really techy-looking stuff.

'Jeez, how much did all this cost?' I say, doing the mental arithmetic, looking at all these miniature designer objects and freaking out.

'Oh, I don't know! Do you like it though?'

'It's very cute.' It looked like an IRL Pinterest board.

'I like the fact it's pink. Fuck the "boy" and "girl" colour norms,' she smiles to herself, admiring the room she's created for Oscar.

'It's very cool. God Cec, I still can't get my head around it. You're going to be a *mum*.' I reach down into the cot and pull out a small, soft bunny.

She puts her hand on my shoulder. 'It's a new beginning for sure, but things won't change too much.'

'But who am I going to call now at 2 a.m. when I'm in the middle of a panic attack?' I laugh. 'And who's going to try out the latest supper club with me? Go dancing and get filthy takeaways?' I'm trying to sound upbeat, but my voice starts to shake slightly.

'Oh, Ol, I'll still be available. I'm not disappearing off the face of the earth.'

'I'm excited for you. I am,' I say, rubbing her arm.

'Thank you.' Cec looks so content. 'C'mon, let's go downstairs. Ooh, I can make you a posh hot chocolate with my new drinks kit from Liberty. It was a gift from Chris's mum: she drives me insane, but at least she gives good gifts.' She winks.

Seated in Cecily's kitchen, I slurp at my hot chocolate, having eaten all the miniature marshmallows that were floating on top in record time. Suddenly, now feels as good a time as any to broach the break-up.

'Talking of new beginnings . . .' I say, with marshmallows still in my mouth.

'Oh yeah?' Cec asks, excitedly.

'Oh, it's not a good thing . . .'

'Oh right, sorry.'

'I don't really even want to say it, to be honest.'

'Go on . . .'

'Jacob and I broke up.'

'Huh?' Cec can't hear as her noisy kettle is making a weird sound and I guess I did have my mouth slightly full.

'Jacob. And me. We . . . we split up,' I say, more loudly this time.

'No?' Cec's eyes widen in shock.

'Oh god, I don't want to stress you out; you're *with child.*' I fold my arms on the table then and hang my head.

'*Ol!* You're not stressing me out. When, what, why? When did this happen?'

'Oh, really recently,' I lie. 'I didn't tell you because, well, I wasn't sure if it was definitely over. I mean it definitely is now. Haven't heard a peep for weeks.'

'Weeks? And you didn't tell me?' She looks genuinely hurt.

'Sorry, I just . . . It didn't feel like something I could say over a message, and I didn't want to be annoying when you've been busy preparing for the baby.'

'Oh fucking hell, Ol. Having a baby doesn't mean I will forget that everyone else exists.'

'OK, sorry.'

'What happened?' she says, handing me a piece of home-made cake.

'We just realized that . . . we want different things.'

'Do you want to talk about it?'

I look down at my mug. Cec's Siamese cat Harvey wraps his tail around my leg, as if he knows I need comforting.

I take a breath. 'Well, I guess we just had one last bad argument that seemed to be the final blow. The last available opportunity to get all those feelings off our chests, but we both knew there was no coming back from that. He accused me of having no emotions, using the people closest to me for story ideas to pitch to the magazine. He would often joke that – when something really terrible or really great happened – he could see the cogs of my brain turning immediately to come up with a headline or caption.'

'Woah, yes, that is harsh.'

'Do you think I do that? Mine people for their stories, for .dot?'

'Not really. Not in a malicious way, anyway. You write what you know.'

'Exactly. He complained a lot about how I was never truly "in the moment" or "living my life". He started sounding like a Buddhist monk and it really started to piss me off.'

'It does sound a bit smug.'

'Very smug! Like, mate, you're not a bloody guru.'

'Olive, was there anything else?' she asks gently. 'I mean, it sounds like a disagreement, but not something to throw away nine happy years for. Is there something else going on between you two?'

'Well . . . actually, yes.'

'Go on.'

'He's ready to have kids,' I say bluntly.

'And?'

'I'm not.'

'OK,' she says. 'And do you know when you might be?'

'I don't know,' I say. 'I close my eyes and try to imagine myself as a mother but, for whatever reason, I just can't.'

'Each to their own, Ol. I remember when we used to chat about the big "baby" question. We both weren't sure for a long time.'

'But then most people move on and decide to do it. I mean, look at you. Can I ask – how did you know, that you and Chris were ready to have a baby?'

'Hmm, well, I always sort of knew deep down, I think. I thought I'd be a much older mum, though, because I wanted to be a partner in my firm before I did the baby thing. But my body sort of took over and I started obsessing over the idea, I guess. Sometime around the end of last year, I woke up one morning and it was like my body wanted it. Craved it like sugar. Like I didn't have a choice. It was weird; I was as surprised as you, honestly. Then, you know, it just happened quite quickly.' Cecily laughs, and runs her hands over her bump.

'Wow. I just feel like everyone's always so surprised when I say I don't think I want kids. Like they're sad for me.'

'Babe, it's your life. I'm proud of you for staying true to yourself even though you must be hurting right now.'

'Thank you.' I hug her. I miss her, even though she's right here.

'Oh Ol. Let's put on a film and get the blankets out.' Cec waddles over to her big wooden cabinet and gets out cosy things like candles, hand cream, room scents and extra cushions. Time to nest. Each moment we have alone together now is a ticking time-bomb before OAP comes. The minute she has this baby, nothing else will matter. She says it will, but it won't. I've already experienced it with Bea: our friendship suffered massively when she had her first baby. We didn't speak to her or see her for six months, maybe even a year. None of us anticipated how much of a shift it would cause. It was like losing a family member – and in some ways perhaps that triggers me. Cec will have a new love, a deeper love. And that's the way it should be. But it won't be the same between us after that. I hug into her closely on the sofa that evening and, when I go to leave later, I linger by the front door awkwardly.

'The next time I see you, you'll be . . . a mum!' I say.

'I know, eeeeek! Love you. So nice to see you, Ol. Remember . . . I'm here if you need me.' She smiles and hugs me before waving me off – she's a ball of excitement.

I walk down the street to Barons Court Tube station with tears prickling in my eyes. I'm so happy for Cec, she'll be a brilliant mum, I know she will. But I can't help feeling that her moving forwards is just a reminder that I'm only moving back.

I sit on the Tube and get my notepad out, and start writing before my brain even feels connected to my hand. My old drinking buddy, Cec. My wild friend. The one who would always dance on the tables and never wanted to go home.

Now, she stays in all the time, she's pregnant and burns scented candles. But she seems to like her new life, the choices she's made. So, what do I really want? Perhaps there is a different future out there that I'm taking for granted. I stare into the distance and struggle to re-focus, the baby/no baby dilemma rearing its head.

Pros for having a baby:
1. I'd get invited to stuff more – such as, but not limited to, mothers' meetings, children's birthday parties, picnics in the park etc.
2. I would feel part of the gang and not like a total gooseberry (see point one)
3. I would feel this 'different kind of love' that people always talk about
4. I would feel more 'normal' in my life choices and wouldn't have to make up fake life milestones at reunions
5. I know what my future would look like 'on paper' – and I would feel part of a bigger family unit
6. I could find a way back to Jacob. Maybe

Cons for having a baby:
1. NO SLEEP!! (I LOVE SLEEP)
2. I would be constantly unsure if I truly did actually want the baby – like is it peer pressure? Wouldn't that be an awful reason to have a baby?
3. Life would be sort of ruined (my bank balance would struggle A LOT)
4. I would feel trapped in general and I wouldn't be able to put myself first or make spontaneous travel plans

5. Long, stressful, screamy airport visits and flights
6. I could regret it and be one of those anonymous mums on Mumsnet pulling her hair out and saying she wants to give it back

I look down at the list. Six pros, six cons. Oh. Crap. Maybe I'm 'on the fence'. Am I on the fence?

'It was around puberty that I became consciously aware that I didn't want children, and I haven't changed my mind since.'

Michelle, 27

7

2011

'Let's see the ring then!' I grabbed Bea's freshly manicured hand. 'Oh Bea – it's lush! Absolutely gorgeous.'

'Thank you, I love it. It's a bit different I guess!' The ring was a deep blue sapphire with small diamonds around the outside. 'Well done Jezza, he nailed it,' I said.

Bea's parents were throwing Jeremy and Bea an engagement party dinner at a gorgeous restaurant in Covent Garden. There were about twenty people altogether on a long trestle table, and the restaurant was loud and full of noisy atmosphere. Cec, Isla, Bea and I were there, plus a few other friends, and around ten family members, including Jeremy's parents and brother. The four of us girls were sitting down one end of the table. Cec had dyed her hair even blonder for the occasion, Bea was wearing a bright headscarf, and Isla was wearing a cashmere beret with her signature fringe poking out. I was wearing a pair of velvet dungarees, hoping they wouldn't give me thrush. Jeremy was at the other end with his family. I liked the fact that Bea had chosen to sit with us. It was a sign, however small, that she wasn't quite 'leaving us'.

'I'm not doing the whole bridesmaids bullshit, by the way, but will you guys please sleep in the room with me the night before the wedding and we can get ready all together in the morning?' Bea asked, folding out her napkin.

'Hell yes,' Cec said. 'I'm *so* excited. Weddings are such fun. What do we wear? Nothing too slutty right?'

'Whatever you want!' Bea said.

'Should we coordinate though?' Isla asked.

'Nah! I find it really weird when brides make grown women wear a lame pastel-coloured dress. I wouldn't want to do that to you,' Bea laughed, ripping off a piece of sourdough from the bread basket.

'Such an exciting next step, Bea. I can't believe you're getting married,' Cec said.

'I know, but marriage changes literally nothing. Just an excuse for a piece of bling on the ol' finger and a big old knees-up with my favourite people! But it feels so nice to know Jeremy wants all the same things as me. We want to get on with it – build a family, you know?'

'Yeah, yeah – but it's also about the *party!*' Cec said, excitedly. We all knew Cec was going to go wild – she had been known to lead many a conga around a marquee.

A cold bottle of champagne arrived in a silver cooler, and everyone was poured a glass by a good-looking waiter in a suit. Bea's mum Sonya tapped a fork on the side of her glass, getting a folded piece of paper out of her pocket to do a little speech.

'My darling Bea! It makes me so happy to see you blossom, to find so many things that bring you joy. The galleries, your best girlfriends, and – of course – the lovely Jeremy . . . You have built all of this yourself with your spirit, energy, and the way you summon such positivity into your life. I'm so proud to be your mum.'

I started welling up. Sonya might be a bit woo-woo, but she was right: just knowing that Bea was on her own brilliant path to happiness, and with her best friends very much beside her through it all, was a lovely feeling.

The whole table carried on eating and laughing and sharing anecdotes, clearly the loudest group in the restaurant. Sonya presented Bea and Jeremy with some crystals that would 'guide their marriage'. We finished our mains, waiters continued topping up our glasses and a giant dessert was brought out, complete with sparklers. We cheered and whooped and Bea and Jeremy waved the sparklers around, smiling the biggest smiles as we all looked on and clapped. The night ended with loud music and dancing on tables, and the restaurant staff seemed to love it just as much as we did, pouring us free shots straight from the bottle into our mouths. Mine and Bea's song suddenly came on – 'Red Red Wine' by UB40 – and we grabbed each other and started singing from the top of our lungs, like we were the only two people in the room.

Even though this was a turn in the road, a new chapter, Bea was still my Bea.

8

2019

I've decided to go and see a Reiki healer this afternoon because I am a Millennial cliché with a free afternoon. I have accepted the fact that since the break-up I haven't really been looking after myself that well. I haven't been to the gym in months and I haven't cooked any nice food for myself in ages either. Cec sent me a huge box of frozen chicken broth in the post, which is very thoughtful. The note read: 'Some nutrients for you! A bit of self-care please. Cec xx'. It doesn't feel very 'feminist' to admit that I am struggling now that I don't have a boyfriend, but it's my truth right now. What's so wrong with enjoying being looked after by someone? Jacob kept me on the straight and narrow. He often encouraged us to cook good meals from scratch; he was fairly healthy and didn't love take-aways; his best mate had started a healthy delivery service and he had free membership; and he'd make us get out of the house on weekends. He even dragged me out to go on runs with him. Without any of that, without any of these small lifestyle nudges, I am immediately back to my natural state, aka filth and laziness. I'm back to being the woman I truly am, who eats noodles in her pants on the sofa and orders Nando's every other night on Deliveroo, even though she can't really afford it now that she's paying double rent. I have no one to impress, no one to suggest ways I could take better care of myself, no accountability. I am being half-arsed with my cleaning – I've definitely not cleared the crumbs from under the toaster for a while. The other day I ordered extra pizza just to keep some cold for breakfast the next day. My teeth hurt from eating badly and spots have erupted on my chin, giving my secrets away. Those fitness blogger gurus always say you should 'tenderly prepare a meal for yourself, like you would for a loved one!' and 'caringly sprinkle some seeds or chilli flakes onto every meal.' Oh piss off!

As I sank into my sofa I'd noticed an old copy of .dot magazine on my very cluttered coffee table, under the half-drunk cups of tea and hardened porridge bowls, and flicked through to see that a colleague had written a feature on the 'Ten best modern-day Reiki healers'. I'm at that point where I'm willing to try anything. I have always been quite cynical of Reiki (what exactly is it? How do they 'heal' you without even really touching you? Is it a rip-off?) but from scanning the article I gathered it's an ancient spiritual healing practice, and it sounds fairly legit – so I've decided to give it a go. I also have very low expectations, so it's always possible that I might be pleasantly surprised. I go with the recommendation at the bottom of the article: a woman named Seal. In the article it says she was trained by one of the 'original masters'. I'm not sure what that means but it certainly sounds impressive. I don't want to put all the pressure on this poor Reiki woman to heal all of my life's problems, but it would be great if she could. Then the £65 price tag would work out to be quite reasonable. I text her. She happens to be free this afternoon so I have a quick shower and head off to her address.

Seal's house-cum-health spa is a twenty-minute walk from my flat, in a very leafy residential area on Holyrood Road. I'm just turning the corner to her place when I spot an old school teacher, Mrs Rudd, walking up the road towards me. I squint. Is it her, here in London? What are the chances. She is wearing a velvet beret and a red Mac raincoat and carrying some canvas shopping bags. I haven't seen her since I was about seventeen years old when she would tell me off for talking too much in English. She did acknowledge on the last day of term that I didn't actually talk the most, but my voice was 'the most distinctive'.

'Olive . . . Stone?' she says now, moving her glasses slightly, trying to place me. 'Hi!'

Ugh, why do teachers always have to say full names?

'Mrs Rudd – it's been so long, what brings you here?' I say, zipping up my coat.

'Oh – please, call me Rachael. We're both adults now! I live just around the corner, we moved about five years ago to be closer to Alistair's sister when she was unwell. How is everything with you?'

'Great thanks, I'm a writer now, I work at .dot magazine, do you know it?'

'I don't, but oh, that's just fantastic, you were always a good writer. Even if you did distract the others in my class!' Her laugh sounds like a honk.

'How is your husband?' I ask. Mr Rudd – Alistair – also worked at the school; there were always rumours that he was cheating on her with the new Biology supply teachers, but I always thought they seemed like a sweet couple, and I always hoped it wasn't true.

'Oh he's great thank you – and our kids are just entering their twenties now. Scary, really, how quickly they grow! What about you Olive – husband, any kids?'

'Um . . .' I pause. 'Yes! Yes, both.' I do a big smile.

'Oh how lovely! How old are they?'

'I have a daughter, she's two. She's perfect,' I say.

'How lovely. So happy for you. The best thing ever, isn't it? Being a mum. Take care. Safe onward travels.'

'Bye Mrs Rudd . . . Rachael,' I say flatly, with an attempt at a smile. I don't feel in control of my words. Why did I lie? What was I saying? I know that was a weird thing to do, but I just couldn't bear for my teacher to see me fifteen years after leaving school, with hardly any major changes in my life.

Feeling distinctly unsettled, I reach a gorgeous house at the end of the street. It's painted white with ivy trailing the walls and windows; the blue dot on my Google map matches with the destination. I look up at the green door. Yes, this is it. Seal's abode. I knock, and a woman with a thick grey plait over one shoulder quickly opens the curtains at the front window and peeks out to see who it is. Then I hear her undoing about four different metal bolts on the door before opening it.

'Olive, is it?' Seal asks, looking me up and down.

I look down at her scrawny bare feet painted intricately in henna patterns. 'That's me,' I reply, stepping inside and wiping my shoes on her doormat.

'Lovely to meet you, Olive. Please remove your shoes and come on through.' I follow her down her carpeted hallway and into a small room opposite her living room. The appointment room has a huge bookshelf and in front of it is a portable massage table covered in towels.

'The toilet is here, if you need it,' she says, pointing to a box room further down the corridor.

'I'm OK, thanks,' I reply, nervously.

'Now if you just lie down on the bed, under the top towel, I'll be back in a moment,' she says.

I lie on the table layered with navy towels that smell of lavender. Seal comes back in carrying some chamomile floral extract in a glass of water and asks me to drink it as it will relax me. I hope she isn't drugging me. I look around the room: there are faux candles flickering, jars of multicoloured sand everywhere and a large twinkling chandelier over my head. Her bare scrawny feet are lightly tapping the wooden floor as she walks, her long plait swaying from side to side. She is wearing khaki harem pants and has a large pastel-pink flower in her hair. Yes, I think I like Seal. She has a very relaxing accent – a hint of Spanish, I think.

She tells me gently that she's going to put on some calming music and suddenly Sade's 'Smooth Operator' booms from the speakers above me and I jump out of my skin.

'Sorry – woops, wrong CD!' she says. 'Now lie back . . .' She pushes me down with her palm as the track changes to something more soothing, classic spa music. It sounds like bells ringing very gently. Then some water lapping against a coast.

'That other song was Sade, wasn't it? I used to pronounce Sade's name wrong. For ages I didn't realize it was actually "Shar-day". I used to just say "Sade" like "shade".'

Seal ignores me and turns the lights down lower.

I blather on: 'Also I used to think Richard E. Grant was called "Richardy", for like my whole life.'

'OK – you have too many thoughts.'

'Hmm,' I agree, closing my eyes.

'I also used to think that people were actually stacked on top of each other during *University Challenge* – it's actually just edited that way.'

'Sshh,' she says quietly.

She tells me she is going to concentrate on my crown chakra first. Sure . . . no idea what that is, Seal, but you just work your magic.

'This is where I channel energy through your body to mine and try to help you to get rid of any of the fast-moving and intense thoughts swimming around your head. It might feel tingly.'

I try my hardest to stay awake and soak up the vibrations of the relaxing music.

'You have a lot of ideas; you are a very confused person.'

'Hmm.' I nod.

'Very tangled. A web. You need to let it all go. Breathe in with me.'

In. 1-2-3-4-5.

And out. 1-2-3-4-5.

'There is such a thing as too many thoughts.' She pauses. 'To be happier, you must try and have less, OK?'

I realize I'm frowning and so I readjust my face. I just nod politely.

She then moves down to my ribcage, aka my 'heart chakra'. After five minutes of nothing, I feel a tingle. She is telling me that my heart is very, very full. You have a big heart, she says. She says it over and over again. You have a big heart. It is so big, my heart's energy is taking up my entire upper body. My ribcage is vibrating. Then, she moves down to my womb chakra. After ten minutes or so, I start wildly hallucinating. She has her hands on my belly. I feel an energy move around inside around my womb area. I am lightly dreaming now, trying to imagine myself with a bump. But I can't do it. Every time I imagine it, after a few seconds it disappears. I imagine myself, five years into the future, getting on the Tube, meeting the girls for dinner in a long flowery dress and with a full, rounded pregnancy bump . . . The picture in my mind evaporates. I wake up to the sound of myself crying.

'It's OK to cry,' Seal says, gently.

I open my eyes and look around the room, trying to find her.

'It can be quite overwhelming,' she says, her face appearing over mine.

'I feel weird,' I say, slightly embarrassed. My mouth is twitching and my whole body feels so awkward and uncomfortable. I feel like I want to move, but I can't.

'It's perfectly normal, just ride it out, you're just getting rid of some things. Always better out than in.' She smiles at me kindly and then her face vanishes out of sight again.

'It feels like you know what I'm thinking,' I say. I don't like how Seal seems to be so in tune with what my body is saying. I feel totally see-through, exposed. It doesn't matter that I'm wearing clothes, it feels as though there is only a thin, frail piece of clingfilm stretching over me and my insides.

'You have some knotty energy in your womb chakra. Something isn't quite aligned,' Seal says gently. 'Is there something that is confusing you, or on your mind – to do with fertility?'

'I don't know.' Tears squeeze out of my eyes, dripping onto the pillow.

'Are you trying?' Seal asks gently.

'Huh?'

'For a baby?'

'Oh . . . no. Definitely not! The complete opposite.'

'Sorry, dear, I didn't mean to assume. It's normally a sensitive area when women are having problems conceiving.'

'I just broke up with someone, the love of my life, actually.' I sniff. 'I feel so alone in my thoughts. I feel nothing there. It's so empty.'

Seal is cupping my forehead with her warm hand now.

'It is OK to feel sad and go through the motions. You are in an intense reflection mode.'

'What do I do now?'

'You must lead with your heart. Make *all* decisions with it.' Seal prods me really hard in the chest with her spiky finger. Her hands are so hard and harsh, probably from years of massaging the hardened backs of stressed-out Londoners.

'Ow,' I say. Seal smiles at me.

She dims the lights, fills the room with burning sage and lights some more candles, and stands there, stroking my temples until I fall asleep.

When I wake up I have a splitting headache, and immediately feel like a failure. How long have I been asleep at Seal's house-slash-spa? As I open my eyes, a suitcase full of negative emotion spills its contents everywhere. I need to get home.

'Have some more water and, please, walk home slowly,' Seal says. As I sip my water my hand is shaking slightly. I insert my card into her payment machine. On the walk back to my flat I feel really spaced out, and when I get there I face-plant on my bed and fall straight asleep. When I wake up again from my second nap, it takes a while for the haze to clear. There are three empty packets of prawn cocktail crisps next to my bed. I just thought that seeing Seal would be a fun thing to do to pass the time, like a back massage, but it's brought up so much more than I imagined. There was a haunting urgency to her voice, like she wanted me to pay attention to her – to my body. I visualize a pie chart of all the different aspects of my life. Seal suggested I write down 'what I know to be true' and start there to ease the confusion.

- I'm still in love with Jacob.
- I feel like my friends are abandoning me and moving on without me.
- I have zero maternal feelings.
- I am noticing that my forehead and hands are getting wrinklier by the day.
- I'm genuinely baffled as to how most people seem to skip out of bed each morning and get on with things.

The next day, still shaken, I decide to work 'from home', i.e. my bed. I lie there, prop myself up with a big cushion, and realize I should probably change my sheets. My phone vibrates on my bedside table, startling me.

Cec: 'HELLO guys just a quick update – Chris is driving me to hospital right now! Baby INCOMING – it's happening!'

Bea: oh my god!!!!

Cec: Chris is speeding lol hope we don't get pulled over

Bea: Well you have the best excuse if you do!

Me: Wow! Keep us updated!

Isla: ♥♥♥♥

Cec: Am I ready for this???? I think I'm ready!!!!

Bea: You are so ready! SO EXCITING CEC

Cec then goes quiet so we assume she's, you know, literally in the middle of it all. I wonder how she's feeling. I don't know what it's like being pregnant (obviously), but nine months sounds, in theory, like a long enough time to get your head around having a baby. But perhaps until it's out, in your arms, it can't feel real.

I hate not knowing what is happening to my friend. The hideous online anecdotes from my late-night Googling about birth stories come back to haunt me, even though I try to block them out. Time ticks by painfully slowly the next day at work – I find myself checking my phone every two minutes. Finally, twenty-four hours later, we hear something from Cec. It feels like an eternity. God knows what she's just been through. Did time stop for her? Or did it go by in a hazy whirlwind flash?

Cec: Guys, he is here.

Cec: He's amazing.

Cec: I . . . made this! I MADE A HUMAN

Cec: shares 16 images

Cec: shares 4 videos

Bea: OMG He is GORGEOUS! LIKE HIS MOTHER

Isla: Totally delicious Cec, huge congrats to you both!!! Ahhh those tiny little hands.

Me: Oh Cec, I'm crying. He's beautiful. I can't wait to meet him. Hi Oscar!

Seeing how happy Cec is, how in love she is with her new baby, gives me knots in my stomach. I'm happy and excited for her, but a slight edge of jealousy creeps in too. I just can't help but wonder: maybe if I did want a baby, I would still be with Jacob, and my life wouldn't feel so tangled up right now.

The flat feels so different without Jacob in it. Outside my window I see bustling outdoor seating areas of cafés, people on bikes with baskets on the front, and greenery from the park over the road. I always hear kids playing, people roll-er-skating, families laughing and groups of friends singing. I used to find it inspiring and uplifting when Jacob lived here, to hear life going on outside. But now it's a stark reminder of how much I am missing out on, as I continue to drink alone in my flat instead of going out at weekends. Everything feels like it's hit a dead-end. No Jacob, no future. I know I have to imagine a different life for myself now, but it just feels too hard. Some days I'm fine, some days I'm really not.

Time for a bath. Anything to feel better. I remind myself

that having a long bath alone is a luxury, something Cec certainly won't be able to do for a while! I turn on the taps and put on an episode of *Desert Island Discs*, and then sink into the hot water, letting out a noise of pure bliss. I put more lavender oil drops into the water and exfoliate my face with a ground mix of botanicals to clear away dead skin. It's harsh and feels like sand on my face. I scrub and scrub and imagine that I am scrubbing away the shit bits of my personality. I shave my legs without concentrating and accidentally cut my ankle. The bath starts to fill with blood and begins to look like a crime scene. Ow.

My ringtone buzzes with the sounds of Eve's 'Who's That Girl'. My sister Zeta is calling me. I'd been keeping her in the loop about the Jacob situation – she's the only person I've really been able to talk to, but most of it has been over text. I wipe my hand on a towel and hang half my body out of the bath to answer it.

'Hey sis! I'm back from my travels and I need to see your face immediately. How are you doing?' It felt so nice to hear Zeta's voice.

God, I have missed her. She works for a refugee crisis charity and was in Bristol at their HQ helping over Christmas and then she went off on a trip to Calais and Greece for a couple of months. I can't believe we are related sometimes, her doing stuff for others all the time. I can't even get myself dressed at the moment.

'Please don't go away for that amount of time again, please. It's been horrible without you,' I say, the water from my body dripping onto the tiles.

'You were in my dream last night, Ol, and it was really weird, you kept barking like a dog and I was so confused about what was wrong. Anyway, you OK?' Zeta laughs, chewing a piece of gum. Zeta and I have always told each other our strangest dreams from when we were very little and shared a bedroom, something I probably wouldn't necessarily tell anyone else.

'Weird. I'm fine, but actually I could do with a chat. Big time.'

'I bet. I haven't heard the full story of what happened with Jacob. I've been thinking about you loads. Wanna meet at the Crooked Cock in a few hours?'

'Yes please,' I say. I rinse myself and pull the bath plug out, listening to the bloody water gargle its way down the hole as I rub my back and armpits. My ankle drips over my bath mat and I stick some tissue to it because – surprise surprise, adult that I am – I have no plasters in the house.

The Crooked Cockerel is an old East End pub with a huge chimney coming out of the top and a bus stop just in front. Apparently one of the Kray twins buried a body in the basement once, or something. It's pretty much bang in the middle from mine and Zeta's flats, between Victoria Park and Mile End. Our fave little meeting spot – a pub that isn't too overly done up and does reliably good food without trying to overcomplicate things with a weird hipster menu. Zeta is five years older than me, annoyingly beautiful and the least selfish person on the planet, to the point where I wish she'd put herself first a bit more. Her looks get annoying because men stare at her and I often feel like shouting MOVE ALONG or asking them to pay if they want to look or take pictures of her. She's not a silent mime artist performing on the streets of Covent Garden, awaiting their approval. Being a full-time paid activist and strategist for a large charity takes up all her time. I know she bottles up a lot of stress, but she also hardly ever complains. She never makes me feel bad for whinging about my smaller problems, though. She doesn't believe in whataboutery. (Thank god.)

I pop on my beaten-up Converse shoes by the door and, as I walk across the road, the bus arrives just on cue. Love it when that happens. I sit down near the front and notice a youngish mum with a thick ponytail get on with a huge double-seater pushchair. She has some mini carrots cut up into tiny pieces in a little Tupperware box and gives them to her identical-looking twins. She catches my eye and I smile reassuringly at her. She looks tired. One of the babies upturns the box of carrots onto the dirty bus floor. The mum scoops them up and puts them in her big Ikea bag. She looks like she's about to cry. I always smile at other women with pushchairs because it looks like fucking hard work and I think there is a special place in hell for people who make new parents' lives even more hellish. Baby karma is real. The mother with the carrots starts playing 'Baby Shark' loudly out of her phone speakers and places her phone in the pushchair with the baby. Everyone in the bus is rolling their eyes or shaking their heads, getting agitated at the fact that we all have to sit there and listen to the song. She has zoned out, looking out through the window, her eyes glazed over. She is clearly beyond giving a fuck what people think of her on a public bus.

When I arrive at the pub, Zeta is outside smoking, in a floral dress and small denim jacket and Doc Marten boots. When she sees me, she outstretches her arms for a hug.

'Ol!' She ruffles my hair as I wrap my arms around her tiny waist. 'I'm so happy to see you!'

I hug her tightly and feel my throat tighten. I just make a 'hmmm' sound as she squeezes me, grateful that she's holding me up for a second.

We go inside, order two small beers and sit down in the back-room conservatory. It's boiling inside and the light is pouring in, reflecting off the tall fern plants dotted around the room.

'Blue skies in England at 6 p.m., cheers to that,' Zeta says. She frowns suddenly. 'Can you believe they are proudly displaying plastic straws at the counter? That's embarrassing.' She refocuses on me. 'Anyway, cheers to you, to us being together again!'

'It's so good to see you. I always miss you when you're away, but this time, I *really* missed you.'

'Sorry for being AWOL at the moment. That is the only downside. It's my dream job but the travelling is relentless, and I feel like I'm growing so distant from friends. It's all right with you and Mum, but it's hard to keep my life here intact.'

'I know what you mean, but even when people live down

the road it's still hard to drag people out to socialize some-times,' I say. 'So, how was it – your trip?'

'It was . . . an experience. I met the most incredible people who are trying desperately to rebuild their lives with prac-tically nothing. It was inspiring. An emotional trip, though.'

'You are amazing; I'd be too scared.'

'You'd be fine once you were there, Olive – we all travel safely as a group, with the charity. Come with me one year. It's motivated me to do even more.'

'OK – maybe!'

'So, what the hell has been going on with you? Tell me everything,' Zeta says, taking a sip of beer.

'Oh Zets. Well, as you know, I had an awful fight – well, series of fights – with Jacob, and it's all over. I've been a total hermit. I honestly haven't spoken to anyone properly in weeks, apart from a few people in the office. And there are some cracks opening up in my friendship with the girls. Maybe they've been there for a while and the break-up's just brought everything into focus . . . I don't know. I just feel so aware that they're miles further ahead in life than me. I'm back at square one and they're raising kids and buying houses and stuff. It's hard to tell if I am ostracizing myself, or if it's the other way around.'

Zeta laughs lightly. 'I understand that. Does Mum know?'

'Well I haven't really wanted to burden her with it all. Seems like she's only just getting her own life back on track. I didn't want to remind her of, you know, men leaving . . .' I still feel a tightness in my chest whenever I mention Dad.

'Hmm, yeah I know what she's like. She's never really been any good at saying the right thing.'

'Yeah, precisely.' I sigh. 'I've just been trying to keep my head down and get on with things. Even if I do feel a bit lonely.'

'Well, I'm here now.' She squeezes my arm.

We all admire Zeta, but she's always away whenever there's a family occasion. She's never been around for Christmas as she's always doing charity stuff. This is the only thing I resent about my sister, that I have to spend so much time alone with Mum. Having a sibling is meant to lighten that load.

'Do you think it's fixable – you know, with Jacob?' Zeta asks. She clearly always liked him.

'I don't think so. The same conversation kept rearing his ugly head. The "baby chat". I knew it was going to come to a full-blown make-or-break moment. It was like a ticking time bomb we both knew was there – it was only a matter of time until it exploded. It got to the point where it was all he could talk about, and there were only so many times I could shake it off or sweep it under the rug or put the conversation off for another day.'

'I see,' she says, biting down on her top lip with her bottom teeth.

'Yeah. It suddenly felt like kids were at the top of his agenda. You know his two older brothers have kids, and it's all very family family family with them. With their perfect little Instagram accounts and group family shots and stupid matching outfits . . . The bloody Brady Bunch. I knew he wanted them, but I didn't know he felt so time-pressured. I thought it was usually the woman who felt some sort of ticking biological clock. I thought I'd *feel* something and then that would push us along. I didn't realize he'd be obsessing over the idea the minute I turned thirty.'

'Oh, Ol.' Zeta moves closer to me and puts her arms around me.

'You know how much I love him.' I start crying in the middle of the pub. How embarrassing.

'I have a question.'

'Yeah?' I sob.

'Do you think your fear of having kids might be linked to Dad leaving us?'

'What . . . no!'

'Sorry. It's just a thought.'

'Why can't a woman just not want a baby and for that to be the end of it?' I say, feeling agitated.

'I know, I know – sorry. But, do you think you'll ever change your mind?'

'I don't know Zets . . . I've been thinking about it a lot lately, though – in fact it's all I seem to think about – and I just can't picture myself with a baby. I just can't.'

'I know it must have been very painful to break it off, Ol, but you've done the right thing. You can't force yourself to be somebody else for him.'

I reach for a napkin to blow my nose into it, hard.

We end up getting raucously drunk after that. Zeta clearly needs a bender after the intensity of her charity trip, and I just want to forget about the ins and outs of the Jacob nightmare. We do a mini pub crawl down the street and end up in a basement karaoke bar singing an old All Saints song.

When I finally stumble home, I stick some chips in the oven and stretch out on the threadbare sofa, scrolling absent-mindedly through Instagram. It is a newsreel of updates of baby Oscar and jolly family album photos of Bea with her kids playing dress-up. I 'like' them with a drunken thumb.

The night out has been a reminder that I have no one to go out with any more, apart from Zeta occasionally, but she's hardly ever here. I realize that I miss these carefree, spontaneous nights. I crave them. I don't want to forget that we are still young. It's clear that our lives are at a major crossroads. We are no longer sat at the traffic lights, though, everyone is already zooming off in different directions. I wish everyone and everything would slow down just for a moment.

9

2012

We were sitting in the sunny beer garden of The White Horse. The outside area was modern and welcoming, lined with deckchairs with striped cushions and big patio heaters. The insides of the old pub building were really in need of a paint job – undecorated since the smoking ban, the pub still reeked slightly of stale smoke, and the once-white curtains remained an off-yellow colour. The girls and I had spent many drunken summer evenings in here. There was normally a cheesy tribute band playing in the evening, or a big football screen with people milling about spilling their beers, or loud, cackling birthday parties. Last time we had a night out here, Fleetwood Bac was the featured act, and I drank and danced with a fake Stevie Nicks until we were both sick in the toilet. This, however, was a more low-key lunchtime affair: Jacob, Cec, Isla, Mike and I were all seated around a big wooden picnic bench. It was just warm enough to sit out, but it felt nice because the evenings were getting lighter thanks to the clocks going back. Mike had just bought a round and was carrying all the pints over on a wobbly tray. We then noticed Bea come in with her big pram, pushing everyone out of the way.

'Excuse me! Coming through,' Bea shouted, loudly.

I went up to her, and kissed her on the cheek. 'So good to see you,' I said. I was acutely aware that I hadn't seen Bea for ages; it was longer than we'd ever been apart before, and I found myself feeling a little awkward around her. A sort of social anxiety, even. A distance.

'Man, I love having a pompously huge pushchair; it's like having a massive lawnmower, everyone immediately moves!'

'How are you?' Isla asked, hugging Bea.

'I'm good! He's fast asleep,' she said, nodding down towards the pushchair. Bea had recently given birth to her first child, Andrew. He was in the land of nod, wearing a bunny hat. Butter wouldn't melt.

'Congrats, Bea,' Jacob said, putting his arm round her. 'He's bloody gorgeous.'

'I'll go get you a drink, Bea.' I stood up.

'Just a lemonade please, love; I'm breastfeeding.'

When I came back out with Bea's lemonade, baby Andrew was wide awake and Jacob was gently swinging him from side to side in his arms. The baby was gazing up at him adoringly, and occasionally taking a swipe at his face with a tiny finger, which made Jacob laugh. I loved it when Jacob laughed, the joy in his face exposed these deep crow's-feet lines around his eyes, which have become deeper every year of knowing him. I always thought his wrinkles looked sexy, whilst mine were a sign of time running out.

'Here you go, Bea.' I passed her the fizzing plastic glass.

'Thanks babe. Look how amazing your boyfriend is with babies!'

'Very cute,' I said, trying not to roll my eyes.

'I wonder who's going to be next then?' Cec said, putting her sunglasses on her head.

'Well, Ol and Jacob have been together the longest,' Isla said.

'That doesn't mean anything, though,' I said quickly.

'I just need to meet someone first,' sighed Cec.

'You will, babe. C'mon, flirt some more with those hot lawyers at your work,' Bea said. 'It's probably you next, Isla.'

'God, I hope so! I'm due an egg check-up soon,' Isla said optimistically. Mike squeezed Isla's knee then and tucked her hair behind her ear.

'You will *all* be great mums,' Bea said.

'I'm so excited for us to have one of our own one day, Ol,' Jacob whispered, smiling at me adoringly, his finger being held on to tightly by baby Andrew. I took a massive gulp of white wine and offered a half-smile as a big black ball of darkness started to knot in my stomach.

'My friend's baby is the cutest baby in the whole world, which made me realize I don't want kids. If meeting the BEST baby in the world can't change my mind, nothing will. Unfortunately, when I phrased this to my friend I just said, "Your baby makes me want to not have kids."'

Sofie Hagen, Twitter, July 2019

10

2019

A week or so later, hungover again to high hell after a few too many at the pub with Col, I message Cecily to see if she fancies a visitor. We haven't heard from her for a while on the group, but maybe if I just offer to come to her, it'll be easier. I am dying to meet Oscar. I also just read this article about 'The Loneliness of Being a New Mum' and how being at home on your own all day can start sending you a bit loopy. Cecily is an extrovert after all and has never been someone who likes having solo time. She never spent any time alone in her bedroom at uni, and always needed someone to chat to around the house. I couldn't bear the idea that Cecily was cooped up with only some goo-goo-gah-gah noises and a few podcasts to keep her company.

When I arrive, there's a note on the plant pot outside that says, 'Let yourself in Olive!' I open the door and hang up my scarf. As I walk into the kitchen, she is sitting in a vintage rocking chair, wearing a pair of stained jogging bottoms, and smiling sheepishly at me. I go over and hug her as she can't move; she just puts her finger to her lips to warn me not to be loud. Oscar is asleep in her arms. Her usual swan-like demeanour seems a lot more ruffled. It's like everything that was once stuck together by superglue is dangling by a single thread. She looks exhausted.

'Oh my god, it's *so* good to see an adult!' Cec whispers in a hiss, balancing his tiny little head on her forearm. I lean down to kiss her on the cheek.

'Ohhh, Cec, he's precious,' I whisper back. 'I like his little hat.'

'Come through to the lounge and you can hold him when he wakes up.'

We both just sit in silence staring at Oscar sleeping for a bit. Watching his little chest go up and down. I am mesmerized; I sit watching him breathe his tiny little breaths. He then opens his small crusty eyes really slowly. Drifting in and out of sleep, showing us the whites of his eyeballs and closing his eyelids again. He eventually properly wakes up and looks around the room suspiciously.

'Aw, he's taking everything in,' Cec says proudly. 'God. Olive, I feel a mess.'

I look around and see there are nappy bags, flasks, muslins, baby wipes everywhere. Her house is normally minimal and tidy. She is sitting in the middle of the mess. Of course it *would* be a state – I am just shocked to see Cec's house like this for the first time. It's like a baby shop exploded everywhere.

'Do you want me to do anything?' I ask. 'Clear away a few bits?'

'Thank you. If you could chuck all that shit on the floor into that big basket, that would be amazing. I can't really bend over very well at the moment.'

'Of course!'

Cec rocks back and forth in her chair, shushing Oscar.

After I've finished tidying up a bit, Cec asks me if I want to hold him. He looks tiny. He looks like a small alien with massive eyes – to me he doesn't even resemble a human yet. My stomach starts to tighten with nerves. I've had so many dreams where I lose or drop babies. This was an opportunity to not fuck up.

Cec very slowly hands me Oscar. His body is like a small, warm hot-water bottle. He curves like a contented baby kitten in my arms and I gently rock him and do all the stuff I've seen other people do countless times. His legs are like little drumsticks, his cheeks are like tiny hamster pouches, with his little tongue poking out involuntarily, and even his dribble is sort of cute. I wipe his mouth with a muslin cloth that has cartoon giraffes on it and touch his flaky little head. Cecily is smiling. *He suits you. He likes you. You're a natural. Ha, look! He's gravitating towards your boob!* All the comments that I normally attract when holding someone else's newborn. Oscar is so small and so helpless, drooping in my arms like a little sack of flour, and yet I feel an emptiness from deep within. Holding a new baby is like a new test every time. Will I now, finally, maybe, feel something? I'd think. Whenever women shouted, 'Oww, what a cute baby! My ovaries! They just twitched!' I would think there was something incredibly wrong with me because my ovaries have never twitched.

There was no desire. Not even a slight, mild ache. Holding Oscar now, in this moment, my ovaries make no movement at all. Maybe they're washing their hair or out for the day.

I cuddle him, and what I do feel is love. The love I feel for this baby is because he's an extension of my best mate, a mini Cecily – he has her blue eyes and the exact shape of her ears. A baby is a symbol of a fresh start, new beginnings, and some new hope for a messed-up world. They make you forget about politics, the news, the chaos the grown-ups have brought about. Something new to fall in love with.

'So . . . how the fuck are you? How is everything? How is your downstairs department?' I say, stroking Oscar's dry little head, while Cec rearranges her boobs inside her feeding bra. 'Whoops, shouldn't swear in front of the baby, should I?'

'I'm OK. Bit sore. A layer of skin came off my nipples today. Clean off. *Ouch*. And I'm tired, of course, but on the mend. He is so lovely, isn't he?' She looks slightly broken, but she's beaming too.

Oscar was starting to get a bit heavy on my arm. Would it be considered rude if I gave him back to her already? I decide to err on the side of caution and hold him for a bit longer.

'I'll tell you though, Ol, I'm so happy to see my feet and my fanny again,' she says.

'So, what was it . . . like? Popping out a baby?' I ask, reaching for a Hobnob. A few biscuit crumbs fall on Oscar's head and onto the perfectly clean white baby-grow he is wearing. I flick them off with the back of my hand.

'Don't look so terrified.' Cec laughs. 'You know you'll be fine . . . if you ever do.'

'Thank you for saying "if". Most people say "when".'

'Well, exactly,' Cec says, rubbing Oscar's back, who is flopping forwards like a miniature drunken old man.

Cecily fiddles with her nursing bra again and I'm amazed and filled with pride at how quickly my friend is getting the hang of it all. My friend, a mother! It seems like only the other day that we were in nappies ourselves. My pride for Cecily turns into a tinge – and then a full-on wave – of sadness. She has been so understanding about the Jacob break-up, but there's only so much I can divulge when she's struggling with a newborn. I'm not sure she really understands how lonely I am feeling, just like I can't truly 'get' all the stuff swirling around her head right now either.

Cec moves Oscar to the nappy-changing table.

'So come on, you have to tell me your birth story.'

'I mean, it was absolutely mental. No one prepares you for what birth is really like. Yeah, it hurts like hell. But it's also, I don't know, the most natural thing? The midwives have delivered thousands of healthy babies. I read lots beforehand, the classic books and some online forums and stuff. I had an idea of all the different ways it could go. I had a "birth plan" but it sort of just goes out of the window. Oscar was in an awkward position, so I needed a bit of "help" with forceps. I'm pretty confident two nurses had their full hands up my vagina as well. Did not see that one coming.'

'That must have been scary?' I ask, chomping on another biscuit.

'Yeah. God yeah. I didn't have a clue what I was doing.

But who does? You just know it's gotta come out of you somehow. You're in safe hands. It was scarier when I had to bring him home . . . the amount of times I've put my ear next to his mouth just to check . . . he's such a bloody quiet sleeper. It's annoying and terrifying.'

'I don't know how you do it – I'm already such an anxious person,' I say.

'I remember the nurse plonking him in my arms and I was just thinking "WTF is this?"' Cec says. 'I know it sounds weird but, even after I gave birth, I thought why is someone handing this baby to me? I was so, so out of it. Like, how is this little thing mine?'

'Wow, Cec.' My eyes widen in admiration.

'I just concentrated on keeping calm because I gathered it would hurt more if I was stressing. I'll tell you something that I think is bullshit, though. This whole "you forget the pain!" malarkey. There is no way I'll ever forget the pain. I know some women who think about the pain every day.'

'Yeah, I think we are all sold that lie,' I say.

Cec puts Oscar down for a nap in his Moses basket.

'A woman called Charlotte delivered Oscar and I think I might send her some nice bits from Anthropologie.'

'That's a lovely idea.' I pause.

Oscar was looking so sweet, but I couldn't help but think babies were also like little vampires. Sucking the nutrients from your bones and brain cells. Obviously not something to say out loud to Cec.

'And how was Chris, was he helpful through it all?'

'Hmmm, I suppose.' She sighs. 'You know what he's like

Ol. Not always the most compassionate man in the world. He did his job and got me to hospital at least.'

'I would say his "job" is to do more than that, Cec!'

'Yeah well. I think we both know I was always going to be the one doing most of the work. I don't think he especially wants his life or career to change,' she says.

'I'm sure you don't want your career to change that much either!'

'Yeah. I've been reading all these blogs and articles about equal parenting . . . but there's just no way that's going to be Chris and I.'

We look down at Oscar in silence. He blinks slowly and stretches out his little hands.

'Well, I'm here if you ever need help or a babysitter.' It came out of my mouth, and I sort of mean it, but the idea of being left alone with a baby also petrifies me.

'Anyway, sorry about the state of the house,' she says, looking around anxiously. It's the second time she's apologized about it.

'Cec. Don't be silly! Maybe you could get a cleaner?' I suggest.

'I could do. I just hate it being so chaotic and disordered. You know what I'm like, I hate feeling like I'm not in control. I could have a word with Chris about helping out around the house I suppose.' She laughs abruptly.

I can sense her frustration already, being strapped to Oscar in that rocking chair all day.

'It's crazy how quickly people expect new mums to "snap back" or "get back to business as usual",' I say.

'God . . . I know. You're telling me. I'm feeling the pressure already, honestly. My boss emailed me a congratulations, but I can tell he has loads of stuff he wants to ask me about,' Cec says, frowning.

'I remember when Julie, the fashion editor at .dot, came back to work after maternity leave, people just said, "Welcome back! Congrats Julie!", gave her a bottle of wine, and then shoved her towards a new desk and computer login and just expected her to get back to it like nothing had happened.'

'Hahaha. Yup.'

'It was like the whole office was totally ignoring the fact that she had just pushed something out of her body, and that her whole life had changed for ever. We were welcoming back a whole new Julie with a new set of challenges, but no one ever really said anything.'

I wondered what the birth had been like for poor old Julie. Birth stories had become a bit of a fascination for me. And every single one put me off more. The gory realities of it all! I noticed, from all the birth stories I'd heard over the years, that yes, they are all entirely different, but also there is always a moment where the mother says, 'I'm probably not meant to say this . . .' Like they are breaking some sort of moral maternal code by feeling a certain way: 'I'm probably not meant to say this but, I wish I could give the baby back, ha ha ha!'

'So anyway, how is work, Ol?' Cec asks, stroking little Oscar's cheek in his Moses basket.

'Really good thank you! Writing some interesting articles, got some travelling coming up. No complaints really.'

Obviously I don't tell Cec that I've been mining online 'mum forums' for scary stories for my 'Millennials & Motherhood' article. One woman had such bad postnatal depression that her husband had to hide all the kitchen knives; another said her husband popped out to get some milk and, by the time he came home, she had practically delivered her own baby; another said the doctors held her organs while they did a C-section. It makes me shudder to think about. It all sounds so barbaric.

I get the sense that Cec might have stuff she needs to do before Chris comes home from work, so I start to say my goodbyes and we have a big long hug.

'You've got this, Cec, and we're here whenever you need us – OK?'

'I know you are, Ol. Thank you.'

I sit on the Tube home, feeling exhausted from just watching Cecily look after OAP. It reminded me of school, when I was given an egg to look after for a month. Mine was called Eggy. It was supposed to teach us how to look after things. Our classroom was quite unruly, and we always forgot to water the classroom plants or feed the pet hamster. The challenge was to not break the egg and return it at the end of the month, when we'd be asked to give a presentation on the most challenging bits. I drew a smiley face on mine and dropped and smashed it on day two. Sorry, Eggy.

I think about all the extra stuff my friends must have to worry about now that they're Mums. The rows and rows of mental filing cabinets stuffed full to the brim with extra information: bottles, school uniform, potties, nappy bags, toy gadgets, shopping lists, dentists, revision, doctors, parents' evenings, the distant family members of Peppa Pig. The list is endless. I already feel I have too much stuff overloading me, weighing me down, keeping me up at night. When I get home, I pour myself a huge glass of wine and close my eyes to focus on my breathing. In through the nose, out through the mouth.

My mind wanders back to the other day in the office, when I was discussing with Colin how wild pregnancy seems to be, after the announcement that someone in the royal family was pregnant again and the whole Internet erupted with gossip and opinion. I've never understood the mania and obsession that surrounds news of another person's pregnancy.

'When people are having a baby, I can't help but think of those little squishy alien toys, you know the ones? Like, having an alien toy inside you, growing and swishing around in your fluids,' Colin had said.

'*Ha!* I know the ones. It *is* all a bit alien,' I said.

'I honestly shudder at the thought. I mean, soz, I know I'm a guy. But still. Imagine casually growing *teeth* in amongst all your organs.'

'Yeah. A little ball of hair and teeth and ears, just growing slowly, in there.' I pointed to my tum.

'I can't,' he said, covering his mouth dramatically.

'I can't, either,' I said.

Thank god for Colin.

I down another huge glass of wine, push the empty wine bottle under the sofa and crawl into bed.

11

2004

Bea and I were going through an Avril Lavigne phase – it was all about pretending to own a skateboard, wearing heavy make-up, dark nail varnish and fingerless gloves for no reason. We would sing her lyrics very seriously from the top of Bea's bunk bed, staring out at the walls covered in Polaroid pictures. Everything felt intense: every text exchange with a boy, every film ending, every friendship blip. All hand-written notes needed to be saved in a box, every train ticket, all tickets to gigs were stuck on the wall. Everything was a memory, being stored into its own filing cabinet.

We were in the sixth form at school, and one week, a girl in our class called Charlize suddenly dropped out. The deputy head teacher, Mrs Paterson, had broken the news to us in assembly. She seemed nervous when reading off her piece of paper, and she kept moving her glasses up her nose as they kept slipping down. 'Hi everyone. Charlize is pregnant and has decided she doesn't need to finish her A levels,' she said, sternly. We were all quite shocked that it had been publicised in this way, such a formal announcement. I'd have expected the school to keep it all hush-hush. The baby was due in a few months and we were welcome to send gifts or notes to her home address. It was the talk of the classroom for a while. It was widely known that Charlize's boyfriend, the father of the child, owned a chain of popular hotels in the area and was going to inherit the family business soon, so they would be fine apparently – financially at least. It was weird that the finances were such a talking point.

'I can't believe Charlize is gone!' Bea said, getting a Twix from the common room vending machine. 'Never coming back. I really liked her.'

'I know, so sad. She really should finish her exams, don't you think?' I said.

'I mean, she was in the year-book as "most likely to get pregnant and settle down", remember? But I think that was supposed to be ironic . . .' Bea said.

'I don't see why she has to totally drop out. It's still good to have some qualifications up your sleeve, isn't it?'

'Totally. I don't think it's a good idea. Her boyfriend is rich as fuck but you've also gotta protect yourself. I personally intend to always have a back-up plan.'

'Same,' I said.

'I really, really can't imagine having a baby,' Bea said laughing, pushing her stomach out.

'God, me neither,' I said. 'Let's just run away when we're older, Bea, go off and travel. No boys, no babies. Can we just make sure we stick together, whatever happens?'

'One hundred per cent,' Bea said, linking arms with me and pulling me tightly towards her.

When I got home, I called Bea from our home landline. This is what happened most days: we spent all day together at school, and then called each other every night. For hours. My mum was often totally baffled that we never seemed to run out of things to say. I liked to sit inside my wardrobe, nestled amongst my clothes, and chat to her in there. It had been my cosy phone spot for years.

'Did your parents get a letter about the Charlize sitch?' I said.

'Yeah, they seemed quite laid back about it! Said it's lovely news. Bit of a weird reaction, really. What about your mum?' Bea said whilst chewing a piece of gum.

'She went mental.' I laughed nervously. 'Said I shouldn't be hanging out with boys. Started quizzing me about what I get up to. She full-on panicked.'

'No way.'

'Yeah. She started drilling into me how much pregnancy and kids will screw everything up. Explained to me all the different ways Charlize's life is ruined. Which was . . . nice,' I said.

My mum's reaction had shaken me, how angry she was. But I'd be lying if I said it hadn't washed over me, too. What was happening to Charlize was so alien, unfathomable. But it wasn't just the topic of common room gossip – it was affecting someone else's actual life.

Part Two

'I've grown apart from friends who have had kids, although
I do have one friend that has a kid who I'm still close with.'

Kelly, 40

Part Two

12

2019

I am working in the sky today, travelling on a flight back from LA, using the free onboard WiFi. I often have to fly there for work, but the trips are never long enough – which can actually be a good thing because I never fully adjust to the time zone and can't get too jet-lagged. I had to oversee a cover shoot for the first edition of the new ungraded print version of .dot, which just meant checking everyone knew what they were doing and then going back to my hotel room to order room service on the company card.

I love the freedom that these trips bring me. I feel a sense of purpose – I love the feeling of being needed by the team. I love the impromptu nature of my life – all I need is my laptop and to chuck a pair of pants in a tote bag, and I can work from anywhere; any hotel room or hotel lobby, preferably with G&T in hand. I know that this is the part that could earn me the stereotypical 'footloose and fancy-free childless friend!' label, which I suppose is, to some extent, true. Weirdly, though, one of the hardest bits about the break-up with Jacob has been that I have no one to text when the flight lands on work trips. I still go to text him when the wheels of the plane hit the runway, to tell him I'm safe; it's still a reflex. That's the strange thing about grief – you often have to remind yourself it happened. Even the little things still bring Jacob to mind; the smell of his aftershave still seems to linger in the bathroom sometimes. I don't know if I'm fabricating senses from memory, or if I really can smell him. The other day I spotted one of his old sports socks under the bed. The sofa seems so much bigger and lonelier with just me on it. I now sleep in the middle of the bed, instead of the one side I'd slept on for years. The bills and letters are still addressed to us both. The money situation is really starting to worry me now, too – instead of £750 each month for rent, I have to pay the full £1,500 now. I will either have to push for another pay-rise at work or get a housemate soon. I don't really want someone else in the flat because I love lounging around naked under my dressing gown, ordering takeaways.

Society rewards couples so much. Life is just so much easier in a couple. Cheaper, easier, more logical: take couple-discounted train tickets for example, or splitting bills, or tax benefits! It's also someone to share the mental load of household admin, someone to share the driving with on a long journey, someone to share a holiday with and be a plus-one to boring parties and weddings. I glare at the couple in the seats next to me, they keep nudging my laptop while snuggling into each other, making the most disgusting slurpy kissing noises. I actually can't believe I was one of those smug couples for so long.

I check the time and I still have another two hours of this flight left. I ask the air hostess for another mini white wine. Then, my phone pings. A WhatsApp from Mum.

Jacob has been in touch with me darling. Shall I 4WRD MSG 2 U?
MUM x

I message back immediately.

Me: WHAT?

Mum: One second darling, I'm just pouring myself a cup of tea.

I feel the fury burning in my chest and take a moment to try and calm myself down. This isn't her fault. The fact that she is the most infuriating woman on the planet to me – also not her fault.

Mum: Sorry. Here now. Just needed to put tea bag in bin. Yes, darling, he wants me to pass on a MSG. He says you've blocked him and no MSGS are getting through?

Me: Yes, I did block him Mum.

(I didn't want to drunk-dial him.)

Mum: He's been in touch with me quite a lot over the past few weeks. Asking me this & that.

(He what???)

Me: Oh my god Mum, what has he said?

She doesn't reply for a minute or two.
I wait.

Me: Mumm????

Mum: I didn't want to disturb U with some of the other messages. I did tell him to stop, and to not think about going around to UR flat. But this time, the boy seems a bit desperate, Olivia.

I hate it when my mum calls me Olivia. Yes, it's technically my full name on my birth certificate, but I hate it. I am Olive. By refusing to call me Olive, she refuses to embrace who I am. I don't have time to call her out on it. I can't help but feel a sense of relief from this news, a surge of happiness. He wanted to visit the flat? This makes me feel . . . weirdly . . . better.

Me: Jesus. Can't believe you didn't tell me all this. Yes you can send on the message, Mum.

Mum: How do I do it, darling? I'm just putting on my glasses.

Me: Copy and paste it, Mum.

Mum: How?

Me: Highlight the text with your finger. Then copy. Then open up my text and paste it.

Another few minutes pass.
There is a long, long pause. No typing.

Mum: Oh.

Me: What?

Mum: I just copied and pasted it back 2 Jacob.

Me: MUM. I CAN'T COPE WITH YOU.

Mum: Sorry darling! He won't know! I'm sure he'll just ignore it.

Me: To be fair, he'll probably just think you're being a weirdo with technology, which is the case.

Me: Mum???

Mum: Yes.

Me: Send me the text!!!

Mum: I am doing it.

Me: God . . . hurry up.

I immediately feel bad and add 'Love you.'

Eventually, my phone pings again. She must have finally figured it out. I start fidgeting, flicking through the pages of my book, and then fiddle with my seat tray, annoying the passenger in front who keeps grunting. I sit on my phone so I can't look. I'm good at distracting myself on the Internet. I'll do that. I put some searches into YouTube.

Why did Geri Halliwell leave the Spice Girls?
Best moments of *Gavin and Stacey*
A look inside Mandy Moore's new multimillion-dollar LA home
Can you be allergic to sperm?
Am I depressed or just lazy?
Are we in the *Matrix*?
Oh fuck off Clearblue adverts.

I look for further distraction. I'm not ready to look at Jacob's message just yet. My journalist instinct takes me to Twitter and I scroll and scroll, immediately reminded what a bizarre place it is.

@leana_scott
Young people, stop saying YOU'RE TIRED. I get major mum

rage when they moan about being tired. YOU ARE NOT TIRED, I'M TIRED, PARENTS ARE TIRED.

@writer_kate
Please DM me if you know anyone that has fallen in love with an inanimate object. Better still, got married to it. E.g. a brick wall. Thanks all #journorequest

@__colin01
Never make eye contact with someone whilst eating a banana. JUST DID THO lol.

@Jane_At_TheDOT
This article is fucking disturbing. Women: read, share, be mortified. This is the world we still live in.

I click on the link to the article that Jane has shared. My fingers tremble as the page loads. Maybe I've drunk too much coffee.

Of course, it's about motherhood. Everything. Conversations with friends, overhearing strangers' discussions, seeing push chairs and 'Baby on Board' badges everywhere, and it's the same on the Internet and in the news. It's like when you learn a new word and you then start seeing it everywhere. The more I panic about being abnormal, the more I think about it, and the more I see babies everywhere. I'm horrified to find that I'm reading an article about a state in America who want to make it *mandatory* for women to have a baby. It sends a shiver down my spine.

'Republicans, empowered by the Supreme Court, move aggressively toward forcing childbirth on women'.

Have you ever seen a more frightening headline? I suddenly feel so lucky: to know that I personally would have the money, emotional support and family network to get an abortion if I needed to. I imagine women without the same rights as me, who for many different reasons might not want a baby, but are forced to have it regardless. They have nowhere to turn, and it's expensive and long-winded to find a solution. Despite my disgust, the journalist in me forces me to keep reading: 'In some states in America, if you want to have an abortion, even if it is only a few weeks in, they make you name it, and bury it.' I feel a wave of sadness and anger ripple throughout my entire body. I read a quote in the article from a (surprisingly female) senator, and then read it again and again, letting the words haunt me as my chest starts to tighten:

Motherhood isn't easy but it's necessary.
Motherhood isn't easy but it's necessary.
Motherhood isn't easy but it's necessary.
Motherhood isn't easy but it's necessary.

My eyes are going blurry from looking at my laptop for so long. I look around and realize that the lights are all off in the cabin, the people around me sleeping uncomfortably in their seats. I pick up my phone and stare at the text message from Mum. OK, OK, I need to face this now.

I breathe in sharply and click 'read'.

HERE IS THE JACOB MSG 4 U, BELOW – LUV MUM.

Hi Olive,

It's Jacob . . . Hope you're well.

I'm sorry for messaging. I've really tried not to, I promise.

I really really need to talk though. Please.

I was wondering if you're around tomorrow afternoon?

I can't stop thinking about our last conversation, there's so much left unsaid.

Please let me know asap if you're about. I can come to the flat, or somewhere near you?

Let me know.

Jacob

Isn't it strange how ex-boyfriends suddenly become more formal the minute they're placed in the 'ex' category? The inversion of how close we once were. This was the guy who once squeezed the blackheads on my shoulders and now he's dotting the Is and crossing the Ts, putting capital letters in all the right places, with a new blunt sign-off. His message seems strangely urgent. I don't know what to say. I need time to think. I always longed to be Sabrina the Teenage Witch for this reason, because she could point her finger and freeze time. I want that. Imagine freezing time for an hour or two so you could sort your shit out. If I could have some time away from work, my phone, my responsibilities to just think, maybe all of this would be easier. I glance back down at my phone. I know I owe Jacob a reply. I stroke my phone screen pensively, and hesitate. I write out the text slowly.

Yes, pick a place and I'll meet you there.
Olive.

I hover my finger over the send button. I reread it a few times. I wait a few more seconds. 1-2-3 . . . Sent.

'Everybody with a womb doesn't have to
have a child any more than everybody with
vocal cords has to be an opera singer.'

Gloria Steinem, *Chelsea Lately*, October 2011

I woke with a world-class hangover and a little sympathy for every hard-drinking writer who tried to construct a whole sentence.

— Anonymous

13

2017

It was Friday night. Jacob and I both got home from work around 6.30 p.m. That was early for me; Gill loved to dump last-minute work on me in the afternoon. Jacob went to the gym (we have a small one downstairs in our building), and while he did that I wrote ten pages of the weird crime novel I was experimenting with in front of the TV. It's called *Blue Assassin*, and centres around a kidnapped dolphin: *Splash* with a dark twist. I was typing, deleting, typing, deleting. I heard the lock turn in the door and Jacob appeared huffing and all sweaty from an intense session. He came into the living room and planted a kiss on my lips and sat down next to me.

'Jacob! Don't sit on the sofa when you're gross.'

'It's only a bit of sweat. You love smelling my sweaty armpits,' he said, laughing.

'Go and have a shower before you sit down, this sofa cost us an arm and a leg. You stink!'

He tried to give me a cuddle and I jokily tried to push him away.

'Come in the shower with me,' he whispered in my ear, and took my hand. I followed him into the bathroom, enjoying the feeling of being wanted by him.

He stripped off. We both got in the shower. We put on some music, shampooed each other's hair, our faces sliding off each other as we kissed, and then we wrapped each other in huge bathroom towels that had been heated up on the radiator. I enjoyed that warmth of knowing someone else's body so well. Every nook and cranny. He nodded to the bedroom. We'd done this hundreds of times, of course. From the shower to the bedroom. But that time I freaked out – majorly. These episodes were turning into a bit of a habit and I think Jacob had started to notice. On the surface, I didn't know why. But then I unpicked it a bit, and I figured out exactly what it was. I had just come off my contraceptive pill because it wasn't 'agreeing' with me. The side-effects were so aggressive: major spots, mood swings, couldn't fit into my clothes any more. I felt as if I'd had a personality transplant and I didn't like the idea of not behaving like myself. He walked out into the bedroom and I followed him.

'You've been a bit . . . off lately, Ol. Are you OK?' he said, turning on his feet.

'Have I? Since I came off the pill to change to the other one, I do feel a bit weird.'

'You said it was being on the pill that made you act weird though,' Jacob laughed.

Why wouldn't he understand that being *on* the pill and *off* the pill and *in between* the pill all means I have an excuse to act totally loopy?

'Please don't make me explain my behaviour, J. My body is confused right now, as I am fucking around with all these different pills. I find it so unfair that women have to go through all this palaver. Men don't have to inject their bodies with all these bloody hormones.'

'Sorry,' he said.

'It's OK,' I said. 'I just got freaked out the other day because I read that the pill I was just on has given a load of women blood clots and one woman died recently from it. There's just always something to worry about.'

'You sound like you're very anxious again at the moment.'

'Maybe I always am.'

I have issues with the pill and I am also allergic to latex, so no condoms for me. I was floating around in no-man's-land, in no-contraception limbo.

'Does this mean we can't have sex at the moment?' Jacob asked gently.

'Yes, sorry. Actually, wait, I'm not sorry. I shouldn't have to apologize for being out of action for a bit,' I snapped.

'I wasn't expecting an apology. I was just asking.'

'Yeah, well, you're going to be on at me to get myself sorted quickly, aren't you, so you can get your end away. It's all men think about. Sex sex sex.'

'Ol, that's not very fair.'

'Well it's true. You're just concerned about getting your leg over.'

'What the hell, Olive.'

'Sorry,' I regretted the words as soon as they came out of my mouth. 'I just feel really vulnerable and weirded out right now. Maybe it's my hormones or maybe it's just *me*.' I put my head in my hands.

'I was actually asking because a) I'm interested in how you are, b) I'm your boyfriend and c) . . . I actually thought that we could discuss the idea of having sex, you know, without any protection,' he said.

Then there was a massive, massive silence.

'Oh . . .' I close my eyes.

'What?'

'Can we just lie down next to each other in bed for a bit?' I asked.

I was feeling really out of control and the thought of having sex made me petrified. With my boyfriend. Of almost a decade. The idea of getting intimate with him was suddenly sending me into nervous breakdown mode. It hit me that I was having the opposite problem to a lot of other women I knew in their thirties. Whilst so many of my friends were paying extortionate amounts to increase their fertility and chances of pregnancy, I was swatting away my partner's penis like an annoying fly. I didn't want to chance it. Whilst Jacob seemed to feel the opposite. It struck me that whenever we saw any friends' babies, Jacob would hold them so naturally. The babies would always warm to him, he was just a natural, making silly expressions that they loved and giggled at. I would smile along, but it always felt like I was hiding something – like I was a fraud.

We sat down on the bed. I wanted to be close to Jacob. I wanted to feel his warmth. I sat on him, folding myself around him. Then, I suddenly couldn't breathe. I climbed off him, feeling like I was having a panic attack. I rushed out, into the bathroom across the hall. I sat on the loo, grappling with my phone, trying to Google my feelings.

'You OK in there, Ol?' Jacob shouted, sounding concerned.

'Yeah, I just need a cold towel on my head. Give me a few moments.'

I sat on the cold tiled floor. My throat felt lumpy with repressed sadness. My body and brain knew the truth. All I needed to do was confront it. Accept it. Think it. Say it.

I just don't want to get pregnant.

That feeling I had with Bea when we sat in the Foyle's toilet all those years ago was not something I wanted to ever replicate. My head hurt. I could hear Jacob as he sat himself down outside, his back against the bathroom door.

I started to cry; I couldn't stop. Because deep down I knew this could be the end of us.

14

2019

'Morning Olive.' I'm picking up the mail on my doorstep, mainly junk, when Dorothy Gray calls over. She is watering a tiny patch of grass outside her front door. I'm not sure why, there are no flowers, just some brown grass, but it's quite sweet. She always seems to be giving herself random tasks to keep busy.

'Morning Dorothy! How are you doing this morning?'

'Yes, I'm very well thank you, Olive – just getting some small chores and errands done. Off to the post office later.'

Please don't launch into one of your long-winded stories, Dorothy.

'Have a great day,' I smile.

'Where are you off to, in that lovely scarf?'

'Oh, just to meet a friend at the coffee shop.' Friend.

'Oh, how lovely. Have you been to that little French one at the end of the street?'

'Yes, that's actually where I'm off to now!'

It's my ex-boyfriend, OK Dorothy? And I'm shitting it.

'Oh, how charming. I do like the crockery they use in there. And the forks are the perfect size. I can't stand a fork that's too small.'

'Yeah it's really nice in there.'

'I'd like to go back there one day. The temperature of the coffee is just right.'

'It is! Very observant, Dorothy.'

'Are you OK, dear – youngsters seem rather stressed these days.'

'I'm fine, thanks Dorothy.' What's giving me away?

'Just remember, when you get to my age, you never remember the little things that used to worry you or keep you up at night – you mostly look back fondly on the good times – they become clearer in your mind,' she says, watering some poppies.

'Thanks Dorothy. You're right.' I pause for a moment. 'What about the big stuff though? The big things that keep you up at night?' Jacob, motherhood dilemmas. Hardly small, silly things.

'Well, you must remember that no decision is ever really the wrong decision. Because it's the decision you made at the time. Respect your past self and her choices,' she says, looking me directly in the eye.

'You're right Dorothy . . . I'm so sorry, but I must get going now . . .'

'Off you dash then, Olive! Have a lovely day.'

She carries on watering and shuffling about with her walking stick. Humming to herself. There is something comforting about Dorothy. I have a feeling she's seen and heard it all.

I'm wearing a white T-shirt under denim dungarees, gold hoop earrings and thin-framed glasses. A bit of mascara and blusher but no other make-up. My hair dried naturally this morning and so is curly at the ends. I smooth it down and pull it back into a low ponytail. I don't want to make too much of an effort. It'll only make me feel more on edge. I meet Jacob at the small French café at the end of my road. It is a small bricked building with the roof painted black on the corner of a busy road and has two big Birds of Paradise plants either side of the entrance. I love the modern black-and-white tiled floors, the bar with hundreds of different liqueurs and spirits, and the friendly staff who always make you feel like their only customer. Even if everything goes to shit with this meet-up, at least I can have a nice hazelnut latte in this place I like. Although, like most things in my neighourhood, it is now tainted by good and bad memories of Jacob. I know I have to start living with that, because the only other option to get him completely out of my mind would be to move to Japan or something.

I see that Jacob has already arrived and is perched on a stool at the window. He hasn't noticed me yet. He's wearing a dark brown leather jacket, jeans, and is sipping a water nervously. He makes eye contact with me before I can try to pretend I haven't seen him, and waves at me sheepishly. I walk past the plants, and in through the main door, feeling his eyes still following me. Don't trip over, Olive. That would be embarrassing. He is wearing a navy-blue shirt that I've not seen before. My heart definitely flutters a bit with familiarity and excitement, but then I suddenly feel a bruising pain immediately after. My brain kicks back into gear, reminding me that he is no longer mine. This man with whom I shared a bed, a flat and my deepest secrets for nearly a decade will, one day soon, become a stranger. It's happening already. I project a horrible thought, imagining walking past him in ten years' time and neither of us saying anything because we are so estranged. I feel overwhelmed at the sight of him, as though I could easily be physically sick. Why has he dragged me out here to meet him? How can he have changed so much in only a few months? New clothes, different hair? I used to know every single piece of clothing that hung in his wardrobe and on the washing line. How can someone become so alien so quickly? It's like waking up from a sleepy dream where nothing is yet in focus and you momentarily forget where you are. Jacob is so close yet so far away now. I want everything to get back into focus, to make sense again.

'Hi,' Jacob says meekly, unsure of how to greet me. Hug, handshake, air-kiss? He hesitates and stands back. 'You good?'

'Hi, yes thanks – you OK?' I say, noticing that he is wearing new shoes too. He looks so different from the last time I saw him.

I take my coat off and sit down on the stool next to him. It feels cosy and, dare I say, romantic. Maybe it's the fairy lights framing the windows. The smell of freshly baked bread is wafting out from the kitchen as a song by Little Dragon

151

plays quietly in the background. Thank god there is music. It dilutes the awkwardness. The last thing I want is people overhearing or snooping on our conversation.

On the table next to us, I notice an oldish man with grey hair and a young woman with long dark hair eating lentil soup with bread on the side. They are speaking loudly in Polish. All of a sudden, the woman stands up and starts full-on shouting at the old man. We don't know what she's saying, but she's angry, it looks like she's about to flip the table. They go outside onto the street to carry on the argument, so they can really raise their voices, but it's muffled through the window. We see her arms thrashing around, and his face all screwed up. It's like watching a fight scene in a movie with the sound turned off.

'Wow – at least we're not like them,' Jacob jokes.

'They've got some beef, clearly,' I say.

'I'm so nosy. I want to know what they're saying. I wonder what he's done? Not sure whether he's her dad or what.'

'Yeah, god knows. Hope they sort it out.'

I'm very grateful for the ice-breaker. We transfer some of our own awkwardness into watching them for a bit. On the table in front of us, a young mum and dad are trying to control their baby twins who are in highchairs. They are screaming the place down. Their screeches pierce my eardrums. Such big lungs for two tiny humans.

'Anyway, you're probably wondering why I got in touch.' Jacob's eyes look sore and bloodshot. He doesn't look great. I feel bad that my first reaction is relief. Relief that he is also human, and also struggling with life. The screaming babies quieten a little. The mum puts Frubes into their sticky hands.

'You look tired,' I say.

'Ha, thanks. Isn't that code for "you look like shit"?'

'No, I just meant . . . are you all right?'

'Not really. Sorry to have messaged you. I know we were going to try having a proper clean break. But. Well, I've been going through a bit of a weird time, and I miss you.'

There's an awkward pause that I don't want to fill. I wait for Jacob to continue.

'Umm. So I just really wanted to see you, that's the first thing. The second thing is I found a lump. It's really put things into perspective.'

'A lump? Is everything OK?'

'Yeah. It's fine now. I got the results back yesterday. It just made me feel really alone, to be honest. I was panicking about it. And I realized that it's something I would have talked to you about . . . You were the person I always confided in. I went to the doctors. I'm just . . . I don't know. Not very good at telling people this sort of stuff. It's not like I can talk about it with the lads. Especially with it being on one of my balls.' He laughs. I chuckle too.

'That's a shame. Friends should talk about that kind of stuff. Friends talk about everything.' I realize the irony in that sentence, seeing how distant my own friends feel right now.

'Yeah. You're right. I suppose I just used to tell you everything. I didn't need them, I guess you were my best friend.'

'I'm glad you're OK now,' I say, trying to ignore how much that sentence punctured me. I am trying to remain neutral and calm.

'Yeah. It was just a cyst.'

'OK. That's good.' I really want to reach out and touch his hands; they are rough and pink at the knuckles with eczema.

'I feel like total shit to be honest, Ol,' he says, rubbing his hands together.

'I'm so glad it was just a scare . . . But you have so many people you could have told. It's not fair to drag me back into seeing you. I'm trying to rebuild things on my own here. It's been absolutely horrible these past few months.' My voice is cracking.

'Sorry. I just . . . I really miss you.' Now his voice is wavering.

'Do you? Or do you miss having a girlfriend? Because I think people can get the two things very confused.' I am shocked at how spiteful that sounds after it's come out of my mouth.

'Olive.'

'Yes?'

'What if we . . . you . . . changed your mind? What if you feel differently about starting a family later down the line? Sorry to drag it all back up but . . . we could have a great life together. I was just angry and upset at how distant you were near the end and . . . I don't know. I didn't mean to shut you out, I want to give you more time,' he says, trying to keep a lid on the desperation of it all.

'I'm sorry that you feel regretful over what you said. You were pretty certain that it wasn't going to work. You know that you want your future to have children in it. And honestly, I respect that. But my instinct's telling me that I don't want children now, and I can't see that changing. You're ready for them, quite clearly. So where does that leave us?'

'But this all feels so wrong. We are perfect for each other. This is, like, the only fight we've actually ever had!'

'That's not true. We had plenty of fights, and you know it. This is the one thing we could never meet in the middle on. We could never meet halfway. We could on all the other stuff. The other stuff isn't as major. This isn't moving to a new house, or choosing where to spend Christmas, or what colour to paint the bathroom. All that is day-to-day decision-making and compromise and we are – were – good at that. But we can't compromise on this, and honestly, I don't think either of us should have to. You're allowed to change your mind about what colour you want to paint the walls – you can just paint over them again. But you can't do that with a baby! With a baby, you cannot just go back to the way things were if you decide you don't like it. We're talking about bringing a life into the world. A human life! A real person, Jacob.'

'Yes, I know that, Olive.'

'We fundamentally want different things. It hurts like hell for me too, but I just don't see how it can work.' I can't look at him now or else my heart and throat will break open and I'll start crying, so I look down at the floor and focus my gaze on his new shoes again. Nike trainers. Blue laces. They look light and springy; light enough to suddenly run off to somewhere far, far away. From me and this mess.

'I've fucked this up. I'm so sorry.' I watch him dig his fingernail into his hand, as if he's trying to hurt himself somewhere to displace the pain.

'No,' I soften. 'You haven't. And no more than I have. This is just two people having different ideas of how they want their future to look. And if I was going to have kids, J, it one hundred per cent would have been with you.' I tilt my head back to hold back the tears. 'It's all I can think about at the moment. I look at Bea, and now Cec, and try to convince myself that my future could match theirs. But,' I gulp as a tear slips down my cheek, 'I just don't want children. And you do. Minds can be changed on some things, but I don't think mine can be on this.'

Jacob pauses, looks down, rubs his eyebrow up and down and then looks back up at me.

'I don't know what else to say.' I stare down at my hands.

He pauses for a while and looks around the café before his gaze turns back on me. 'Maybe you could see someone?' he says. 'You know, talk it out?'

'I don't need to "see someone", Jacob! I don't need therapy just because I don't want kids!' I take a big breath. 'I know it's a huge deal to you, so I understand it's hard to get your head around, but your life isn't worthless or any less valid if you don't want a family!' I realize my voice has crept up and that people around us have started to stare. 'Maybe you need to go and see someone to get your head around *that.*'

'OK, OK. I know that, Olive. That's not what I'm saying.' Jacob lowers his head.

'Maybe people who want kids or live for their kids will never get it why I don't want them,' I went on. 'But here are a few reasons: kids would ruin our relationship. Kids are hard work. Kids will destroy my body, and my freedom. Kids will destroy my bank account, and I don't have any money as it is. The world is overpopulated! The world is a mess!' I was ready to burst into tears.

'OK,' Jacob said hurriedly. 'I'm sorry. I'm just so sad without you, Ol. Life feels so meaningless without you there.' His heart was on a plate and I felt bad for losing my temper with him.

'I'm sad too. But what can we do? Get back together and then I'd disappoint you for ever? And take something so huge away from you? I can't do that.'

A waitress with a resting-bitch-face comes over with a pad and pen, and a tattoo on her face. 'Sorry for the delay. What would you like to order?'

'Err, the classic hazelnut coffee for me, please,' I say with a fake smile, shuffling the different paper parts of the menu.

'Same please.' Jacob's tone is blunt. The waitress nods and leaves.

'You hate coffee,' I say.

'I know,' he laughed. 'I panicked.'

I laugh at this and the tension between us disperses a little.

He takes a deep breath in then and says: 'Look, I am trying to backtrack a bit here. I've realized that I am losing you over something, a thing, a person, that isn't even born yet. That's stupid. Yes, I want kids. But I want you too. I want to be with you. This entire break has been miserable, and I feel lost.' He reaches for my hand. 'It's so stupid. I made such an effort this morning to scrub up nicely for you. Trust me, I've looked an absolute state for the past few weeks. I had a massive caveman beard up until yesterday, if you can imagine it. Even Steve said what a state I've looked.'

'That's rich coming from Steve.'

He tries to touch my hand again, but I recoil.

'Look Jacob . . . Your family – your mum, your brothers – it's all they talk about. Asking us about babies. I've found it so hard. I never know what to say to them!' I pause and take a deep breath: 'I'm scared that if we stay together, I will get pregnant. I'm scared I will just do it for you because I still . . . love you so much. And I'm scared it will be the worst decision of my life and I will never forgive you for coercing me into it.' I close my eyes. The realization that I will always love him sets in like a rising tidal wave. What if I feel this awful and sad for ever?

The waitress plonks our coffees down on the table.

After she moves out of the way, he grabs my hand. 'Olive, I love you too.'

'Don't, Jacob.'

'I would never force you into it,' he says, desperately but gently.

'No, I know. I just . . . this is all going to end in tears.' I edge my stool away.

'Please.'

'We both know you will be happier . . . without me.'

I know that, deep down, Jacob understands how awful the situation will become later down the line if we don't end it now. But this still feels physically painful, saying goodbye to someone you still love so deeply. We've already spent years sweeping it under the carpet. Years deferring it. Years doing the whole 'ah we have loads of time'. But it has got to the point where we can't continue to sweep. If I get pregnant, I won't want to have it, and that would absolutely kill Jacob. He is desperate for kids and I am actively hurting him by holding them back from him. I've surprised myself with how adamant I've become. I just know being with him would be unfair to us both.

'OK.' Jacob breathes in, sharply. 'Well . . . I've changed my mind then. I want to be with you. I don't care about anything else. I am willing to miss out on the other things.' Jacob's eyes are welling up.

'No, Jacob.' I push back my stool. I replay what Zeta said to me not long ago: Remember Olive, it's cruel to be kind. 'It's over. We're over. I don't want to be with you any more.' I steel myself. 'I'm not in love with you any more. Babies or no babies. It's right that we end this now.'

I fight against every natural impulse in my body to kiss him and just forget it all – pretend it was just another silly argument. But, for once, it wasn't a silly argument. For the first time ever, we were both really hurting one another. It would be pointless to go back to normal; we'd only find ourselves in another café a few months down the line, putting ourselves through all this again.

'You know what, Olive. I will probably look back on this moment one day in the future and love you even more for having the strength to do something I couldn't,' he said, tears balancing on the ridges of his eyes. One falls then, and starts to gently trickle down the side of his stubbly face. I lift my hand instinctively and touch his arm and then wonder if this will be the last time I ever touch him.

He knows that this needs to happen, and so do I. Our path together has reached a dead end. We both have a new chapter to embark on, but the beginning of it will feel as if we're being dragged through a forest of thorns, jagged rocks and stinging nettles, bleeding everywhere for everyone to see.

The waitress comes over again and takes our empty glasses, placing a voucher for a free coffee on the table. I put it in my pocket. Jacob politely packs up his bag, pays the bill, and then gets up to leave.

'Right.' He coughs, straightening his shirt, like he's trying to rid himself of any last remnant of emotion. 'I'd best be off then.' A cold goodbye. A hard goodbye. A stranger's goodbye.

And, before I have a chance to respond, he walks right out the door. I feel physically sick; it feels finally, in some way, finished.

When I get back to my flat, I stop outside Dorothy's door and rummage inside my handbag for a pen. I pull out an old biro and lean the voucher against my leg to write on it: 'For your next cappuccino, Olive x'. I post it through Dorothy Gray's bright orange letterbox.

'Finding child-free friends does get harder as I get older.'

Emilia, 36

15

I walk into my kitchen absolutely exhausted from staying up all night on my laptop, deep-diving into online hate forums where 'mum bloggers' rip each other to shreds. All for my article at work, of course. I'm trying to understand why these parenting forums encourage so much competitiveness and insecurity, and whether or not they alienate child-free women (or indeed reinforce their decision not to get involved!). I went down so many rabbit holes and woke up with random scribbles in my notepad that now don't make much sense.

I open my fridge and realize I have run out of milk and need to pop to the shop. I pull on my coat, pop on my shoes and as I open my front door I'm nearly deafened by a motorbike that screeches past. As I'm about to shut the door, I catch sight of Dorothy out of the corner of my eye. This time she is not watering her plants, she's lying in the middle of the road, motionless.

'Dorothy! Oh my god, Dorothy. Are you OK?' I rush over to help her back onto her feet. 'Quick, up you get. A car might come. Jesus.'

'Oh, thank you sweetheart! Silly me! Thank you for helping. I will even forgive you for blaspheming,' she says, heaving herself up against the weight of my arms. 'I felt extremely dizzy – and then before I knew it, I was on the floor!' She starts laughing heartily.

'Gosh, I'm glad I saw you. Are you all right, do you want me to call anyone for you?'

'No, it's OK. I wouldn't want to worry anyone. I'm alive and kicking,' she says cheekily, back on her feet.

'Do you have a walking stick?'

'I do, but I hate it. Reminds me of how old I am. I don't want to look old, darling.'

'I think you should use it; you'd probably find it really helpful.'

'Oh, I suppose I should,' she sighs, huffily.

'I was just thinking Dorothy, I should give you my number in case of emergencies.'

'Oh that's very kind, Olive. I promise I won't pass it on to any young chaps I know.'

We both chuckle.

'Why don't you come in for a minute? I should give you mine, too. I don't know my number off by heart. I could write it down though.'

I want to say no. I have things I need to do. But there's something about Dorothy, and she's obviously vulnerable at the moment. 'Yes. Of course.'

I follow her into her house. She has an old patterned carpet in the hallway. It smells of TCP, a smell I find comforting as it immediately reminds me of my grandparents' house.

Dorothy opens a creaky drawer on a table next to the stairs with a very old-looking phone sitting on it. She takes out a tiny piece of paper with some numbers scribbled on it and puts on some very thick-lensed glasses to read it out.

I scribble down the numbers as she reads them out slowly, her hands shaking as she holds the piece of paper.

'Would you like to stay for a cup of tea, dear? After all, it was so lovely of you to post the coffee voucher,' she says, beaming.

I don't have the heart to say no to her. 'Sure! I can't stay too long though.'

We both walk into her front room and I sit on an old small circular futon, a piece of furniture that looks like it might once have been the height of fashion. She has six different clocks all making different tick-tocking sounds. How does she not find that irritating? How does she sleep? I notice she has stacks of old VHS tapes piled up high next to a big old TV. She also has piles of stuffed address books next to her sofa, and stacks and stacks of thick envelopes with letters inside. There are picture frames perched on every surface; relics of Dorothy's past. It's like I've tumbled into an *Alice in Wonderland* of memories.

'So many videos! What a collection you have,' I comment, pointing at the pile, as Dorothy potters in the kitchen, clanking mugs together.

'Oh you know! Doris Day! Betty Grable! Gene Kelly! The classics!' she says enthusiastically. 'My favourites. My generation!'

'I'll have to watch some of these old films one day,' I say.

'I watch them on repeat,' Dorothy shouts from the kitchen.

She wanders back in, her hands shaking again, nearly spilling tea everywhere. I jump up. 'Sorry, Dorothy! I should have helped you,' I say, taking the cup and saucer and placing it slowly onto her glass coffee table.

'So, what's your favourite thing about these old films?'

'Well, I suppose they remind me of being young! The stars in them were young when I was young. Very good looking too. I *love* the clothes – oh, the wardrobes were magnificent.'

'And these framed paintings on the wall. They're beautiful,' I say, looking up at a row of painted ladies in different-coloured dresses, all wearing cloche hats. Funny to think I might be rewatching old episodes of *Girls* or *Sex and the City* when I'm older. I think those will be the shows that will remind me of being young. My version of Doris Day.

'Thank you, I love dresses,' she says. 'Even this one I'm wearing today holds so many memories.' She looks down at the floral buttoned-up dress she's wearing. It's faded, but beautiful.

'Did you used to collect them? Dresses?'

'I used to make them, dear – for the stars. In Hollywood.' Her eyes light up as she speaks.

'Wow . . . really?'

'Yes . . . I travelled the world, dressmaking – it was the dream job. And my lovely husband was so understanding. I was the breadwinner, which in those days seemed very odd to our friends and family.'

As Dorothy goes into the kitchen to get a slice of lemon drizzle cake (she won't take no for an answer), I Google her quickly. Because I am nosy. Her Wikipedia page instantly comes up.

'Dorothy Katherine Gray was known for her stylish and iconic garments, including the famous strapless diamond leotard worn by Betty Grable in the 1946 film *Diamonds*. She designed a selection of couture gowns and coats for many of Marilyn Monroe's film premieres, which are currently immortalized in a photo gallery in the Palm Springs museum.'

I'm slightly blindsided. I feel a twinge of guilt. I'd somehow put Dorothy into a small box of tradition and convention. It's just what I'd associate with her generation. Her little life across the road. But I suppose it goes to show, people can surprise you all the time. There doesn't have to be one given path for anyone.

We finish our tea and cake and I gather my bag to go. I'm meeting Isla and I don't want to be late, but I'm realizing that I could stay all day listening to Dorothy's stories. I want to know more about her life.

I say goodbye and thank her for the tea – she definitely put too many sugars in it and, with the cake too, I am on a slightly buzzy high.

'Have a good day, Olive: seize the day! And thank you so much for helping me earlier,' she says, jiggling her bad arm at me. 'I hate to think what might . . . well, thanks for helping me.'

Our conversation from earlier replays in my head, her

voice ringing in my ears: No choice is the wrong choice, because it's the one you make at the time with the information you have.

'It was lovely to chat to you. And remember to use your stick. Bye, and see you soon!' I find myself giving her a big hug as I leave.

Turns out it's the kind of day where it really does matter if you leave the house and forget to wear deodorant. It's four in the afternoon and my iPhone tells me it's still 22 degrees. It's like 'yay shorts weather' slash 'oh shit global warming'. The shade of London's parks looks like an old faded sepia Polaroid, like those stained photos that have been passed down in an old dusty jewellery box from grandparent to grandparent. The parks are brown, dry and crispy already, and it's not even May yet. I'm scared of it getting any hotter. I don't feel quite myself if I'm not wearing big baggy jumpers and woollen beanie hats.

I get the tube to Green Park station; it is pretty disgusting in this heat and results in droplets of sweat dripping down the backs of my thighs and into my socks. I hope no one notices. I'll assume everyone is too busy worrying about their own sweaty crevices.

Isla and I have decided to meet for an afternoon picnic in Green Park, in a nice patchy bit of grass near Buckingham Palace. We decided earlier this year to do more 'London things' together. But this sunny, La-La-Land weather is bringing far too much pressure to be sociable. I know I've been too busy moping around of late, hiding away from the world in my flat, but I sense Isla really needs some support. She'd been ignoring all of our calls, while continuously posting some old photos with long waffly captions to Instagram, which is really unlike her.

I meet Isla by the Tube and we go to the M&S food shop. We buy a soft French baguette, some cheese, some olives, a bottle of wine and some alcohol-free beer for Isla. We scan the park and find a spot with some dappled shade under a tree. A group of young boys are kicking around a football, two teenage goths are on a date and they sit flirting and flipping through a magazine about tattoos and piercings. We sit near a young hot dad and his toddler daughter who are reading a David Walliams book together. He is doing different voices for the characters and she's laughing along encouragingly. It's very sweet.

Isla and I like doing nothing together. We mainly just lie in silence, or read books in restaurants together, and if we're outdoors we will listen in to everyone else's conversations around us and one of us will occasionally pipe up with a deep, existential question for us to interrogate. One of our favourite games to play is coming up with someone's whole life story based entirely on their style and choice of shoes: Clarks shoes = accountant with a mistress; Russell & Bromley boots = stay-at-home mum running a secret illegal business; Stella McCartney flatforms = retired artist who once shagged Mick Jagger; metallic Converse trainers = tattoo artist or body-piercer who used to be a policeman. You can tell a lot about a person from their choice of footwear. Sometimes we would elaborate wildly on these stories, as it would distract Isla from her pain, even if it was only for a few minutes.

'How are you feeling today?' I ask her gently, as I waft out an old picnic blanket for us to sit on. It feels like a while since we've sat down, just the two of us. She looks sad, as though she needs a chat. And I feel deflated from thinking about my lonely cat-lady future. I don't even like cats, I am totally screwed.

'Not good, to be honest, Ol,' Isla says, noticing me sizing her up. She looks pale and her posture is awful. 'I'll tell you in a sec. Pass me one of those fake beers, will you, please?' She gets herself comfy and crosses her legs. 'God I wish I could just have a glass of wine, but my doctor would kill me.'

I pour my wine and her beer into plastic cups, splashing the drinks slightly onto my jeans.

'I feel awful. This is the first time I've been outside in *days*.' Isla puts her sunglasses on. *Same here*, I think. For different reasons, but hey. I try to quieten the anxious thoughts that are fighting for room in my own head. Isla will be my sounding board, but for now she needs to offload.

'We don't have to stay out very long if you don't want to,' I say.

'Thanks,' she takes a sip from her plastic cup. 'So, I'm about to start IVF round two soon, but I have to wait and I don't know how long for. The question is: can I handle the strain on my mental health, my body, the unknown, the potential disappointment *again*?' She lies down on her side, sighing, taking another sip of her drink. 'The amount of people who are telling me to "think positive". I want to punch them all.'

'Oh Christ, poor you. Here, take this.' I give her a small pillow I packed in my bag.

'You're so sweet, Ol. Thank you.'

'So what happens now?'

'I have to wait a couple of months, have two normal periods before trying again. I guess I feel stupid for thinking it might happen during the first round.'

'Oh, you're not stupid.' I lean across and hug her. But I feel so conscious of not holding her too tightly, scared to hurt her more, like she has a 'fragile: handle with care' label on her body.

'And if that's not shit enough,' she starts saying after we pull away from the hug, 'it is hurting so much to have sex with Mike. He's being so good and nice about it all, but it's kind of affecting our relationship. He knows it's not him and I still fancy him and everything, but it's just super-frustrating. It was our anniversary the other day and it just ended up with me crying endlessly and him lying there until I fell asleep. I'm just so exhausted. All the time!'

'You poor thing.'

'Sex has sort of weirdly changed a bit for me now, because of all this,' Isla says. 'So much pressure.'

'That's understandable,' I say.

I don't know what the right thing to say is. I often feel like the worst person in these awful situations. I laughed very loudly at a funeral once, not out of malice, but from sheer awkwardness. This time, though, I instinctively just know to sit close to her, our crossed-legged knees touching as I listen.

'You know, a few years ago, I wasn't actually sure I wanted kids,' Isla says with a sigh, 'until I realized that I might not be able to. And now I feel like something's been taken away from me. It really wakes you up. How silly of me to think I could just click my fingers.' I feel surprised hearing this from Isla, and guilty that I didn't know. I used to have the 'will we/won't we' conversation with Cec a fair bit growing up, but for some reason Isla and I never really discussed it. Isla's attitude towards kids always felt like a mystery to me.

I feel a twinge of ickiness in my stomach. I technically have a choice still – babies could be in my future – and I'm choosing not to use it. I have access to something she wants. The big, fat, inappropriate elephant in the room.

'It's weird,' Isla continues. 'I think every one of us has a *Sliding Doors* moment, whether we know it or not. This is mine. I might never be a mum. Well, in the biological sense, I mean. It just makes me really fucking sad to say that out loud.' Isla takes a bite of the baguette. She chews it with her mouth open, like she's completely given up on the world. 'I'm so lucky that my uncle keeps funding my treatments. It's so pricey.'

I think about how much time Isla has spent in her bed feeling depressed, or suffering from endometriosis flare-ups over the years, plus the horrific tragedy of losing her parents at such a young age. Luckily her uncle has stepped in and done a great job and continues to help her financially. Poor Isla, spending her life suffering in more ways than one, and now fertility issues are unfairly being added to her pile. Making an active choice about motherhood is one thing, but having that choice taken away is another. How do you do the whole 'Where do you see yourself in five years' time?' when you don't even have free rein to choose? Every time someone we vaguely know announces their pregnancy in some elaborate way on Instagram, we all hold our breath and hope that Isla doesn't see it. She has good days, and then is triggered all over again by seeing something online and then won't be able to leave her house for ages.

'I feel so lucky that my job is flexible right now. I don't know how people do it if they are chained to a nine-to-five. How would you fit in all these fiddly doctors' appointments?' Isla says, propped up by her elbows.

'You're right, I still have to fill out a form and send it to my boss to have time off for a bloody smear test. And I work at a feminist magazine! I'd like to think people would be more understanding – especially when it comes to women's issues.'

'I hope they will be. I've decided to basically close my practice and just take some of my top-paying clients from home – it's been really nice actually.'

Isla had opened her own therapy practice four years ago and it was thriving. Word-of-mouth (and social media) recommendations counted for a lot these days so, when a famous Millennial author had recently written a book with a chapter on therapists, and had told her millions of Instagram followers about how great Isla was, literally overnight she was inundated with emails and texts from young, wealthy girls wanting the same magic fix. Isla had always been interested in the inner workings of other people's minds, and she knew from an early age that she wanted to do something that involved talking about feelings. She called it 'Headonism', which was a shit pun the girls had all come up with at Jono's years ago, but it stuck. It made sense: therapy had become much more normalized now, at least with women in their late twenties and thirties. 'Off to see my therapist!' was the new 'Off to get a haircut!' If anything, you were weird if you didn't have one these days.

Isla pours herself more fake beer, dribbling some onto the grass, and gets herself in a different comfortable position on her front.

'So this woman came to see me the other day. Obviously I can't use her real name or anything – let's call her Marnie. She had paid the premium amount that comes with last-minute bookings, she sounded desperate, so I agreed to do it. I asked her to fill out a form online beforehand, which had some big questions on such as, "What's your relationship like with your parents?" to "Have you ever been in a traumatic environment?" She left most of it blank, so I had no idea what she was coming for.'

'Right,' I nod, chewing on a grape.

'This was a first session, so it was technically a chemistry meeting, getting to know each other and generally having a warm-up session, but she seemed very adamant that she wanted to dive on in. She had been struggling to come to terms with the fact that she had recently had an abortion, and the deep feelings of regret that followed shortly afterwards were haunting her. She'd had the termination at seven weeks and, immediately after the operation, she just wanted to make a U-turn. Marnie kept saying she wanted her baby back. She said she couldn't leave the house. She couldn't be around anyone. She cried at everything. She was worried that she was innately bad. That she might kill someone else.'

'Wow, poor woman.'

'I know. But I really struggled to find my empathy, Olive. "Poor her" wasn't my immediate reaction, and it really scared me. I tried to cover it up but I felt my face get hot in the session. I was so angry. I would do anything to get pregnant. And there this woman was, opening up to me and paying me to give her zero judgement. I wanted to call her an idiot.'

Oh God, I thought, and here *I* am, wanting some sympathy over my break-up with Jacob; desperately wanting to talk to Isla about the obstacle that tore us apart. How can I ever get Isla's empathy in the face of this?

'I feel awful, Ol.' She slumps her head into her hands. 'I am a fully trained therapist – and a good person, I hope – and yet there I was, judging this other woman so severely for her choices. Maybe I shouldn't have gone back to work so quickly.'

I swallow my own queasiness. 'But you weren't to know. Yes, you're a therapist, but you're not superhuman.'

'And I obviously don't have any issue with abortions. It's just, all I can think about is my own body right now.' She awkwardly moves her glasses up her nose as she talks. 'I'm a monster.'

175

'No, you are not.'

'Maybe I shouldn't be a therapist any more,' Isla says.

'Isla. No. No amount of training can make you become immune to your own open wounds.'

'Hmm. You know, I can't treat her now, but when Marnie left she shook my hand and thanked me for a brilliant session. Through my pain, I guess I still managed to help her in some way. She said she felt so much better. Then I closed the door, smiled, waved, went back indoors and sat on the sofa. I stared at the wall, then I cried and cried and cried into a cushion until my face hurt,' she says, and starts to cry again.

'Oh, Isla.' I move and sit next to her, wrapping both my arms around her.

'I just want my own fucking baby so fucking much,' she says, this time with a snot bubble coming out of her nose.

We sit in silence, me holding her. She feels so small, her shoulders so petite. She has lost weight. She is closing in on herself.

So, this is what it must feel like to really want a child.

I close my eyes tightly and try and imagine it for a second. To imagine wanting it. To imagine that feeling in my own body and mind, of wanting to create a new life.

Still nothing.

The more I hide it, the heavier it becomes. Each woman I know carries it – shame – but it's a different shape for us all. There is always a hidden shame related to motherhood; whether you want a baby, or you don't, or whether you hate being a mother or whether you love it more than anything else in your life. I know what it's like to want something, to pine and long and cry for something. I have longed for boys who didn't love me; I have longed for a new version of myself, longed for a dream job, longed for my cosy bed after a week of camping . . . But this lack of longing for a baby feels so lonely. And not having Jacob in my life any more seems like some kind of punishment for my decision.

I desperately want to say all this to my friend in this moment as I sit there, hugging her, rocking her gently as she cries into me. But how can I, in the face of Isla's pain?

'I think I should go and lie down now,' Isla says, in a monotone, and starts packing up her things.

She does this sometimes. When we were younger we'd be having a nice time at a party and she would suddenly grab her bag and leave. A French exit? An Irish goodbye? I understand this time, though. We put the ends of the baguette and plastic cups in the bin and brush the dirty grass off our clothes.

'You are so loved, Isla,' I say, gently. 'No matter what happens, you have me, and you have Bea and Cec.'

'Thank you, Ol. You know, when we were younger, I just never imagined all of these problems. Adulthood looked like the dream.'

'I know, me neither,' I say, hugging her tightly.

'People have started to look at me with pity. Society really wants us to get married, have two children and move to a house with a driveway still. I'm more likely to go and live abroad and travel more.'

Lily, 43

16

It's late afternoon on a Friday and I'm planning to spend the evening getting drunk on the bottle of chilled rosé sitting in front of me on my desk. It was a gift from Gill because Chrissy Teigen retweeted one of my articles last week, and the website practically broke because so many people were clicking the link. It was an amazing feeling and it's a pretty rare occurrence to have your article go viral. On that note I need to finish Gill's 'Do Millennials Want Kids?' article – I've really started to enjoy the editorial tunnels I've been going down. It's almost become a sport. It's all I can think about and I have so many notes, more than I know what to do with.

I want everyone to leave the office, so I play some podcasts loudly as a hint. Everyone is slacking off, slumping in their chairs, writing personal emails, eating loudly at their desks, ready for the weekend. Someone is playing a Phil Collins song and Colin is starting to pour Buck's Fizz into plastic glasses because the company has just met its quarterly financial target.

'Beverage, m'lady,' Colin says, planting one down next to my mousepad.

'Thank you.'

'Excited for the weekend? I am gonna get *leathered*,' he says, knocking back the liquid.

'Meh,' I say. 'To be honest Col, I've got sod all planned.' Colin is literally the only person at work who knows the real me. He squeezes my shoulder and then disappears to the other side of the office, distracted by a colleague who has brought their new dog in.

I feel like it's a taboo thing to say that I never really find the weekend that exciting. I prefer the working week more than the pressure of having a perfect two days outside of it. I put my headphones in and hover my fingers over my keyboard, as if I'm about to play a grand piano.

My phone beeps, interrupting my flow. It's Cec sending me a pic of Oscar with the caption: 'We just had a poo-nami.' I shudder.

It's the first peep I've heard from Cec in weeks, but I need to get into my stride with this article. Focus, Olive. I Google: 'Why am I not feeling broody?' No harm in mixing my personal interests with the professional. I look over my shoulder to check no one is watching me.

Over two million results suddenly pop up on the screen.

An article comes up from an online magazine listing '9 signs you're feeling broody!!!!' The website doesn't look very legit, but I'm intrigued all the same.

- You romanticize the idea of morning sickness (hell no)
- You feel your ovaries twitch whenever you see anything really cute (no)

- You are jealous whenever someone posts a pregnancy bump on Instagram (nope)
- You've often stood sideways in the mirror and imagined a bump (lol no)
- You've often put a pillow up your T-shirt to imagine a bump (wtf no)
- You randomly find yourself going into Mothercare and look at/touch baby clothes even though you're not pregnant yet (no, what's wrong with people please?)
- You love holding your friends' babies (it's OK, but no, not really)
- You write down baby names in your notepad (no)
- You absolutely love the show *One Born Every Minute* (hmm, no.)

I look around at the party atmosphere in the office. Colin is doing a samba routine with Julie, the head of design at .dot. Julie has her hands on Colin's shoulders, and Colin has one leg back, like he is doing a lunge. 'I Like It' by Cardi B is blasting out of the radio.

'What are you two doing?' I shout across the office. 'Some people are still trying to finish their work for the day!'

'Julie's got a date tonight,' Colin says, mid-step and a bit breathless, 'so I'm teaching her some new moves.' She steps on his foot and they burst out laughing.

Next to these two jokers, a meeting is trying to happen on beanbags on the floor, and someone else is shouting over the music about cover lines.

'Can everyone be a little quieter? It's like a zoo in here,' I say.

'Agreed,' says Jason, one of the lead editors who looks stressed out.

Yes, everyone is a bit annoying and I have to tell them to shut up, but deep down I do still find the madness really comforting. It's my second home here at .dot.

Ping. My internal thought-bubble bursts as I see an email flash up on my desktop from Gill. I've set them to 'high priority' and they make a horrible noise that actually makes me jump.

From: editor@.dotmagazine.com
To: olive@.dotmagazine.com
Subject: YOUR ASSIGNMENT

All right Ol.
Re that Millennial article you're writing . . . here's something that might be interesting to investigate and add into it.

Have you heard of The Moth? It's a non-profit storytelling night based in New York. Well, there's a Moth-inspired (not actually The Moth) evening – ANYWAY it's an open-mic night happening on Tuesday night in Shoreditch for 'childless women'. I think it could be useful for your article. It's called the CFBC 'Child-Free By Choice club'. Interesting, eh???

I'm quite tempted to go myself to be honest but I'll be in Ibiza . . . shagging a hot DJ hopefully ;)

I reckon you should go along, take notes and write something juicy up. Don't let anyone know you are a journalist though obvs. Undercover style, please!

Toodles,

Gill

.dot magazine, editor-in-chief

I take a sip from my topped-up wine glass and start typing my response, fizzing with excitement. I can feel this whole topic getting deeper under my skin.

From: olive@.dotmagazine.com

To: editor@.dotmagazine.com

Subject: RE: YOUR ASSIGNMENT

Yesssss - fab idea! Enjoy your hol.

O x

Ping. Gill replies.

From: editor@.dotmagazine.com

To: olive@.dotmagazine.com

Subject: RE: RE: YOUR ASSIGNMENT

Great. Make sure you get some juicy testimonials from these childless women pls ;)

Best wishes,

Gill

.dot magazine, editor-in-chief

I feel Colin lurking behind me, waiting to interrupt. I can smell his pungent cheap aftershave. Love him, but not his choice in male grooming products.

'Yes Col?' I say, still typing.

'Do you fancy going for food in a bit, babe? You've been looking a bit stressed out lately,' Colin says, sitting on the side of my desk.

'Ah, maybe – where are you going?' My eyes are glazed over.

'A few of us are just gonna go to that Thai place on the corner. It's a bit dingy but the food is really good.'

'I might join you later. Still got a load of stuff to get through,' I say, still not really taking my eyes off my screen.

'You've literally only got Google open,' Colin laughs.

'Yeah, well,' I say defensively, turning on my chair. 'I've got to Google some stuff. For an article.'

'OK.' Colin takes my reading glasses that are on my desk and starts cleaning them with a cloth from his pocket. 'These are filthy.'

'What would I do without you, eh?' I laugh.

'I'm gonna send you an angry shouty email in ALL CAPS if you don't come join us in the next hour. OK?'

'Fine, OK.'

'You work too much,' Colin shouts as he walks off, putting his leather jacket on.

We both know that I won't go. Too much to do. Too many rabbit-holes to dive into. My mind flickers for a second: have I become slightly obsessed?

People start to trickle out of the office and, finally, I'm the only person left. I start to do some undercover Googling, ready for my night out at the CFBC night 'Moth style'. I crack my knuckles. I am excited by this.

A chance to meet new, interesting people both online and at the club.

I'm surprised the first thing that comes up when I Google 'Support for child-free women' is the CFBC – I've never come across this before. I click on the CFBC website and it's just a landing page. To see the rest of the website I have to 'request access' by signing up as a member. All I can see at this point is that the group was founded by a woman called Iris who had set up a private Facebook group called 'Child-Free Women by Choice', but again I have to request access first. On the website the only thing I can read is the 'about me' and the 'contact' section, with Iris's email address. The 'about me' section is dedicated to explaining why everyone must respect child-*free* as the correct phrasing and wording. I look around, just checking again that no one is lingering and looking over at my monitor. I'm not embarrassed to be searching for this stuff, but something's telling me to keep it close to my chest. It feels oddly private.

About The CFBC club

First things first, we are a club exclusively for women who *choose* not to have children. Please do not get this confused with women who are struggling with fertility or can't have children. Those women are of course welcome here (we welcome you!!). But the focus of this group is for women who fundamentally do not want to live a life with children, so they can share, discuss, find like-minded friends and most importantly, not be judged. When getting in touch with us, please make sure you check your terminology. Child-*less* is suggesting that something has been taken away. No. Child-*free* is who we are. We are all free to make our own choices in the world. We look forward to hearing from you.

I click open on the 'contact' section of the website and notice that Iris lives near Islington in London, not that far from me. Iris is nearly fifty and passionate about women feeling that their lives can be extremely whole, without kids, at any age. Her bio really highlights how much she absolutely loves her colourful, rich, sexy, adventurous life. Fair play, Iris.

In the contact section there are also links to helplines that could help women who are child-free *not* by choice, explaining perhaps that this might not be the group for them and suggesting other groups that might be more appropriate.

My eyes light up reading something so resonant. A group for women who simply choose not to have children, and are totally OK with it. As they should be!

I open up a new email from my personal email address.

From: only.olive@gmail.com
To: iris@CFBC.com
Subject: CFBC Query

Hello Iris,

I have been doing some late-night Googling, wondering if I am alone in my feelings of not wanting children. I can't tell you how relieved I felt stumbling across the CFBC! I was wondering if you had any space for a newbie, and how I can sign up. I'd love to come along to the next event if you'll have me!

Best wishes,
Olive

I throw back the last dregs of rosé and call it a night. I unplug my phone charger and put it into my tote bag, and swap my heeled boots for my old trainers. I go to message the girls to see what they're up to this weekend and, as I reach for my phone, I notice the ping sound of a new email:

From: Iris@CFBC.com
To: only.olive@gmail.com
Subject: RE: CFBC Query

Hi Olive,

How are you? Lovely to hear from you. You caught me just at the right time, I only check my emails once a day!

Things are very busy for me at the moment – well they always seem to be these days! I'm doing all sorts of projects, a new yoga school, an art exhibition that needs finalizing and my new boyfriend is in town ;) Life has never been better!!!! ;-)

So glad you want to come along to a gathering. The Child-Free By Choice (CFBC) open-mic night is at the Book Club in Shoreditch. Please don't share the address with anyone else – but of course feel free to bring a friend or plus-one. I know it can be quite nerve-wracking coming to these sorts of things on your own, but I promise you everyone is super-nice and I will be there to make sure you are OK! We offer a nice safe space where we can all share our stories together, judgement-free. You could even do a reading if you want?

We only ask that attendees donate a small amount to our CFBC charity fund, at your discretion! Here's the link to make your payment.

Let me know and I can confirm you, we'd love to have you there!

I x

Iris seems fun. I like that she is making it clear that she has a full-to-the-brim life that she loves. My first question when I meet her will be whether she feels any pressure to be seen to be 'having it all' in a different way: travelling, sex, friend-ships, hobbies. Having to 'make up for' not having kids, in some weird way. Ambition with a capital 'A'. I feel like this with my friends sometimes. When they give updates about their families, partners or babies, I seem to fill my silence with career news. I also wonder if she ever feels like she has to be seen as outwardly happy all the time, in case people think she's made a huge mistake. Either way, it feels so inspiring to hear from a woman like Iris, who seemingly has no regrets about her life choices. You hear these stories of women over fifty who suddenly think, 'Oh shit, I'm never going to be a grandmother, what have I done?' These are the stories I see a lot of. I'm not saying they aren't valid, but they can be scaremongering. It feeds into the whole 'it's better to regret what you've done, rather than what you haven't done!' theory. I worry then that some people might go into motherhood even if it's not right for them. I am excited by getting to know Iris. Gill will be pleased that I've already secured a place at the CFBC club – sometimes these closed groups are hard to access. Journalistic brownie points to me! What about bringing a friend or two? I have no idea who the hell would want to come with me. Maybe I'll ask Zeta. Or maybe Bea? Or, oh my god, Colin would be funny, plus he's judgement-free. Bea could pretend and come as a child-free woman in disguise. Isla's so vulnerable right now, it wouldn't feel right to subject her to this – she might see it as a sort of betrayal.

I feel tight knots of excitement form in my belly – I am going to be around a hundred women who might feel exactly the same as I do.

17

That night, I wake up in the dark, pouring with sweat. My entire back is drenched. Despite my growing excitement about the CFBC club, my troubled subconscious is rearing its head. I rub my eyes as the dream comes back to me.

I am carrying a huge heavy baby car seat with a big handle. It's important, this baby seat and its contents. I don't know what my baby looks like inside this seat, but I need to protect it, and we need to reach our destination. I am carrying this big bulky car seat down a busy street. My legs feel heavy and I can hardly lift up each leg. It's like they're not my own and they are made of something different, like metal or stone. The baby seat is perched on my arm like a handbag. But it's so heavy. Everyone is walking slowly, and my arms are aching from the weight of it. I am pushing past, battling through the crowds, stressed, needing to get somewhere quickly, weighed down. My knees are buckling. Cracks appear in the pavement. The weight is getting worse, but I have to avoid falling down the cracks. The roads are ripping apart and I am balancing on the edge. My stomach is lurching. I can hear a baby crying.

There is gunge on my feet. Green slime. It's sticky and it's making it so much harder to walk. I feel an urgency.

When I look down, the thing is empty. There is no baby in the car seat. Why was it so heavy? Anxiety overwhelms me then; something is missing.

I look around me and familiarize myself with my room before face-planting back into my pillow. That was too real. I reach for my laptop and Google 'hot yoga class'. I book a hot yoga session at a 'luxury hotel' for the next bank holiday weekend. In these anxiety-ridden witching hours I always feel a desperate need to book something to make me feel less alone and afraid. So this time: not just any old sweating – some luxury sweating.

'I have a difficult enough time getting motivated to take good care of myself. I cannot imagine having to always put a child first.'

Maria, 26

18

There's a plain-looking envelope on my doormat. I shuffle along my tiny hallway in my thick socks and grab it. I slice it open with a knife and inside I find a letter from TFL and a 'Baby on Board' badge. Huh? Oh. Crap. I suddenly have a flashback of me searching on eBay for a second-hand badge on Friday night as I drank myself into the weekend with a massive glass of wine in hand. Looks like it's arrived. Guess if you say you're pregnant, anyone would just believe you, eh?

I put the badge on, clipping it to the outside of my jacket. I look in the mirror. It looks weird on me. Probably because you're not pregnant, Olive! But I feel different. Like it's a tiny piece of armour, a temporary shield against the real horrors of the world. A shortcut to feeling like I might have my shit together.

I call Mum on the way to the bus stop. Sometimes I feel guilty about how long we can go without speaking to each other. She bought me a fridge magnet last Christmas that says, 'Call your mother' and I have to admit it's worked. Every time I look at it, I'm given a little nudge to make more of an effort with her.

'Hi Olive!' She picks up after quite a few rings.

'Hi Mum.'

'How are you doing darling? Good week?'

'OK, thanks. Just plodding along with work and seeing friends. You?'

'My friend Steph came round last night and showed me pictures of her daughter's new baby. Then we did some gardening together. Was so exciting using my new gardening gloves!'

'Oh lovely.'

'What are you up to today?'

'Oh just work, Mum, and seeing my friend Col at the pub.'

'You've been doing some printing?'

'Printing?'

'When you make the magazines.'

'Mum, I write for the magazine and the website. I don't physically print them.'

'Sorry darling, I still don't one hundred per cent understand your job.'

'It's not that hard to understand, Mum.' I sound huffy now.

'All I know is that you are doing *very* well. I'll have to show you pics of Steph's grandchild soon; she's got the smallest, cutest ears! Reminds me of when you were little, actually.'

'OK, Mum. I don't really know Steph, so I don't need to see her baby photos. Speak to you soon though.'

My heart sinks. My achievements never seem good enough.

I reach the bus stop. I always get the same one into Soho, but this time it's like I'm in an episode of *Black Mirror* – everyone is smiling at me. It's so weird. A woman with a pushchair grins at me; a young guy collecting money for charity, who normally hassles me, just nods warmly in my direction; a man waiting at the bus stop gets up quickly and offers me a seat.

'Congratulations!' a man with a toupee and briefcase whispers, looking me up and down.

Creepy.

Congratulations on what?

Then I realize. Oh shit: the badge.

I take it off before I see someone I know – that would be a very hard lie to wriggle out of – and I feel instantly invisible again.

I'm half an hour early for my drink with Col. My phone beeps; I assume it's Col running late but it's actually a new WhatsApp message from Cec. It hits me that it's been a while since I heard from her. She hasn't replied to any of my latest messages asking her how she is. I mean, I completely get it, she's busy with a new baby and all. But I realize I've totally stopped expecting any replies from her.

Cecily: Hi guys – I wondered if you were up for organizing my baby shower! Well, I'm calling it a 'baby party' because it's not really a baby shower as Oscar is already here. Wanna do it next weekend. YES I KNOW IT'S THREE MONTHS AFTER I'VE ACTUALLY GIVEN BIRTH but I'd always had it in my head to do it this way. I wanted Oscar to be there, celebrating with us!!! It can be my baby shower slash his sort-of three-month birthday? Anyway, nothing major, just bringing people together (I'll send you a list) and help with some of the decorations.

Bea: That sounds like a lovely idea, Cecy. I'll make a cake!

Isla: Sure x

Cec: Ah fantastic, thanks guys! I thought we could plan it together tomorrow when you all come over! Are we still on for the little rendezvous at mine? Oscar is excited to see you all!

Me: Cool – looking forward to seeing old OAP.

Cec: *eye-roll emoji*

Bea: Wouldn't miss it for the world. Can't wait.

Isla: I'll be there x

I don't mind helping, neither does Bea, but to ask Isla, while she is struggling with IVF appointments and other stuff? Not cool, Cec. Not cool at all. I understand that Cec might be in an awkward position, not wanting to leave Isla out and all. But it feels like a bit of salt in the wound.

I give Isla a call to check how she is. It rings and rings, but no answer.

When I arrive at Cecily's house the next evening, Bea and Isla are already there. Bea is busying herself in the kitchen, opening cardboard boxes and unwrapping wine glasses from bubble wrap. I walk into Cec's giant living room and she's put the fire on, which is making crackling noises. I can immediately feel the warmth on my face. Cec is kneeling in the middle of the room on a grey fluffy rug, gesturing and muttering something about 'the plan of attack'. She has lots of folders spread out, highlighters and stickers and Post-it notes.

'Hello love!' she says, acknowledging my arrival and then continuing to hastily cross things off her to-do list. 'Right. Decorations, tick. Colour scheme is nailed. Just need to follow up with the caterers – the woman there is being very vague about the canapé sizes – and then I need the addresses written out in my special gold pen and then stuck onto these envelopes.'

I am genuinely taken aback by the scene in front of me. Cec was never this manic an organizer before – we used to laugh together about how seriously people take these sorts of things. She was my laid-back friend who rolled her eyes with me at the endless Instagram posts of cheesy engagement shots and baby reveal parties. Where has her cynicism gone?

'OK, Amelia and I can help with that bit, can't we?' Bea says, as Amelia licks a sugar-free Chupa Chups and nods along.

'Great, thank you – here are the envelopes.' She hands a stack of paper to Bea. 'The list of names is on my laptop, over there,' she says, pointing to a shelf next to the TV.

'Cec, give Olive something to do,' Bea says, gesturing at me while I stand there aghast at Cec, who has turned into a micro-manager overnight.

While Bea and her kids are writing out invitations, I start ringing up a catering company about a vegan option for the charcuterie boards. I suddenly notice that Isla is nowhere to be seen.

'Where's Isla?'

'She's in the kitchen making decorations,' Cec says, frowning at her clipboard.

I find Isla sitting at the large kitchen island, crying quietly, with a Pritt stick in hand. She sobs gently as she pulls the glue stick across the paper decorations.

'Isla! What's wrong?'

'Nothing. Cec just asked me to glue these decorations together,' she continues, pulling the stubborn stick against the grain of the paper, sniffing. I yank it from her.

'It's fine,' she says, picking up another baby-shaped blue paper cutting and gluing its bottom, wiping her snot with her sleeve.

'It's clearly not – look at you, you're crying.'

'Ugh, I am surrounded by all this baby stuff and it's so bloody hard.'

'Oh babe. It's not fair for you to be doing this. I'm booking you an Uber home right now. Stay in here. I'll deal with Cecily.'

'Please don't make a fuss, Ol,' Isla calls after me.

I march back into the living room. My cheeks feel hot and red.

'Cec. I'm booking Isla a car home. It's really not OK to ask her to do all this baby-shower stuff with what she's going through. It was a bad idea.'

Cec looks up from her baby-shower folder and stands up. 'Well, that's fine, obviously. Why didn't you say anything before? I don't want to upset anyone,' Cec says, tucking her bob behind her ears awkwardly, and then putting her hands in her back pockets.

'Yeah, well. I'll get Isla home, and you can give me another task to do.'

'I'm sorry guys. I just want everything to be perfect,' Cec says innocently.

'Just a bit of sensitivity, maybe Cec.'

Isla mopes into the room.

'Is that true, Isla?'

'Cec just leave it,' I say.

'I don't know. I'm just finding this baby overload a bit much right now.' Isla looks down at the floor.

'I understand. Sorry . . .' Cec pauses and looks down. 'Oh god, I've been really self-obsessed.'

'No you haven't, Cec,' Bea pipes up. 'You've just had a baby. You're allowed to be centring everything around that right now. Isla, I'm very sorry you're finding things so hard right now, but this day is also really important to Cec.'

'Of course you would side with Cecily, Bea,' I say irritably.

'I'm not siding with anyone, Olive.'

'I'm just saying: there are more important things than this baby shower,' I say.

Cec's mouth drops to the floor. 'You can go home now Olive,' she says, in a monotone, not looking at me.

'Oh Cec, don't be like that darling,' says Bea.

Then the baby monitor goes off, and Oscar starts screeching.

I feel as though some sort of invisible battle line has been drawn.

19

I'm in the bath with avocado-flavoured shampoo in my hair.
My laptop is balancing on a towel on top of the toilet and
the soothing voice of a mental health themed podcast where
famous authors discuss their lowest moments is playing in
the background. My phone pings. It's our WhatsApp group
again. What now? Usually I crave hearing from them, but
I've been stewing on the fallout at Cecily's all week, getting
the fear about whether or not I was too outspoken, and
now I'm terrified of the situation getting worse.

Cec: Hi guys

Cec: So I'm going to be organizing the baby shower myself
now.

(10 minutes pass)

Cec: Guys? That OK??

Me: Fine by me

Isla: me too

Bea: OK, love! xx

I sink further into the water. Really, she should have just done it all herself from the start. She was micromanaging us anyway. It looks like she's been curating a Pinterest board of pastel-coloured inspiration for this party (room dressings, food, decor and invitations) for months. Her hen do was a slap-up meal for ten people in a sticky pub, for God's sake. Where has my friend gone?

By the time the big baby shower day arrives I can feel my nerves jangling in my belly, a sense of impending doom. I'm wrapping some presents in my kitchen, and Zeta is sitting at my kitchen counter, drying some plates. I accidentally get some very sticky Sellotape stuck to a small blister on my hand and shout expletives.

'Big day today then,' Zeta says.

'Yep, I'm still a bit annoyed with Cecily, to be honest.'

'Has she been bossing you all about?'

'Yeah – well, it's her bossing Isla about that bothered me. Imagine getting your mate who's struggling with IVF to spend *all* day Pritt-sticking your "It's A Boy" bunting for you. I don't know, I just thought it was quite cruel, and so not like Cec.'

'Are you taking a present?' Zeta asks.

'Yeh, I've made some cupcakes. Not just any old cupcakes: they are vulva-themed and nappy-themed.'

I show Zeta the cupcakes, loaded with pink icing on the

top with a slit down the middle with lips and a clitoris. I have also made a few that have icing on top resembling a soiled nappy, with realistic-looking chocolate for the poo coming out of a white iced nappy.

'They are *disgusting*,' Zeta screams, laughing.

I can't wait to take them to the party.

I struggle to carry multiple bags onto the Tube because of all the cake tins, so – with a pang of guilt – I get the 'Baby on Board' badge out of my bag again, to ensure that I definitely get a seat. It's only fair to sample the travel benefits of pregnancy every now and again. Maybe. I spot a few people walking ahead of me as I get out at Barons Court Tube station. I know they're on their way to Cec's party because they look a bit posh. A man in chinos and loafers is carrying a huge card that reads: 'Congrats on your new baby, don't drop it!!!' There's also a woman wearing a fascinator (what?), and a yummy mummy (said with an ironic tone) with a big yoga bag and a bunch of flowers who's shouting at her son 'Horace', calling him to hurry up. Oh god, this whole thing is going to be hell.

At Cec's, I hang up my coat, shaking out the rain. I slide into the kitchen wearing a red satin jumpsuit and slippery socks. The kitchen has been taken over by gold balloons that spell out 'OSCAR'. Cecily's dad, Todd, makes a comment as I enter the kitchen that I 'look like Father Christmas!', which I try my hardest to take as a compliment.

'What have you brought in those huge bags?' Todd asks me, peering over his glasses.

'Oh! Some cakes!'

'Let's have a look.'

'I can't really open the lid right now, Todd, they might topple over.'

'Come on, let's see! I do love to see what you girls get up to in the kitchen.' I subtly shudder and try to ignore the casual sexism.

'Here.' I get out one of the plastic tubs.

'Are they . . . ?'

'Yes! They are, Todd.'

Todd nearly falls over backwards.

'Vaginas!'

He splutters at me before excusing himself to go and find his wife.

I am suddenly quite hot from the awkwardness. I place them down in the centre of the kitchen island. I look around at a sea of bald men in blazers and middle-aged women in kitten heels. I know no one. Where are Bea and Isla? I can see Cecily through the kitchen crowd, laughing and mingling with family friends of all ages. She's wearing a long black sequined dress with a small slit up the side. And there is a chorus of 'Don't you look good?'/'Wow, you've lost so much weight already'/'Where is your dress from?'/'You've snapped back' echoing around her. It's true, she looks great. Cec's husband, Chris, is holding Oscar against his chest with a muslin cloth over his shoulder.

'Hey Chris.' I touch OAP's wet, dribbling chin. He does look really cute in his dinosaur patterned onesie and it melts my heart a little.

'All right, Olive?' Chris says in his usual deadpan tone.

'How are you? Feel like I've been asking Cec how she is but I haven't had a chance to ask you yet!'

'Yeah, all good thanks. Cec's doing most of the work, to be honest, like she should be.' He does a wink.

'I'm sure you've been helping a lot.'

'Not really. Busy time at work, can't leave the lads, I mean the team, dangling.'

'I see.'

'Cec's been amazing, running around like a headless chicken. The silver lining is that she's losing her baby-weight quickly at least.' He laughs, heartily. God, he is such a dick. 'I'll be getting her back in the gym soon. She'll have to keep up with my six-pack,' he says, slapping his stomach.

Chris is the worst, but somehow we always find a way to forgive him, because he's clearly not going anywhere and Cecily does really love him. Unfortunately.

Phew, I spot Bea. She has just walked in with her army of kids behind her. Arnold is wearing a VR headset as a hat, Amelia has wild hair and a giant bow headband on, and Andrew is hitting people with a plastic light sabre. I've never been happier to see them all.

'How lovely is this?' Bea says, making her way over to me. 'It all came together in the end! How are you, sweetheart?' She leans over to kiss me on the cheek.

She is wearing a large hat – big, white and ruffly. It kinda looks like that Ikea lampshade, the one that everyone in the world has. It keeps poking me in the side of the head when she leans in to speak to me.

We take a glass of champagne from a silver tray and thank the waiter. This party is ridiculously fancy. It doesn't feel like Cec's kind of thing.

'Where's Jez?'

'Working, of course. He is really sad to miss this, though. He sends his love,' Bea says. 'Amelia, come here, let me wipe your nose with this tissue, darling!'

'Is it hard with him being away so much?'

'Yeah. It's basically just me dealing with these three on my own but, you know, I just get on with it.' Bea pinches Amelia's nose with the tissue while she wriggles away. 'It would be nice if he called or texted occasionally, though; it's difficult to keep telling the kids that Daddy's too busy to talk,' she says, stiffly.

Bea is usually unflappable, but she seems a bit stressed out, and hasn't made eye contact with me. It feels like she's not telling me something.

'Amelia love, will you go and put this tissue in the bin over there?' Bea says, pointing to a very expensive tall bin in Cec's kitchen. A bin that might also be a robot that cleans the house. One of those bins.

'When's he next back? Would be nice to get together.'

'I don't know, Ol.' She sighs, acting all defensive. 'And how's Jacob doing?' she asks, turning it back on me, desperately wanting to change the subject.

'Oh . . . um . . . well actually—'

Isla suddenly pops out from behind the kitchen counter, interrupting us.

'Hi gang!'

She's holding a bottle of Veuve Clicquot and looking slightly manic.

'I probably shouldn't be drinking, but I'm in between IVF cycles and one or two can't hurt – just don't tell my doctor OK?'

She seems to be holding it together, but I'm worried she's going to find today hard with all this baby paraphernalia around her. Mike is working late, apparently, so I make a mental note to keep an eye out for her. In case she gets too drunk.

Cecily comes tottering over, trying to remain balanced on some very high-heeled, gold strappy sandals with zero support.

'Those shoes look very uncomfortable.' The words have left my mouth before I have a chance to stuff them back in.

'They're fine, Olive,' she says abruptly. 'Thanks for coming guys.'

'What normally happens at a baby shower then?' I whisper to Bea. I almost feel like I've paid money to be here, and I want a performance.

'Olive, stop overthinking everything. Just muck in,' Bea says.

'Yeah, just mingling really,' Cecily says, having clearly overheard. 'Try and have fun Olive,' she adds snippily.

'I'll try,' I reply, gritting my teeth.

The tension feels as if it's growing – not lessening – between us. I suddenly need the loo or, at least, a little breather. All the guests are piling in now and a lot of women are screaming and hugging and squealing in Cecily's face. Eurgh.

On the way to the bathroom, I bump into Cecily's mother, Tiff. Tiff is really quite something. Everyone knows Tiff. Or, should I say, everyone avoids Tiff. She's loud, smells of Elnett hairspray, wears pearls, and has long red nails. She's judgemental, rude, opinionated, political, un-PC and extremely overbearing. Over the years, I've learned to humour her and take what she says with a pinch of salt. She's always been slightly passive aggressive and ghastly with her comments. Every time she came round to our student house she would Febreze everything and bring her own blanket to sit on in the living room. Cecily's family appear nice enough on the outside, but they are very controlling and it has been difficult sometimes, watching Cecily being cornered into making decisions that just suit her parents. Like the time they hijacked Cecily's wedding and made her rearrange it and change the location to suit them. We all looked after Cecily when she was crying in our beds so many times during that stressful time. We knew deep down that she didn't want to be a top-dog lawyer; she had been forced into that too. What she really wanted was to be an interior designer, and she would make such a great one. I hate it when people get stuck in career paths they don't love because they want to impress their parents. I guess this is the only upside of having an emotionally distant mother – she never gets involved with my life choices.

'Hello darling!' Tiff air-kisses me and nearly suffocates me with her intense levels of hairspray. She has quite a lot of red lipstick on her two front teeth.

'Tiff! Lovely to see you,' I say, my faux smile appearing again.

'How glorious does our Cecily look?' Tiff remarks, looking over at Cecily in a self-satisfied way.

'So gorgeous. Just like her mother,' I smile, and then realize I'm clenching my teeth again. My level of sarcasm has suddenly become risky.

'So, do you think you'll be next?' Tiff says, sipping her champagne, hand on hip.

'Sorry?' I decide to play dumb.

'You know, next to have a baby!' exclaims Tiff, flapping the hand that wasn't wrapped around a champagne glass.

'Oh . . . Ha! Who knows!' I reply.

'Go on . . . have a baby,' Tiff whispers smugly, leaning in to touch my arm, and fluttering her eyelashes with delight.

'Maybe one day,' I squirm.

'Oh go on!' she replies.

Oh yes, Tiff, of course, because *you* have told me to, I will get on it, tomorrow!

'Oh, you'd look *just divine* with a bump, darling. Having babies is just glorious, I loved being pregnant.'

'That's nice to know.'

'It sounds silly but I really recommend it, darling. Also, you know, I don't want to sound like a nag, but the clock is ticking for you girls. I was thirty when I had Cec, and honestly? It was way too old, really.'

'Well I—'

'You don't want to be a geriatric mum,' Tiff interrupts, loudly. 'Well, actually, you probably already are, I suppose!'

Isla appears behind me and hands me a glass of champagne. 'You look like you need this!' Isla says, smiling at me.

'Thank you,' I say, relieved to see her, saving me from this conversation.

Tiff fake-laughs and enters the conversation again with gusto. 'Isla, hello darling!' Tiff air-kisses Isla. 'We were just talking about babies! What are your thoughts, hmm?' Tiff says, taking another sip from her wine glass.

'Babies are cute, sure!' Isla replies, looking at me for support.

'Do you think you'll have one?' Tiff asks, leaning in to Isla.

'Um . . .' Isla looks awkward.

'Er, it's not really an appropriate question Tiff,' I say.

'No, it's fine . . .' Isla says.

'No it's not, Isla,' I say firmly. 'It's not something she wants to discuss, Tiff. In fact, it's not really something I want to discuss with you either.'

'Oh goodness. I see!' Tiff squawks, awkwardly.

Cecily notices us with Tiff and knows to come over and try and save us. 'Mum, what are you saying to the girls?'

'Oh, nothing much, darling. We're having a lovely time. Lovely champagne, this is.' Tiff turns to Cec to change the subject: 'I do worry about how you're going to raise your little one in London, Cecily. London is so . . . polluted, and grubby, and Oscar will need some proper fresh air to run around in. I don't want my grandchild being raised in such a polluted city. Hardly any green spaces!'

'Oh Mother! I've told you. Loads of people have kids in

London. London is fine. More than fine. Lots of parks. Keep your voice down too, please.'

'I have plenty of friends brought up in London,' I say. 'They turned out all right.'

Tiff nervously laughs. 'Let's hope Oscar becomes very streetwise then. Lots of crime here. Druggies,' she lowers her voice, 'lots of stabbings.'

'Mum . . .' Cecily rubs Tiff's arm gently. 'Please. Life is great here.'

Tiff gets distracted by her husband Todd, who has just accidentally dropped a glass and is shouting Tiff's name loudly, an angry vein popping out of his head.

We sip our drinks and I am about to open my mouth to ask Isla if she wants to sneak off for a cheeky cigarette, when a woman appears out of nowhere and introduces herself to us all.

'Hi girls, I couldn't help but overhear your conversation with Tiff. I work with Cecily. I'm Jool.' She puts a hand out for us to shake. We do so, limply. 'Apologies for butting in, but I couldn't help but overhear your conversation and, you know, woman to woman and all that, Isla, I want to say it also annoys me when people ask presumptuous questions about my situation. Gosh, it makes me angry that people are so insensitive.'

'Thank you,' Isla looks at me in a panic. Her face saying it all: Who is this woman? Why is she talking to us?

'You know, it took me ages to get pregnant, just in case you wanted any consolation or to hear any stories that ended well. *Years!* I was getting grey hairs, wondering if my baby would ever arrive.'

'Thanks, but it's a long story,' Isla replies politely, her cheeks turning pink.

'Thing is, you just need to think positively.'

'Jools—'

'It's actually just Jool.'

'Whatever. Thanks for your help, but that's quite enough,' I say. 'It's not always helpful to share advice, that's all.'

'Wow, tough crowd. I was just trying to help,' Jool says. 'I had problems too. But everything changed when I changed my attitude. You should start manifesting. Start a mood board. It starts with you.'

Isla and I roll our eyes. Jool sighs at us in a patronizing way and then wanders off in search of a canapé. We go to the loo so we can reapply our lipstick and then wander back to find Bea and Cecily.

As I walk through the kitchen, I overhear Jool say to someone that 'time away from her kid for a poo and scroll on Instagram Stories feels like a holiday in the Maldives', and that's the icing on the clitoris cake. We need to get out.

'Can we go outside for a sec?' I ask Isla.

'Happily,' she says, grabbing her scarf from one of the kitchen stools.

We go out into the front garden, streetlights twinkling; she declines a drag on my vape. She wraps her scarf round her shoulders to stay warm.

'Where's Jacob by the way?' Isla asks innocently.

I suddenly feel really hot. I have got used to ignoring it, bottling it up. I've now started to dread one of the girls actually asking me any real questions about what happened. Because I know I'll be forced to look in the mirror.

'That's kinda what I've been wanting to tell you about.'

'Oh?'

'We actually broke up a while ago.'

'Fuck . . .' Her eyes dart around, not knowing what to say. 'Sorry.'

'It's OK. Well, it's not. But everyone has so much else going on . . .'

'I'm so sorry. Is there anything I can do, Ol?'

'Not really. Just the occasional chat and hug is good,' I say, sucking on my vape.

'Ugh, Olive, I've been so distant lately.'

'I understand,' I say, exhaling my flavoured vapour.

'I've been so focused on one thing. You know, I've just had the worst cramps all night and haven't really told anyone. I just feel awful.'

'You should go home if you don't feel well. I can break it gently to Cec.'

'Do you mind? Sorry, I just suddenly don't feel good at all.'

'It's totally fine,' I say.

'Can we carry on this conversation asap? I hope you're OK, Ol.'

We hug and kiss each other on the cheek. And, just like that, she leaves. I'm left standing alone. A million things unsaid stretching between us. Once, Isla wouldn't have just left – she'd have tried harder. She would have sat on my bed and chatted it through with me. But we have different things going on now.

I go back inside and tune in momentarily to the background noise of everyone milling around. When did Cec become friends with these awful people? There is a man with a giant moustache who is bragging about how his darling son just got into their private school of choice.

'It is £30,000 a year, so of course they made room for him! Ha ha ha! You can get whatever you want with the right amount of cash, am I right?' He cackles smugly. I notice his logo'd T-shirt reads: 'I LIKE TO PARTY. EVERYBODY DOES'. Then he starts slagging off state schools. I shudder at the thought of ever having to dig around for 'The Perfect School' for 'The Perfect Child'. The competing. The pompous rich people. The catchment areas. The pettiness. The potential for crippling disappointment. The constant Keeping Up With The Joneses. The Insta-Mums with their perfect marriages and perfect houses and perfect post-baby bodies. *Yuck*.

I really want to get out, or maybe even do an Irish goodbye, but an old school friend, Rose, has spotted me through the milling crowd and is making a beeline for me. Oh god, I really need to devise an exit strategy, quick. I should have just left with Isla.

'Olive!' She reaches out to hug me. 'It's been years, how are you! I thought you'd be here.' She sort of falls into me, instead of a hug – Rose has clearly had a few rosés.

'Rose, hi! I'm great, thank you – you look well!' I say, remembering to smile without gritting my teeth this time.

'So do you. I haven't seen you since we left school! I kept

asking Cec to arrange a reunion, but we never got around to it. Our parents are friends, so we've stayed in touch.'

'Gosh, school was so long ago now. You're making me feel old now,' I say, pointing at my face.

'We both need a top-up!' Rose reaches for a fresh bottle of champagne on one of the side tables and pops it open, filling us up. Both glasses overflow and spill onto the floor. 'Woops!'

'So what's new with you?' I ask, swallowing a big mouthful of bubbles.

'Oh, you know. *Life*. I'm feeling pretty shattered, to be honest. I just had a baby.'

Just like everyone else, I think.

'Well, six months ago now,' she continues. 'A little boy. He's over there with my husband.'

I look over reluctantly. I see about five men with babies in papooses.

'Oh, congrats! He looks lovely,' I say.

'Can I tell you something?' She lowers her voice. 'I hate it.'

I laugh, nervously.

She continues: 'Seriously, Olive: don't do it.'

'I'm sure it's not so bad!' I say awkwardly.

'It's bad. It's fucking bad.' Her lip wobbles a bit.

'Oh, Rose . . .'

'It's OK. My husband, he loves it. He's a total natural. I suppose that makes me lucky, it's not like I have to do everything on my own but . . . I . . . I just feel weirdly flat about it all really.'

She's glugging down the champagne pretty fast and pours

more from the bottle, almost missing her glass. She pours me another overflowing flute.

'Shall we go and sit down over there?' I point towards the corner of the kitchen where there are two comfy velvet chairs in a bay window. We squeeze past some people who are lingering and drinking around the kitchen island, nodding and smiling blankly to strangers until we get to the seats.

'So, what is so bad exactly?' I ask, drinking more and more with every question. I realize I've picked up the wrong glass – it's not mine, it has a different-coloured lipstick mark on, but who cares at this point?

'Oh lord, where do I start?' She is speaking in a hushed tone. 'We didn't bond at the beginning, me and the baby. I suppose that's normal though, is it? But I just miss my old life. God, I miss it so much. I miss having five minutes to myself, to gather my thoughts, to send an email, to just think for a second. I am so sleep-deprived. I feel like I am going totally insane . . .' She gulps.

'It sounds hard,' I say, feeling genuinely intrigued.

'Mmm-hmm. The other day – don't tell anyone – my husband was out and I just turned the baby monitor off. I just left the baby to cry in the other room. I ignored my own baby. For ages. I just couldn't face it.'

'I mean, I'd probably do the same.'

'I just can't help thinking that I've made a huge mistake. How terrible is that? My husband barely looks at me now that the baby is here. I don't even get a cuddle or a kiss. It's all about the baby. Which is fine, but – like – I exist too!'

'That must be weird.'

'I recommend not having one, or at least waiting for another ten years.' Rose knocks back another huge mouthful of her drink and I follow suit, getting more and more tipsy.

'You know, you should speak to Cec. She hasn't said too much, but I'm noticing that she seems to be finding it hard too. I think that is totally normal. I know she looks like a swan swimming around on the surface, but her legs are really splashing around underneath.'

'Oh, maybe I will. Sounds like me. We mums have to stick together.'

'Indeed,' I say.

'I'm guessing you are a godmother then, Ol? Cec is lucky to have you girls around to help.'

I feel slightly wounded, a pang in my chest. 'Oh, we're not actually . . . I don't think she decided to do the whole godparent thing.'

'Ah, fair enough. Just assumed you girls, as you're so close, would have been given that sort of role. Well, thanks Olive. You've actually made me feel so much better. Just being able to talk to someone who won't judge me makes a change.'

'You're welcome. You've given me a lot to think about too.'

She air-kisses me, and excuses herself, making her way over, reluctantly, to one of the many men bobbing babies up and down on their chests.

I neck half of my drink and look again at this odd

assortment of people I don't recognize. I then spot Cec standing with Bea and go bounding over, knocking a wine glass off a table and onto a man in a papoose.

'Hey Cec, I have a question for you!' I say, tugging on Cec's arm. I realize my breath smells of champagne.

'OK, Ol,' Cecily says, eyeing me suspiciously.

I am swaying a bit, now.

'Why are we not godparents? Are we not good enough for you any more? Is that why I feel like I barely see you?' I'm right up close to Cecily's face. Bea's mouth is hanging open.

'Sorry, what, Olive?' Cecily hands Oscar to Tiff and shoos away all the nosy people standing around, including Tiff.

'I just think . . . Isn't a baby shower about godmothers and stuff?' I am slurring now.

'We've decided not to do it, actually.' Cec watches as I step backwards. I realize one of my bra straps is showing because my jumpsuit has come off my shoulders.

'OK. Fine. I'm heading off now, then. I just . . . I thought I'd be godmother material, to be honest, considering all the history we have.' I pick up my bag and stagger – with as much dignity as I can muster – out of her £1 million home, scuffing my shoes as I walk.

'*Who needs a velvet couch anyway?* And I hate that duck-egg colour you're clearly obsessssed with,' I shout behind me.

I make my way outside. My phone is blurry. I press Uber. I sit down in a small patch of grass outside Cec's house and suck on my vape.

'No vaping on the property,' a voice comes out of nowhere.

'Eh?' I look up and see a very hot man with a beard and a checked shirt.

'Only joking.' He waves his vape at me.

'Right,' I say, rolling my eyes.

'Are you OK? Can I help with getting you a ride home?' says Checked-Shirt Guy.

'Why would you do that?'

'Just wanting to check you get home safely. It's pretty late, and you seem a little—'

'I've got an Uber coming, thanks.' I gesture out towards the road. 'Wait, I seem a little what?' I slur.

'Nothing. Cool.' He takes a puff of his vape.

The Uber rocks up and a woman in a baseball cap puts her lights on and hollers '*Olive?*' out of the window.

'*That's me!*' I shout back at the car. I turn around to this random guy. 'I don't need a man, *or* a baby!' I tell him as I trail awkwardly across Cecily's front lawn, trying to reach the Uber.

'Sorry?' the man shouts, not hearing me.

'Nothing!' I giggle, and burp, finding myself hilarious.

Hot Checked-Shirt-Beard Guy does a little salute, I get in the cab and frown through the window at him before he gets smaller and smaller and is eventually out of sight. Bit disconcerting when people are randomly really nice like that.

I pull out my iPhone and open my 'notes'. I write: 'I'd rather freeze time than my eggs.' Sounds poetic. But then again, I am very drunk.

20

The next day, I wake up with an excruciating headache. When was the last time any water touched my lips? My tongue is furry, my throat is sore, and my stomach is rumbling, even though the thought of food is making me want to vom. I am only able to open one eye as the light seeping from the blinds in my bedroom is so bright, adding to the throbbing pain in my temples. I pick up my phone from the floor: 10.03 a.m. There is a wine glass next to my bed; I faintly remember getting a bottle of wine from the fridge and finishing that in bed. Oh dear, oh dear. I see there's a notification in the group WhatsApp chat, making my stomach lurch. I go and make myself a cup of tea before crawling back into bed to face up to the damage I did last night.

00.30 a.m.
Bea: Oi, did you get home OK? Pls let us know.

00.34 a.m.
Bea: Hello? text us when you're home.

08:02 a.m.
Bea: OL?

10.30 a.m.
Me: Sorrrrrry just seen this. I'm alive. Just woke up. Feels like a diseased pigeon has died in my mouth

Isla: What happened last night after I left? You OK?

Me: Sorry to anyone I offended. I don't remember the last hour or so of the night

Isla: I missed the ending. Sorry again for leaving early Cec. Such a great night :)

Me: What did I do?

Bea: We were just worried about you

Me: That's a first

Bea: Huh??

Cecily is typing

Cecily is typing

Isla: It's OK, Olive

Bea: Ol. Please don't alienate yourself from us

Cecily is typing

Cecily is typing

Cecily is typing

There is a long pause.

Cecily is typing

Cecily: I'm so disappointed in the way you were yesterday, Olive. I'm already feeling vulnerable, at home all day, missing my career and old life and I just wanted a day to celebrate my new baby, as it's not been easy. At all. And somehow, somehow you managed to make it about YOU. As usual. WHEN WILL YOU REALIZE THAT NOT EVERYTHING IS ABOUT YOU!!!

Monday. And I'm feeling the full effects of a two-day hangover; I'm exposed and vulnerable. I look in the mirror in the .dot toilets and can't see the strong Olive I thought I'd built up. I don't think Cec has ever been this angry at me. Not even that time when I accidentally lost her entire handbag on a night out. I feel terrible. I am a shell, and I know exactly what I am about to do.

I look under the toilet stalls to check for earwigging

employees and press my phone to my ear. It starts to ring. The knots in my stomach feel tighter and tighter, and I feel as if I might be sick. He picks up straight away.

'Hello?'

'Hi,' I croak, and then cough. 'Jacob, it's Olive.'

'Oh . . . hi!' he says, a mixture of surprise and confusion. 'Everything . . . um . . . OK?'

'I know we haven't spoken in ages. I wanted to pick up on our last conversation.'

'OK . . . what exactly?' he asks. I can hear him fidgeting around, trying to find somewhere for a private conversation, probably.

'I don't know. Just the idea, that, we could . . . one day . . . patch this up or find a way around it.'

'Oh, Olive . . . I . . .'

'You said you wanted to make it work, and I just wanted to call you to say I'm willing to have a more open mind. About us. All relationships are different.'

'Olive.' He sounds serious suddenly. He coughs. 'Olive, I've actually met somebody.'

I am now sitting on the sofa watching *Sister Act* for the 172,282nd time. I don't know what to do with myself. I contemplate calling Zeta but I can't muster the energy. I wrap a fleecy blanket around me and wish it would swallow me whole. I put my WhatsApp groups on mute to try and forget they exist and scroll mindlessly through Instagram:

@Jamie Langdon

I have asked this amazing woman to #BeMyWife. She is #MyRock, my #OtherHalf, my #DreamWoman. I will treat you right forever soon-to-be Mrs Langdon!

@Katie Michaels

Welcome to the world little guy! You have changed our lives forever and forever! Our life before will never compare to this amazing moment! WE LOVE YOU!

@Lucy Lominer

I have started a crowdfund for donations for mine and Michael's honeymoon. Even if I haven't spoken to you in a while, I would really appreciate anything you can spare for our dream holiday :-)

I need a break from the dreaded scroll and other people's stupid lives. I decide it's time to have a social media detox because it is driving me up the wall. The pregnancy ads. The announcements. The bumps. The engagements. The constant couple selfies. The 'I said yesssss!' staged pics. I put on my big camel coat over my unwashed pyjamas and walk to the local corner shop. I pick up some milk, crisps, measly bits for dinner and a random glossy magazine, and tuck it under my arm. When I get back upstairs, I flick through the magazine and begin eating crisps out of the big bag, getting crumbs everywhere. As I turn the pages, it's mostly inane celebrity gossip and questionable agony aunts giving young people questionable life advice ('Just stop buying avocados and then you might be able to get on the housing ladder!'). And, then, in the back pages, I see her. Like a magic poof of smoke, she appears. A photo of Cyril Snow. A smiling woman with wonky, glistening teeth, long thick grey hair, sitting on a clean white sofa, next to a huge plant, wearing bright red trainers. My eyes widen with intrigue as I read the advertisement.

ARE *YOU* LOOKING FOR FERTILITY ADVICE?

For the first time in YEARS, renowned homeopathic fertility expert Cyril Snow is opening her doors to new clients. Having only taken on a small number of repeat VIP clients for the past few years, Cyril is looking for a handful of new private clients, on a first-come, first-served basis. Cyril Snow is an award-winning female health expert with over thirty years of experience within the wellbeing and fertility sector. Are you struggling with your fertility or personal wellbeing? Cyril wants to see you. Go to CyrilSnow.co.uk for more information. First appointment is a one-off 'chemistry session' to test the waters. Get in touch asap to avoid disappointment.

I look down at my 'I Woke Up Like This' stained T-shirt and smell the stench of cigarettes in my hair. You know it's bad when you're ditching your vape and drunkenly buying a pack of twenty Malboro Reds. Since I split with Jacob I haven't been looking after myself – not beyond token yoga classes and shellac manicures – and I know something needs to change. Something deeper. Seeing Cyril's friendly looking face in the magazine ad feels like a sign. Her eyes look welcoming and kind and empathetic. I think of my article on Millennials and motherhood, and the angle that meeting Cyril could add to my work. But, deep down, I know this is more personal. Closer to the bone. I'd love to know if she has clients who feel similar to me, women who are apathetic towards motherhood, or struggling to navigate their future life choices. If I got back with Jacob, I could have my old life back. I wouldn't be stinking of stale smoke, I wouldn't be sitting here alone feeling helpless and desperate, and I want someone to just take over the reins of my life – Cyril feels like as good a bet as any. I open my laptop and place it on my stomach as I lie down on the sofa. Biscuit crumbs fall out of the keyboard.

To: CyrilsPlace@CyrilSnow.com
From: only.olive@gmail.com

Dear Cyril,

Noticed your ad in a magazine and would love to book a chemistry session. What is your next availability? I am struggling with some negative thoughts to do with my future and would love to get your opinion.

Best,

Olive x

To: only.olive@gmail.com
From: assistant@CyrilSnow.com

Hi Olive. You've come to the right place. Can you do next Wednesday at 8.00 a.m?

Please note there is a no cancellation or refund policy and you will need to pay for the consultation up front, as soon as possible. Thanks.

Money money money. I suppose women's fertility (like everything in life) is still a business, isn't it?

I pick up my phone to WhatsApp the group but put my phone back down again. I stare at its screen, hoping to see a notification. I want someone to offer an olive branch. Someone to check in. I know I'm being stubborn but I can't help it. As much as I try and ignore it, I feel so bad about how I've treated Cec, especially in her vulnerable just-had-a-baby state. We've had fights before. We've not spoken and then made up before. But for some reason, this feels different. A bigger fish. It's rattling me.

'People my age be on baby no. 3,
and I'm still on "Mambo no. 5".'

Instagram meme

21

2010

Jacob and I first met when we were working in a bookshop on Broadway Market. Funnily enough called Broadway Bookshop. We both had low-paid junior roles at big companies during the week (him at a film editing agency, me as an intern at an online magazine), so we both needed the extra cash from the weekend job too. I guess that's how we first bonded. Both knackered, young and broke. You get to know someone very quickly when you work with them in a tiny bookshop (or: you end up wanting to murder each other). And soon, with us, I began to question whether I just saw him as a friend, my bookshop pal – or something more.

The bookshop had a small coffee shop attached to the back, which I loved. I would have about four coffees a day and, although it was probably bad for my health, it made me very productive. During the summer, Jacob and I would put some of the sale-items or second-hand books on display on the shelves outside on the street and sit on little chairs drinking our iced lattes in the sunshine. It was a really great place to work, plus being around books all day seemed to have a good effect on my soul.

'Did you know six minutes of reading can help reduce stress levels by up to sixty per cent?' Jacob said, reading this information from a small book propped up on the till. 'That's sixty-eight per cent better than listening to music, one hundred per cent better than drinking tea, and three hundred per cent better than going for a walk.'

'Did not know that,' I said.

'No wonder we're quite happy here,' he mused, tapping his fingers on the counter.

Jacob and I had been working together for a few weeks and it all felt very easy. We just got on, we loved discussing the books we were reading. And then little things started to happen: the odd touch of the hand, brushing past each other between the bookshelves. And then more personal – we began to leave notes for each other behind the till on books we thought each other would like. This went on for weeks, with the notes getting more and more intimate. Then one morning, Jacob came in, dumped his bag behind the till and looked at me suspiciously.

'Olive – really random question. There's this Facebook page called "Hot Dudes Reading", where people submit pictures, I'm guessing, of err . . . men reading . . .' he said.

'Oh, right?' I replied, innocently.

'And my mate Steve has just texted me to say that I'm on there.'

Oh God. I went all hot. Full-on sweaty back. Bea had

recently pointed out that I spoke about Jacob non-stop and that I must fancy him. We'd got really drunk and posted a pic of Jacob on 'Hot Dudes Reading' as a joke. I'd forgotten all about it, until now.

It was technically Bea's idea. She'd posted it. But how did I explain that?

'Really!' I laughed, while rearranging a table display.

'Yeah . . . weirdly it's a photo from the other night when we were packing away some stock and I was reading something quickly behind the till . . . Did you take this photo?'

'Erm, let's see.' I grabbed his phone, wondering if I could just delete the whole thing.

'Yeah . . . I suppose I took that,' I said, anxiously.

'Did you . . . submit it? To the page?'

I paused and considered lying. 'Yeah, I did. Sorry. I was in the pub with my friend and we were just being silly. Bit of a laugh really,' I said, bracing myself. He would have every right to think that was very weird.

Instead, his face softened, and he was smiling at me. 'So . . . does that mean . . . you think I'm hot then?'

I turned bright red. My cheeks were like miniature hobs.

'Well,' I said. 'Um, I guess I do.'

Admittedly it was a very strange way of us 'breaking the ice'. But, from then on, we were inseparable. Every Saturday, after our shift at the bookshop, we'd go for dinner or drinks, or a walk around the park. Then we started seeing each other in the week. Then we met each other's colleagues. Then we were introduced to the family. We were fully joined at the hip. He was my person, and I knew I wanted to hang up his Y-fronts on the washing line when we were both old and wrinkly.

Our favourite thing was to get a roast dinner together on a Sunday afternoon around 4 p.m., and drink red wine and eat crispy potatoes until it was dark outside and we could roll home together, hand in hand. One weekend we went to our favourite pub in Islington, The Duck's Arms, with pattern-carpeted floor and grand fireplaces and a bright green bar. We sat at our usual table by the window, and it was starting to get dark outside already. We were both wearing oversized cosy jumpers.

'It's on afternoons like this when I actually do love the winter,' I said, as I reached for Jacob's hand.

'Me too. I mean, winter can be nice when you have someone to share the cold nights with,' he said, smiling at me.

'We're lucky, aren't we?' I said. 'To have each other.'

'Ol, there's something I need to tell you, that I can't believe I haven't already said.' Jacob looked serious for a moment.

'Oh?' I said, trying to ignore the worry in my gut.

'I . . .' He paused for a few seconds, 'love you,' he said, smiling widely, staring into the black centres of my eyes.

I almost choked on my red wine with relief.

'I love you, too.' We leant over the table and kissed, our noses scrunched up against each other. If I had been a stranger looking over at our table, I would probably have been sick. But to us, it was the best feeling in the world, and we were in our own little bubble.

I suppose if I knew back then all the pain that was to come, perhaps I would never have set foot in that bookshop at all.

22

2019

I go through my work emails next door to the .dot office in a new co-working space on a big squidgy sofa and drink a latte from a paper cup, which is kind of gross but it's sustainable and blah-blah. I love the flexibility of my job. Today I'm planning next month's editorial pieces for the website and commissioning some of our favourite freelance writers to put together articles about polyamory. I've arranged to go over to Bea's this evening, so as soon as it hits 5.30 I leg it across London to get to Waterloo and then nip into Foyles and buy an interesting book that's advertised in the shop window – a new novel about a luxury surrogacy farm. I sit down on the creaky train to Surrey and pop the 'Baby on Board' badge on again as I can't bear anyone bothering or bumping into me – I feel a twinge of guilt as it's become a bad habit, but I'm not too worried about it yet.

I realize I'm still wearing my badge as I ring Bea's doorbell and quickly scramble to remove it. She answers the door dressed in art overalls.

'Hello gorgeous!' Bea says chirpily as she answers the door.

I hand her a bunch of flowers, a belated birthday gift. 'Happy birthday for the other day. Sorry it's late,' I say, wiping my shoes on her doormat.

'Ohh, thank you, they're gorgeous.' Bea is covered in paint, her hands are dry and coarse from the many years of using them to cook from scratch, rolling pastry, sculpting pottery, painting, using needles and threads. Her hands look ten years older than she is, but they're still beautiful. Her hair is balanced haphazardly in a bun on top of her head, with stray hairs everywhere.

I follow Bea through to the kitchen and she starts arranging the flowers, snipping the stems and running them under water as she starts chatting away. She doesn't mention the whole Cecily Baby Shower Fiasco from the weekend, which I'm grateful for. Bea is a good listener. Sure, she is constantly shouting *Don't eat that/Don't touch that/Get off that/Be nice to each other/Stop doing that/Don't break that/ Where have you put that piece of Lego?* to her kids, but all whilst having a genuine conversation with me. Her ability to actually listen to her friends whilst maintaining her mad life is a real skill. She is like a dolphin: they sleep with one side of their brain wide open as a defence mechanism as they drift through the deep sea. A rare breed: a successful multitasker. She can genuinely talk with you on any topic and still have one side of her brain on kid-watch. Maybe she isn't one hundred per cent present (who is?), but she isn't like other mum friends who only pretend to be listening to me. *Ah-hmm. Right. Oh yes. Oh poor you. Depression? Oh dear. Sounds nasty. One minute.* While literally looking straight over my left shoulder at what the kids are doing. I get it, you have to keep them alive, but you also have to keep your friendships alive.

Bea places the flowers on the middle of her big wooden dining-room table in a large hand-painted vase. White, pink and yellow lilies, her favourites.

'They look lovely. Thanks, Ol,' Bea says, finessing the stems so they spread equally in the vase.

I brush my sleeve past them as I sit down at the table and get orange lily-pollen powder on my jumper. 'Fuck's sake,' I mutter.

'Don't worry, I can get it out, just need a bit of sticky tape to lift it off. Just *don't* rub it.'

'Thanks . . . and well, thanks for not making a big deal of me being a dick at Cecily's at the weekend,' I say, after a sharp intake of breath.

'Ah, it's fine, you're always a bit of a dick,' Bea says, winking and rummaging around for sticky tape in a broken kitchen drawer.

'But seriously, I don't know what came over me. It felt like something was building up, and I snapped. And poor Cec got the brunt of it. I feel awful.'

'It's OK. I get it. It's a strange time, Ol. We're all going through some big changes, and it can feel scary,' Bea says, carefully dabbing at my sleeve with tape.

'Yeah. That must be it. I just feel very removed at the moment. A little lost,' I say.

'And you think Cecily has it all together?' Bea asks, with an eyebrow raised.

'Yeah I do. Cecily has it all together, and I don't. So I said some things I didn't mean.'

'I think you have more things in common than you think, it's just accepting that your situations are different. Cec definitely doesn't feel like things are all together,' Bea says.

'But she has everything. The husband, the baby, the house. The fucking roll-top bath.'

'Come on. You're a grown-up, Ol, you know those things don't equate to magically having all your shit together. She's finding adjusting to her new role as a mother really hard. We all have things we are finding hard, and those things might come at different times for each of us. The important thing is, we need to be there for each other. Life isn't a race. For all you know, she could be jealous of your life, your freedom, your glamorous job.'

'You're right.' I look around at her living room, it's like Toys 'R' Us has exploded everywhere. 'I cannot believe you keep three small humans alive every day,' I say, looking around at the stack of toys in every corner of every room. 'It's just so . . . impressive.' What I really mean to say but don't is: your life is so alien to me and I don't understand how you do it.

'Thanks. These bags under my eyes wish they were going on holiday, though. Ugh, I look haggard.' She goes over to the big mirror by the dining table and pulls her fingers down her face. 'I look old as fuck.'

'Don't be silly . . .' I throw a stuffed rabbit with one creepy eye at her.

'I suppose I miss having a bit more time for myself, but sometimes I actually think I would get really down in the dumps if I had too much spare time – you know? Too much time to think. Sometimes that is a curse in itself. But maybe that's just me.'

'Zadie Smith once said something like being a mother and being busy makes her more creative, not less. Like, the fact that she can't sit around all day is a good thing.'

'Yes exactly! So, update me on your life please. How're things, how's work? What exciting things are you doing while I sit at home making papier mâché masks, Play-Doh spaghetti and get toys thrown at me?'

'Well, hunkering down with takeaways most nights is hardly the high life. Oh Bea, I have so much to tell you.'

I am just about to open up about the Jacob break-up, when Amelia gallops in wearing a huge Liverpool FC football shirt and muddy wellies, and hands me a small fresh daisy from the garden. 'This is for *you*,' she says, handing me the crumpled flower in her sweaty palm, 'because you are very nice and priitttty.'

My face melts into a smile. I gasp overdramatically, 'Aww, Amelia, thank you, you sweetie.' I take the flower and give her a big hug, picking her up.

Bea has to take an urgent call in her home office; it's her nanny, apparently. She says sorry a million times and promises she won't be long. I walk over and stand at Bea's deep farmhouse sink with chrome taps, I wash up some of the mugs that are lying there, stained with tea. I look through the big window that overlooks a huge garden, full of swings, a treehouse with fairy-lights and beautiful flowers – chaotic, like everything at Bea's, but the perfect family tableau. It's raining outside. The window is smudged with trickling water and my eyes start to well up, making the view even more glazed over. This love and devotion that my friends have for their children, this undying never-ending sense of love, why don't I want it?

When Bea comes back into the kitchen, she is glancing down at her Nokia 3310 which we *love* to mock her about – along with all her other Nineties tech.

'I'm *so* sorry,' Bea says, looking flustered. 'Our nanny is really ill and it's fucking absolutely everything up. I really do rely on her.'

'It's OK. You're spinning so many plates. Don't apologize.'

'Also, Ol, I've made a terrible mix-up. I just got a text reminding me – I totally forgot I have another friend coming over today. A mum friend. She's a darling, though. I think you'll like her.' Bea smiles at me a little nervously. 'We can have lunch all together?'

My heart sinks slightly, but I smile reassuringly. 'Great! The more the merrier then,' I say. I don't want to make her feel bad for double-booking – she's a mum, she's already consumed with guilt on a daily basis, so the last thing she needs is a dose from me.

The doorbell rings and I go to answer it as Bea is finishing off some final things in the kitchen for lunch. She is also baking banana bread and the house is filled with a warm and toasty smell. It drifts down the corridor and under our noses just like a Tom and Jerry cartoon. When I answer the door, a woman with very voluminous hair smiles and says hello before grabbing my shoulders and kissing me on both cheeks.

'Hi! I'm Belle!' Her face is radiant, her cheeks peach with expensive-looking blusher. 'Are you Bea's lovely nanny?'

'No – I'm Bea's best friend, Olive.'

I thought it best to lay down some facts. Best friend.

'Oh, gosh, I'm so sorry. So lovely to meet you. This is my daughter Florence. Or Flossy as we call her. Flossy say hi – don't be rude to the lady!'

The lady? I look down and Flossy is picking her scabby nose. I bet she wipes bogies on sofas.

Belle is wearing a beautiful cashmere jumper and her hair is immaculately blow-dried. When she pulls back from the air-kissing, I get a whiff of her perfume; she smells amazing. She looks like a walking, talking filtered photo.

I move back and signal with my hand for them to come in. Belle smiles at me again and walks through to the kitchen, holding Flossy's hand. She follows reluctantly, like a small, lazy dog.

Belle gallops into the kitchen to find Bea. 'Ahh Bea! Long time no . . . *Flossy please stop tugging my sleeve* – so good to see you!'

'Thanks for travelling to me this time!' Bea says, hugging her, holding a spatula.

'Of course, my pleasu— *Flossy I already gave you a tissue* – what a lovely house this is!'

'Thank you – tea? Breakfast or Earl Grey, just making up a pot.'

'Breakfast please, wow this view – *Flossy stop that noise darling please* – it's a little slice of heaven, this location!'

I stand there like a lemon. Flossy has snot running onto her top lip. Belle smiles at me again. Your kid is gross, I think to myself, smiling back.

It is quite unnerving, this feeling when I am in the company of two – or more – women who are mothers. They have this unifying, unbreakable bond that I can't compete with. It's as if they have an invisible thread that ties them so closely together. A thing, a secret code, that they know about, and I don't. Bea has only known this woman for a few months, I have known Bea since we were five, but it's not a simple comparison or equation any more. In some ways, Belle and Bea clearly have a deep-rooted connection; they inhabit a different territory that I wouldn't be able to elbow my way into even if I tried. Literally the closest thing I can compare to being a mother is cat-sitting for Cecily and having to put some food out on a tray a few times a day. I don't even look after plants. I only have cacti and aloe vera, because you can ignore them and they don't die.

'Your names sound quite similar,' I say awkwardly by the sink, struggling with what to say.

'Ha, yes! "Bea & Belle" sounds like some cool restaurant, doesn't it! One day eh? When we grow older and run away to Malibu?' Belle jokes, taking a seat at the wooden dining table and de-robing her scarf. I smile through gritted teeth.

As if you're taking my best friend to Malibu. I look down at Flossy, who is sucking on a strand of her own hair.

'Do you want to play with Amelia, sweetie?' Belle crouches down and talks to her like she's a puppy about to fetch a ball. Flossy nods.

Jeremy is apparently looking after the kids in the living room. On his days off from being a glamorous film director, Bea's husband hardly ever leaves his armchair; reading the newspapers and watching the rugby. He's quite quiet and reserved; I like him. I notice that Flossy is holding a baby doll by a clump of its faux hair.

'That's a cute little doll,' I say to Flossy. 'I used to have one just like it!'

'You are the baby's mummy, aren't you, Flossy!' Belle says. Flossy nods manically.

'I used to feed my doll this weird powder and it would poo it out,' I blurt.

'Olive!' Bea laughs.

Belle takes Flossy's hand and takes her to the room next door where Jeremy and Amelia are playing with plastic bowling pins. The room is a mess.

'Don't you think it's kind of creepy that we start programming little girls into being "mummies" from such an early age?'

'Yeah I suppose!' Bea says.

I do find it strange that little girls are given miniature pushchairs and fake kitchens. They have the rest of their lives to be adults and constantly do things for other people, but we start teaching them their 'role' as soon as they can walk.

'How old is Flossy, Belle? Three?' I ask.

'Actually she's four,' Belle says, sounding affronted as she walks back into the kitchen.

'Right,' I say. Same difference, I think.

Bea takes off her apron and puts it in a big drawer.

'Right, now that Flossy and Amelia are all settled in the next room. Hurrah – a chance for some "us time"! Anyone for a mid-afternoon drink, if you know what I mean?' Bea gets out a bottle of Malbec. It has some dust on it, which suggests that it might be an expensive one. Better than my usual from the Co-op bargain bucket. 'This is what Sundays are for!' she says, pouring from the heavy wine bottle.

'So how are you Belle?' Bea asks.

'I'm good, actually. Work's going well, and the kids are blossoming! I still fancy my husband. You know, can't complain honestly,' Belle says, flicking her hair over one shoulder.

'How many kids do you have?' I ask, sounding politely intrigued.

'I have six,' Belle says.

'Fucking hell,' I say, before I can get control over my mouth.

Bea looks at me with widened eyes.

'Ha-ha. That's a fair reaction. I know, it's a lot!' Belle says, brushing her long silky blown-out hair over one shoulder.

'Right, here you are,' Bea says, handing us both a glass of red. 'Cheers, to us!' Clink.

'So how do you do it then – balancing six kids and working?' I ask, taking a sip.

Bea gives me a look that says I should stop grilling her mate.

'Sorry if I'm being nosy,' I continue. 'I'm a journalist, and sometimes I can come across a bit strong, a bit like I'm interviewing someone instead of talking! Terrible habit!'

'Oh no, it's fine,' Belle says, wiping some red wine from her chin.

Here's the thing: most people love to talk about themselves.

'You know, we just make it work. My husband works full-time too, but he will do what he can to help. I just . . . we find the time, I guess. It's amazing what you can fit into one day. I do the drop-off and my husband picks them up. What's that saying: we all have the same amount of hours in a day as Beyoncé!'

'I actually find that saying really depressing,' I say.

'Oh?' Bea says.

'Well, like, yeah we all have twenty-four hours in a day, but Beyoncé has caterers, personal trainers, chauffeurs . . .'

'Yeah I know what you mean – I guess I just make it work with what I've got,' Belle replies.

'It's super interesting to hear about other people's routines, though . . . I'm in awe.' I laugh nervously. Six kids. *Six!*

'I love how you just get on with it,' Bea pipes up. She is now restocking the fridge on the other side of the kitchen.

'Yeah well, maybe we are just lucky. The kids are bright, they're doing well in their exams, very sporty too. You know, I genuinely think I might turn the spare room into a trophy cabinet room. They bring some new award home most days!'

I look over at Bea who is smiling at her. I can't help but raise my eyebrows.

'Every day is a bit mad, things can and do go wrong. It's not perfect, but we just have a really good system in place. I wouldn't have it any other way. You know, people say you can't have it all. But you can! You can have whatever life you want.'

I watch Belle as she speaks: she doesn't have any bags under her eyes; her nails are freshly shellacked, her hands look soft and perfectly manicured; her hair is glossy and clean; she smelt nice when I greeted her – of fresh flowers and clean linen. She speaks slowly, she doesn't seem frantic at all: she is calm. I mean, what the fuck? I can't even look after myself. How do you dress yourself and dress six kids, and go to work, and feel calm at home, and do all the kids' admin, and your own admin? And the next burning question on my lips is: how do you make dinner for eight people every night? That's effectively like running a small, inner-city restaurant! I can't get my head around it. Belle is the living, breathing real-life version of the stock image photos that I scoff at, or the 'mamas' on the cover of *Goop* magazine. I didn't know these women actually existed. But here I am, sitting across from one. I feel like David Attenborough, eyeing up a rare new breed.

'How do you look after all your kids and still have good hair?' I ask, tilting my head to one side.

Bea laughs, and rolls her eyes at me.

'Ha-ha, you're so sweet!' Belle says, stroking her perfect hair. 'But you know, there are so many apps now. You can basically order anything to your house – massages, pedicures, hairdressers. A total godsend when you are housebound.'

Belle has her shit together and there is no denying that it is making me feel a few rungs lower down the ladder in the race of life. Am I awful for judging another woman like this? Bad feminist. I should be happy that this woman has found a good balance that works for her. And yet I long to find a big ugly smudge in this perfect oil painting.

'Anyway, enough about me,' Belle says. 'Bea has told me so much about you, Isla and Cecily. You're a writer, aren't you? I've heard some incredible things about your work. You're practically famous!'

'Ha. Well, I'm lucky that I find my job fulfilling. I love writing and telling stories, it's all I've ever wanted to do and a great way to spend my days to be honest,' I say, smiling. I do love it, but it does also get to me a bit that I'm often labelled as Career Woman™ in the friendship group, because I don't have kids.

'Wow, that does sound wonderful – not many people can say they make a living from writing. And you're in a relationship? Married?'

'Well, no . . .' I look over at Bea who is mopping up a spillage on the table.

'No boyfriend on the scene?' Belle presses.

'No . . . I'm actually not with anyone,' I say. I look over again at Bea whose mouth is now hanging slightly open.

She gasps. 'What? Why? When?'

'Well, actually,' I take a big breath. 'Ages ago now. Like . . . a couple of months. I'm OK now though. Really.'

'How could you not have mentioned this to me sooner? What happened exactly?'

'Well, we disagreed about a lot of things, but well . . .' I gulp down a huge mouthful of wine, Belle in my eyeline. This is so not how I imagined having this conversation with Bea. 'I suppose the main reason is because I don't want kids. That was a deal-breaker for him, sadly.' I've just said it, ripped it off like a plaster.

Belle looks shocked and sad.

'God Ol, I can't believe it. I feel awful that I didn't know. You've been dealing with this all on your own?' Bea says gently, putting her arm around my shoulder.

'Well, Zeta and Mum knew.'

'I can't believe this, love.'

'It's fine, you guys have had your own stuff going on. There never seemed to be a good time to bring it up, and I didn't want to be a burden.'

Bea slaps her forehead with the palm of her hand. 'Oh Olive. I am so, so sorry. I had no idea you needed us. I really regret how we all left that evening at Jono's. Is that what you wanted to talk about that night?'

'It's OK, Bea. It's actually been quite good for me, in the deep end on my own. At least I didn't drown.' I know what I'm doing. I'm trying to make Bea feel guilty, even if I'm not entirely sure why.

'How are you feeling now?'

'Better. Still plodding along I guess.'

'But Ol, you've got so much going for you, you're doing brilliantly with your writing.'

'Is that enough, though?'

'Of course. Your life doesn't matter less because you don't have a boyfriend or husband. Come on.'

'I know.' I wipe a tear away from my eye and wriggle my body slightly on the stool so that they move away from me a bit. They have dragged their chairs too close.

'And I mean, who knows Ol, you might just be going through a phase with all the baby stuff. Hey, weren't you looking into child-free women for an article at work? Maybe these doubts are coming from all that research. Obviously if you did decide to have kids – one day – you'd be a great mum!'

And there is was again, the old 'if you change your mind'. This is the classic response to the statement: 'I don't want to have children.' It's almost a reflex, a safe word, a way of softening the blasphemy. I know we haven't spoken about it properly, but I sort of expected better from Bea, I can feel my body itching with frustration. I can understand random strangers delivering that line without really thinking, but from my best friend? Who knows me better than anyone?

I open my mouth to reply but then quickly close it. I have no response. Belle is playing with her jewellery on her fingers, spinning her engagement ring around. She looks at me stiffly, smiling with her mouth closed.

'I don't hate kids, by the way,' I joke in Belle's direction.

'Oh god! Of course not! I would never think that,' Belle says, almost choking on her wine.

'I just feel really paranoid that people think I hate kids

just because I don't want them. I love kids. Well, I love some kids. My friends' kids.' *Oh shut up Olive!*

'Of course,' Bea and Belle both say in unison.

There's a silence.

'Whilst we're opening up here, I suppose I have a confession to share,' Belle says. 'I do this weird thing where I sort of feel like I have to show off when I meet a new person, in case they're a better mum than me. I wasn't sure if you had kids or not.'

'Well, even if I did, it's definitely not possible that my lifestyle would beat yours in any way,' I snort. 'There's clearly no competition here.'

'That's not true! I don't know what's wrong with me,' Belle laughs back. 'It's silly but my walls go up. I'm a bit embarrassed now.'

'Hey, don't be hard on yourself, love,' Bea says.

'I guess, the truth is, I might have it all on paper, but I do have help,' Belle says.

'It's good that your husband helps you,' I say. 'So he should.'

'No, I mean, I have a lot of help – Bea, promise you won't judge me?'

'I would never!' Bea protests.

'I have two nannies and a night nanny,' Belle blurts out and clasps a hand over her mouth.

'So?' I say.

'Exactly,' Bea said. She refills our glasses and we clink them together again. 'I sometimes let Amelia watch stuff on her iPad for hours. When Arnold was born, I sometimes used to put him in another room in his basket and leave him to cry. Sometimes I buy ready meals! Sometimes I let them fully attack each other because I am so tired and I don't have the energy to intervene,' she says, guiltily.

'Bea, you are allowed to do all of this and more,' Belle says, cupping Bea's hands.

'Can we just do a little cheers to giving ourselves a bit of a break, please?' I say, holding out my glass. The others join in. Clink clink. We're acting normally in front of Belle, but there is an edge of tension between Bea and me lingering in the air, which neither of us can ignore.

23

I open one eye, which takes ages to adjust to my surroundings. My neck is sore from sleeping awkwardly and I'm being abruptly woken up by my alarm which is going off loudly next to me, but I can't remember why. I roll over and grab my phone. Oh crap. Appointment with Cyril, 8.00 a.m. Shit. I totally forgot. Why did I book an appointment so bloody early? I quickly shower, get dressed and jump on the number 8 bus. I forget my badge and have to stand like the other non-pregnant muggles, dammit.

When I arrive at Cyril's clinic in a posh bit of Central London, Adam Street, I stand awkwardly outside for a bit, checking my phone. I suddenly feel a little silly and exposed. I'd booked this on a real down, hungover moment, wallowing in the messiness of the Jacob situation, and now I'm wondering: why am I here?

I'm a little bit surprised when I step inside. I don't know what I was expecting. Something a bit more . . . clinical? I suppose I was imagining some kind of doctor's surgery, but this is very different. The walls are a bright coral colour, with framed photos of beaches lining them. Cyril's awards and placards are also scattered around ('Winner of The Family Future Awards, 2017'), but mostly she's hung up seashells and old fossils. The reception table is in the corner of the room and it has dream catchers dangling over it, and there is an essential oils diffuser wafting out a light lavender aroma. There are books and magazines on the table with titles such as *The Heart Manual* and *Your Spirit Guide*, which have huge stickers over them saying 'DO NOT STEAL THESE FROM THE CLINIC'. I go over to the water machine, fill up a paper cup and accidentally spill water over the carpet.

'Hi hun, can I help?' the receptionist asks, swooping in beside me.

It sounds a bit passive-aggressive and I feel as though I shouldn't really be here. She has train-track braces and wavy hair.

'Hi, it's Olive Stone. Here for an appointment with Cyril Snow.'

'Yes, lovely. Cyril is running a tiny bit behind schedule with another client but will see you soon. Please, take a seat.'

As I sit and wait, I scroll through my phone and pop Isla a message. It's been ages since I've spoken properly to her, weeks since I've seen a message with the two blue 'read message' ticks on WhatsApp. I hope she's OK.

'Excuse me hun, but Cyril doesn't like phones being used in her sacred space, the radio waves interfere with her practices. Do you mind switching it off? Thanksomuch.'

'Oh, yes sure.'

'Maybe you could read one of Cyril's books instead? She likes it when her patients take an interest in her work.' She nods in the direction of the books.

I notice the little pager clipped to the receptionist's belt. It beeps.

'Cyril is now ready for you, hun.'

'Howdy! Hi! Sorry to keep you waiting there.' Cyril appears in the doorway to the reception, dressed in a long white tunic with floral embroidery around the collar. She is wearing dangly earrings, mini dream catchers, has long blondish-grey hair up in a messy bun. She has multiple silver rings on each finger, big sandals, an anklet on both feet and unshaved legs.

'Hi! Not at all. Lovely to meet you,' I say, getting up from the waiting room sofa.

'Come in, come in!' She leads me down a short corridor, down some steps and into her room. 'I replaced all the chairs in my office with these yoga balls because they are good for the hips and the pelvic floor! Please, do sit down,' Cyril says. I feel a bit silly as I rock backwards and forwards awkwardly on the ball. Trying not to fall off.

'So, dear, tell me everything. I am so happy to meet you! It's been a while since I've had any new clients in the building. It's very exciting, for me and the team. Your name is . . .' She looks down at her iPad. 'Olive! What a lovely name.'

I nod. 'Thank you.'

'So, Olive. What is your story?'

There's a comfortable, easy vibe about Cyril's room. There are plants all around, pictures of her family on the wall and her handbag on the floor. It feels laid-back and intimate.

'Do you mind if I record the session on my phone? I often suffer with short-term memory loss and like to listen to things back again,' I say. A little white lie. I want to record the conversation for myself, but maybe for a future article too.

'Of course, dear. Whatever works for you,' Cyril says calmly. I click record.

'Well, I don't know what exactly brought me here. I suppose I was intrigued and wanted to discuss my current situation. A feeling of indecisiveness.'

'You followed your intuition, darling. You came here for a reason. You must always give yourself credit for the decisions you make.'

'I guess my issue is not the usual one your clients come to you with, though.'

'All stories are welcome.' Cyril puts her hands in a prayer position and leans her chin on her fingertips before closing her eyes. I wait a minute for her to open them. I continue.

'Well, I'm not actually trying for a baby at all. It's the opposite really. I wanted to ask whether you're coming across a growing number of women who are opting out of having children? Ya'know, deciding the whole baby thing isn't for them. It's just well, when I try to picture myself with a baby, with a kid, I feel . . . nothing.'

Cyril's eyes ping open.

'Oh! Olive my dear,' she coughs. 'Are you suffering from any recent trauma? Anything that has made you feel this way?' Cyril reaches for her iPad again, looking concerned.

'Umm no, I don't think so. I have never wanted to have

children, in fact, but for some reason it's all I can think about at the moment. I feel consumed by it, by the decision to *not* have them. Perhaps it's because my friends' lives are filled with babies at the moment.'

'Ah, yes. It makes sense that it is all you are thinking about.' Cyril raises her hands upwards. 'We often repress our deepest desires, and they come out in our dreams. Have you been dreaming about children at all?'

'I have yes – but they're usually nightmares.'

'We often think nightmares are reflecting the things we don't want. But often we have fearful dreams about the things we want deep-down and secretly desire.'

'I guess I just feel quite abnormal compared to my friends. It used to be a level playing field, but now it's like we're all veering down different paths. Plus I've broken up with my boyfriend over it. I wanted to seek your reassurance – do many women feel like this?'

'Of course, many women go through these phases.'

'Phases?'

'You may have a hormone imbalance. You may be oestrogen dominant and naturally have low progesterone. It's only biology – it's not you! You mustn't put yourself down because of this.'

'I suppose I'm wondering from your research and experience with other women, if these feelings might be normal, and whether you think . . . I might change my mind one day,' I say.

'From my experience, you will most probably change your mind,' Cyril says, not skipping a beat.

'I will?'

'Oh yes,' Cyril sighs. 'I have heard thousands of these stories, stories just like yours. You must not let this worry you. Some women repress deep feelings of desire for children at first. It's fear. This is how we often deal with fear – we shut it down, shut it off, bury it deep down and teach ourselves to hate it. This is when we have to dissect it, explore it before your brain connects to your body. It's just about coming to terms with the idea before your body takes action and releases all of the chemicals to make you *feel* ready. Perfectly normal.' She taps her iPad again.

'Right,' I say.

'As women, unfortunately, we cannot trust our own hormones.'

What?

'It's annoying, but such is life. You shouldn't read too much into these intense feelings. Try not to.'

'So, you're telling me I can't trust these feelings I'm having?'

'Indeed. It's just your mind playing a trick on you. Very normal.' She pauses. 'So how would you like to move ahead and work together? Our approach is highly personal and holistic. We offer acupuncture, diet and nutrition advice, testing for fertility issues, and emotional support. Don't be afraid, we will find a solution to this problem.'

'But . . . are you saying you've never come across women who genuinely never wanted children – and felt fine about it? I'm pretty sure these women do exist,' I say.

'Oh, of course they do! But from my experience they always

261

end up wanting one after our sessions. It's about getting the body ready to *welcome* a new life. We get to the bottom of it, whatever that issue or block might be, and we realize those maternal feelings were there all along,' Cyril says, smiling. She is now sitting on the floor in the lotus position. 'Sorry, darling, I do like to move around a lot while talking. I like to stretch, sitting in one place for too long isn't good for you. Come down here and stretch with me.' She flaps her hand at me.

I get on the floor, on a giant mat, and she tells me to kneel on all fours.

'Right, first let's do the "cow": lower your back so it's flat.'

'OK,' I do as she says.

'Say moo with me,' Cyril says.

We moo.

'Now, we do the "cat", arching our backs. Lift upwards, you'll feel a nice stretch. Now say meow as you breathe out,' says Cyril.

We meow.

We do this mooing and meowing for some time. Cyril seems to be getting more and more high-pitched with the meows and really 'mooing' from her core. It's really hard not to laugh. She is deadly serious. I look at the clock.

'Feels so good to stretch, doesn't it?' Cyril says, when she finally stops. I follow her lead, and we both get up and sit back on our springy balls.

'Right. So, Olive, I'm glad you booked this chemistry session,' she reaches for the drawer next to her and pulls out some papers. 'Please fill out this form at home and send it back to me. It's quite long, we're asking for a lot of personal information, but obviously it's all confidential. Then we will contact you with a bespoke treatment plan and fee for going forwards. Oh, and we do monthly price plans too, if that helps at all. Obviously if you don't send back your form soon, we will take that as a sign that you do not want to go any further. But I must say, I'm excited for you to really dig into this and face the truth of these feelings.'

I take the form. It's a thick wedge of paper in a plastic wallet.

'OK, I'll have a read-through.' I already know that I won't.

'Wow, where has the time gone, eh?' Cyril says, glancing down at her watch. 'Well I hope we'll see you again very soon, Olive. Make sure you drink lots of H_2O.' I mean, she could have just said 'water'.

Cyril leads me out and points me in the direction of the reception area again. She bows and says: *Namaste*.

I feel a little dumbfounded. All the Google searches I've been doing run on loop. I liked Cyril at first, she was being nice and gentle with me, but I could also sense her fierce judgement. Suddenly it all feels a bit sinister; what is this? A type of conversion therapy? I wanted to meet Cyril to have a frank conversation and talk to someone who has seen it all. And perhaps, deep down, I did wonder if I could change, if I could get Jacob back.

I shake my head. I decide in that moment to march back in. I tell the receptionist I left something in the treatment room.

'OK, but please be very quick,' she says, bluntly.

I walk down the carpeted corridor and knock.

After a long pause, I hear Cyril's calm voice reply: 'Come in.'

I open the door slowly and peek round. Cyril is meditating, cross-legged on the floor.

'Sorry to interrupt, but—'

'Go ahead,' she says, opening her eyes very slowly.

'I don't feel like you took me very seriously just now.'

'Oh. How so?' Cyril says, breezily.

'I was watching a TED Talk the other day about a woman who had her tubes tied – did you know one in five women don't want a biological child?' I say. 'Next week, for example, I am going to the Child-Free By Choice event. With hundreds of other women who feel the same as me.'

She gasps, loudly.

'Please do not say such things inside my clinic, Olive. We deal in positive energies here, and such dark thoughts about sterility will not be tolerated. We will not have negative omens brought into this space. I have a lot of women who come through these doors who desperately want children. And I am their only hope. We must always think positively!'

'But this is the whole point: I think you're being pretty insensitive to my feelings.' Many women's feelings.

'I'm sorry to say it Olive, but it is insensitive of you when so many women are struggling hugely with conceiving. Women whose eggs have not frozen properly. Bodies and wombs that aren't working. You have a healthy womb, I can sense it.' She closes her eyes and stretches out her palms. 'You have nothing to complain about. You're pursuing need-less drama.'

'Hey,' I say, stepping back. 'Stop visualizing my womb. That's private.' I put my hands over my stomach area.

'Look, I understand. But you have to understand that your feelings of not wanting a child will never be as important as a woman who desperately wants one but can't.' I feel guilty again for even being here. Cyril is describing women like Isla.

'What is that supposed to mean?'

'The women I meet, who want kids, or have miscarriages, *those* are the women that our society needs to support. These women who come through my door desperate for my help. The women who have lost partners because they can't conceive, the women who have suffered multiple miscarriages and are putting themselves at risk, the women with illnesses, the women who are desperately grieving and coming to terms with having missed their biological window to have a baby. You will be fine; you have made an active decision. You will go on holidays and live your own life. Statistically, you will live longer and be richer than women with children! You will do as you please. We must think of those women whose lives are on hold until they have a child. It is their dream. And it is my dream to help them.'

I gulp. 'Well,' I know I sound defensive, but my mouth keeps moving, 'how do you know that there aren't women out there, like me, suffering with the fact that they feel a bit like an outcast?'

'What you are talking about is loneliness. Loneliness can be cured. But it does not compare to the desperate women I help and tend to in my clinic. These are vulnerable women.'

I am hot with rage. I don't know if I'm angry because Cyril is so right, or so very wrong.

I get out my Dictaphone and start to talk into it as I walk to the bus stop. Ranting, asking rhetorical questions, describing what just happened. I'm sure I could write a piece on this. On Cyril.

'Olive recording. Part two, notes. Research Cyril back story. Why do homeopath fertility experts rub me up the wrong way? Is it because their position makes me feel inferior and jealous? Because deep down I wish I was "normal"? Interview some of her past clients – see what they say. Has she ever convinced someone that they want kids, when deep down they might not? Do we not care about women with no maternal feelings in society? Must we change them? Or disregard them? What did I like about Cyril? What did I not like? Unpick own emotion vs what factually went on in the room.'

I'm still seething as I get on the bus home. I WhatsApp Colin – an unlikely oracle, but I need someone to offload to.

Me: Oh my GOD just went to see that Cyril woman I was telling you about

Colin: The fertility woman?

Me: YES. She made me feel like a freak. That I was going through a 'phase' and for a price she could 'convert me' into wanting a baby – it was actually kinda gross??

Colin: Jeezuuuss. Isn't it odd how some human beings make their money? How does she sleep at night?

Me: Seriously

Colin: It was a bit weird though, Ol. Going to see a fertility expert when you don't want kids

Me: I needed some perspective! Besides, she was pushing the whole 'homeopathic' approach on her ad. I'm a sucker for that stuff

Colin: Wait was this for an article for the mag?

Me: Nope, spent my own cold hard cash on it, but I might pitch it to Gill

Colin: Youch $. Yes. You should

Colin: How are you feeling now?

Me: A bit stupid for doing it. But OK, actually. Do I care if some homeopathic woo-woo woman thinks I'm not living up to my full human potential – no! Do I want to live my life in a way that suits me? YES

Colin: Exactly. And also even bad experiences make great anecdotes as Caitlin Moran would say

Me: Definitely. Makes me realize that splitting up with Jacob was right. My feelings are valid. And that woman Cyril is BANANAS

Colin: That shit IS bananas b-a-n-a-n-a-s, as Gwen Stefani would say

Me: Thanks Col

Colin: Anytime. Go and have a nice G&T, and immediately wipe this Cyril woman from your brain please

Colin: RELAX – as Frankie Goes To Hollywood would say

Me: omg please stop quoting people *laughing emoji*

I want Colin to think I'm fine. That I'm tough, with my outward-facing armour on. Why can't I even admit the truth to him, the most relaxed person I know? Yes, the meeting with Cyril was silly and flippant, a bit of an experiment. But really, if I'm being truly honest, I have a feeling it's going to take a while to wipe away the feelings that Cyril stirred up in me. She made me feel wrong. She made me feel overdramatic. She made me feel like I had no right to explore my fear. Even though I don't want a baby, I have to admit that I am petrified of my own uncertainties, the demons that might come back to haunt me later on in life. The fact that Jacob is moving on, and I am still in the same place.

'Are you really viewed as any less of a woman because you don't have children? What do you think?'

Coleen Nolan, *Loose Women*, 2016

24

2018

We were out at a sushi restaurant celebrating because Cec had been given a promotion at work. I didn't know much about the legal firm hierarchy system, but I did know that she was now only one step away from becoming Partner – which was the ultimate dream goal.

'I'm paying tonight – I'm feeling flush after Gill gave me a bonus, so let's go wild,' I said. It wasn't quite lawyer-standard salary, but I liked to treat my friends.

'That's generous! Thank you Ol,' Cec said as she poured everyone a glass of water.

'I'm gonna get the lobster I think,' I said, scanning the menu.

'Ooh me too,' agreed Isla.

'What's everyone going to drink?' Bea said, grabbing the wine list. 'I'm in the mood for some rouge.'

'Aren't you meant to have white wine with sea food?' Isla suggested.

'Oh, I hate all those snobby rules,' Bea said, waving her hand.

'Think I'll just go for fizzy water, you know. I've got an early start tomorrow,' Cec sighed.

'No! C'mon Cec. Just have the one at least – my treat!' I said.

Cec shuffles around in her seat. Sitting on her hands. Slightly pink in the cheeks.

'I really shouldn't, actually,' she said quietly.

'I promise it won't be a late one,' I said, pressing.

'It's just that . . .' We all looked up from our menus. 'Um . . . Well. I'm . . . actually . . . pregnant,' Cec said, quietly, breaking out into a huge grin.

'Oh my god!' Bea yelled.

'Amazing!!' Isla screamed.

I opened my mouth to speak, to offer my congratulations, but I was frozen, totally frozen.

They both jumped up to hug Cec, and started making such a fuss over her, hugging her and squeezing her shoulders. I suddenly felt like the walls of the restaurant were coming in around me, closing me in, alone. Like the world had suddenly tipped.

'Ol?' Bea nudged me under the table.

'You OK, Ol?' Cec's voice started drifting into my ears.

'Sorry . . .' I leapt up. 'I was just taking it all in. I'm . . . just . . . surprised! Wow!' I said, pushing my chair back, making a slight screech and joining in the group hug.

I can't believe it. Cec. Pregnant. Wild Cec. My Cec. Deep down, I always felt she was my ally, my partner in crime. How did we suddenly get here?

* * *

272

On the drunk side of tipsy, I WhatsApped Cec on the way home in a cab.

Me: Sorry for my delayed reaction about the baby news. I was just so surprised. So happy for you, Cec, it's amazing news

Cec: It's all good, Ol! It's taken me by surprise too *cry/laugh emoji*

Me: Have you been feeling OK though? Any cravings? Crazy hormone rages?!

Cec: Not really yet. Although I've started dreaming about salty McDonalds fries

Me: I would happily take you there!

Me: Wow, it's so exciting. I can't believe it :)

Cec: I know

Me: I found this old photo of us from 10 years ago that came up on Facebook yesterday. Look at us!

Cec: Oh my god. We're so young. So slim!!!! Haha. Oh Ol. We've been through so much together

Me: And more to come xxx

I felt tears forming in my eyes. Talk about hormones – I wasn't sure if it was a tangle of emotions about Cec's good news, or the fact that everything seemed to be changing. Maybe, a bit of both.

25

2019

It's the night of the CFBC! The night I've been waiting for. I'm on the phone to Bea, who promised to come for moral support.

'Looking forward to seeing you later. Thanks for agreeing to come with me,' I say. 'It genuinely means a lot.'

'Of course, love – I always want to support your work.'

'It feels a bit more than just a work assignment though, I'm excited to go and meet these women.'

'Yes I know, but it'll be exciting to research won't it?'

'Yes – but I also feel excited about just checking things out. I think I'll take a lot away from this, Bea.'

'I thought you always tried to stay neutral when writing an article?'

'Bea, this isn't something I can be neutral about – it's like I said, I'm not sure if having kids is for me, so this isn't *just* a work thing.'

'Sorry yes, I know I know – let's chat more later,' she says.

'All right, see you soon. By the way, Colin is coming too!' I say.

'Amazing!' she says, then hangs up. I can't help but feel slightly annoyed by her flippancy, assuming this is only a work project.

Bea is staying the night at my flat afterwards, so she comes over to dump her bags before we go. She puts on a layer of lipstick in the bathroom mirror.

'So I did something a bit weird the other day,' I say, hovering by the doorframe.

'Oh yeah?' Bea says, rubbing her lips together and putting the lippie back in her pocket.

'I went to see this hippie homeopath woman. About the fact that I'm not getting, you know, the baby urges.'

'That kind of thing doesn't sound like you,' Bea says, turning to look at me.

'Yeah well, Jacob has a new girlfriend and it has sent me slightly loopy.'

'Oh Olive. Really? I'm sorry. That must feel way too soon.'

'It really does. How can he flip the switch on his feelings like that? Nine years with me, and now, suddenly, he's into someone else? It's only been a few months.' I feel my eyes water. There's something about talking to close friends that brings these emotions out in me, even if I think I'm controlling them.

'I think people move more quickly when they are older. More decisions to make, you know?' Bea says, calmly and gently.

'Anyway, tell me something good. How's Jeremy?'

'Well,' Bea takes out a clip in her hair and readjusts it. 'Unfortunately, not great, actually.'

'Oh?' I say, genuinely taken aback.

'Yeah, things aren't good at all, to be honest, Ol. But I'm just putting it down to "married life". You know. We've been together for so long and marriage is hard.'

'Yes, of course. Anything in particular that's bothering you?' I probe, gently.

'Nah don't worry about it, forget I said anything, it's just us being boring married old fogies. It can't be passion and fireworks the whole time I guess.'

I know she's not telling me the whole truth.

Saved by the bell, our Uber arrives outside the front door and we jump in. Magic FM is playing Spandau Ballet's 'Gold'. The Uber driver is wearing a shawl-necked grey sweater and has greyish stubble to match. He has one tiny hoop earring.

'All right ladies? Good evenin' to ya,' he says.

'Hi, thanks. We're off to The Book Club bar, please.'

'Yup, no probs. Twenty-minute drive it says on 'ere, all in all,' he says, tapping at his GPS.

'Cool, thanks,' I reply.

There is a pause, and the driver keeps looking at us in his rear-view mirror enthusiastically, like he wants to chat. Bea is sending a reminder to Jeremy about the leftovers in the fridge and where to find the Calpol in case Amelia's cough gets any worse. I open the latest email from Iris with our tickets attached. The driver then turns down Magic FM slightly and clears his throat.

'Did you girls watch that *Good Morning Britain* this

mornin' with what's-his-chops?' he asks, face bobbing around trying to make eye contact in the rear-view mirror.

'Er, no, what was the topic?' I ask, looking at my phone.

'Gender-fluid kids,' he says.

'Oh right,' Bea says. We glance sideways at each other.

'It's properly ridiculous, isn't it? Gender-fluid this, gender-binary this, non-binary that.'

We make a sort of neutral 'mmmm' noise.

He goes on: 'You know, they had a seven-year-old boy on there. Said he was a girl! Ridiculous. He's not a bloody girl! I wore pink dresses and all, when I was younger! My cousin Donald, he liked dolls! World's gone mad. Just cos you are playing with girly toys doesn't mean you should write down "gender fluid" on your school forms. Am I right?' He starts laughing to himself, snorting through his nose.

We both know to just nod and smile. I want to challenge this idiot. But late at night, in a busy city, it probably isn't worth it. It is aggravating having to hold your tongue in so many ways. You don't want to run the risk of being chucked out of a taxi late at night, or getting verbally abused, or you know, murdered and chopped up into little pieces and put in someone's freezer.

'Honestly,' he continues, 'I think it's dangerous. Making these young'uns think they know themselves and what they want at such an insignificant age. I wanted to be a vet at seven! And an astronaut. Doesn't mean nothing. I mean, look at me now!' He laughs.

'Huh!' I grunt.

'Moral of the story is, you don't know what you want at

seven. And you definitely aren't gender bloody fluid.' He takes a sharp left down a small narrow street and Bea and I swerve to one side.

'I wouldn't mind if my kids wanted to put that on their form,' Bea says. 'I don't think it's that important as long as they feel they're being heard, to be honest.'

'Fucking hell, really?' he says, staring at Bea through the rear-view mirror and spouting off again.

We stay quiet after that. The onslaught goes on and on, until (thank god) we eventually pull up next to The Book Club bar-side entrance and hop out, utterly relieved that the journey is over. Bea slams the car door.

'Good riddance. Jeez, is it possible to go anywhere in peace in this city? Everywhere you go, someone is there, waiting, ready to make you feel awkward with their opinions. So. Many. Opinions.'

'Agreed . . . Anyway, remember, you are Child-Free tonight. You have no kids! No mention of them, OK?' I prod her arm.

Colin is waiting, leaning on the brick wall outside the club in a leather jacket, sucking on his vape. He thinks he is James Dean.

'Hey bitches!' Colin says before air-kissing us.

'Excited?' I ask, linking arms with him and Bea. They both nod, although they look a bit uneasy, too.

'I mean, excited to see *you* guys, not sure what this whole shebang is gonna be like.'

'God I know . . . I'm glad you're here with me,' I say, shrugging, but feeling a tug of excitement in my stomach.

We knock on a big black door. A tall woman lets us in, crouching slightly, and says the main doors will open in five minutes. She tells us we can wait in the central bar. We walk down the carpeted staircase and order three wines and a packet of nuts.

When the main doors finally open, a woman with a clipboard ticks our names off and ushers us quickly down some more stairs. The basement room looks pretty, with thin draped reddish curtains. It is dimly lit with fairy lights, smells slightly of stale beer, and has chairs laid out in a horseshoe shape, with a lone microphone standing in the middle. It just looks like another innocent open-mic night. Eventually people start to trickle in, and the room starts to fill up. I look around as more and more women of all different ages pile into the room one after another, laughing all around us. It's mainly women, and only a handful of men.

'If I pick up a date or take someone home from this night it'll be the weirdest fucking thing,' Colin whispers to me. Trust Colin to be eyeing up the dating pool in the room. 'But then again, at least we'd both know where we stand on the whole kids thing!'

In the corner of the room we spot a tray of ice-cold G&Ts on the side of the bar with edible flowers floating in them, next to a little sign that says: 'Take one and pass one to a new friend!' We neck our wines and grab a floral G&T. Everyone here seems to know each other, and it is slightly intimidating to be the only visible newbies in the room. I then notice the host, Iris, walking down the stairs wearing a turquoise kaftan. I recognize her from the website, her stylized portrait photos. I notice books are on sale on a table by the door, including signed copies of *Selfish, Shallow and Self-Absorbed: Sixteen Writers on the Decision Not to Have Kids* by the author Meghan Daum, on special discount.

'We should probably muck in,' I whisper, nudging Bea. 'Else they might be suspicious that I'm a journalist, you're a nutty mum of three, and you're just here for the free gin,' I say, elbowing Colin.

I look across the room and notice tons of Post-it notes covering a cork board. Each note seems to describe something that relates to or celebrates child-free life. I look more closely and one Post-it note reads:

'Maternal urges drop by 25 per cent with every extra 15 IQ points' – Satoshi Kanazawa.

Another one:

'By the time you finish reading this sentence, the number of people on Earth will have increased by 300. Don't add to overpopulation.'

'Brutal!' Bea mutters, laughing heartily.

It suddenly hits me that everyone in the room has something in common: they have actively chosen to not be parents, whatever their reason or back story. It's starting to feel a little 'culty', putting me slightly on edge, but I have to admit there is something powerful in the shared outlook.

The laughter and chatter increase in volume around us and there's a loud tapping of the mic. Tap. Tap. Tap. It's Iris, in the middle of the room, next to a standing microphone. There is a collective shuffle, and people strain their necks to see over each other's heads. Iris's bracelets and long necklaces are hanging over her kaftan, making a loud clanging and clinking against the microphone.

'Welcome everyone. Welcome! Can you hear me OK?'

There is a generic 'woop!' sound.

Iris holds her clipboard in front of her and runs her finger down the list. 'Right, first things first, everybody! Oi, please, *sshh* at the back there! Right, some ground rules before I introduce the amazing speakers we have for tonight. And, of course, if you have something that you'd like to say there'll be time for any volunteer speakers at the end. Just put a piece of paper in the hat that's on the bar at the back! So, a quick intro about me, in case you're new to us: I'm Iris, the founder of CFBC. We went from a small supper club meet-up with a few child-free friends, to, well, a global community for hundreds of inspiring women – and some men! – such as yourselves. I started this group because I felt like it was needed. It's been quite the whirlwind. I'm so glad you are here, that you have spread the word, and reached out to friends who might feel the same. A reminder that this is a safe space! We don't stream anything online! We don't judge each other! Our prerogative is to support and encourage and share and say whatever we want. Some women here tonight will be articulating their thoughts for the very first time. We must listen to each other. All phones must be off. And not just airplane mode, please, *off!* I have made some incredible friends through the group, and we hope you do too. We want people out there to know that it is perfectly normal to be child-free, and more than that: a fantastic lifestyle choice! Right, let's begin. First up, we have Miranda, a radio DJ who has travelled all the way from Wales. Up you come, my darling, the mic is yours.'

Miranda shuffles towards the centre of the room and takes a while to place her feet in a comfortable position, before adjusting the microphone in line with her mouth:

'Hi everybody. Yes, I'm Miranda. Bit nervous about kicking things off . . . This is my first time doing anything like this, so bear with me . . . I'm only going to speak for a few minutes about my story. I feel enormously privileged to be able to actively choose my life's path, to be alive right now, in this year, in this version of the world. My mother wasn't really taught about contraception, and her family was crazily religious, so me and my brothers weren't planned. She never had a choice, she never once sat down and thought, "What do I want?" So, my twin brother and I, we weren't necessarily "wanted". I don't think my parents were ready for kids. They would go off and leave us to fend for ourselves quite a lot, when we weren't really old enough to look after ourselves. I suppose what I'm saying is, I am not my mother. I don't have to be in a situation I don't want to be in. So, I'm going to feel empowered by my choice. I don't want children, and I feel lucky that I know how to manage and maintain that decision. Thank you for listening to the shortened version of my story.' Miranda bows, and leaves the stage.

Everyone claps loudly. That was strangely confessional, so personal – which, I suppose, is the point. I don't know what to think.

'Thank you, Miranda! Up next, Marie!' Iris bellows from the mic.

Another woman, wearing a dark red silk top, walks onto the makeshift stage and does a big nervous cough into the mic. There is a piercing screech of feedback.

'Hi, I'm Marie McDonald. A children's nurse working in London. I am pretty sure I don't want kids. I don't get any maternal urges, but I feel like I should because I work with children and I love my job. I care for ill children every single day and I get extremely close to them. But I don't want to have a child of my own. I hate the fact that people assume I'm "less of a woman" or "less of a human" because I cannot commit to motherhood itself. Even though my job is so giving, I feel like I'm seen as selfish by the outside world. This is what my friends hint at, anyway. I feel like whatever I do, however much I give, I'm still not enough to some people. Thanks for listening.'

The audience claps and lots of people hug her as she comes off stage.

Bea nudges me and whispers: 'Where's she getting that from, do you think, that people would think she's selfish?'

My stomach tightens because I understand what Marie is saying. The small reminders every day that people think you're different, living outside the lines.

Before I can properly answer, Iris's voice is booming through the mic and the next woman is ushered onto the stage. She has short red hair, hoop earrings and is beaming into the crowd.

'Hello. I'm Dee. I think that the Internet as it is – and how it is evolving – is fucking terrifying. Sorry, Iris – I'm allowed to swear, aren't I?'

Iris hollers back from the crowd: 'Yes – please do!' Colin puts his hands up too and shouts, 'Woop!'

'So yeah, social media. Do I really want my kid growing up in a world where kids are exposed to porn before they even go to secondary school, and have the dangers of privacy issues and information leaks before they even hit puberty? The environment that kids are forced to grow up in today is absolutely despicable. I don't want to bring someone into this horrible shallow world, with all this data hacking, privacy issues, trolls, robots!'

'I'm going to get another drink,' Bea whispers loudly to me. 'Want another gin?'

Colin and I nod and hand over our empty glasses. A night like tonight certainly demands a good amount of social lubricant to get us through.

Bea waits at the bar and a woman with shoulder-length blonde hair, arm tattoos, a nose-piercing and a bandana around her neck perches on the barstool next to her.

'Omg, look, Bea's getting chatted up,' Colin says. We both giggle and sidestep towards them in unison so we can listen in on their conversation.

'First time here?' the blonde woman asks, looking Bea up and down.

'Yes, actually, enjoying it so far though,' Bea says, politely.

'I'm Koko,' the blonde woman says and puts out her hand.

'Bea.' They shake hands.

'Nice to meet you, Bea. What brings you here, then?' Koko asks, swigging on her bottle of Corona.

'Oh, you know . . . wanting to be around some like-minded

women! Feels like it's become increasingly hard to find that,' Bea says.

'Oh man, same.'

'So, no kids for you then, ever?'

'Nope. I cannot stand the idea of having anyone running around depending on me twenty-four/seven. Imagine!'

'God, same,' Bea rolls her eyes. The barwoman slides three gins across the bar towards Bea. 'Thanks.'

'When did you know, really know, that you didn't want to be a mother?' Koko asks, leaning in.

Bea nearly chokes, swallowing her drink too quickly. 'Oh, immediately! From birth! Never felt the urge, to be honest.' Bea scrunches her face up into a ball. She is clearly hoping that Koko can't magically see into her brain and realize that she has birthed three children whom she absolutely loves more than anything else in the world.

'I find most mothers to be rather irritating. Very holier-than-thou,' Koko says, making intense eye contact with Bea.

'Oh, agreed.' Bea brushes her fringe out of her eyes awkwardly.

'The worst. Like, who cares about your little bundle of joy? Mothers become *so* self-absorbed once they have kids. They turn their back on everything else. Their friends, their own health, their own dreams. It's so, so sad,' Koko says, picking at her beaded bracelet on her tattooed wrist.

'So sad!' Bea agrees, glancing over at Colin and me.

'Like, we get it, you pushed something out of your vagina, but there are a lot of women out there, making scientific breakthroughs or launching things into space – you know?

It's not actually life's biggest achievement.' Koko rolls her eyes, shaking her head.

'Well . . . some women are able to launch a rocket into space and have a baby at the same time.' Bea forces a laugh, the corners of her mouth twitching slightly.

'You wanna know another reason I don't want a kid?' Bea knows she doesn't need to consent to an answer; Koko is going to tell her anyway. 'You see, I have a lot of money . . . I really don't want to sound like I'm showing off about it, but you know, I live in a really nice part of London and I've worked for it. Born to working-class parents, I have grafted away and my artwork has been selling and I've managed to make my first mill. And you know, I'm worried that my kid would grow up to be spoilt and awful.'

'Oh, you can't think like that!' Bea says.

'Do you know what I mean though? Rich people's kids end up being really terrible. Like that famous chef. You know the one. Have you seen his son? Tattoos, drugs, the lot. Really, if you have money, your kids will most likely be awful human beings.'

Colin bursts out laughing. Bea glares at him. We can't blow our cover.

'It's a very interesting . . . observation,' Bea says, diplomatically. What she means to say is: you are generalizing, and you also sound totally mad. 'But I think that kids can totally transform a life – they can actually pull you out of the depths of your own issues and give you a whole new perspective. They are cute as babies, and then they can grow up to be your best mates.' Bea's eyes glaze over with love.

Koko slowly backs away. 'Right. It was, er, nice meeting you. Must dash to the bathroom.' She practically legs it. Bea turns to Colin and me, smirking.

Iris starts tapping the mic then. 'Right everyone! Attention please! Next speaker!'

A woman with a beautiful multicoloured scarf round her head and shimmering, flawless make-up steps onto the stage.

'I am here because I have chosen not to bring a baby into the world for many reasons – the main one of them being that I don't want my relationship to suffer. I love my husband; we have a fantastic life together. We truly believe that with children in the mix our lives would change too much and that it could impact negatively on our very loving and happy relationship. I know that might sound bleak, but I think it's important to protect a good relationship when you have one. My husband and I, we want to prioritize each other. I hear all these horror stories of people no longer having time for their partner, or they just don't feel like they can love each other and love their kids. I don't know, maybe these stories have got to me a bit! But I'd rather not risk it. My relationship with him is too important to me. Thanks for listening.'

More clapping and murmuring. I feel a tightness in my chest. A sharp, immediate sadness that almost takes my breath away, as if I've jumped into an icy lake. I suppose that's what I wanted with Jacob – I wanted him. I wanted a long fulfilled life with him. Time and space for us to focus on each other and grow old together. But, ultimately, that was not what he wanted.

The clapping subsides and Iris asks the crowd if anyone has a question, reminding the audience that they have to be safe, welcoming and kind. A woman stands up in the back row. She has a strong presence; she is older, probably mid-seventies, with a sour, frowny face. She clears her throat and someone hands her the sweaty mic:

'I have a question, but really it's more of a comment.' Everyone lets out a groan. 'The overarching themes seem to be that one should remain childless – sorry, child-*free* – in order to dedicate time to be a creative, or an academic or a writer, or to have better relationships or to travel the world. Why are you *justifying* yourselves? Yes, maybe you'd be bad parents. But nobody here is identifying the truth. Parenthood is a bad idea because children are annoying and parenthood is boring. Tonight would have been more stimulating if it hadn't been so monotonous and repetitive. Be honest. Stop making excuses! It's fine to just say: I don't want kids. End of conversation.'

Iris is clapping politely and looking around the room, checking that no one is offended.

Colin nudges me, suddenly recognizing someone in the crowd. 'Hey Ol, look!' He subtly points across the room, clutching his chest: 'I fucking love her. Kweeeeen!'

'Who is she?' An old friend from school? A colleague? Who?

We then hear whispers and muffles from all around. Ohh, shit, it's Jemima Jenkins, a real British actress standing right there. She starred in *Six Women*, a popular Channel 4 sitcom portraying the cosmopolitan dating lives of women in

London. And here she is: in a leather jacket with a faux fur collar and chunky boots, and hugging Iris like she's some long-lost sister. She settles down on a bar stool and is handed a tall glass of prosecco by Iris's helper who is also wielding a clipboard.

Iris strides into the middle of the crowd again with the mic. 'Hi everyone! I hope you're enjoying your drinks and meeting new people. Now, we have a really special guest here tonight. Please don't overwhelm her, I know you won't!' Iris glances over and gives Jemima a reassuring smile. 'Up you come, Jemima! You can intro yourself – as if you need to!'

Jemima shrugs her jacket off; underneath she is wearing a top that glitters like a Seventies disco ball. Her boobs are suspiciously high up and unmoving. Her shiny top reflects sparkling shards of light all around the room.

'Hello. I'm Jemima. I'm a TV actress and I've had the pleasure of working with HBO on a few different sitcoms, some of which you might have watched. They were the best few decades of my career, actually – the absolute time of my life. I don't do public speaking by the way, so bear with me! I hardly ever do interviews; I just don't like the nosiness. The press, the paparazzi – they are all intrusive idiots as far as I'm concerned. Anyway, I'm here because I care deeply about this community. This amazing safe space that Iris and her team have created. Thank you, Iris. Let me tell you a bit about my story.'

Jemima clears her throat. Every woman in the room is totally captivated, hanging onto every word. I grab my notepad and a pen from my bag. A famous actress is sitting right in front of us – I think of how much Gill would love this scoop.

'I'm sure there's loads of you, especially you young women in the room, who just know, you *know*, you don't want kids. That's the young woman I was, too. I was snapped up by the film and TV industry at a relatively young age, I studied in the UK at an acting school and got my big break in theatre before auditioning for *Six Women*. I became very famous, very quickly. I had the best time, made the best memories. But at one point I also blamed that show for what it robbed me of too. I'd accidentally left it so late – putting the effort in to try and start a family. But then I thought to myself, I have twenty-hour days working on this sitcom. My mornings would start at 3 a.m., I'd nap in my trailer for a bit and then work through until 1 a.m. some nights. How would that work? How could I do that, and be a good mum too? Years later, I started letting dark thoughts slip through. Had I let some TV producers take away my chance to have kids? But no, the truth is, I clearly didn't want them enough. I could have made it work, or made the time, or worked less if I'd really had a desire to have children – just like I made time for everything else in my life that I wanted – but I didn't. I now mentor young actresses and I get to be maternal in a different way. I just want everyone in this room to remember to look deep inside and know sometimes we don't have to stifle ourselves with the pressure. We don't have to build up this huge unanswerable question in our heads: *Do I Want Kids?* It hangs over us, but why? Sometimes we can just roll with it, make smaller natural decisions as we go along and follow what makes us happy daily, and in doing so we will make the right decision for us in the end, without turning it into something so pressurized. Do you know what I mean?'

This is the first speech that has deeply resonated with me. Some of the others felt a little forced, or something just didn't quite add up. But Jemima's story felt so heartfelt and real. She hadn't chiselled the fact that she didn't want kids into stone; she came to it naturally, gradually. It was just something that made sense for her as she lived her life. Sometimes we don't 'know' for sure, and maybe we never will, but we just have to live each day in the way that feels most natural to us. I feel a weight lift off my shoulders.

Everyone in the room starts nodding and clapping. Bea puts her fingers in her mouth and blows a whistle. 'I like her,' she whispers to me. 'She's right – it's not as binary as two sides of a coin; we all just make decisions as we go along.'

'Yes exactly,' I say. Maybe we're having a breakthrough here; I feel another wave of relief that Bea seems to understand.

'Thank you, Jemima,' Iris says. 'On behalf of everyone here, I just want to thank you for coming along tonight and making so many of us feel seen and supported. Please can I ask that no one asks Jemima for a photo or autograph tonight.'

Well, that settles that then. I put my phone away. What's wrong with me? I never usually get starstruck like this.

'Right, next up, we have Laura, let's give her a huge clap please!'

Laura appears on stage and quickly ties her hair up in a high bun and pushes a pencil through it to hold it in place before speaking.

'Hello everyone! It's actually my birthday tomorrow – forty-four years old! All my life I've known I didn't want kids, but things bed in a little easier as you get older. 1) You know yourself better! And 2) People don't ask you as much! Once you reach a certain age as a woman, it seems like society just kind of forgets about you anyway. Where are the over-forties and -fifties on billboards, or on the covers of magazines? We're kind of invisible, apparently. At least we stop getting nudged. I fucking hated my thirties, there was so much pressure! But I guess I should also say this: I am the CEO of a corporate child-free support network, a network I founded in my early twenties as an adamant child-free woman. And, well . . . I'm expecting.' She places both her hands on her belly, looking a little sheepish but proud.

The room is silent. Iris looks around and I sense she's going into crisis-management mode. Everyone's mouths are hanging open. I look over at Bea and Colin and shrug. Someone drops a glass. Smash. The silence continues; time seems to stop still. Iris goes up and gently edges Laura off the stage, while the people in the crowd whisper amongst themselves. Laura looks as though she's in a world of her own, stroking her belly.

Then one woman shouts: '*But think of the environment, Laura,*' and tuts loudly.

* * *

Colin, Bea and I share an Uber home at around 10.30 p.m., gossiping in the back. So much drama in one evening! I get my Dictaphone out:

'Olive checking in, recording part one of notes from Child Free By Choice evening. Ask Bea and Colin thoughts, will add to part two later. Do research on women who spoke tonight, see if there's anything on Google. Write down bullet-point themes. Freedom. Money. Judgement. Work. Environment. Emotion. What felt weird about the club? What felt empowering? Where do I stand now? Pitch profile of Jemima separately to Gill. Follow up with Iris tomorrow.'

Colin smirks at me, he mocks me when I do my Dictaphone voice. Then, Bea's phone goes off loudly – it's Isla calling. The radio isn't on in the Uber and the roads are quiet, so we can all hear the audio coming out of Bea's phone as clearly as if Isla was sitting here next to us.

'You all right, lovely?' Bea asks, warmly.

'Yes I'm OK – just really needing to talk to someone. Are you free now for a quick natter?'

'Of course, darling. Just been out with Olive and her colleague Colin.'

'Cool – where did you go?'

'Oh, just a club thing.'

'What kind of club?'

'Well, it was for Ol's work, for research – we were keeping her company.'

'Sounds interesting, what was it about?'

'Well.' Bea pauses. 'It was a club night for child-free women.'

'Right,' Isla replies, curtly.

I lean forward and glare at Bea who raises her shoulders in a I-couldn't-help-it-what-was-I-supposed-to-do kind of way.

'It was interesting,' Bea glances over at me, showing her gritted teeth.

'But why did you go?' Isla sounds shocked and upset.

'I just said, love, to keep Ol company. She was a bit nervous.'

'Bit weird, Bea.'

'Why?'

'You pretended to be childless to get in?' Isla says, sounding appalled.

'It's child-free actually,' Bea says.

'I . . . Sorry. I just . . . it's a strange move, and I could really use some support at the moment, myself.' Her voice wobbles a bit.

'I'm sorry, I didn't mean to upset you. I know I was meant to call you yesterday, I got distracted making a bumble-bee costume for Amelia for that thing at Rainbows and my day went out of the window.' Bea slaps her head.

'No, it's OK. I suppose I just want my old self back. Is Amelia OK?'

'She's fine, love. At home with Jeremy, on the mend. How are you, Isla? What's going on?'

'I'm . . . it's just . . . I can't afford another round of IVF. My uncle has said no to giving me more money, think he's embroiled in some legal fees with his ex-wife or something. He's cutting me off, basically. And I feel like a total monster because I need the money and I am so jealous of Cec and Oscar. I can barely stomach the photos.'

'Oh Isla. It's totally understandable that you're feeling low.'

'I know I'm being sensitive. I just feel a bit lonely and left out.'

'I'm sorry, tonight was just a silly thing. No one was taking it seriously; it was just a random thing for an article Ol's working on.'

'It's OK,' Isla's voice is really shaking; it's obvious she's about to cry.

Colin and I look at each other. Just a silly thing? Just a laugh? I hadn't realized my life choices were so ridiculous to Bea.

'I am sorry, Isla, I hope you feel a bit better tomorrow,' says Bea.

'Don't worry, I'll call back another time.'

'OK, I love you. Have a good rest tonight. I'll call you first thing tomorrow,' Bea says gently.

Bea looks over at Colin and me, and mouths 'sorry' as she hangs up.

I can't hold back, anger is coursing through me. 'Tonight wasn't some joke thing, Bea.' I feel my voice cracking.

'I know, I know, Ol, I just said that to Isla to make things easier. I know it's not.'

'You must have thought it, a bit?'

'No! I was just trying to make Isla feel better. And you were here for a work thing, right? I was just giving Isla the facts.'

'Why are you clinging on to that? I've told you, Bea. This was *more* than a work thing for me.'

'OK, Ol, I'm sorry. Look, if I'm totally honest, I guess I always just presumed you would settle down one day. Maybe that's wrong or naïve of me. I suppose on some level I just always imagined us raising kids together, doing the same stuff like we always have, you know? I don't want you to rule anything out.'

'Bea, if I wanted to settle down, I'd still be with Jacob. No one is understanding my pain at the moment – no one!'

'But look at it from a different angle: what if Jacob wasn't the right guy?'

'He was, Bea, he was the perfect guy!' I break down in tears. 'It's not that hard to believe, is it? That I don't want a family? I feel like you literally don't know me at all.'

'Ol, please, don't do this. We need to support each other,' Bea says, desperately. 'I promise I'm hearing you.'

'Come on Olive,' Colin says, quietly.

'Can you pull over please?' I ask the driver.

'Really, now, love?' he says, surprised.

'Yes, now. Please.'

'Ol, don't do that,' Colin pleads.

The CFBC was not a silly thing at all. Far from it. The driver pulls over to the side of the road on Shoreditch High Street, I grab my bag and slam the door, hard. I know I'm drunk. Maybe I'm being dramatic. But I can't stop myself.

'You childless people, you have no idea! What's the biggest drama you have to put up with?'

Michael McIntyre, 2013, *Live at the Apollo*

26

My phone rings loudly. Phone calls make me anxious; voice-mails even more so. No one actually calls any more and, if they do, something's most likely up. So it's no surprise that I don't leap for joy when Bea's name pops up on my screen. I'm still annoyed with her. I pick up with a 'Hello' which has the perfect amount of bluntness and maturity. I think.

All I can hear is hysterical shouting and screaming in the background. I can barely hear Bea. I recognize Cecily's voice. Why is she screaming? Bea speaks quickly, panting in between sentences.

'Oscar is locked inside the house.'

'*What?*'

'Cec accidentally shut the door and it locked automatically. With the baby inside.'

'Fuuuuuck . . .'

'Yeah, can you come here and support? She's really panicking.'

'Yes, yes I'm coming now.' I hang up. Whatever's happening between me and Bea, it sounds like Cec needs me more.

Luckily, Bea had been doing a recce for work, eyeing up a warehouse space for a new exhibition that happened to be close to Cec's house in London. Thank god she's there. I run to the Tube, putting my coat on as I jog; my 'Baby on Board' badge is still stuck onto my top coat pocket.

'All you lot are too busy staring at your phones to notice this *pregnant woman*!' A very old and wrinkled lady is pointing her walking stick aggressively at a row of men in suits on the Tube. 'You ought to be ashamed.'

'So sorry, so sorry,' one of the huge manspreading men splutters, scrambling to his feet. I turn bright red and realize they are all making a fuss over me.

'And while you're at it, you can move for me too. I'm eighty fucking seven!'

The men look shocked and most of them move out of the way at the speed of light.

The old woman takes a seat. 'Much more comfortable sitting down, isn't it dear?' she says to me, smiling sweetly now.

When I finally arrive, sweating lightly after running from the station, I see Cec sitting on the ground in her front garden, howling.

'My baby is inside. Somebody get him out, please!'

Cec and I still haven't properly resolved anything since the bust-up at the baby shower, but when big shit hits the fan, everything else fades in comparison. We have bigger fish to fry.

Bea is on the phone pacing and it looks like a tall, hench guy with stubble has decided to take control. He has lots of tattoos and he's wearing a navy hoody with a skull and crossbones graphic on the back.

'Everyone calm down. I am going to climb to the top of

your garage and I can easily get into your top window from there. I might have to break it,' Skull Guy says.

'Break anything, just get my baby *out!*' Cec cries, her hands resting on her forehead.

'Don't worry,' Skull Guy says, flexing his muscles. 'Where is Oscar exactly?'

'He's in his car seat, just by the front door. Please don't scare him,' Cec sobs.

'Who is that guy?' I ask Bea, pointing at Skull Guy.

'He's Cec's neighbour apparently; he ran over when he heard all the commotion.'

As we talk, Skull Guy strips out of his jeans and stands in just his boxers – the heavy jean material would only hold him back, apparently; he needs to be able to 'manoeuvre'. He then runs and jumps onto a ledge on the side of Cec's house, stands on the garage roof, jumps over onto the top of the conservatory and smashes open a window on the middle floor with a hammer. Bloody hell.

Cec starts hyperventilating again.

Skull Guy climbs in through the broken window and nearly cuts himself on the shards of glass. We watch, squirming. He throws the hammer off the garage roof and it flies through the air, nearly hitting Bea.

'*Jesus!*' she shouts.

Then we all cheer because Skull Guy is finally inside and has given us the thumbs-up. He emerges a few minutes later at the front door holding Oscar, who actually seems fine, not even a tear in sight.

I feel physically sick. Cec is now holding Oscar in her

303

arms and is shaking from head to foot. That was the worst half hour that we have ever witnessed.

Cecily's husband Chris arrives soon afterwards; we hear his red sports car pulling up. I've never been a fan of his at the best of times. Perhaps it's unfair to judge your best friend's partner, and maybe it's rare to completely understand what your friend sees in them – after all, you're not the one shagging them. Perhaps Chris was cracking in the sack. (I highly doubted that, though.) He was a top-dog lawyer in the City, and perhaps he could be accused of being a little too performative when it came to his 'wokeness', if you know what I mean. He always pulls out the 'I'm a male feminist' card, a modern-day liberal Lothario, talking about how women are equal and quoting facts about the gender pay gap over a canapé at a dinner party. Yet the way he treats Cecily is often questionable – and this time he completely loses it and starts going mad. Sure, he's a dick, but we'd never seen anything like this before.

'You locked our son inside the house? How the hell could you do that? You stupid woman! What's next – leaving him on the side of the road while you drive off?' Chris bellows in Cecily's direction.

'Chris, please, let's just focus on the fact that everything is OK now rather than apportioning blame,' Bea bellows back, standing in front of Cecily in her usual protective manner. Cec doesn't say anything, she just stands there, looking shell-shocked, expressionless, and clutching Oscar tightly in her arms.

'Everything is *not* OK, Bea,' Chris growls.

He rolls up the sleeves of his shirt, wipes his forehead and starts pacing.

'I cannot *believe* you could be so stupid,' he barks, sort of to himself this time as he walks around in a circle.

'Everything is under control now, mate,' Skull Guy cuts in.

'And who the fuck are you?' Chris replies, looking Skull Guy up and down. It probably doesn't help that he isn't wearing any jeans.

'Chris. This kind man – our neighbour – was across the street. He just *saved* your son. You should be thanking him, not shouting at him,' Bea says.

'It's no bother, honestly,' Skull Guy says.

'Chris, please.' Cec gives Chris a sharp look and it seems to bring him to his senses.

'OK, fine, sorry mate. You can leave now, though, we're all OK now. Thanks everyone.' Chris looks around the garden and waves everyone off. About ten people have gathered just to have a look because it turns out most people are nosy. But now the commotion is over. 'Nothing to see here, all right! You can go now!' Chris shouts, shooing everyone away.

'I feel like the worst mum in the whole world, you're right, I am a total failure. A crap mum,' Cec says, closing her eyes and squeezing tears out.

This seems to sap most of the anger out of Chris. His shoulders drop, his face softens. 'Oh Cec, no you're not.'

'I am, Chris, you just said I was. You're right! I fucked up!'

'No, no. You are the rock of this family, Cec. I'm sorry, we all just freaked out.'

'I don't even know who I am anymore, I can't do anything

right.' She starts shaking her head, tears sliding down her face. It's heartbreaking.

'I'm sorry,' Chris tells her. 'I need to be there for you more.'

'I'm so sorry for what happened today. I am an idiot.'

'No, I'm a fucking idiot. I'm sorry.' Chris puts his arm around Cec. She blows her nose on her sleeve.

'Ugh, what a horrible day,' Cec says through a bunged-up nose.

Bea and I suddenly realize we are ear-wigging and should probably head off.

'Babe, I'm going to go now. I'm glad everything is OK,' Bea says. 'Please, please don't beat yourself up about this.' She puts a gentle hand on Cec's shoulder.

'Same, message us later OK? Are you going to be all right?' I ask.

'I'll be fine, girls. Thank you, for always being there.' We hug Cecily and give Chris a nod.

I make to move away with Bea, but then slow my steps. I need to stick around and talk to Cecily. I don't want to leave her like this.

'Chris,' I say, diplomatically, 'why don't you take Oscar inside and I'll take Cec for a quick coffee, just to take her mind off things and chill for a sec?'

'Sure.' Chris lifts Oscar out of Cec's arms. I feel quite impressed with myself for taking the reins. 'See you later, Cec.' He kisses her on the lips, locks his car with his key blipper and walks into the house, chatting nonsense to Oscar.

Cec's shoulders drop and, despite her lingering tears, she

looks happy with my suggestion. 'Thank you,' she mouths at me.

We pop into a coffee shop on the corner near her house; it's falling apart a bit, the walls have paint flaking off and there's a funny smell coming from the kitchen, but it's not the time to be picky. There are loads of posh cafés in this area, but Cec needs something simple. We just need a hot drink and a moment to breathe.

I buy Cec a latte and a cup of hot tomato soup and a mint tea for me. I can tell she's really spaced out because she's not mentioned what a dive the place is. There's an old guy behind her, plugging five different gadgets into the plug sockets and complaining about the tap water.

'I'm sorry you're going through a hard time, Cec . . . Oh look at you, you're shaking a bit – are you cold?' I ask, pouring her some water.

'I'm OK,' she says, pulling her cardigan over her shoulders. 'Just the world's shittest day.'

'Cec, this stuff happens, I bet everyone has done it, just no one really talks about it. Honestly. Don't beat yourself up, you are doing brilliantly,' I say.

'Ol, I just can't stop crying. Literally on the verge of tears the minute I go to bed and the minute I wake up.'

'Oh babe. Have you tried taking anything?' I say, not knowing at all what the 'right' thing to say is.

'No, but you're not the first to ask, or suggest that I could do with some help. I'm going to see the GP next week; it's just been impossible to find the time – I never have a minute to myself.' She looks down at her chipped nails and rubs one of her tired eyes. 'Things between me and Chris are bad. I think he expected me to be this Superwoman Perfect Mum who could just adapt her entire life overnight and Do It All but . . . I can't.'

'Of course you can't. It is not fair of Chris to expect that.' I could go further and really bad-mouth Chris, but I hold my tongue. They are still married, after all.

'I can't breastfeed either. Too sore. But Chris doesn't really get why that's bothering me. Everything is a fucking mess and I can't see a way out.'

'Cec, it will get easier. It has to,' I say, holding both of her hands over the table.

'It has to,' she repeats, staring into space.

When we leave the coffee shop, I walk Cec back to her front door. I hug her goodbye and tell her to call me whenever she needs to. I look her in the eyes and make her promise to call me if she needs a babysitter or someone to come and watch Oscar while she sleeps. I book an Uber home. In the back of the car, I stare out of the window as passing trees, parks and tall buildings whoosh past. Poor Cec – I feel so worried for her right now. Any element of self-care has gone out of the window and she's clearly struggling badly, only beginning to open up to her friends. I feel helpless and suddenly really, really guilty about the horrible fallout at the baby shower.

An image of Cec kneeling on the grass and looking desperately at her front door comes back to me; tears running down her face as her baby waited on the other side. I never want to experience that level of fear for myself . . . I remember someone at work highlighting the dangers of sleep deprivation after birth. She said she was so exhausted that she left her baby in a car once. She said the lack of sleep had turned her properly mad and she had actually forgotten she even had a baby for a whole hour. Luckily a passing neighbour heard the baby cry and alerted her to it. She said it was absolutely horrific and gave her major anxiety attacks for years afterwards. How can your own brain betray you in such a way and make you forget such a vital detail about your life? Like, a very, *very* key detail.

I don't think I could put my heart up for risk like that. If you have children, you have no idea what might happen to them. You have no idea who they will grow up to be, you have no idea if they will survive a long life, you have no idea how your relationship will pan out. All of these things frighten me to the core. People who say, 'Oh but who will look after you when you're old?' always assume that you'd be friends with your kids later in life, and that they would live in the same country as you. But, actually, they might avoid you like the plague or badly fall out with you. It's happened to me with my dad. He moved away, left my mum. My relationship with my dad is nonexistent, and I don't think having a baby is a one-way ticket to having forever happiness or a new best friend. Children also move away, they might fall in love with someone on the other side of the world, reducing your relationship to an inconveniently timed Skype call. The idea of having a child frightens me for so many reasons, so many more than the horrors of childbirth itself. Perhaps I'm scared of having that much love. Too much love, to potentially lose.

27

2018

'Are you telling me that you've strung me along for all these years?' Jacob was marching up and down the living room, pulling at his hair. I'd never seen him look so stressed. Not even after that time he accidentally transferred £1,000 to the wrong account for his friend's stag do.

'I haven't strung you along Jacob. I just . . . I didn't really know,' I said, defensively. *I didn't want to face it*, I think.

'Olive,' he said, breathing heavily now. 'You must have known. You must have thought at some point, during the nine years we've been together, that you didn't want a family.'

'I didn't think about it that much! It wasn't front of mind! We got together when we were twenty-four, I didn't *need* to think about it.'

'You must have had an inkling that we would get to this point, and you never said anything to me. Ever.'

'Either one of us could have changed our minds over the

last few years. How was I to know that you so desperately wanted this?'

'I think when you have an idea that you probably don't want kids, it's something you should tell your partner, like, at the earliest opportunity.'

'I knew we would cross that bridge when we came to it.'

'*I hate that phrase, crossing the stupid bridge.*'

'Jacob, stop shouting.'

'I'm not shouting,' he said, forcibly lowering his voice.

'And please stop pinning all the blame on me.'

'I'm not. I just don't know what to say.' He looked increasingly strained as he spoke, his face bleached of colour.

'There's nothing to say. We clearly want different things,' I said, coldly.

'Olive, I need a *plan*. Life is about having a plan.'

'Well I don't need a plan, J.'

'Is there any way we can compromise on this?'

'How? I feel like you're putting me in a corner.'

'And you're putting me in a corner too,' Jacob whispered. I'd never seen him so frustrated. We were both trapped. Flies stuck in a sticky web.

'Either one of us makes a huge sacrifice, or . . .'

We both knew what the 'or' was, but neither one of us had the guts to say it out loud. That would make it real. We didn't want it to be real, neither of us. The 'or' was a horrible, horrible thought. 'Or' meant the end.

'Olive. You're the love of my life. For nearly *ten* years. Please, I can't bear this.'

I burst into tears.

I hugged him close to me.

I got mascara all over his white shirt.

We both shook silently in each other's arms.

We had always compromised and negotiated, and we had always solved things. Got to the bottom of a problem, together. We knew how to sort things out. We were good at it. But this wasn't a situation where we could meet halfway. In short: we were fucked.

In the middle of the night, around 4.30 a.m., I got up and went into the bathroom and sat down on the bath mat next to the tub. I didn't know what to do, so I went online and posted on an anonymous forum: 'I don't want kids. My boyfriend does. Any advice?'

The replies came in thick and fast:

Answer 1: Good job you're not married. You should tell him before you say 'I do'. Otherwise that is very unfair.

Answer 2: Set him free. Leave him.

Answer 3: Wow you need to separate immediately. You're wasting his time babe.

Answer 4: Tell him the whole truth and nothing but the truth so help you God.

Answer 5: You must let him go so he can be a father asap.

Answer 6: Maybe you could adopt a puppy instead.

I voluntarily hit my head on the side of the bath. I can still remember the hollow thudding sound it made.

'You OK in there, Olive?' Jacob asked through the locked bathroom door.

'No,' I replied. 'I'm not.'

Part Three

'I don't know how I'll feel about it when I'm eighty and I don't have any children and grandchildren. I don't know if that will make me happy, or sad.'

Donna, 49

Part Three

28

2019

It's Friday evening and I spend an hour at hot yoga to calm down from the week and sweat it all out. I have to admit that I love having the time and freedom to do anything I want to, whenever I want. Doing yoga in a hot room, practically a sauna, with strangers (including an old man in his Speedos) isn't something I thought I would enjoy – but I really do. The teacher is telling me to let go of all my pointless thoughts, to let them swim away like little fish. But I'm struggling to concentrate on 'being zen' with all the drama that is going on with my friends. I leave the class early and a few of the keenos give me a dirty look for disturbing their downward dog. Just as I'm arriving home from yoga, sweaty and pleasantly sleepy, I put my keys in the lock and my phone beeps with a message. It's Dorothy Gray.

SORRY TO TEXT YOU OLIVE BIT OF AN ACCIDENT CAN
YOU CALL

Christ. Poor Dorothy! Sounds serious. I was looking forward to putting on my new silk pyjamas and watching Netflix, but my heart's hammering at the thought of Dorothy in trouble. When I call her she doesn't pick up. Hmm. I notice her lights are still on, as usual. I ring again, but nothing. So I go and knock on her front door. I knock louder and louder. Dorothy!? I can hear someone shuffling to the door, dragging their slippers along. She eventually opens it.

'Oh Olive, thank god,' Dorothy says. She has a blood-stained tea towel around her hand. Something is really bleeding a lot. The tea towel is practically completely red.

'Oh my god, what's happened?' I feel sick at the sight of it.

'I was cutting up an apple and my hand slipped . . .'

'Can I see?' I peel back the tea towel and all I see is a very red, bloody and messy hand. I suddenly feel light-headed. I am not good with blood. I'm worried she might have cut a vein or something. Her hands are so pale and thin. 'Oh Dorothy! We should take you to A&E, right now. I'll book us a cab.'

'Really? OK dear. I'm sorry to text. When I first did it, there really was a lot of blood . . .'

I am starting to feel very woozy. 'Come on, do you want to put some proper shoes on while I sort the taxi? Keep the tea towel on and keep pressing down on it.'

I hate the fact that Dorothy lives on her own. I mean, she might like it. But the fact that I'm the first person she contacted makes me wonder if she has any family or if anyone ever calls her. I shudder, as though a cold wind has suddenly blown over me. Maybe that could be me one day – living all alone? It can be fun now, but what about in fifty years' time?

The cab pulls up outside and it's a young woman driver. I wonder how that must be for her – on the nights when she picks up drunken louts from East London pubs and clubs. She seems relieved to see me and Dorothy. An odd, unintimidating pair.

'Hi. The closest A&E please. Think the nearest one is Homerton,' I say to the driver.

'No problem,' she replies.

Luckily she doesn't pick up on the likely chance we might get blood on her car.

'Do you have any family, Dorothy?' I ask.

'My late husband Benjamin and I, we have a son called Max.'

'Oh lovely – do you see much of him?'

'Sadly not, dear. He lives in Australia.'

'Does he not come back and visit?'

'Afraid not. I haven't seen Max in twenty years.'

'Really?'

'It used to keep me up at night, but now I realize he's someone who needed to go off and do his own thing. He never felt close to us, even though we felt close to him.' Dorothy's voice suddenly sounds hoarse and dry. 'He never felt the need to keep in touch.'

My eyes prickle with tears. Maybe I'm due my period soon.

'I'm so sorry, Dorothy.'

'It's OK. I do miss him. But it was a long time ago, Olive. He is in my photo albums at least. Although it does hurt to look at them,' she adds, looking out of the window of the cab.

She pauses. 'My husband and I, we had such a wonderful life together. Boy, did we travel and see things.'

'That's wonderful.'

'And you know: so many friends of mine, in the same state I am in, they don't see their kids either. It's very sad. Their children have either moved away and aren't really close any more, or sometimes they're just emotionally distant. You know, people often believe that having children means unconditional love guaranteed, and someone to care for you as you get older. It's just not the case.'

'Well, I'm just glad you texted me,' I say, trying not to well up again.

'We're all human beings aren't we. I knew you'd help if I asked.'

'Of course.'

I like helping Dorothy and being available for her. I am really warming to her. I feel myself softening, slowly letting people back in.

I think I'll go so far as to say she is my friend.

I have decided to try and 'meet new people'. Not in a dramatic way, just so I can leave the girls to it for a little while. Give them some room to breathe. It's clichéd, maybe, but I have signed myself up for a 'class' in a couple of days' time. I had a look on Groupon and good deals for improv classes kept resurfacing. Sounds like something failed actors do on weekends, but learning to make things up on the spot with a bunch of new people could be fun. So much has been going on lately, but I finally feel like I'm coming out of the other side and willing to try new things. It's time to properly move on, and maybe that means getting out of my comfort zone. I also look up 'the benefits' online and it says it's good for mental health, relieves anxiety, boosts creativity and encourages you to 'let go'. That's what my reflexologist told me once: she could feel a sign somewhere in my feet that I struggle to let go, insinuating that I have bowel problems: 'You need to let go, you know, when you go the toilet, and in life.' What a beautiful motivational quote that is! On paper, improv is my worst nightmare, because I often find comedians quite depressingly desperate. But I'm in need of a Cheryl Strayed in *Wild* moment, minus the 2,000-mile hike, obviously. Maybe this will be mine.

My buzzer rings and it's Isla, waiting on my doorstep with a big leather overnight bag and a squishy travel pillow.

'What's up?' I ask as I let her into the flat, taking her coat and guiding her to the sofa. Her face looks puffy and her eyes sore from crying.

'Mike and I have had a massive bust-up. This horrible pressure to get pregnant is really getting to us, clearly. We aren't in a good place.'

'I'm so sorry.' I give her a squeeze. She feels smaller than usual.

I know she was annoyed with me after the CFBC night and that phone call with Bea and – although she is here, needing me – I can feel a simmering tension still there. An invisible barrier between us. But her arriving here speaks volumes about our friendship. At the end of the day, she knows I will always give her a roof if she ever needs it, even if things feel far from resolved.

'Our lives have turned into apps and spreadsheets and calendars and meticulous planning and we just aren't getting on at the moment,' she continues.

'Does he know you're here?'

'Yeah, I didn't storm out or anything. Can I stay?'

'Of course, stay as long as you need to. I'll get the sofa bed out.'

After a few nights of Isla staying, though, she is starting to drive me up the wall. She's cooked for me every night, which is nice, but she's taking over my space. I can't boot her out, but this has made me realize how much I like living alone now. Funny how you can get used to things when they are forced upon you.

'I'm off out tonight,' I say to Isla as I grab my keys from the hallway table.

'Oh cool – a date?'

Why do people in couples always assume that newly single people are constantly dating?

'Nah, not ready for that kind of shit yet. I'm doing an improv class.'

'Really! You're so great, Ol, trying new things. Can't wait to hear how that goes,' Isla says from the sofa, swinging around the remote control.

'Yeah, we'll see! Have a nice evening.'

'Thanks again for having me, Ol,' Isla says sweetly.

'No problemo!'

The improv class is above a pub called The Chesterfield in Islington. I'd been there before with Zeta for a pint. It's one of those recently revamped hipster pubs with pastel-coloured walls that serves pretentious craft beers with long names. Accidentally Wes Anderson. Anyway, perhaps this class is exactly what I need. I can disappear into being someone else and wear zero make-up and baggy clothes whilst doing it.

I walk into The Chesterfield and a man called Areeq with a long, very dark beard and a turban greets me. He immediately makes me feel welcome, and ticks my name off a list. He tells me to go up the stairs to the top floor. I make my way up them, feeling as though they could crumble beneath me at any moment. What am I doing? Going deeper into a darkened basement? Am I about to get murdered by wannabe comedians? I walk in and gasp.

A woman with grey curly hair turns around. I cannot believe who is in there, in the centre of the room. It's – Iris. I almost leap onto her.

'*Iris!*' I kiss her on the cheek.

'Darling! We meet again.' She's wearing a different coloured kaftan this time – with pink and orange swirls. She looks fantastic. I think it's fake tan, or she's been away somewhere hot in the time that has passed between now and the CFBC night.

'I didn't know you did improv?'

'Yes, I'm teaching the class! Been a qualified improv

teacher for years; I discovered it when I was finding healing practices. Did you know that improv classes are great for helping with anxiety?'

'Good to know,' I laugh nervously.

'I had a break from it but now I'm back. I'm having a whale of a time rediscovering lost parts of myself through different artistic mediums. Improv, open-mic nights, singing, dancing! I'm going to discover poetry-writing classes next. Looks like you're doing the same, it's no accident that we meet again! Are you rediscovering yourself?'

'Rediscovering myself?'

'Well yes, are you?'

'I suppose. I recently went through a bad break-up with someone.'

'Ah. I see. Well, good for you. Most people would be moping around, but here you are! Ready to explore and meet new people and show yourself to the world, you should be proud of yourself. For refusing to let life trample all over you.' I smile. She doesn't know that I've literally been moping around the house for weeks on end, crying in the bath.

'Thanks Iris. I'm trying.'

Iris steps back, puts her hand on her heart and clears her throat:

'The time will come / when, with elation / you will greet yourself arriving / at your own door, in your own mirror / and each will smile at the other's welcome.'

I stare at her, a little baffled.

'It's "Love After Love" by Derek Walcott. Beautiful piece. A reminder to *feast* on one's own life. Let go of your guilt,

Ol. Women are made to feel guilty for everything. The food we eat, the bodies we have, the relationships that don't work out. We must accept the challenge and refuse to take on this guilt.' She is looking me dead in the eyes.

'Yes, I suppose you're right,' I say, slightly confused, but feeling motivated. 'I'm a newbie to all this,' I add.

'Darling, you will be *great!*' Iris starts twirling around the room. 'Just like you were at the CFBC event.' I glance around the room wondering if anyone heard. It still feels like a swearword to announce that I am a member of the CFBC. But I bet no one here knows what it is anyway.

I find my nerves starting to fade, mainly because I don't know anyone here. Being surrounded by strangers feels weirdly relaxing. 'Right!' Iris claps her hands above her head. 'Over here! Please, come here and stand in a circle. Thank you! That's right.' We all shuffle awkwardly around her. There are about twelve of us. A tall man wearing a checked shirt; a brother and sister (I think twins); a woman with blue hair and several others.

'Right, *hello!*' Iris rubs her hands together like she's rubbing in moisturizer. 'For those of you who don't know me, I'm Iris. I've been leading improv classes for years and it's all about getting back to your childlike self. We will be learning about the acting craft and comedic timings, but mostly everything will be unplanned or unscripted; created spontaneously by you guys, the performers. It is about un-learning all the bullshit in the world that tries to squash us down and force us to become smaller. Kids are joyful! Kids don't get creative blocks, they just pick up the crayons and draw! We must reconnect with our younger selves. When we grow up to be adults, we don't have *fun* any more. We are so self-conscious! So embarrassed! So British! In these classes, you will leave your self-consciousness at the door. I want you all to take a piece of paper from this hat.' Iris walks around with an upside-down straw hat. 'That's it, take one and pass the hat on. Here are some pens. I want you all to write down the one thing you hate about yourself, or are self-conscious about, and then we are going to burn them.'

We all look around at each other nervously.

'It'll be hard to choose just one thing,' I say, and most people laugh under their breath.

'Same,' says Checked-Shirt Guy.

I realize that something about him looks really familiar.

I write down: 'Being jealous of my friends.'

I fold the piece of paper into a tiny triangle.

Iris kneels down to burn all the bits of paper in a little copper incense-burner on the floor, and all the tiny bits of paper go up in flames.

'There is no need for us to read them out. The important thing is that you each know what you wrote down.'

Then Iris puts everyone in pairs and I'm joined up with the tall guy in the checked shirt, who introduces himself as Marcus. He looks around mid-forties and has salt-and-pepper hair. He puts his hands in his jeans pockets and stands next to me.

'I know this might be a bit weird, but . . . you don't remember me, do you?' says Marcus.

'Uh, no? Oh god, how do I know you?'

'You're friends with Cecily, right?'

'Yes . . .'

'I was at her baby shower. My mate Tom works with her and I was his plus-one for moral support. You were outside and—'

'Oh shit,' I laugh. My mind flashes back to the drunken haze. How embarrassing. I was outside with my vape, shoeless, slurring, waiting for a cab. 'Sorry, god knows what I said to you,' I say, cringing in front of him.

'You were fine,' he laughs, kindly. Crow's-feet appear around his eyes when he smiles.

'Now, guys! In your pairs, I want you to link arms. That's it, get quite close to each other please. Get cosy!' Iris shouts across the room.

We all do as we are told. We are scared not to, as Iris's enthusiasm is enough to knock you over. The room suddenly feels quite hot.

'Now, we are going to be doing another ice-breaker called "Conjoined Twins". I want you all to pretend you are twins joined from the waist up. You must move together and even speak together in unison if anyone speaks to you.'

Oh my god. I am dying. I link arms with Marcus and we both burst out laughing.

The good news is that absolutely nothing could be worse than having to pretend to be a conjoined twin with a hot man when your armpits are really sweaty on a day when you have forgotten to wear deodorant. The bad news is that Iris wants us all to go to the bar downstairs afterwards, so I can't go home and scream into a pillow with embarrassment. I have to ride it all out. A group of around seven of us go for a drink. We all order pints and it feels really good to have bonded with a group of new people: people who don't know the real me; people with whom I've only had a stupid laugh; new people who aren't sharing their emotional baggage.

Iris comes back with a tray of beers and plonks herself down next to me, her earrings jangling.

'That was fun. Cheers! To Iris, and everyone who made it until the end!' Marcus holds his drink up in the air and we all clink in unison.

'I'm still dying inside, honestly. This has put me so far out of my comfort zone,' I reply.

'You were great.'

'Thanks.'

There is an awkward silence, and even though we have been 'breaking the ice' all afternoon doing cringe exercises, sitting here exchanging small talk suddenly feels rather personal.

'How did you end up here then? Doing this class?' I ask.

'Oh, my kids bought it for me as a birthday present. I think it was a sort of joke present, but I've actually really enjoyed it.'

I surprise myself by feeling a bit gutted to hear about his kids. Having any sort of romantic feeling for a guy right now could not be further from my mind. Of course he's married, with kids. I obviously read too much into it – I don't know what counts as 'flirting' these days anyway. So out of practice.

'You?' Marcus takes a sip.

'Oh, you know, escaping my life by trying to learn how to become someone else for a bit,' I say, also taking a sip of beer. 'One big cliché.'

'Of course. An improv course reeks of a midlife crisis,' Marcus replies. 'Sorry, quarter-life crisis for you.'

'And, midlife crisis – for you?'

'Well. Do you want the long story, or short story?' he replies.

'Hmm, what about a medium-length story?'

'OK. Well . . .' He pauses. 'I am . . . living the second chapter of my life, I suppose. I am . . . enjoying myself. Part one feels over.'

'I like the sound of that,' I reply.

'My wife died, ten years ago now. Ten years ago tomorrow, actually. . . But, you know, I'm finally feeling like my old self again. The loss will always be there, of course, but I've finally come out the other side.' We both smile gently at each other. I do like a man who can open up unprompted. A rare breed.

'I think that deserves a little cheers. To coming out the other side, I mean.'

'Yes, it does.' We clink our glasses.

'I'm so sorry,' I add.

'Long time ago now.' He breathes in, pushing his chest up and out and coughs away his emotion.

'And your kids? How old are they?' I ask, changing the subject.

His face lights up again. 'I have two kids. Magical kids.

They are fifteen and seventeen now. Very independent, strong young women. So, now, I am free! Sort of.' He laughs. 'Although I feel like a one-man taxi company. Weekends going all over the place dropping kids off, picking the kids up from parties. I enjoyed looking after them, but, oh my god I am so glad to have some time back for myself now. Rediscovery, as Iris calls it.'

'Do you think people judge you for saying that? That you kinda want your life back now?' I ask.

'Maybe. But I'm getting the impression you won't judge me.' Marcus laughs. We lock eyes and it feels awkward, intrusive, too deep almost.

I look away, a slight blush in my cheeks, and change the conversation. But I'm excited that someone – someone new – is making me feel like this.

When I get home, Isla is there stretched out on the sofa, watching a David Attenborough documentary. Something about penguins.

'All right?' I say, placing my keys on the table, slamming the door shut, feeling a little tired from the walk home.

'S'pose – still feeling a bit meh. Sorry I've eaten all your kettle chips.'

'Ha, that's OK, what's yours is mine. How you feeling today? Have you spoken to Mike yet?'

'Here and there. He's being very understanding and sweet. Says it's totally normal that I might need some space. I think he needs some too.'

'That's good.'

'I'm not annoying you by being here, am I?' Isla asks.

'No, it's OK. I do have some work I need to do tonight though.'

'That's fine! Shall we cook some dinner together, like the good old days? Ooh, we could cook a roast.'

'Ah, I'm sorry, I was going to order something and just do some work at my desk in my bedroom,' I say. It's true. I need to crack on with various unfinished assignments.

'Oh, OK. I just thought we might be able to spend some time together, maybe tomorrow instead?'

'Yeah maybe, I'll have to let you know.'

'Is something wrong, Olive?'

'No – not at all. I just . . . I suppose . . . I have a lot going on and I guess I've just got used to being a bit more independent, with you guys always being busy.'

'Right.' Isla folds her arms and crosses her legs.

'Look, I've been worried about you and I'll always be a sounding board, Isla. But I can't help feeling that you haven't properly spoken to me about the fact that I broke up with Jacob. No one has really.'

'Oh sorry, you just didn't really open up about it, you were getting on with things. I just assumed you were fine.'

'Isn't that the problem, though? Everyone assumes I'm bloody fine all the time. I'm really not. We were together for nine years, what makes you think I'd just be "fine"?' I say, exasperated.

'Sorry, Ol, I should have asked more questions. I assumed you were busy finding yourself with the child-free club stuff.'

'Maybe I am.'

'Well, it sounds like you're spending more time on work than seeing your friends.'

'That's not fair, Isla. You know my work and life blur. Plus, you guys never spend any proper time with me any more. You're always late, or tired, or distracted by other things.'

'Distracted? By what? My fertility issues? Or perhaps it's the immense amount of stress being put on my relationship? Wow, thanks Olive.'

'I don't mean it like that. And it's not a competition.'

'You think we are all self-obsessed, just admit it. The only self-obsessed one here is you,' Isla says with a piercing look. 'Time to grow up, Olive.'

'If that's how you feel, I think you should go home.'

'Yeah, I think I should too.'

Isla quickly gathers her bag from the sofa bed in the next room and I hear the door gently slam shut as I stand in the kitchen, boiling the kettle, tapping my fingers on the counter.

'I think society secretly envies women like me who live precisely the way they want to without buckling to outside pressures or expectations.'

Sarah, 43

29

2014

We had arrived at the airport super early, checked in bags, slowly made our way through security, and Isla was now pacing up and down the perfume aisle in Duty Free, getting more and more anxious.

'I just hate flying. Ugh, I should know better, I'm a bloody therapist,' she said, rubbing her arms and then rummaging in her bag. 'And I've forgotten my Rescue Remedy,' she sighed.

'Hey, you'll be fine, we're all sitting together and we can distract you,' I said. Every year we'd go away together as a foursome, somewhere hot and sunny, and every time Isla would have a meltdown in the airport because of her fear of flying; it was almost part of the tradition.

'Just think about the lovely sunshine we're about to have, Isla!' Bea said, wearing her big sunhat, testing out a new Gucci scent.

'And the fact that statistically you're more likely to

become President of the United States than die in a plane crash. Or something,' Cec added, picking at her nail polish. I give Isla's shoulder a reassuring squeeze.

Once we were on the flight, and inevitably hit some crazy turbulence, Isla yelped from underneath a scarf she had placed over her head.

'Here,' I said, taking Isla's wrists and spritzing some lavender spray to calm her nerves.

We touched down at Faro airport and hopped in a cab for a forty-five-minute drive to Lagos. Despite having our luggage in tow, we asked the driver to drop us off at the beach and we immediately plonked ourselves down on the sand, feeling its warmth between our toes and the sun on our SPF-covered faces.

'This is just what we need, isn't it?' Isla said, breathing in the sea air.

'God, seriously,' Cec said, stripping off her top and lying down in her bra.

'Can we promise we will always go on holiday together, like, every single year forever?' Isla said.

'Absolutely. Always. We've not missed one year so far,' I said, as Bea handed each of us a Calippo ice lolly that she'd bought from a man on the beach.

Later that night, Isla and I sat on the balcony of our hotel, gin and tonics in hand, looking out to a pink-purple sky. I loved these little moments with Isla; the two of us linking arms, feeling close, and reflecting on life. The very attentive barman kept coming out and bringing new drinks. It was happy hour, so we obliged.

It was late now and we could hear Bea and Cec splashing around in the pool below. They'd had a few different cocktail concoctions from the hotel bar, and were doing that thing of trying to 'whisper' but doing so very loudly. They had decided to skinny-dip, had thrown their wet bikinis up at us in celebration. Despite their efforts, the bikinis didn't quite land on our balcony, but on the neighbouring hotel's sloped roof. Isla and I were bent over laughing, already imagining them having to tiptoe back into the hotel fully naked.

A few drinks later, Isla suddenly started spinning out. 'I think . . . I've had one too many,' she said, trying to hold back the sick building in her throat.

'Oh dear,' I said. I knew full well how much of a light-weight Isla was. Drinking often brought out a vulnerability in her too. Oops, I should have gone easier on the drinks. I texted Bea and Cec to say I was taking Isla back to the room.

I walked her slowly through the hotel lobby and then into the lift. Her eyes were closing and opening each time the lift made a 'ding' as we ascended from one floor to the next. I slid our keycard into our door lock and went straight towards the bathroom. I slid the glass door across and she practically slid down the wall onto the tiles and was almost sick on the floor before I turned her towards the loo seat. She chucked up her seafood dinner, and all the gin. I brushed her hair back out of her face, like I had done countless times before, and found one of Bea's hair bands next to the sink to tie it back.

'It's okay. Let it all out,' I said, rubbing her back gently as she coughed up the last bits of vomit.

'I love you . . . Ol,' Isla said. 'You always know how to look after me.'

'I love you too,' I laughed, hugging her close.

She then flopped onto me, leaning her sicky face on my shoulder, and fell asleep.

30

2019

I'm on my way to meet Bea for a drink at our favourite cocktail bar near the V&A museum. She has just had a meeting at a gallery nearby and anytime she is in central London we try and get a quick drink in before her train home. I'm trying not to bump into anyone as I walk, simultaneously checking my phone because I have a message from Marcus and obviously need to read it immediately. I don't know why, but it makes the insides of my stomach do a little dance. I feel fourteen years old again. It's an old-school dopamine rush.

> Hey Olive, look, I'm not getting any younger. I think the kids call it 'yolo', but do you fancy going for a drink?

He had clearly got my number from the group improv team WhatsApp group (it's called 'Mission Improvable'). I decide to ignore the cheesiness of his message. It's hard out here for new daters – I should know. I reply saying yes and asking when and where. He replies: tomorrow, Barbican, 1 p.m.

I quite like this decisiveness. It's refreshing.

Bea is sitting at the bar by the window. She has bought us two margaritas and is already licking the salt off the rim of the glass. She waves.

'Hey, hey – sorry I had to order, was desperate for a drink,' she says.

'Good idea,' I say, giving her a kiss on the cheek and taking off my coat. 'You OK?'

'Fine thanks. Just life, eh?' she says, with a half-smile.

I notice she seems a little glum, and I assume it's because of our little spat in the taxi on the way home from the CFBC event.

'Life indeed. Cheers to the ongoing messiness of it,' I say. We do a little clink and put our drinks back down. I decide to bite the bullet. 'Look, I'm sorry about the other night, by the way, at the CFBC. It all got a bit intense, didn't it.'

'No, Ol, it's me who should be apologizing. Let's just put it behind us shall we? I think we both know it was a misunderstanding.'

I'm not sure if that's strictly true, but I just want to make peace with my best friend. I hate all this group tension, it's not like us.

'Agreed. But really, everything OK?'

'Kids are doing great. Touch wood it stays that way.' She touches the table.

'And Jeremy?'

'Well.' She coughs, and takes a massive sip of her

margarita. 'I *cannot* believe what I'm about to tell you.' There is a long pause. She closes her eyes and inhales, and then opens them again slowly. 'Jeremy . . . he's been cheating on me.'

'*What?*'

'For a whole year.'

'*What?*' I feel like my eyes are going to jump out of my head like in a cartoon.

'Yeah. I know. It's just awful at home at the moment – if we're in the same room we start arguing and the kids are now noticing, so we just need to be apart from each other as much as we can while we sort this all out.'

'I'm *so* sorry, Bea. When did you find out?'

'Last week, although I'd had suspicions before then. It didn't sink in. Still hasn't. I suppose I didn't want it to be true? I was in shock. I knew he was working away a lot, but I never thought he would jeopardize our relationship. I found emails and texts on our shared iPad.'

'Jesus. I can't believe it either. What a fool. How *dare* he?' I'm enraged, and to think we all liked Jeremy, he seemed like one of the most genuine guys. I might expect this from Chris, but not Jeremy.

'It's like suddenly my biggest insecurity has come true. I've been feeling unlike myself recently, my body has changed so much since the third kid. And he's been hooking up with his twenty-three-year-old intern, of all people. It makes me feel like a sack of spuds.'

'What a fucker. You do not deserve this. I mean no one does, but especially you. You do *so* much for him and those kids and your home and—'

'I suppose it's not been *great* for a while.'

'But still!'

'I wonder whether I was just too eager to chase the marriage and kids thing so early and didn't really put much effort into the maintaining of it all. He clearly felt trapped – it goes some way to explaining all the travelling. And, well, I could never be bothered to have sex. And even when we did it, he was always the one to initiate it.'

'But this is not your fault, Bea. Please. Don't go there,' I say.

'I just feel like I've pretended everything is fine for so long, to the point where I've almost ended up convincing myself that it was.' She sighs.

Bea's body language is so different. She is slumped over, slouching. A far cry from the Bea we are used to, who always stands so solidly and confidently, normally taking on other people's problems and devising solutions.

'Anyway,' she sighs. 'How are you? Let's change the subject. Distract me.'

'Oh Bea.' I squeeze her knee. 'What are you gonna do next? How can we help?'

'I don't know. He's going to move out for a bit. Have some time apart. I suppose it's going to depend on whether I can forgive him. But I don't think I will be able to.'

'That's understandable, I suppose you're going to have to give it time. I've heard some marriages can be better after a bad shake-up, or . . . perhaps it is just unforgivable. What do you want to happen, do you think?'

'I do still love him, Ol. But, I think it's just run its course now. I don't know. How can it ever be the same after this?'

Her eyes look tired. 'Please tell me about you, my brain hurts from it all.'

'I'm OK.' I almost feel bad now sharing my news, but I can tell she's also desperate for some escapism. 'I'm actually going on a date tomorrow.'

'Oh my god! That's exciting. That's crazy. What's he like? Where did you meet him?'

'At this random improv night. He's quite a bit older. He's really sexy. I know it sounds weird but I am relieved that I actually fancy someone. I thought I never would again.'

'You really deserve some good vibes in that department. Come on, Cupid.'

'I know. I'm up for it,' I say, smiling. I catch my reflection in the window in front of us, and see that I feel and look so much better. If only I could say the same for Bea.

I look in the bathroom mirror, comb my hair through and clip it so that one side of my hair is pulled back behind my ear. I put on a creamy glittery eye-shadow I got free at work and then immediately wipe it off. What am I doing? I am going on a daytime date, I do not need glitter. God, it's been so long since I've been on a first date, and it shows. I decide to wear a floral dress and white high-top Converse shoes. Marcus has decided we should meet at the Barbican arts centre for an exhibition and a coffee. He has a lifetime membership pass. Honestly, my first thought was thank fuck he hadn't booked crazy golf.

As I approach the building, I see him waiting in the lobby area wearing an oversized denim jacket. Hands in his pockets.

A man self-confident enough to wait on his own without needing to scroll on his phone. His eyes light up when he sees me.

'Hey!' He walks over and gives me a hug. 'So, I got us tickets for this exhibition all about AI.'

'This series will explore the relationship between humans and technology,' I read off the ticket. 'Sounds intense for a date. We've skipped the crap film and bowling bit?' I pause. 'I'm into it.'

'Great. Let's go and pretend we're intelligent and then have a nice big drink after.'

We wander around the exhibition and it is a little strange. There are half-eaten robots, big metal talking dogs, self-driving car simulations, USBs plugged into skeleton heads and holograms that feel so real, I flinch. One of the digital projections on the wall reminds me of a mix between Nineties Windows Media Player and the eyes of Kaa, the snake in *The Jungle Book*. The next projection makes a huge, unexpected bang and emits some fake smoke, and I find myself grabbing Marcus's arm.

'It's a weird time we're in, isn't it? We're so close to having self-driving cars, but then also have an HMRC website that is so slow and shit and politicians who don't know how to tweet properly.' I laugh.

'Ha. I gotta say, I do hate how much time my girls spend on their phones. Art-directing countless selfies,' he says, shuddering.

'Yeah, I bet. It must be hard to know what's doing damage and what stuff is actually a positive influence on them.'

'True.'

'I'm not perfect. I am glued to mine,' I say.

'It's just difficult to know what they do all day on their phones. I can't monitor them that closely any more. They are nearly adults, and it feels wrong to ask what they look at.'

'You need a secret squirrel,' I say.

'What's that?' Marcus laughs.

'A secret squirrel is the James Bond of the rodent world,' I say, sticking my front teeth out over my lip.

'You are so weird,' he says, taking my hand.

We go to the bar, sit on stools. I awkwardly climb onto one, making a squeaking noise.

'That was the chair,' I say. I cackle. I notice it's a sound I haven't made for a while.

'Sure,' he says, laughing. 'Two small beers please,' he says politely to the barman who nods.

We cheers our glasses.

'Thanks,' he says.

'What for?' I ask.

'You've put a smile on my haggard old-man face.'

'You're not that haggard,' I say, with a grin.

We both laugh and hold each other's stare a little longer than usual before resuming our strange, rambling conversation. Is this what people mean when they give you cheesy advice that there will be a light at the end of the tunnel? The dark cloud above my head is still there – but it's feeling lighter now. For the first time, I can actually imagine it disappearing altogether. Today feels like a sort of fresh start.

31

Isla is in hospital looking frail. She is sitting up in her bed, the white covers draped over her. She is whispering to me, so I go closer.

'What can I do?' I ask desperately, kneeling at the side of her bed.

She starts talking but goes mute. I can't hear her.

'What are you saying, Isla?'

She is babbling, but no words come out.

She curls up into a foetal position in the bed, sad and vulnerable. A female doctor knocks gently and comes in holding a clipboard to her chest.

'She's a thief! You're a thief!' Isla shouts at the doctor in a hoarse voice. Her voice is coming back. I have a notepad on my lap and I start asking Isla questions.

'Stop writing, Olive.'

'Sorry,' I say.

'Please stop doing that. This is my story. Not yours.'

'I know.'

'Everyone is stealing from me. Thieves!' she shrieks.

The female doctor puts black Sellotape over Isla's mouth.

* * *

I wake up suddenly, sweating. A bad dream again. I sit up in bed and glance around in the dark, waiting for the tightness in my chest to loosen. The dream has shaken me to the core. I reach over to my bedside table and pick up my phone. My last conversation with Isla on WhatsApp was a week ago. It shouldn't feel surprising at the moment, given the trajectory and how we left things, but it still feels like a long time.

I don't want to generalize 'about women', but I do think that we just know when something is up. That female intuition. We have pure gut instinct. We don't need to ask for an explanation or scientific reasoning. We just know, we get a whiff, and then most of the time we are proved right. For example, if you ask most women, they will probably tell you that they knew way before any evidence surfaced that their partner was cheating on them. We are not paranoid, or silly, or hysterical: we have intuition. A deep-rooted emotional compass. So, I knew something was up with Isla.

As soon as it feels like a sociable hour, I pick up my phone and ring her. No answer. I suddenly feel sick and don't know if it's just worry, or hunger. I root around to prep something for breakfast and realize I have no food in the house. I need bagels and milk and some fresh air in the form of a walk to my local corner shop down the road. I think about pulling on my new navy onesie out of habit, but actually, I'm feeling different. Brighter. I can see a speck of a silver lining. I decide to get properly dressed and pull on a pair of jeans that are frayed along the bottom and an old black-and-white-striped woollen jumper. I put my Bluetooth headphones in my ears and Emma Thompson's

Desert Island Discs episode blares out into my ears as I cross the road by the pub and pass the train station. I go into Tesco and pick up a copy of *The Times* and walk to the bread section at the back of the store. Bagels pre-sliced, only one bag left. I then go to the wine section and pick up a cheap but OK-ish one for later – a claret. Then I put it back. I don't need to get drunk on my own tonight. I start wandering towards the till and spot a woman who has the same hat as Isla looking at the biscuits. It's a red cashmere beret I bought her from Reiss for her birthday years ago. I realize quickly that it *is* Isla. She is walking quickly away towards the exit.

'Isla!' I shout.

She carries on walking away.

I stride after her, and my walk turns into a bit of a gallop.

'Isla . . . !' I grab her arm. She turns around, reluctantly.

'Oh . . . hi,' she says. Clearly she'd seen me. She looks at the floor. I notice how tired she looks.

'Are you OK? I was getting worried I hadn't heard from you. I'm so sorry things have been so awkward between us. I really hated leaving things like that.' We step to the side, by the magazines, so as not to block the entrance to the store. I set the alarm off. It goes off loudly and the security guy gives me side-eye.

'I'm OK. Can't stay and chat though,' she says.

'Of course. Sorry it's just . . . I don't know what to say.' This feels so alien to me. Not knowing what to say to one of my best friends. I feel nervous, like I'm going to put my foot in it.

346

'Yes, I'm sorry if I have been a bit distant lately. Not feeling myself, I guess.'

'Can we talk? Sort things out?'

'I can't stay and talk about this here,' she whispers.

'OK. I don't want to be paranoid but I'd really like to know what's up.'

She pauses and rolls her tongue around the corner of her cheek. 'Honestly? Having a child is all I can think about at the moment. And I feel like not having a child is all you are thinking about. It's OK. It really is. But I personally can't hack it right now.'

'I'm . . . sorry,' I say, surprised and deflated.

'Maybe it's me being selfish, or maybe it's you, or maybe it's neither of us? But it's all-encompassing and it's painful and I'm just really trying to make this reality happen for me.' She gestures towards her lower body.

I don't know what to say.

'I don't mean to make you feel bad, but it's just the truth. I don't want to be around someone who speaks so openly and cynically about motherhood right now.'

I'm glad she is being honest but, also, it feels like a sharp little dagger being sliced into me multiple times.

'I'm so sorry. For what you are going through, and the things that you feel are out of your control. I'm sorry if I've upset you.'

Fuck, I should have said sorry *for* upsetting you. Not *if*. Semantics, Olive.

'It's fine. I'm just feeling shit about everything. And the worst thing? I know this is probably jealousy, or something.

But you don't care – you don't need this to feel complete. I do. You might never have to go through all of this shit.'

I open my mouth to reply, but nothing comes out.

'I feel like it'll never happen for me. And I don't want you to feel like you're treading on eggshells because of me. You're allowed to do what *you* need to do. So, I just need a break.'

I've never had a friend 'need a break' from me before.

'OK. I'm sorry,' I say.

'Yeah. Well. I dunno. I know you're not actually trying to hurt me. I know that one person's choice isn't a personal attack on someone else. I just need to protect myself right now, OK? I have to go.' Isla readjusts the handbag on her shoulder and leaves the store. I just stand there, and then accidentally drop my packet of bagels. We are so close to the exit that the bagels trigger the store alarm to go off again, loudly. My face turns bright red and the security guard follows me to the till.

One thing is for sure, Marcus has taught me how to sort my shit out. My flat is much tidier now, with home-made food in the fridge. He made pastry from scratch the other night and baked a lemon tart. There is a huge vegetable lasagne in the freezer with a handwritten sticker on it. He bought me a new fluffy rug for the living room. Marigolds under the sink. He bought me two massive cheese-plants and told me to talk to them so they grow. I never thought a fairy godmother would be a forty-something man with a beard.

'Do you think I like Marcus because he like . . . "fathers" me a bit?' I ask Zeta on the phone that night as I lie hanging upside down off my bed.

'Calm down, Sigmund. You might just like him because he's a proper adult, not a dick, and has experienced a bit more of life than you,' Zeta replies, with a hoover blaring in the background. She turns the hoover off.

'I'm just worried that I like him because he's a bit older and wiser or something.'

'Why are you worrying about this? Oh, wait . . . it's because it's your birthday soon. You always get really weird and intensely introspective around this time of year.'

'Do I?'

'Yeah, you have a massive freak-out, every year. But really, you're doing just fine, babe.'

'Thanks, I feel good at the moment, actually. I finally feel like I'm in the right lane. That following my gut has ultimately been a good thing.'

'I'm proud of you,' Zeta tells me, before carrying on with her hoovering. My phone calls with Zeta were never about anything crazily exciting, they were just normal everyday chatter – and I began to realize that they have been the extra piece of Sellotape holding me together all along. The little, mundane, lovely bits of life.

My phone flashes with Bea's name whilst I'm out having a cigarette break at work. I stump out my cigarette and pick up.

'I'm excited for Friday!' she says, while telling one of her kids to be quiet. 'Thirty-three, eh! Girl, you're getting old.'

'I know. Me too, excited to see you. I was worried you were calling me to say you couldn't come.' I laugh nervously.

'I knew you'd say something silly like that. Birthdays have always made you so paranoid, ever since you were little!'

'God, you're right. Zeta was saying the same thing. They really do turn me a bit loony, don't they?'

'Well, I'm glad you are actually celebrating this time and not just hiding away in a cave like you usually do. I'm looking forward to meeting Marcus!' Bea lets out a little squeal.

'Yes, I can't wait for you guys to meet,' I say, sort of meaning it. My nerves are fighting to take over.

'And, Ol, it's lovely to see you so happy again,' Bea says in her motherly tone.

'I'm feeling good. Even though thirty-three sounds really, really old. Did you know Jesus apparently died at thirty-three?'

'Oh shush. I reckon you'll outlive all of us, to be honest.'

Statistically I probably will, I think, if I don't have kids.

'Ha. Do you think Isla will come?'

Bea pauses. 'I hope so.'

'Me too. OK, I better get back to the grindstone, see you later Bea . . .'

'See you then, Ol. Can't wait. Mwah.'

Cecily offered up her house for the birthday party, which I really appreciate, especially as her garden is the biggest. The space is big enough for a medium-sized marquee, which is lucky as the weather is predictably rubbish when the big day rolls around. Bea has brought a wheelbarrow full of booze and huge packets of ice and she and Cecily got up early to put bunting all around the garden, which has letters spelling out 'Olive'. Fairy lights are strung up too, ready to twinkle later. It does look amazing.

The kids are now on the trampoline singing 'Happy Birthday to You' in a very high-pitched, out-of-tune way. I look around and realize that the fourteen brilliant people in this garden are the only people I need. Zeta, my friends, Colin, some .dot colleagues, and then some additions: Marcus and some of Marcus's pals who I've started to get to know recently.

'Cec, this is the loveliest thing, thank you,' I say, scanning the garden. 'How are you feeling?' My question was deliberately vague, but I'm all too aware it hasn't been too long since the OAP locked-in-the-house incident.

'Much better thank you, Ol. My therapist has been teaching me some ways to "forgive myself". Blips happen, I suppose. I'm doing better, each day is a little easier.' She starts cooing at Oscar who is strapped to her chest in a cute papoose.

'I'm really glad to hear that. Oscar is very lucky to have you as his mum.'

I look over at Marcus who's in charge of the barbecue. He's wearing a novelty apron which says: 'I cook as good as I look'. I can only assume it was a joke Christmas present. He is singing to himself while turning over the vegetarian sausages, before looking up as the garden gate creaks open. It's Isla.

She looks around sheepishly and creeps through the gate.

'Hey! Sorry I'm late. I've brought drinks,' she says, holding up a tote bag. 'You must be Marcus, I've heard so much about you.'

I appear behind Marcus with a gin-in-tin in hand. 'Isla! You came. I'm so happy to see you,' I say.

'Great to meet you, Isla. I would hug you, but I'm covered in BBQ fat,' laughs Marcus.

'It's cool. It's nice to meet you in person, finally.' She nods.

'Thanks for the drinks – just pop them in the wheelbarrow that's filled with ice. Glad you could make it.' Marcus smiles.

'Hey, Isla, you're here!' Bea says, as Colin also appears next to us. We do a group hug.

'Yeah, of course. Good to see you. I like this,' Isla says, tugging on Bea's new grey cashmere Acne jumper.

'Thank you.'

'Don't you just love how Ol's boyfriend takes control?' Colin says, looking over at Marcus.

'You crack me up,' I say. 'I'm just going to fill up the snack bowls, back in a sec.'

As I'm about to head inside, we hear Marcus clanking a glass with a fork. Ding ding ding! He's standing there looking a little nervous, his silly apron still on.

'I'd like to make a toast,' he says tentatively. 'If that's OK!'

'Yesssss, love a speech!! Gather round everyone!' Colin says, ushering everyone closer and opening another bottle of white wine.

'Oh god.' Isla and I look at each other and grimace slightly.

'There she is! Birthday girl!' He smiles in my direction. 'I know this is a bit bold, but I'd like to say a few things about Ol.' He coughs nervously. 'I checked with her friends, and they reassured me that Olive wouldn't die of embarrassment and she likes speeches.'

Bea and Cec look over at me and smirk, raising their glasses jokingly. I might kill them. I do not like speeches.

'I know we've only known each other a short while in the grand scheme of things.' He laughs. 'But it's been the best few months of my life.'

To my absolute amazement, I am not grossed out. My cheeks are not that red.

He continues: 'There are so many things I like about you, Ol. I admire how strong and independent you are, the way you put yourself first. I think it's something society envies: someone who doesn't people-please or do things "just because". You really are unapologetically YOU! Never change. Happy Birthday Olive!'

'Happy Birthday Olive,' all my friends say in unison. Except Isla, who I notice has just slipped back inside.

I kiss Marcus and take a few minutes to enjoy the moment. 'That was lovely, I'm just going to pop inside for a minute.' When I get to the kitchen, Isla is leaning over Cec's big kitchen island. The one she broke down on just a few months ago when she was making Cec's baby shower bunting.

'Isla – what is it?'

She sighs. 'Let's go into the living room.' I hate how serious her voice sounds.

We sit on Cec's squishy sofa. It feels eerily quiet. Everyone else is outside in the sunshine.

'What have I done? Have I murdered someone in your family without remembering?'

'OK, let me get this off my chest. I'm really sorry it's your birthday but I'm just desperate to clear the air. And before I do, I know you are going to think I am bonkers.'

'Go on.'

'There's a deeper reason why I've responded to things so badly recently – your journalism about being child-free and, you know, anti-birth—'

'I'm not anti-birth,' I laugh. 'That's ridiculous. Birth is pretty necessary for the human race to carrying on surviving. I don't want a kid, but that doesn't mean I want the whole human race to die out.'

'OK, but you've been writing a lot about how you find the idea of birth and motherhood traumatizing.'

'Yeah, I do, though. That's how I feel about it, that's just my point of view. I am entitled to that, Isla. I don't judge you because you want a baby, so why are you judging me because I don't?'

'OK, well, I don't know if you remember, but a couple of years ago, on a drunken night out, we were discussing . . . my options. And I know it perhaps wasn't a totally serious conversation, but I remember you saying that, if it ever came down to it, and I couldn't have kids, that you'd be a surrogate for me.'

Did I? What what what?

Oh my god, maybe I had watched that episode of *Friends*. The one with Phoebe and her brother. She made it look really easy. It would not be appropriate to joke about this right now, Olive.

'Isla, I'm so sorry, but I really don't remember that.'

'It's OK. I feel really weird bringing it up after all these years.'

'I don't know what to say.'

'We were in that pub on George Street and I was talking about my health issues and how, one day, I might need to use a surrogate. How it's a totally feasible thing these days. Obviously, Bea and Cec were trying for their own, but you said . . . you said something that I took to mean you would be open to it. You said you'd do that for Mike and me. I know this sounds a bit crazy, and it was such a long time ago, but it just really stuck with me. You sounded supportive.'

Sounds like I'd had one jar too many that night.

'I can't believe I'd offer up something so huge and not remember it. I'm sorry, Isla.'

'It's OK. I'd just latched onto it . . . And now things are looking incredibly unlikely for me, and so when I kept hearing you talking so negatively about everything . . . About how much birth grosses you out . . . I mean, you went to that child-free meet-up and pretty much all your articles at .dot are centred around this topic nowadays.'

My eyes widen. 'I know I've been slightly fixated on it over the past few months, but can you blame me? I've had a massive life overhaul after breaking up with Jacob – I've been questioning everything whilst feeling behind everyone else! I'm really sorry, but I also really needed this.'

Isla sighs and looks down at the floor. 'This is all such a mess, and now I feel totally weird for even saying anything about the surrogate thing.' She takes a step back.

'You're not weird. You're in pain right now. There's a difference.' We stand there awkwardly and I make the first move. She lets me hug her and we hold each other tightly. It feels good. Like things might start to go back to how they should be.

'You will get through this, Isla,' I say. But of course, we don't know for sure. Isla doesn't look up, she doesn't look at me. I can't help but fear an invisible wedge has grown between us. What if there's no way back?

'Here, I got this for you.' She passes me a small box, tied with gold ribbon.

'Happy birthday Ol,' she says.

'Oh wow, Isla.'

I open it, and a gold chain with a green olive-leaf pendant sits on a velvet cushion.

'It's gorgeous.'

'Sorry that it's been so tense,' she says.

'It's OK.' I say. 'I'm sorry too.'

Bea and I stay the night at Cecily's after the party. No sign of OAP as Chris's parents are looking after him for the weekend. Isla decides to go home. We leave things on a good note, but I am too embarrassed to tell the others what happened. Am I mad, or is Isla mad? Cec shows each of us in our couples to her fancy guest rooms, complete with folded White Company towels and lavender sprays on the pillows. Cec's house is modern but it is still cosy and has all the fancy tech: press a button to lower the blinds; press a button to lift the bed up, dim the lights, or play some music when showering. Before bed, we all watch a film on her big corner sofa under cashmere blankets. We put the electric fire on, finish off the last of the red wine and I flick luxuriously through some magazines that line the coffee table. I love snuggling into Marcus. My friends seem to like him too, which I am happy about. Bea clutches her heart dramatically whenever she spots us holding hands.

The next morning, we all sit around drinking coffee in our dressing gowns. Marcus has gone off for a morning run. I call him a crazy fitness freak.

A text appears from my mum. Love how she is texting a day late.

HAPPY BIRTHDAY OLIVE!

Thanks Mum

HOPE YOU HAVE A LOVELY DAY WITH YOUR FRIENDS AND NEW PARTNER. SORRY I COULDN'T ATTEND. M x
ps. SO LOVELY RE JACOB'S NEWS ISN'T IT?

What?

What news?

I can't help myself.

BABY NEWS.

I throw my phone on the floor. Then, I pick it back up. I can't breathe. And I do a bad thing. It could practically be classed as self-harm. I go onto Jacob's Instagram account. He hasn't updated his account for months, but I go through everyone he is following. And find her. A girl called Julia. My brain ticks. I feel that triggering, uncomfortable feeling that I thought I would have moved on from. After all, I'm happily settled down now.

'What's up?' Cecily asks. She can tell when I start getting tetchy, I start to twirl the front pieces of my hair. Apparently the colour has sort of drained from my face.

'Nothing . . .' I reply, manically looking into my phone.

'It's the weekend, you're not meant to be working,' Cecily says, trying to snatch my phone from my hand.

I turn away: 'I'm not.'

'What are you doing then?'

'Searching for—'

'What?'

'Fuck.'

'What?'

'Nothing.' I go into the kitchen. Cec follows me.

'Olive?'

'Jacob. His new girlfriend.' I pause. 'Pregnant.'

'Oh . . . god.'

'I know,' I say.

'Well,' I can see Cec's brain cogs do the mental arithmetic, 'do you care?'

'I don't know.'

'You were always going to feel this way, whether it's now

or in five years' time. It was always going to hurt when Jacob moved on.'

I check. Yes, my heart is fully intact. I haven't exploded. The ground is still sturdy beneath my feet.

'I thought he might have told me,' I say, 'considering the reason we broke up.'

'I suppose you haven't written to him about Marcus.'

'I know. I don't know. It's just – you know, I'd finally managed to push him from my mind. But now, he's right back there. And I'm happy for him. But I'm also sad. Jacob's getting what he wanted, finally, and he deserves that. No one deserves that more than him.' I feel something knot up inside me. 'I suppose it's just a reminder that, it could have been me. That was supposed to be me, but it was never really going to be.'

'Yes, Ol, because you didn't want that. You could have had it, and you didn't want it. Look at your life now. You're happy. Please don't distract from that.'

'I'm actually. . . happy for him.' I blow my nose into a tissue. 'I think it's hay-fever.'

'Come here.' Cecily pulls me into her. Bea's kid Andrew wanders in and hugs my legs while I cry. Then Marcus comes in, hair scruffy and his face all red from his run. He doesn't ask why I'm crying but he just strokes my hair anyway. He stretches his long arms and hugs all of us. A conga line of hugs. I have so much, right here.

'The positives [of a child-free life] for me are more time and money, to do all the things I want to do in life.'

J, 32

32

Marcus and I are sitting side by side with our laptops on his small kitchen island, going through emails and other bits and bobs for work. He's wearing a pair of light brown glasses that he only wears when at this computer and a big knitted jumper – I keep looking up just to catch a glimpse. He's deep in thought, with frown lines across his forehead. He then looks up, takes off his glasses and turns to me.

'Ol, I've been thinking,' he says.

'Yeees?' I reply, clicking 'send' on an email to Colin.

'You should meet my girls soon.'

'Really?'

'Yeah!'

I gulp, feeling caught off guard. 'OK, I would love to.'

'It just feels wrong now to be tiptoeing around them. They'll love you,' he says. The only reason I am sat in Marcus's house right now is because they are both away on holiday with some family friends.

'That would be wonderful – just let me know when,' I say, smiling.

'OK.' He nods. He makes us both a cup of tea while singing to himself and I tell him to 'sshh' because I'm trying to write. A sign of closeness.

The idea of meeting Marcus's two girls is, of course, terrifying. It's a relief that they're old enough to hopefully welcome new people, but they're also old enough to really analyze me and question me in ways I'm not sure I want to be questioned. For once, the tables will turn, and I'll be the interviewee. When we first started going out, Marcus would call his kids 'the fifteen-year-old' and 'the seven-teen-year-old', I assumed as a distancing technique so that I wouldn't start getting too attached in the early stages. They didn't even have names until recently. Now I know: Caitlin and Sally.

When I get back to my place, I pick up my keys and bag to leave the house and find a note wedged in my letterbox. It's written in old squiggly writing, I can hardly make out the letters:

Happy Birthday OLIVE – thank you for being a great friend to your old neighbour. Dorothy x

I smile and fold up the note, and put it in my pocket. The air outside is warm, and everything finally feels like it's moving along just how it's supposed to.

The following weekend, I follow a pebbled path in Hampstead and finally arrive at the Mason's Head, a big grey pub with foliage growing around all the windows. There are orange lights framing the arch of the doorway and a festive feeling in the air. Old lampposts flicker like a scene from *Mary Poppins*. I push open a heavy wooden door and the barman, cleaning some glasses, says hello.

I can see Marcus waving; he is sitting at the back at a corner table. A girl with a dark brown bob is seated in front of Marcus, with her back to me. She turns around and waves coyly. That must be Caitlin, the seventeen-year-old. She is wearing a leather jacket which has 'God Is A Woman' painted in gold on the back. On closer inspection she has bits of blue dye on the tips on her hair. Sally, the fifteen-year-old, has longer, darker brown hair and heavy winged eyeliner. She is seated next to Marcus and is wearing a long black dress, a black cashmere beret and Dr. Martens boots. Her head is resting on his shoulder.

'Ol! Over here.' Marcus scoots up out of his chair and comes over to kiss me on the cheek. I am a ball of nerves.

'Sorry I'm a bit late! Traffic was bad! Hi,' I say towards the girls, my voice suddenly sounding a bit squeakier than usual.

Sally smiles at me. Caitlin doesn't.

'What do you fancy to drink?' Marcus asks me, rubbing my back.

'A white-wine spritzer would be great,' I say. My armpits are sweating a bit.

'Dad, can I have a white-wine spritzer too?'

'Sorry, Sal, not yet, you're nearly there! Few more years I'm afraid or . . . do it behind my back.'

'But I think I look old enough,' Sally says, flicking her hair.

Caitlin gives her a playful punch on the arm. The girls

clearly get on well with each other, but Marcus said they used to be awful to each other when they were little, which reminds me of Zeta and me. He said they used to have the most vicious fights, and even cut each other's ponytails off while the other was sleeping. Zeta once broke my arm by pushing me so hard that I fell over a football and smacked into a brick wall. Young girls can be brutal.

'Did you guys have a nice walk on the heath?' I ask Marcus.

'Really lovely. You should come with us next time.'

'Would love to.' I had made up an excuse that I was working this morning, when really I just needed a lie-in and a lazy 'me-time' morning . . . books, bath, moisturizer. There are just some things I'll never sacrifice, even if I'm in a relationship.

Caitlin comes back with a tray of drinks, piping up: 'Dad, you have to join us on the march on Saturday.'

'What's this one about?' Marcus asks, taking his shandy from the tray.

'It's to support a campaign about lowering the voting age! So younger teens can vote. Please come. You *can't* say you support it if you don't turn up. Honestly, it drives me crazy, people tweeting a hashtag from the warmth of their sofa,' Caitlin says.

'True that,' I say, nodding.

'I understand, Caits. I'll definitely try and make it,' Marcus says.

'Will you come, Olive? Look at this banner I made.' She gets a big piece of rolled-up paper out of her rucksack.

'Yes, of course!' I say. 'Wow, that's really good.'

'Do you ever go to protests or anything?'

'Yeah sometimes! I work at a magazine and we do lots of write-ups about that sort of thing.'

'Oh cool – Dad said you were a writer,' Caitlin says, sipping her Diet Coke and crunching small cubes of ice.

'Yes I am – I'm an editor at .dot magazine. Do you know it?'

'No way – I *love* .dot magazine,' she says, no longer playing it cool.

'Really? Some of the team are going to the march; if we meet up, I'll introduce you. They're a fun bunch.'

'Oh my god.' She looks interested and I want to hang onto it. 'What is it like working there?' she asks, pulling the sleeves of her jumper over her hands.

'It's really fun – I head up the lifestyle and culture section; we've got so many amazing writers. I love writing the stories and features, scrolling through social media is sort of part of the job these days too, but I kind of hate that bit. Maybe I'm getting old.'

'You're not that old. Dad's quite a lot older than you,' Sally says, cracking open a pistachio nut.

'All right, all right,' Marcus says.

We order food, and everyone goes for a cheeseburger, except Caitlin who orders a vegan burger. It arrives quickly. Too quickly, if you ask me. Pub life.

'I like your name,' Sally says as she squeezes some ketchup onto her plate.

'Thank you.'

'Is it short for Olivia?'

'Yep, but only my mum calls me that when she's angry with me, which is most of the time, to be honest.'

Sally flinches slightly at the word 'mum'. I hope I haven't made a big faux pas.

I look over at Caitlin and she's moved her two pieces of burger bread to one side, nibbling only on the salad.

'And how's school going, Sal?' Marcus asks.

'It's OK. Writing an essay currently in my English class on why Disney films are incredibly sexist. I mean, Ariel from *The Little Mermaid* – she *literally* loses her voice, for a man, and is also at the beck and call of her weird controlling bearded father,' Sally responds.

'Nothing wrong with a bearded controlling father!' Marcus says jokingly, in a deep booming voice.

'You're the opposite of that, thank god.' Sal laughs and nudges him lightly on the arm. 'Mr Totally Laid-Back.'

'Shall we go back to ours for another drink after this? The wine is a bit of a rip-off here, I've got better ones at home,' Marcus says.

'Sounds perfect,' I say.

Seeing just how much Marcus's daughters adore him has made me like him even more. We finish our drinks and I feel so warm and loved up, knowing that I get to go back to their family home with them, and that I've been accepted. I feel welcome. I feel relieved; I was expecting the worst.

We hop into the car and listen to *The Greatest Showman* soundtrack on the drive. Sally starts belting out 'This is Me'. She is very out of tune, but I can't help but take it as a compliment that she is comfortable enough around me already to sing so loudly (and badly). Caitlin is resting her arm on the car door and daydreaming out of the window. I get out of the car and the girls walk ahead towards the front door. Marcus kisses me. His jumper smells cosy, of bonfires and aftershave.

When people say 'You will meet the right person when you least expect it', I want to rip one of their arms off and beat them with it. It's the most fucking annoying phrase in the world. *But*. It is kind of true. That is what makes it even more annoying.

Later on, when I get home, I rummage around in my bag to get my keys out, and notice Dorothy's light is off; it's odd, as she usually leaves it on throughout the night. It's part of my routine to look up at Dorothy's light and know she is there. It's a comfort. I hope she is OK. The next day, when I wake up and draw my curtains, Dorothy's light is still off. I make a coffee, add sugar, and sit at my kitchen table, scrolling through the *Guardian* app. I tap the table nervously. Something doesn't feel right – perhaps it's that female intuition again. I pull on some jeans, use some deodorant, spray some dry shampoo in my hair and throw on a big jumper. I knock on Dorothy's door. No answer. I try peering through the letterbox. The door opens, and a woman with a bob and a hi-vis jacket stands there, probably wondering why I'm crouching down weirdly.

'Hi, can I help?' Hi-Vis Woman says.

'Hi I'm Olive, Dorothy's neighbour . . . and friend. Is she in?'

'Oh. I'm sorry. Haven't you heard?'

'No?'

'Dorothy was found unconscious yesterday. Poor lady. We heard this morning that she died in hospital overnight. The postman noticed her lights were off – which was unusual – so he flagged it, thank goodness.'

'No.' I feel a lump forming in my throat. 'Was anyone with her?'

'Her friend Rupert was there; she died very peacefully.'

'Oh my god. Poor Dorothy.'

'I've been told to pass on that Rupert is planning the funeral. Do you know Rupert?'

'No, I don't. How can I contact him?' I ask. She passes me a piece of paper with Rupert's number on. Sadness overcomes me and I feel physically sick.

Olive: Hi Rupert, this is Olive. Dorothy's neighbour? I'm so sorry to hear the news. It's such an awful shock. I'd love to attend Dorothy's funeral. Do you know the details? O x

Rupert: Hi Olive. It is in three weeks' time, St Martin's Crematorium. I'm sure Dorothy would love that.

His words hit me hard, like a physical blow to the stomach. It sounds as if Dorothy is still here. I didn't know my neighbour for very long but I felt close to her. Like we understood one another. She softened my heart again after my break-up with Jacob. She helped me to heal.

33

'I hope your girls are starting to like me,' I say.

Marcus and I are in Sainsbury's, looking for some inspiration on what to cook. We go past the fruit and veg and I toss some lemons into the basket.

'Stop fishing for compliments,' Marcus says.

'I'm not! I wanna know,' I say.

'Of course they do. They're not judgemental girls. I'm proud of that.'

'So they won't judge my cooking next week then?'

'Well, I can't promise that,' he laughs.

'I mean it's fajitas. How wrong can it go?'

'But seriously. They are old enough now to accept meeting someone outside of the three of us.'

'Have they ever met anyone else you've dated?'

'I haven't really dated anyone else in a serious sense. I was scared to meet someone when they were younger, and I didn't ever want to lie to them or sneak around.'

'Like Jude Law in *The Holiday*.'

'Not seen that film.'

'We must rectify that immediately.'

I can't help but feel slightly relieved that there's not been anyone else serious before me, or at least recently. It makes things slightly simpler.

We push the trolley around, and I stop by the oatmeal wraps.

'Would you want any more kids, do you think?' I say, reading the back of a packet.

I can't believe how casually I just dropped that in.

He frowns, and then looks at me. 'Wow, that's a big question.'

'I know, sorry.'

'I don't know, I don't think so. No,' he says, sheepishly.

'Interesting,' I say.

'Is that the wrong answer?'

'Why would that be wrong?'

'Well, I don't know, why were you asking?'

'My last relationship broke off because I don't want kids.'

'Oh, I see.'

'Yeah.'

'Well, you told me you didn't want kids the first time I met you, so I suppose I knew that already.'

'No, I didn't.'

'Yes you did, on the lawn at Cecily's. You shouted.'

'Yes, OK, I don't need a reminder on what I shouted.'

'Having children is . . . the most magical thing in the world,' Marcus says, and I can hear him swallow down a lump in his throat. 'But also, I understand where you're coming from.'

'Yeah, as it turns out . . . it's not very me.'

'That's fine, Ol. Your body, your rules. Not for everyone.'

'Well, quite.'

'C'mon, we need to get some sour cream,' he says, putting his arm around me and pushing the trolley at the same time.

I sit on the loo, scrolling through Twitter. I realize, suddenly, that I need to call Bea and check in with her. I wonder how she's coping with the Jeremy situation. I press her number in my favourites and Bea's face flashes up on my screen, just a picture, saying 'calling'. For a moment I thought that she could see me on the loo. I mean, it wouldn't matter if she did, but still – boundaries.

'Hi!' she answers quickly.

'Hey!' I say, pressing the flush.

'You on the loo?' Bea laughs. 'You call people at the weirdest times. I hope you wipe down your phone with a Dettol wipe afterwards,' she says.

'Sorry we didn't get the chance to talk properly at my birthday. Are you OK?'

'Honestly Ol? Everything been has totally flipped upside down, and I feel absolutely horrendous. The kids have heard us shouting at each other, and they keep crying. I think it's really affecting them so he's gone to live with his mate for a while.'

'Oh, Bea.'

'It's horrible seeing him now, living in a shoebox with a friend while I'm in our family home.'

'Yes, but Bea, he did this. Not you. He fucked up,' I say.

'I know.' She sighs. 'I do still love him, despite everything.

But I honestly don't think this can be repaired. Our whole relationship was built on trust, especially as he goes away so often; now I just don't know what to believe. Has he cheated once, or more than once? Am I a total mug?' Her voice cracks and she starts crying.

'You are not a mug. You do absolutely everything for that family, and he's a total, total idiot for throwing it all away. This just doesn't seem like the guy you married, or the guy we know.'

'I thought so too,' she says, sniffing.

'Maybe some things, no matter how right they were at the time, do change. Maybe nothing is actually within our control and we can't prepare for anything.'

'I miss the old days. The old Jeremy.' She sniffs.

'We are here for you Bea. And that's something that will never change. I promise.'

'Thank you, Ol. That's actually exactly what I needed to hear,' Bea replies, blowing her nose into a tissue.

Later that night, after my sort-of-successful fajita cook-in with Marcus and the girls, he and I are sitting in the living room watching a film on Sky Cinema. We have some crisp white wine with ice cubes in, and the fairy lights around my window are giving off a soft, golden light.

'I was thinking,' Marcus says, reaching for a handful of peanuts, 'that you could maybe take Caitlin out soon, just the two of you?'

I feel a pang of fear in my belly. I'm not good at this stuff.

'Oh, er, sure. Any reason?' I say.

'I think she's a bit low at the moment.'

'Oh. Really? Oh god, poor thing.'

I haven't been the best person around sad friends recently. I've cared, but I know in hindsight I probably said the wrong things. I once read a list online of 'the top ten things you shouldn't say to a depressed person' and I had been guilty of them all. Like, 'Don't worry, the sunshine is shining!' Or, 'Don't be sad, just cheer up!' I suppose I'm worrying that I will accidentally make things worse. I think about Isla, too.

'I think that spending time with you might make her feel a bit more inspired about what she could do with her life, and her career.'

'Me? That's really nice but—'

'I think she needs an older female figure around, just to observe and learn from a bit. No pressure, maybe I shouldn't be asking you this. It's just she tells me nothing and I thought she might be more open with you.' He sighs and I see the worry in his eyes.

'You want me to be your secret squirrel?'

'Yes, I want you to be my secret squirrel. If that's OK and if it doesn't make you feel uncomfortable. I just need to know she's OK. You don't have to tell me what she says or anything.'

'That's good of you.'

'I would never ask you to betray her trust – that's like reading her diary! I just need to know she's OK. That she has someone, other than her old man who she can talk to, if she needs to. I'm sorry, Olive. Is that too much? I don't mean to overstep the—'

'No, don't be silly. It's fine, I'll talk to her.' I smooth his cheek and kiss him. We go back to watching the film in silence, my head on his chest.

The next day, after Caitlin comes back from a jog, I knock on her bedroom door and poke my head around into the room.

'Hey,' I say.

'Hey.' She doesn't look up from her phone, curled up on her bed, in pyjamas, post-shower.

'Can I come in?' I ask.

'Yup.'

'Sooo, I was wondering. I have two free treatments at a new spa in central London. Do you fancy coming with? Could be fun?'

'Is Dad going?'

'Just us, I thought that would be nice?'

She hesitates a little. 'OK, sure. Thanks.' She goes straight back to her phone. Success. Ish. I'm so happy she's agreed to come with me, but also nervous. What if we have nothing to talk about? What if she doesn't like me?

I go downstairs, excited to tell Marcus that Caitlin has agreed to hang out. Sure, our exchange was short, but she said yes! I bounce down the stairs and he is sitting at the kitchen table, glasses on, doing a crossword.

'She's in. Next Saturday. Hopefully some bonding time.'

'What? No way! You squirrel fast.'

'Yes, well, I had some treatments at a really nice spa and

was going to invite Colin but it would be lovely to go with Caitlin instead. Don't tell Colin!'

'Great. By the way, she struggles with any sort of public transport now and she will probably ask you for a step-by-step description on how to get somewhere and then home again – just warning you before she starts asking you endless questions.'

'That's totally fine. Good to know,' I say, ruffling his hair.

'I took her to a therapist a few years ago. They said her anxiety comes from a fear of change and being out of control. It's apparently something to do with the rug being pulled from under her when her mother died, and so now she fears change.'

'Yep, I get that,' I say. I think about how Dad left suddenly, all the bruises from that.

'I'm really glad she's agreed to go out with you, I was pretty sure she'd find a way to say no.'

'Don't worry, she'll be OK. I'll talk to her too and check that she's not struggling.' It felt good to help. To have a new task at hand.

We arrive at the spa the next weekend. It's called Glow Up, which sounds tackier than it looks. A woman wearing big pink furry slippers greets us at reception and gives us a key to a locker, plastic flipflops and a folded-up white robe each. She plonks it all into our arms.

'Press a four-digit code to lock the lockers and don't spend too much time in the sauna – fifteen mins max, otherwise you'll pass out, OK?' she says, sternly.

'OK!' I say.

'So, you're both booked in for the seaweed wrap bath and a full-body massage, correct?'

'That's right,' I say, feeling upbeat.

'OK, great, I'll just ask you both to fill out these forms, change into your cossies and then come hang out in the waiting area in your robes. There's a lovely selection of herbal teas in there too.'

'Lovely, thanks.'

We go into the changing rooms.

'How's school at the mo?'

'Rubbish.'

'How come?'

'Don't really like anyone.'

I'm really aware that all my chat with Caitlin would be classed as small talk. I hate small talk, so kind of hate myself for it.

'I used to feel that way at school,' I say.

'I don't really want to wear these flipflops, I might get a verruca.'

'You don't have to,' I say chirpily.

'Bit nervous about the wrap massage, I have some bruises.'

'Don't worry, Cait. They'll be gentle with you,' I say, trying not to act taken aback by all of the signs pointing in the same worrying direction.

We get changed, and when Caitlin re-emerges, she is in a red crinkled swimming costume that is hanging off her. We go into the waiting room and then shortly afterwards go in for our treatments. There is no greater chance for self-reflection than looking out onto a rainy London road while covered in green slime.

'How was your seaweed wrap?' I ask her afterwards, sitting in front of the changing room mirrors, my hair in a towelled turban.

'Nice . . . bit slimy. Bit . . . seaweedy?' Caitlin replies, combing her hair.

'I never know if these beauty things are a massive con. Or whether we'll wake up tomorrow with dazzling mermaid skin. Shall we go in the sauna for a little bit?' I ask.

'Sure,' Caitlin replies flatly. She's still being reserved with me, which is understandable.

We sit on the warm wooden seats, and I put some more water onto the coals.

'Mmmm, it's nice to be warm,' Caitlin says, closing her eyes.

'Feels good to get all the bad stuff out of my pores. Mainly gin,' I say, laughing.

We sit in silence for a bit, my wet bikini bottoms occasionally squeaking against the bench. I once read somewhere that it's important not to steer the conversation too much with teenagers. Even if it's awkward, it's best to occasionally go quiet and let them come to you with what they want to say.

'Dad seems really happy.'

'Does he?' I say, smiling.

'Yeah. I was kind of wanting to hate you. That's the easiest narrative when your dad finally meets someone like you.'

I wondered what she meant by 'like you'.

'But it's hard,' she continues, 'you know, to hate you, when my dad is always in such a good mood. You really do seem to make him happy.'

'That is honestly so nice to hear. Thank you.'

'He's not always this jokey and smiley, you know. It's a recent thing.'

'I am really grateful, Cait,' I say, breathing in, 'that you're allowing me in.'

'I'm grateful too,' Caitlin says. She gives me a smile.

My eyes well up.

We return our items to Fluffy-Slipper Woman, and go outside to head home. It's clear the temperature has really dropped. We can both see our breath in front of us. I try to order us an Uber on the corner of Tottenham Court Road but it's too busy. We walk on a bit, and I link arms with Caitlin. It's always best to order a cab down a quieter road than risk getting piled up in a bundle of honking cars. I notice how frail her arm is; she is like a tiny Polly Pocket. She is cold, shaking slightly. We shelter under a bus stop until an Uber finally arrives, and I make him blast the car with hot air. We both stare out of the window as Magic FM plays.

When we get home, I pour Caitlin a cup of tea. I offer her a Rocky bar; milk chocolate with biscuit and caramel goodness inside. She takes it.

'Dunk it in your tea. It melts, so yummy,' I say, showing her the technique.

She slowly unwraps it and nibbles its edges.

After what feels like ages sitting in silence, she speaks.

'What were you like at seventeen, Olive?' she asks, still nibbling.

'Oh god, that's a question!' I say. 'Well, I hope you don't mind me saying that you're one of the most clued-up seventeen-year-olds I know . . . I, on the other hand, had *no* idea who I was or what I wanted. Truly no clue. I thought I was mature, though – now I realize I wasn't. I was very, very self-conscious. I remember, once, I threw a footballers and WAGs party and I went as a WAG – thought my worth was based on how many boys would look at me. Now, it's funny, but appearance is the last thing I base my value on.'

'Must take a while to get there. To . . . actually . . . like yourself,' Caitlin says, stirring her tea. 'That seems like a totally distant dream to me.' I notice she's unwrapped but barely touched the chocolate bar.

'Oh god, it really does. I remember – around your age – breaking up with my first boyfriend, who was so wrong for me, and just starting afresh. I love how many times you can reinvent yourself in life. You can experiment with anything.'

'I just don't really know what I want to do with my life.'

'You have tons of time, I promise.'

'People always say that.'

'I know, it's probably an annoying thing to say, because it doesn't really mean anything until you're older and on the other side.'

There's another long pause. I hold my tea, staring out of the window, up at the very few London stars I can see.

'Olive?'

'Yes, love?' I say, zoning back in.

'I'm scared.'

'What about?' I turn to face her. Focused.

'My periods. They started a few years ago, and now they've just . . . stopped.' She clutches at her thin silver chain necklace; it's like she keeps forgetting to breathe.

'Oh darling, it's OK.' I take her hand, which is resting on the table. 'Have you been to the doctor?'

'Not yet.'

'I can come with you.'

'Do you think it's . . . really bad?'

'We will get you better again. I promise.'

I once read in some 'advice' article that it's important to say 'we'. It's important she knows she's not going to go through this alone. We will get through this.

'Thanks Olive.' She hugs me. I can't believe she's hugging me.

I feel honoured that she's opened up to me but now I am responsible for it, and her. Marcus said I only need to tell him when it's crucial to, and I know that time is now. I really don't want to screw it up.

34

Life could not be better right now at .dot magazine. Gill has basically hinted that I'm getting promoted because she wants to go on a sabbatical to 'find herself' and try Ayahuasca. So that would make me Editor-in-Chief, which is one of the hardest ever promotions to get in this industry, because editors hardly ever leave. They normally have to die first. I am on cloud nine – my absolute dream job is finally mine. For the first time I feel like both sides of my life are evening out. My professional and personal are matching up with my idea of 'success'. Even my mum was delighted for me when I rang her, understanding the magnitude of it all. The seesaw is finally becoming evenly weighted.

The sun is shining and I am sitting on the .dot rooftop terrace, a recently renovated space that overlooks the London skyline, feeling full to the brim with possibility. It's a team-building day, but mainly training for junior staff. I have therefore managed to wiggle my way out of it, and there's no one else up here. I have the terrace to myself. I have just Skyped a creative agency that's helping us out with some billboards for the big relaunch of .dot. We are plastering bold feminist statements across London's bus stops and Tubes, which I'm really excited about.

I go to close Skype and realize that Jacob's icon is still in my contacts – and that he is online. Texting and calling would seem so incredibly personal, but for some reason Skype feels like the right medium through which to message him. Formal, yet friendly, like a softer version of Linkedin. I stand up, with my headphones in and my laptop balancing in my hand. Without taking a moment to think, I press 'call'.

There is a dialling tone but, after a few minutes, I hang up. No answer. I feel nerves in my stomach, but it's fine. It could have been an accident – one of the interns playing around on Skype. I turn around to go and sit back down, and then my laptop starts making a noise. He's calling me back. I make sure my camera isn't on. I can't do that.

'Hello?'

'Hi . . . Olive?' Jacob says, sounding inquisitive. His face appears on my laptop. He obviously has his camera on. I see that he is sitting in a home office, with some paintings on the wall behind him. Must be where he lives now.

'Hi!'

'Hi.' He laughs at the back and forth. 'Did you . . . ring?'

'I think it was by accident,' I lie. 'But . . . how are you?'

'I'm . . . good. It's been ages. It feels really weird to hear your voice.' He laughs nervously.

'I know. It's always going to feel weird, isn't it?' I say.

'What's new with you?' he asks, scratching the back of his head.

'The usual, really. But, I'm good. It's taken a while, but

I really am,' I say, meaning it. I pause momentarily. 'Mum . . . told me. About your news.'

'Oh.' He gulps. 'Yes. Yes it's . . . exciting. I didn't know whether to say anything or, how . . . or . . . whether you'd care or . . . or what to say really. It's all happened rather quickly to be honest – bit of a surprise.'

'It's OK, Jacob. I'm not ringing you to be weird with you. I just wish in some alternate universe it could have been me.' My voice tightens. 'But . . . you're going to be a fantastic father.' I want to ask about his new partner, but I bite my tongue.

'Olive, what we had was really special. That doesn't just vanish. Maybe it never will.'

I sniff. 'I'm glad this is happening for you.'

'Thank you for everything . . . over the years, Olive.'

'You too. We had fun, didn't we?' I smile.

'We did. It's hard to know if we could ever be friends; maybe you think that would be impossible. Or, maybe I would. But, you know, I'd love you to meet the baby when it's here.'

Tears start to form.

'I would love to. But let's see,' I say.

We say goodbye, using work as an excuse. I close my laptop. I look over the London horizon as the sun starts to go down and realize that two things can always be true at once. I can still love Jacob, in a different way, from a different angle, and still love my new, uncomplicated life with Marcus. I can still accept that my path with Jacob was intense and wonderful and special, until we reached the fork in the road and had to change direction. I can be happy and sad. I can be happy for him, and sad for the circumstances. I can mourn the past, and be excited for the future.

It hasn't gone unnoticed with Marcus that I don't see my best friends as much as I talk about them. He made a passing comment the other day that I hadn't seen them since my birthday. I should message them. I could be bitter and passive aggressive and mention the fact that it is always me trying to get us together, but the truth is, I want to see them more than I want to prove I'm right. Yes, I am usually the one to instigate things in the WhatsApp group, but I also don't want to sit around just waiting for them to call; life is too short. I feel the need to bite the bullet now. Our friendship might have been changing and wavering and blowing around in a stormy wind, but I know it needs some grounding. WhatsApp is the worst for communication. We need to get in one room together, facial expressions, body language, awkward atmosphere and all. There have been so many times where I have been tempted to cut it all off, to run away, to shrug and say, 'Perhaps we aren't the friends we used to be.' But I am absolutely determined to set it right again. Our friendship means too much.

I sit on my bed, take a sip of tea and open WhatsApp, trying to block out the possibility of a tumbleweed-shaped rejection.

Me: Hi guys

Me: Can we go to Jono's next week? Would love to see you all

A few hours later, some replies trickle in.

Cec: Course! Great idea. Chris can babysit x

Bea: Would love to Ol – long overdue

Isla: Sure

Cec: It's been too long

Bea: I miss you all x

There is something about returning to Jono's – our old haunt, full of so many memories – that highlights how much we've each changed and how far we have drifted. When I arrive the next week, I try to hide my surprise that everyone has actually made it. We each drag our chairs out from under the table and they squeak awkwardly along the floor. Then, the silence feels quite deafening. This feels very awkward suddenly. There is so much unsaid, so much hanging in the air.

'Girls!' Jono says enthusiastically, placing down menus in front of us. 'Been so long!'

'I know, but we're back – so good to see you,' I say.

'Work good?' Cec asks Bea. Clearly skirting around the elephant in the room.

'All good. Lovely review in *The Times* for the recent

exhibition, which is great. You been going back to work a bit now? How's Oscar?' Bea asks Cec.

'Yeah, been checking in. He's fine, and I'm doing OK,' Cec replies, twirling her ring around her finger.

'And . . . everything OK . . . at home?' Isla asks Bea. We're all relieved she's asked.

'Well, it's still over. He's renting a flat in London.' Tears prickle in Bea's eyes.

'We're so sorry, Bea,' Cec says.

'You've dealt with it all so well. Must be so hard, but sounds like it's for the best,' Isla adds.

'You'll be OK, Bea,' I say, gently.

'Yeah . . . I will. It's just hard on the kids,' Bea says, quietly.

'Is there anything we can do?' Cec says.

'Honestly, no.' Bea wipes away some tears, and looks away, a cue she wants us to change the subject.

'Everything OK with you Isla?' Cec asks.

'Yeah, still working from home a lot. Officially on my next round of IVF – our third time now, so we are just hoping for the best! I'm not telling anyone apart from you guys,' she replies.

'That's amazing!' I say.

'Oh Isla,' Bea says, squeezing her hand.

'Got everything crossed for you, darling,' Cec says.

'And you, Olive?' Bea asks.

'Oh, I got a promotion. Editor-in-Chief. Gill's gone!'

'Oh wow, Olive! You've always wanted that,' Cec says.

'That's incredible – but what happened to Gill?' Bea asks.

'She's booked a trip around the world. *Eat Pray Love* vibes.

Off to find herself and do some Ayahuasca,' I say, laughing.

'Good for Gill. She was always a bit of an odd nut,' Bea says. 'And amazing for you, Ol. You deserve it.'

Luckily now that Gill's gone, I don't actually have to publish that 'Millennials vs kids' article, and I don't have to include anything about the CFBC either. Thank god. I realized I didn't want to write about those women and expose them for the sake of a headline. I want their stories to be kept private. I want them to be respected and understood beyond a few hundred words. I know better now, though, than to raise this subject again in front of Isla. There'll be a time and a place for us to talk about this kind of thing. Right now, it's too sensitive.

I twiddle my thumbs and breathe through my nose deeply. Why is this next bit so hard? 'I just want to take this chance to say . . . I'm really sorry for the way I've been acting, if I've caused anyone any hurt or upset. Or, if you feel like I sort of disappeared with Marcus for a bit, during the whole honeymoon period thing,' I say.

Isla stays quiet.

'I don't think you have, Ol,' Bea says, unfolding her napkin on her lap.

'Well, I guess I felt pretty alienated when you guys went to that . . . child-free event together,' Isla says tentatively.

There goes keeping quiet. 'Isla, we didn't invite you for obvious reasons. And, the CFBC really helped me. I might not be signing up anytime soon, but being around like-minded people made me feel less alone. I was in a really bad place after all the stuff with Jacob,' I say. 'It meant a lot.'

'Well the bullshit problems I've been having with my fertility mean a lot to me,' Isla replies, getting more heated.

'Both things can mean a lot to both of you,' Bea snaps. 'Come on, let's put this all behind us, please.'

'Agreed, we are four very different women. Very different to when we first met,' I say.

Jono comes over and takes our wine order. He obviously senses the awkwardness.

'Everything OK, ladies?'

'Hmm,' we all sort of murmur back.

'Would you like to order?' Jono gets his notepad out.

'Ah, I'm not ready yet, sorry,' I say. The theme of my life.

'Yeah, few more minutes please. Thanks Jono,' Cec says.

'Girls!' Jono flaps, putting his pen behind his ear. 'I don't know what's going on here, but all I know is that you have all been coming here for almost ten years. I've never known four women who are as close as you four. Come on! I'll be back in five!'

'Look, Jono's right. Our friendship is worth more than all these silly fights,' Bea says.

'Let's go around the table and each apologize,' Cec says.

'That's stupid,' Isla says.

'No it's not. It's adult,' Cec says.

'OK, go on, then,' Isla says, huffily.

'I'll go first,' Bea says. 'I'm sorry for not being honest with you, Isla, when I went to the CFBC with Olive. I'm sorry I joked about the importance of it, Olive. I'm sorry I didn't open up to you guys properly when I found out Jeremy was cheating on me.'

'Bea – we get it, it's been horrible and hard,' Cec says.

'I know, honestly one day I might laugh, it's *that* much of a cliché to run away with a younger, hotter woman. Anyway, I'm slowly, slowly getting my head around it. But look, my point is that none of us round this table has a perfect life, none of us will make identical choices – let's just be a little bit gentler on each other, OK?' Bea says, softly.

I nod.

Cec speaks next. 'And I'm sorry, Isla, for making you feel like shit at my baby shower by putting demands on you. For being distant since I've had Oscar. For rejecting your help, Bea – I just felt like a weirdly different person once I became a mum, my mental health was in a really rocky place. It was so scary, I didn't know how to just be "me" any more,' she says, solemnly.

'We get it, Cec. And look, I'm sorry too. I feel like these past few months I've been a total self-obsessed monster. I've been awful to you Cec, especially when you were pregnant with Oscar,' Isla says.

'You weren't that bad,' Cec says.

'And I'm sorry Isla,' I say, 'for being insensitive to what you've been going through. I'm sorry I called you selfish at my house. Bea, I'm sorry for pushing you away when you were trying to help. Cec, I'm sorry again for making a scene at the baby shower.'

'It's OK. I often assume you are doing fine, Ol, and I shouldn't,' Cec says. 'You can stop calling the baby OAP, now though,' she adds, with a half-smile.

'I've been the worst,' I sigh.

'Olive, we understand. You really don't have to make it into a huge deal that you don't want a kid. It doesn't change how we feel about you – it really changes nothing, as long as you're happy,' Bea reaches for my hand.

'I know. I see that now. And I am happy. I really think I am,' I say, relieved.

'Have you ever questioned that maybe nothing was wrong with you in the first place? That nothing needed fixing? That you are right where you are meant to be? There are so many ways to live a fulfilled life. What you do, the people you impact, it's all so valuable.'

I reach for a napkin, lean my head back and blot away my suddenly runny mascara. 'I guess I've just been on a bit of a rollercoaster and it was difficult to reach you all because it felt like there was this ginormous chasm between us. I just don't want to drift away from any one of you.'

'Ol. None of us want that either.'

'I am feeling so much better in general now, though, and I want to just say sorry and put all that icky stuff behind us.' I really believe what I am saying for the first time in ages. I am happy with who I am. Where I am. With my life choices.

Bea is now holding my hand over the table and squeezing it. The girls reach out and squeeze it too.

Our food arrives. The atmosphere finally settles. The air feels clear. Or at least, clearer. I am starving. All of that confrontation has made me ravenous.

Just as we start chatting normally, with the dark cloud lifted, my phone starts buzzing in my bag. I've been ignoring it during our heart-to-heart. I have a look before tucking into my pizza. Eighteen missed calls! Jesus. It's Caitlin. My stomach lurches.

What's going on?

My heart pounds and I call her back straight away. No answer. I ring again. Still no answer, so I text her:

Me: You OK? Have you sat on your phone?

My throat is suddenly dry. Bea pours me some water. They all notice something's up.

My phone pings and it's a text from Caitlin:

Caitlin: I'm sitting on the floor in Paddington Station, I just had a massive panic attack. Can't swallow or breathe properly. Please help. Not sure where Dad is :(((

I grab my bag and stuff my phone inside. 'Guys, I'm sorry to leave, but it's Caitlin. She's not very well.' I throw down some money on the table.

'It's OK babe, you go, just text us later and please let us know everything is fine, OK?' Bea says.

'Take your pizza with you in a box!' Cec says.

'See you soon, Ol,' Isla says.

I leave with a thrilling feeling of purpose.

I feel needed.

Caitlin.

I want to be there for her.

'It makes me a little sad sometimes to think that I won't have anyone to take to Disney for the first time, or read *Harry Potter* to for the first time. But that's a flash of sentiment that in no way endures, or has any impact on my decision to not have kids.'

Sienna, 39

35

I sit on the edge of the bed, with my hand on Caitlin's forehead. She is very warm and clammy all over and I hang a thermometer out of her mouth. She is still feeling anxious and has been in bed for a few days. I have bought her one of those 'heavy duvets' from John Lewis; they are meant to help with anxiety as the weight of the blanket can make people feel comforted.

'We won't be long, Cait,' Marcus says, kissing her forehead.

'I'll bring you back some sausage rolls in my bag,' I say, leaning down to hug her. I realize, with a jolt, that I love her. It feels scary. A double-edged sword of love. I have let her in now, and she relies on me for support. There's no turning back. Now I have to carry around this constant worry for her. I can't just turn my phone off for hours like I used to. I might get something wrong. But Caitlin has given me a newfound responsibility, something I've been forever running away from, but with her I don't seem to mind too much. It has surprised me.

'Sally is downstairs, OK? And she knows to text me immediately if you need us,' Marcus says. 'We're not going far.'

'Yes, let us know if you need anything,' I say, gently squeezing her shoulder.

I've asked Marcus if he will come with me to Dorothy's funeral. He never met her, but he could see how upset I was, so it's nice that he's coming today and I won't be a lemon. Marcus is wearing a black T-shirt with a black jacket and trousers and dark Ray-Ban sunglasses – he looks a bit too hot for a funeral, in my opinion. I'm wearing a thin black polo-neck cashmere jumper, tight black jeans, and a PVC black coat from Topshop over the top. We look as if we are going to a wanky fashion show, not an elderly woman's funeral, but it's the only clean black clothes we had. The details of the funeral were posted in a Facebook group called 'D's Funeral'. I didn't know old people used Facebook. They do now, apparently. I copy and paste the address from the Facebook group into Google Maps – it's at a crematorium next to the cemetery where Dorothy's husband is also buried.

We get off the train and jump in a cab. We then walk up the sloping hill towards the large funeral room where the service will take place, and everyone is waiting outside, standing around with paper cups of coffee. I'm holding a bunch of flowers and the water in the little plastic bit at the bottom is starting to drip all over my black boots. I look around at all the varying gravestones, all the messages and birth dates engraved. My heart lurches when I see a date that is too short, too young to be on a grave: *1991–2003* RIP. I shudder, and link arms with Marcus. I am aware that this must be awful for him; no one likes being reminded of death. But his body is like a radiator right now, warming me up.

Funerals are funny things. These sorts of enclosed environments always make me nervous that I'll say something super-inappropriate, or I'll look too happy at the wrong moment. Everyone is so formal in their posh, stiff, black clothes, but underneath it all, people are screaming out for a bit of light relief. When we go inside we sit three rows back, out of respect because we hardly knew Dorothy and we're sure her nearest and dearest might want to sit at the front. We are among the first to arrive, and I'm wondering how many people even knew Dorothy, or that she's died.

'If no one turns up, we should move to the front,' I whisper to Marcus. He nods politely.

Before we know it, the rows are filling up and, when I turn around, we see people standing at the back, squeezing in. I hear someone gossipy murmur in front of me – something about Dorothy's son turning up. Someone subtly points as he walks down the aisle to sit in the front pew. He is around six foot tall with dark, floppy hair; he is holding a baby in his arms and his partner is walking slowly behind him wearing a black pashmina and thin-framed glasses. My heart beats fast, and I feel both sad and happy that he is here. Dorothy had always seemed quite down that they hardly saw each other. I understand that Australia is far away, and perhaps time does run away with all of us. But you know what they say: funerals bring people together. I keep staring at him as he bounces his baby up and down, dwelling on the sadness and the irony.

It's suddenly quite hot and crowded in here. Hundreds of people are piled into one small room. The celebrant does his spiel. It's not very religious, which surprises me. Just upbeat, celebratory and reflective. Mary, Dorothy's eighty-five-year-old cousin who's sitting next to me, tells us she is doing a little speech. When her time comes, she takes ages to get to the stage with her walking stick and her son helps her hobble up to the podium. She puts on the tiniest reading glasses and reads off a tiny scrap of paper.

'Life is not a dress rehearsal. Life is not about waiting for the storm to pass. It's about learning to dance in the rain. You should be nice to those on the way up, because you don't know who you might meet on the way down. You can't be an everything to everyone. After all, it's not the number of breaths we take, but the number of moments that take our breath away. Yesterday is history, tomorrow a mystery and today is a gift. That's why we call it the present . . .'

Marcus and I try not to laugh. I mean, she's literally Googled and read off some inspirational quotes. But, you know, the thought is there. When the service is over, everyone slowly makes their way out of the room, smiling solemnly to each other and muttering 'great woman', 'a really lovely woman'. I manage to catch Rupert as I leave, overhearing others greeting him.

'It's Rupert, isn't it? I'm Olive. I texted you about coming to the funeral. I am – was – Dorothy's neighbour.'

'Oh, hello Olive. Thank you so much for coming. I know Dorothy would have appreciated it. I remember her speaking very fondly about you.' Seeing the way Rupert's eyes light up when he talks about Dorothy makes me wonder whether he might have been her boyfriend. It makes me smile to know she had so many people who loved her.

'Really? That's so lovely. You know, I always thought of Dorothy as a bit lonely,' I say. 'But there are so many people here, celebrating her life.'

Rupert laughs. 'Why, what made you think that, dear?' he asks, warmly.

'I don't know. She once gave me her number as she was worried about falling over.'

Rupert laughs, lightly. 'I think Dorothy thought *you* were a bit lonely.'

'*Really?*'

'I remember her saying you seemed a little sad, and she said she wanted you to know she was there if you needed her.'

'That's . . . really lovely,' I say, and reach for the note she wrote to me a few days ago but realize it's in a different coat.

'Dorothy had lots and lots of friends, Olive. And you were one of them.'

At this, I burst into tears. Marcus, shocked, scrabbles for a tissue in his suit jacket. Rupert says goodbye and Marcus and I sit down on two wooden chairs nearby.

'That is the sweetest thing, because Dorothy was right. I had been sad. I was really sad and lonely. She must have seen me stumbling home late and watched me taking the bins out in my tracksuit after another long weekend in the flat on my own.' I laugh through the tears. Marcus hugs me tightly.

Some people die too young. Some people die old. Some people get what they want. Some people never get what they want. Some people have different priorities, different dreams. Some people change their minds in small ways, some do a total 180. We're all out here, making up our lives as we go along. There is no 'better' path. There is no 'worse' path. Each of us tries our very best to get through the weeks, months and years using what we have and what we were given, and the rest of it is just down to sheer luck. We make our own family – kids, friends, pets, neighbours, strangers, passions, memories – and we can shape other people's lives in so many ways.

Leaving something behind isn't just about having a child who will roam the earth after you've gone. A legacy is made up of everything you've ever done. It's everything you leave behind. It's every choice you make. It's every person you meet. It's every feeling you've passed on. It's every story you tell.

Epilogue

2025

Marcus and I have moved further into the city. Further in. Not out. First, I moved out of my flat and in with him, but this was always going to be our natural next step: a place of our own. Ours. He sold his house and his girls were upset at first, understandably. But they were OK with it in the end, and I feel their genuine happiness for us, which is more than I could ever have asked for. It's not easy to sell a house with so many deeply engraved memories embedded in its walls. Instead of feeling like we needed to 'upgrade', or buy somewhere with lots of space, we decided to downgrade – a cosy flat for just the two of us above a family-run Swedish furniture shop in Soho. What responsibility do we have? None, really. We wanted to take advantage of this and live freely, in the heart of the city we love. We are next to one of our favourite French restaurants, and we can walk to the Curzon Soho cinema to watch films, or go to the theatre whenever we want. I work from home most days now and sometimes sit on our little veranda with my laptop, overlooking the London cityscape. I feel so happy and contained in the rhythm of our daily life together. We have a small spare room for Caitlin and Sally, of course, but they are busy living their own independent lives now. Caitlin has moved in with her boyfriend, a lovely tall boy called Callum, who was also a family friend (so Marcus approves, which makes things a tad easier). Her health is back on track – has been for years now – and her relationship with food has been reframed through an entirely different lens with the help of a therapist and Callum's ongoing support. She is healthy and happy, but we still check in often. Sally is studying History of Art in Bristol. She lives with a big group of girlfriends, who work hard and play hard. It feels like Marcus can relax now, knowing that his babies are settled. Of course he will always worry a bit, but everything feels . . . in place.

Marcus is out with his friends tonight, and I am excited to be hanging out with mine. It's the first time they've seen the flat, and I've tidied and cleaned extra hard for their arrival.

'Congratulations Olive! *Home-owner!*' Cecily says, popping open a big bottle of champagne in my new kitchen. Isla ducks as the cork goes towards her head. It spills onto the wooden floor, but I don't care. Bea finds a tea towel and mops it up.

'*Thank you!* And thank you guys for my gorgeous present, I love it.' They have clubbed together to buy me a vase –

and Bea has painted a face on it. They've also bought me a big bunch of sunflowers, which are now sitting on my kitchen table, the bright yellow petals reflecting how I feel inside. Bea pours a glass for us all. She has made us some smoked salmon nibbles too. We all say 'cheers'.

'Show us your room, then!' Bea says, sipping on her bubbles and linking arms with me. Cec leaves her glass on the side.

We run down my tiny corridor as though we are sixteen again. I swing open the door and reveal my huge custom-made bed, positioned in the middle of the room, plants either side, with a view of the bustling streets of Soho. Light is streaming into the bedroom and reflects off the shiny leaves of the new plants. Everything feels like it is so full of life.

'Huge bed!' Bea says, she practically face-plants in it, her body planking and bouncing upwards. Isla and Cecily join her. Then me, trying not to spill my drink on my fresh linen sheets. Four in the bed again.

'Where the magic happens,' I say, leaning back with a smirk.

'This is the life isn't it, Ol?' says Cec, looking out of the big window onto the Soho streets below.

'It's lush. Maybe I could bring a date back here one night when you and Marcus are away,' Bea laughs, smoothing out the duvet and flicking her hair around.

'Oh my god – yes,' I laugh. Bea and Jeremy's divorce was finalized around three and a half years ago now, and she is loving her new single status and the freedom it brings her. She is glowing, physically fitter than ever, and still manages to somehow remain friends with Jeremy while they co-parent – separately but pretty happily.

'At least Oscar now sleeps in until at least 8 a.m. most days; I think the bags under my eyes are just about disappearing,' Cec says.

'Cheers to that,' I say. Oscar is now five, and very polite, with a totally adorable side-parting. He has really grown on me. He calls me Auntie Ollie, which is pretty cute.

'So, guys,' Cec clears her throat. 'I have a little housewarming gift for you, Ol, but it's actually something for all of you.' She reaches into her handbag and hands us each an envelope with our names on.

'Oh, you are so sweet, Cec! Thank you,' I say, taking the envelope. 'Should we all open them together?'

'Yeah!' Cec says, shuffling around on the bed with excitement.

'OK,' I say. 'One, two, three!' We all tear the envelopes open, and pull out another small thin piece of card.

It is a scan. Of a baby.

I can see the shape of its tiny nose.

The curve of its back.

The outline of a foot.

Tears are suddenly brimming, fresh salty water that falls down my cheeks and into the corners of my mouth. Bea and Isla have the same reaction. Isla is smiling with her mouth closed, her face resting in her hand. Bea and I have our mouths hanging open.

At the bottom of the scan is Cec's handwriting. It reads: 'Will you be my godmother?'

'I'm sorry I didn't ask you guys the first time round, you know, with Osc. I was totally overwhelmed and had a lot of postpartum stuff going on, I just wasn't thinking about anything like that. I was feeling too sad and scared,' Cec says.

'Oh Cec, we totally get it – this is so lovely!' Bea says, practically hugging the piece of the paper.

'Isla, I hope you don't mind me doing this, I just . . . I didn't want to be weird . . . I love you and want you to be involved, if you want to, that is,' Cec says, feeling nervous, biting her lip a bit.

'Oh Cec.' Isla moves to sit right beside her. 'You're so sweet for saying that. I am OK! I really am, we don't need to tiptoe around it any more, I promise.'

None of us knows quite what to say yet, so we wait for Isla to continue.

'I still have my moments when I feel sad about it all, but honestly, I am genuinely making peace with it. It's not that I feel I "have" to get over it, it's just that I know it sounds weird, but I don't have the same urge as I did. As you know, I've just opened my new practice, work is better than ever, Mike is happy too – we are happy, we are OK with how our future is looking, even if it's not the one I expected.' Isla puts her hand on top of Cec's.

'That is wonderful, Isla,' Bea says.

'It's funny how things change, isn't it? I'm happy and feel like I might want different things now. And anyway, down the line, if I do still want a family, I could always consider adopting.'

'I am so glad to hear that, Isla,' Cec says, as if the words 'phew' were written on her forehead. 'She is so lucky to have you as a godmother.'

'She? *A girl!* Oh Cec, I am so excited to meet her,' Isla says, kissing Cec on the cheek. 'Thank you guys for getting me through those horrible few years. I couldn't have managed without you. I'm so glad to be out the other side now.'

'Of course, Isla. Thank you, guys, for being there,' Cec says, to all of us. 'Being pregnant feels . . . different this time round.'

'Enjoy it, Cec, they grow up so quickly. Mine hardly need me any more,' Bea says laughing, clearly enjoying her own new phase of motherhood.

'We've all come a long way, haven't we?' I say, holding my three best friends as tightly as I can.

There are things we can choose – and things that we can't. But one thing is for sure: I choose these friends. Over and over again.

Acknowledgements

You know what they say about novels. It takes a village.

The biggest thank you to the team at HarperCollins. Kimberley Young, for seeing something in my first draft. Charlotte Brabbin, for inspiring me to go that little bit further with each edit. To the best Marketing and PR squad in the biz: Sarah Shea, Fliss Denham and Liz Dawson. To Ellie Game for creating one of the most beautiful covers I've ever seen. I can't believe it gets to be mine.

Thank you to my friend and literary agent Abigail Bergstrom for reading and reviewing countless drafts before we sent it out. (And for the wine and chats. A very important part of the process.)

Thank you to Kim, Justin and Lynsey at Diving Bell for your support, friendship and the enthusiasm you have for all of my creative projects.

Thank you to all the women I spoke to in confidence when researching the themes in the book. You helped me build Olive from the inside out – you are all amazing, it's no wonder I fell in love with her.

To Elizabeth Gilbert, Marian Keyes, Louise O'Neill and all the fellow authors who read early proofs of *Olive* and provided me with such generous support during your own busy book schedules. I really appreciate it.

Thank you to my past self for sitting down and writing the damn thing. I've tried so many times and failed. This one stuck.

To my amazing friends, family and Paul for making my personal life so supported and full of love. Thank you for always putting up with my overactive imagination.